PRIMAL
Storm

Other Books by R. A. Smith:

Oblivion Storm
The Grenshall Manor Chronicles - Book 1

Enjoy!

THE GRENSHALL MANOR CHRONICLES - BOOK 2

PRIMAL Storm

R.A. SMITH

Xchyler Publishing,
an imprint of Hamilton Springs Press, LLC
Penny Freeman, Editor-in-chief
www.xchylerpublishing.com

1st Edition: January, 2014

Cover and Interior Design by D. Robert Pease, walkingstickbooks.com
Edited by Penny Freeman and McKenna Gardner

Published in the United States of America
Xchyler Publishing

To Joy. Thanks for keeping me ticking.

If you don't overcome, you won't become.

—Sebastien Foucan

CHAPTER ONE

Everyone who ever lived has known fear at some stage in their lives. For some, the dark. For others, spiders. Or perhaps heights. For every individual, there exists a tailored nightmare.

The trick is to not let it get the better of you. And Jennifer Winter knew that better than most. She'd been a fighter from her first heartbeat. During childbirth, a rare complication for the modern age took her mother. But Jennifer kept breathing even after everyone had given up on her.

And just a year ago, she clung on again, with the help of a friend, when Death came for her.

She once had strength well beyond that of a mundane being—speed, power, toughness, and a ferocious battle posture, traits that brought a bestial warrior to the surface from the depths of her soul.

Now, she may have been a solid athlete, at best. The power she possessed previously had seemingly deserted her. Before she could look after others again, she would have to relearn to look after herself. Through some strange logic, that had led her to the dangerous challenge she had set herself: free-running the rooftops of London.

Whilst bedridden, she demanded to be shown sports and exercise videos to keep her inspired. Thankfully, Kara, her employer by formality, housemate by convenience, and best friend by lengthy history, duly obliged with a series of extreme sports clips, but the one which had caught Jennifer's eye the most had been a short movie on *parkour* versus *freerunning*. She had found it fascinating, *motivating*.

Just as it was getting dark that day, she had set out from her starting point of Grenshall Manor, a location once mystically obscured in Mill Hill, North London. Some basic stretches, which attracted the unwanted attention of a group of spotty teenagers, preceded a gentle jog. Her idea of gentle still allowed her to overtake a few of the regulars in the neighbourhood as they wound down from their commute in the best way they knew.

After a couple of miles, when she reached Islington, she decided to break into something more interesting. It was time for an exercise of balance. She looked to the skies and started to climb the face of a block of flats until she reached the rooftop.

She moved to the edge of the high-rise and rocked forward on to the balls of her feet. One slip and she would have a very long drop down. *One minute*, she said to herself. *One minute without falling*. The first challenge of several.

As it had all her life, the world continued to pick fights for her. When her stepmother entered her life, Jennifer hoped that things would improve. But nothing good came of that. Oh, she remembered. She would never forget.

That was the day the fear started.

When hers became a tale of two stepmothers, however, her life changed irreversibly. The second, the enigma she knew as Alice Winter, had her deal with most of her fears head on. Like now.

Thirty seconds.

She stood taller, stretched. It felt good.

She'd had a lot of time to think about her past; lots of time to consider a new exercise regime, as well. Months, in fact—months of stagnating in a bed in a mansion hardly any living person knew existed until her friends, Kara and Mary, found it. Their discovery of Grenshall Manor yielded much more than a property of significant value, but her part in its discovery ended a day sooner at the hands of a violent, undead entity.

The assault she withstood would have killed just about anyone else several times over.

Her balance was perfect; her strength, better than she gave herself credit for. She stretched out her arms, a movement which produced only the merest hint of teetering on the edge. She looked good for achieving her goal.

Twenty seconds. Not good enough. Push harder.

Still on her toes, she leaned another inch forward, another inch out into empty space. Again, her balance held true. As she endangered herself further, staring out over the cityscape, she chose her route of descent.

Time. Challenge done.

She lowered herself back to the soles of her feet and stumbled backward as she did so. She had spent weeks intensively building up her calf muscles after their period of atrophy. They did not let her down, but they ached like hell.

She cursed herself for feeling so weak. She wiped sweat from her brow as she allowed herself a little recovery time, but only a moment. She turned to the left and bolted to that edge of the building. As her feet hit the ledge, she sprung as hard as her legs would permit . . .

Not hard enough. She was going to be a good foot short. She grabbed a satellite dish just in time—but misjudged that, too. Instead of grappling the top, she fought to grip the bottom of it. The bolts came loose with the tiniest pop, and the dish tilted under her weight.

Quickly, she pushed her legs wider and braced herself against the building. She nudged herself upward and shifted her grip repeatedly up the surface of the dish. Her balance returned, her hands reached the top of the dish before it took further strain, and she propelled herself to the right. Her feet landed on a balcony railing. She crouched, then leapt for an overhang on the roof. She pulled up and onto her intended target.

Jennifer continued her run, her immediate future no longer mapped. She ached, but that was a good thing. She was still moving. That was the important part. She built up more speed, and propelled herself using all her limbs for the next building—that one slightly lower down than the last. She had the momentum this time, but the ground came at her fast.

Brace!

She hit the concrete first with her right leg, absorbed the impact with an elegant forward roll, then came straight out of it. Back on her feet, she continued at almost full speed to the edge, then flung herself into space. The opposite roof was too far below to roll.

She flailed in the direction of a high pipe on that building. Catching it just before landing blunted the pace of her drop, and with that, she fell safely to the roof. Perhaps not quite as intended, but decently all the same.

Jennifer had already marked her next building. She leapt more confidently, allowed herself no hesitation, and launched again, that time straight down at an angled wall. She hit with her feet firmly planted on the top. She had to combine speed with balance, and ran with her arms held out to either side. The slightest slip would leave her very little chance to react safely.

The first few steps were fine, more momentum than judgement, but the next had her crossing her own feet at a high speed. Just as she had her footwork together, she ran out of wall. Impossibly off-balance and still travelling too quickly to stop, she threw herself into an elegant swan dive to make the most of her motion. She got quickly under control and tucked into a somersault.

She caught another protruding pipe and her feet hit the wall at her own pace. She took another quick look but swung around, then pushed herself clear, and dropped neatly on to a passing truck. One final spring took her to the pavement, just in front of an alleyway. Her feet planted with competent gymnastic form.

She winced as the self-punishment decided to catch up with her. Every muscle gave crippling protest. She propped herself against the wall of one of the buildings and rested before pushing on.

Jennifer stepped into a canter, then worked herself into a flat-out sprint for a full minute. She breathed heavily. It used to take her ten to fifteen minutes to get anywhere near as tired. Her stamina had abandoned her on the day that the fear returned.

That fateful, near-fatal day had been almost a year ago. Of those many months holed up at Grenshall Manor, for half of those, she had been unable to sit up by herself, let alone move under her own steam. Mary, the heir to the mansion and one person she could genuinely say had been through the wars like herself, had looked after her on almost every one of those days, a unique nurse. She kept her company, in touch with the world, and well-fed.

But Jennifer began to resent being cared for; worse, to develop a strange animosity for her caregiver. She couldn't help but notice that

Mary blossomed by the day as she learned increasing control of that dark art of hers.

But more than that, Mary looked genuinely happy in herself. She had, figuratively and literally, laid old ghosts to rest in the time she and Jennifer had known each other—most significantly, as Jennifer assessed matters, the lingering case of her parents' deaths at the clumsy hands of an irrational ghost.

Jennifer had achieved none of this. The mother she never knew died a victim of natural causes; nothing more to say on that tale. The woman she most wanted to call her mother after that, who helped her through her darkest days and introduced Jennifer to the basics of her talents, Alice, was taken from her, too. No resolution had come of that, and she no idea even where to start.

That pale touch of death had faded from Mary over the recovering months, and she had become a completely different person from the one-time half-dead amnesiac Jennifer first rescued. The raven black hair had grown full-bodied, a streak of red in there by her own choice.

When not improving her more mystic arts, or working on building repairs, Mary would sacrifice entire days to keep Jennifer company. Sometimes, she would improve her tailoring skills, but she would keep herself busy every day with one thing or another. And for most of that time, Jennifer remained hobbled, weak and unsteady. It proved maddening.

The most recent couple of months had been better. At least some of Jennifer's coordination had returned, her mobility such that she could once more get around the building. She even helped Mary with her clothing design. But her ordeal that night in the Bond Street Station would not leave her be. It always hit her when it was it was least welcome. Like when she was catching her breath.

~*~

"MARY!"

Jennifer roared, enraged into indiscipline, leaping straight at Violet and attacking with her sharp, clawed hands. She pummelled her opponent repeatedly, shredding away at normally vital organs. But that did not slow her opponent. Instead, Jennifer found herself hearing echoed laughter from . . . somewhere . . .

"Rage . . . power . . . madness . . . yes . . . you must join us . . ."

One of her clawed strikes was caught in mid-air and Jennifer's fury degenerated into fear as she stared into shadowy eyes. She moved for the necklace, even now gleaming at her, but a numbing cold washed over her, freezing her in place, leaving her defenceless.

Jennifer grew paralysed when needle-like fingertips dug hard into her arms. Her mind scrambled, her breath shortened, she could think of nothing but the biting chill, the pronounced thumping of her heart beating; slowing rapidly.

As the voices laughed in concert, she lay helpless, unable to cry out, even though her guts felt torn from her—immobilised as darkness encroached upon her sight, a vision of death and shadow no living mortal eyes should have seen; the last thing they would ever see. The girlish giggling continued, taunting her even through that slow, excruciating process . . .

~*~

The first day she regained consciousness after that fateful assault, Mary and Kara told her that Violet had been defeated. But that memory lingered, the pain inflicted in that struggle unlike any other she had ever experienced. Every part of the creature's touch felt like raw, unbottled death.

The worst thing about it, though, was that it had taken her out of the fight. She'd left her best friend Kara with no more help than a broken woman as protection—someone she hadn't known for forty-eight hours. Being dead, or just gravely wounded, meant that she could not save them, whatever they faced.

And if she went down, what chance did they have? That would have been two others she couldn't help. And proud as she was of Mary and Kara for defeating the most powerful enemies they had run into to date, she resented the fact that they reminded her of her failure that day; the most dangerous time either of them had ever faced.

There would be more danger; she *knew* that for a fact. And because of it, she had to prepare. Get herself at least fighting fit again. She amazed Mary with the speed she was able to run, after returning to her feet. "It's a bloody miracle you're still with us at all," she had told her. It especially reminded Jennifer that Mary kicked the life back into her when they retrieved her from, of all places, a morgue. Yet another favour owed.

So it started with runs around the mansion. As she worked on her conditioning, Grenshall Manor's own condition also improved. Every day, Mary and her new staff toiled to restore a former glory—or to add a contemporary touch in a way only the new lady of the manor's artistic eye could. In the more recent evenings, Jennifer helped out wherever possible, hefting stones and climbing to parts others had difficulty reaching for repairs. It was all good for her natural return to shape.

She'd been running for longer than she thought—now in unfamiliar territory. She looked up, trying to find a landmark, a street name, anything to tell her where she'd gone. It was probably time to head home.

Against the moonlit sky, she saw a flash of shadow amidst the darkness. It had gone as soon as she picked it up, but there had definitely been something. She looked around, and nothing seemed out of the ordinary elsewhere. There couldn't have been anything there. She shrugged and continued running.

She made it ten steps before another shadow flitted by. Too late to be birds. Too densely populated and bright—unlikely to be bats. Too big. Wrong movement. It had just leapt across a building. But cameras pervaded the streets of London. The police would rapidly look into it if they deemed it suspicious.

Her hair stood on end. Then, she closed her eyes as a blinding flash sizzled around her. Vehicles stopped and darkness fell. The visual effect was reminiscent of what she had seen of an electromagnetic pulse. But the rest did not follow.

Physically, she had no evidence of a device of suitable power being unleashed around her. But a quick scan around told her nothing new about the situation. The only thing she had seen came from looking up. It was just the one lead. She found a foothold on a nearby building and followed it.

Jennifer started climbing, the stone on the side of the slippery building. But, she fought for every grip, and clung with great strength. She wobbled, the balance awkward. Arms and legs coiled, she forced her way up, finally gathering momentum and gaining her stride.

She reached the top and looked across the rooftop. She was alone, as far as she could tell. But this was a better vantage point than where she had been, and, at least she reinforced her technique in the climb.

Surely the emergency power would kick in before too long? Almost as she had the thought, there were brief flashes from hundreds of lights as far as the eye could see. But, as suddenly as they had come on, they flashed off.

What gives?

She saw several flashes of movement. More shadows, climbing the surrounding the roofs nearby. She heard a whizzing sound behind her. Without thinking, she dashed for the nearest extractor fan and leapt over it, forward rolling as she landed. She dragged herself to the edge of the vent and sat up, peering from behind cover.

Jennifer spotted the hook before an individual clad completely in dark, loose clothing and a face mask reached the top. He retrieved his climbing equipment and moved towards her. An electronic whisper sounded as the climber approached. She slid around the opposite side of the fan and watched. He was armed, but as far as she could see, bore no resemblance to any local police team or military squad. She'd walked right into something else.

"Number Four in place," he whispered, not beyond her strong hearing. A year ago, she could have leapt the fan and taken him down before he knew she was there. She still had a chance, but she needed to know more. Staying low, she crawled closer, waiting as he positioned himself on the edge of the roof.

There it was again. That flash of shadow. It went past, well before she had any idea what it was. Still a large shadow. Still flowing.

Then again. An adjacent rooftop. Right by the standing guard. The shadow flickered into sight again, then vanished just as soon as it appeared. She got a better look this time. Person-sized. Wings? No. A cloak was more likely. But the vanishing was more difficult to explain.

She could sense a trail. That smell. She had grown accustomed to it. That was why she hadn't picked up on it faster. It was like . . . distilled *death* to those with senses as acute as hers had been, but it wasn't forgettable either. It was the same stench that Grenshall Manor reeked of, if one knew where to check. Not like Mary. The aura around her had changed.

No. This was more like that awful Gate Chamber Mary had told her about, but she had never seen for herself. Mary claimed to be in full control of it now, but Jennifer could still sense it. Jennifer had no reason to doubt her friend, for anything the rightful owner of Grenshall Manor had said to her since they met had been right.

But it—the shadow—had gone again, whatever . . . *whoever* it was. What she knew: the squad had spread out around the buildings. Yet, she had never checked her exact whereabouts. She intended to do that when she had given up for the day to head home. Time to check the nearest landmarks and work it out.

She recognised one of the buildings, not too far ahead. The British Museum. A useful reference point. And one that the intruder had been staring straight at. They were *all* pointing in that direction. She guessed that must have been their concern.

As she stared, the shadow returned, right there. It moved quickly, flitting around down there, near other figures. They had dropped to the ground as she stared. This thing was causing harm. It was time to act.

She leapt on to the fan and then down behind the guard. But she stumbled.

"Wha—?"

She launched an uppercut from the unbalanced stance. She caught him and eased him to the ground, smashing a fist into his facemask. Certain he was unconscious, she dragged him out of sight and slipped him out of his fatigues, putting them on herself. It wasn't a perfect fit, but it would do.

Then she plotted a route and moved back to the other edge of the building. She launched at speed and vaulted on to the fan, then on to another protrusion on the building, before propelling herself with all her strength over the edge to a slightly lower building.

Jennifer knew someone was on that rooftop too, but her landing was sloppy, putting her right in front of him. She punched him hard in the gut and reworked her footing before seizing him by the head and throwing him over her own. She brought a foot down the side of his skull, taking him down and out.

With no time to hide him anywhere, Jennifer left him and ran again. She leapt, looking for flag poles, lowered platforms and hanging ledges—anything to descend quickly but keep from alerting them. Down she went, across and around, but her lack of practice and familiarity with the scenery caused her to slip a couple of times.

For an ordinary person training daily in the art of *parkour*, freerunning, that would have been dangerous enough. For an untrained individual, it was damn near suicidal. To Jennifer, who needed only watch once and was as good as trained, but so very off her game, the risk fell somewhere in between.

Her grip slipped once too often and she fell on her back, winding herself. But she picked herself up and moved before she could bitch too hard about it. There were still too many armed villains in the area. That bump was nothing compared to the prospect of being discovered.

The nearest guard had heard the fall, try as she might to mask it. She pressed herself against a wall around a corner and waited for him to check. But he looked spooked. They were in communication. At least two of them had failed to report. They were aware they had been compromised. There was no turning back for her now, even if she had foiled their plans.

No such luck. They held their positions but pulled out their weapons. Jennifer leapt in full sprint and, using a fixed camera, swung herself straight onto a lower building. Even as her feet hit the ground, more smoothly this time, she made the connection.

The pulse had put the cameras out of action, as much as the power. The assault was anything but spontaneous, and couldn't have been easily planned. Whatever situation she had landed herself in, she could probably have used backup—but that was impossible now. It was either let it happen or finish the job.

She noticed herself blowing again. She was normally better than this. Clinging onto the edge, she lowered herself down and found herself on a hotel, the *Kingsley by Thistle*. A good vantage point. Maybe she could figure out what was actually going on from there.

People milled around below her. They seemed edgy. Many held small objects in their hands, no doubt mobile devices they realised were not functioning at the moment. There was no light coming from them, but her eagle-like eyesight gave her a hint. They had nothing to do with whatever was going on around them. Most were moving away, trying to retreat to find a source of illumination. It was one of the most reliable, most primordial instincts of human behaviour. To find safety.

A tempting alternative, but Jennifer knew such an elaborate operation no doubt meant someone or something was in jeopardy. Against the tide of the crowds, one other person stood stock still, but not dressed as the others she had seen. The individual stood too distant to see in great detail, but with such calm poise amidst the upheaval that it caught her attention. She leaned in for a closer look.

To her left, another of the mysterious squad raised a rifle. Long range. And aiming downwards at the person she was looking at. She powered herself upright, and flew at the gunman, first throwing him off his aim with her lunge. Her momentum took him to his knees, and she wasted no time. She kicked the gun from his loose grip and slipped her arms around his throat, squeezing as he thrashed around to escape. She leaned backwards and snapped her legs around his waist, ensuring maximum leverage and squeezed harder. His resistance quickly stopped as he slipped from consciousness.

"Number Ten: I said take the shot!"

She seized his radio and the grappling hook from his belt. She then ran to the edge of the building, securing the hook and tying the end of the attached rope to her waist. If Number Ten wasn't available to take that shot, someone else would very soon. She took the plunge, rappelling down the building with professional precision. She kept one eye on her target all the way down.

Near the bottom, she could see the intended victim: a young female police constable who had been playing with her radio but had given up and searched the street. She spotted Jennifer's descent, and headed over, pulling her asp from her belt and flicking it to full length. "Stop right there!"

"It's not me you want, Constable."

The officer hesitated, reaching also for another pocket. Jennifer detached herself from the rope and stepped forward.

"Stay where you are!"

"Look, this whole thing's deliberate. Something's up—we haven't time to waste."

"I know."

"Someone just tried to kill you. Someone else will probably try in a moment. You need to move. Right now."

"What do you mean, somebody—?"

"Talk in cover." Jennifer ran to a nearby alleyway and beckoned the policewoman to do likewise. The constable followed with extreme caution.

Jennifer kept a good look around, but was aware of the understandably jittery officer ahead of her. "Inspector Hammond." It was a long shot, but it was the only name she had; the only link that had any chance of saving the woman without resorting to violence. "I need you to stay out of sight, get to the working power and call in. Ask for Inspector Hammond and tell him this is from Dr. Mellencourt's friend."

"Look, I can't just—"

"Whoever this is, they've gone to a lot of trouble to do whatever it is they are planning. I think they're hitting the British Museum."

"Even with the power down, they'll have no chance."

"There's a bunch of them. They're armed and they've got something the museum guards really won't be able to handle. Nor will you."

"And you will?"

"Prior experience. But I need to hurry. Please do this for me."

With that, Jennifer turned and made her way out of the alleyway. "Hey!"

Stop shouting. You'll get us both killed. She turned and threw a finger to her lips before bursting into a sprint.

Jennifer had lost little of her speed and quickly covered the ground to her intended destination. It wasn't going to be easy, but she had to go for it. As expected, the entrances appeared secure, but a closer look inside revealed several guards on the floor. They were motionless, not even breathing. Her physical enhancement may have gone, but her additional senses had not dulled.

More lives may be in danger in there. She had no time to waste. She tried the front door. Locked. She ran to a trade entrance. Also locked. "Damn." She would have to hit the roofs again.

The presence of several of the robbers on the roof came as no surprise to her. But none were doing anything other than standing on an over-watch pattern.

"Thirteen. Hostile located, directly below. Remember mission protocols. Over."

"You have a better shot? Over."

"Confirmed. Taking now. Out."

All pretences of subtlety now gone, she released her grip from the rooftop as the shooter grazed her shoulder on the way down. She gritted her teeth and suppressed a howl as she hit the ground hard. Rolling backward, she cursed as she lay flat, her legs dead from the fall. Anyone else, on a good day, might have broken them both.

She rolled across the ground before the second shot could find its target. She forced herself back to her feet and leapt behind a pillar, just as the third slammed into her cover.

"Seven. Why isn't the target neutralised?"

"Target just leapt off the roof."

"And still moving?"

"Fully active."

"Mission compromised. Prepare to abort."

"Negative." This voice was female, a strong French accent evident. "First team are about to acquire the targets. Deal with the problem. And any witnesses."

If she stayed there, Jennifer was dead. Even if those shots remained inaccurate, the strike team was coming for her. She made a dash for the side, weaving as pot shots smacked around her. But it wasn't as if there was a convenient window. Roof glass was likely her only way in. That was going to hurt. Even if she survived the armed robbers.

She scaled the building again but, this time, searched for the nearest guard. Clinging to a ledge, she edged across until she was closer to a pair of boots. The guard looked in the other direction—but not for long.

With all her strength, she lifted herself further up with one arm and with the second, swept at his heels. He landed on his backside, kicking her in the face, but she clung on grimly. The guard swung his feet at her, but she blocked with her free hand before catching one of his ankles.

She launched the other hand straight at his face. He caught her arm but soon realised his life was in her hands. His delay allowed her to drag herself up. He began a muffled yell, but she rammed her forehead into his nose, then straddled him. She swung several punches until he stopped moving.

The noise had alerted the others. She pulled herself up to a crouch and stayed low as she ran across the roof, looking for any glass areas. Another guard took aim. She threw herself down on the glass and rolled as the shots came in, until she found cover once more.

She waited for the robber to close in and rolled around to the other side of the glass dome. When he came within reach, she launched to her feet and grabbed his rifle, twisting the barrel away before he could raise it, then kicked a hamstring and dropped him to one knee. One well-aimed chop to the back of his head finished the job.

Retaining the rifle, she ran back for the glass roof and took a flying leap to evade a series of shots. With all her might, she slammed the weapon butt into one of the bullet-cracked panes and shattered it. She repeated this several times until there was a suitable gap and then threw herself into the hole, just as a hail of rounds flew over her.

Another long drop, but she was more prepared for it this time and rolled as if it was a tenth of the height. Now, she needed to find the first team. Almost in total darkness, she crouched behind one of the centre exhibits and looked around, hoping for other light sources. Instead, she found another downed guard. She reached for his neck, checking for a pulse. Nothing. She shook her head and looked deep into the darkness. Another body. In a swift but crouched hustle, she checked him, too, on the way past and again saw no signs of life. But he led to another.

She soon picked up a different trail. That cold, abhorrent whiff of death that she picked up on the rooftop. That was the trail to follow. She moved fast, all the while focusing on what was at the end of the scent.

Mistake. The cloaked figure flew out of nowhere and tackled her to the ground, but her momentum freed her as she rolled backward.

Jennifer got to her knees, but the shadow moved faster, punching her twice in the face and knocking her backward. As the assailant closed in for the kill, Jennifer swept hard with her leg, and floored the opponent. She crawled forward and leapt—

But the figure vanished into thin air. Jennifer landed on nothing. She tried to re-establish the scent, but a knee connected with her face. The lightning-fast attacker then kicked her hard, leaving her flat. Jennifer heard a sword unsheathing, but even with her sight, could barely see it. Punch-drunk, she offered no resistance as another kick rained in on her jaw and the sword tapped her neck with a cold touch of death she remembered intimately. Panic set in. She knew this was the end.

"Face of war."

It was just a whisper, but it echoed across the museum just as the sword rose. The killer hesitated. Jennifer attempted a sweep on her adversary, but her strike simply passed through the cloaked figure. She doubted a repeat attempt would produce different results. She continued to roll and made a run for it.

The grey death appeared from nowhere in front of her and thrust a powerful kick into her face, quick as a flash. Jennifer fell backward, the ethereal onyx blade against her throat. It chilled to the touch. In her experience, only Mary could move like that. But this blade-wielder could fight.

A woman with bright red hair emerged, her arm around a tall, lean, tattooed man with a shaven head. Neither were uniformed. The red-haired woman clung to the tattooed figure like glue.

"Are you certain?" the cloaked figure asked. The voice was accented, female, possibly Asian.

"He said it. When is he ever wrong?"

"Then why was this so easy?"

The red haired woman frowned. "Do you want to explain to *him* that you killed her? Let him make the decision."

"As you wish."

The cloaked woman swung a rapid kick at Jennifer's head.

"She certainly has resilience." The second and third kicks sent everything dark.

CHAPTER TWO

E verything ached—an unusual occurrence in itself. On the plus side, it meant Jennifer felt the effects of the fight, simple aches and pains, cuts and bruises, instead of the cold, debilitating torture of months before. At least she felt *alive*.

How long had she been out? A few seconds? A few hours? And also, *where* was she? Lying under covers on an uncomfortable bed which was reminiscent of a ship's cabin, in a room she could barely stretch out twice in. The ceiling didn't look to give her much clearance either.

The next challenge was how to get out of there, wherever there was. She got out from under the sheets—and realised she had been relieved of all clothing, other than her sports underwear.

What?

An uncomfortable situation just became even more so. She looked around for her clothes. The room was sparsely furnished. Other than the bed, not even a rug covered the stone floor.

However, on a very low table lay a stunning, blue silk dress. Jennifer lacked Kara's expertise on matters of fashion, but felt quite certain the gown was of exceptional quality, and definitely expensive. *Someone* was dropping an unsubtle hint as to how they wanted her dressed.

As much as the wardrobe demand aggravated, the real question was why they didn't off her when they had the chance, especially if they knew what would happen when she got out of there. Unless whoever held her just didn't care.

Her thoughts drifted on to who the hell the robbers were, and how the cloaked one took her down so easily. That ruffled her greatly. Sure, her condition remained some way off a hundred-percent full strength, but she had no idea she was *that* rusty.

Her opponent moved faster than anyone she had previously encountered. Organised, disciplined *and* well-equipped; it seemed quite clear the gang members were no common criminals. And some of them also had additional . . . advantages.

She returned to thoughts of how to escape. The walls were impenetrable old stone, whilst the door was wooden but looked solid. Jennifer went over and gave the handle a try, unsurprised to find that it didn't turn far. Leaning hard against it didn't budge it either. It felt unshakeable. If she was anywhere near full strength, it would have been worth testing harder, but at the moment, futile.

She supposed there were some advantages to not running at full strength—opponents would likely underestimate her. Because, besides healing her recent wounds, it was fair to say she was feeling better than she had in a while. Maybe if she just stayed there for a couple of days, they'd have the real Jennifer to contend with. And then they'd be in trouble.

Only problem was, someone clearly wanted her to keep an appointment with them. And she made her own damn appointments.

Justified paranoia rather high, she checked for cameras in the room. A cursory scan, followed by a more detailed squint, revealed nothing. If they were hidden, they'd done a really good job of it.

Cheap perverts ruled out at the least, she went for the dress and dived into it. She began to zip up the back—it was better than nothing after all—but then an idea came to her.

"Hey!" she called, in half-zipped attire, and battered the door. "I'm awake. But I need a little help getting into this thing."

She cupped an ear to the door and heard footsteps close by. A key turned in the lock and she leapt backward and to the left, alert and waiting.

The door opened but not to full width. The guard, dressed as most of the others she'd seen, appeared with nobody behind him, armed and aggressive. "Get ready," he said, a French accent to his voice. "The boss wants to see you."

Good. She was too valuable to shoot. "Looking forward to it," she purred, turning her back to him. "Now give me a hand."

"Stop messing around and get dre—"

Jennifer was already where she wanted to be. She smashed an elbow cleanly upward into his chin, then grabbed his arm. With total control, she twisted it, turning him the opposite direction and drove him head-first into the wall twice. Guiding his unconscious body down on to the bed, she peered outside in all directions. Only one guard in sight—the one she'd knocked out.

Sloppy of them—*or too easy.*

She wasn't going to make a run for it dressed for an awards ceremony if she could help it. She stripped the guard before ditching the dress in exchange for his body armour and more practical clothing. She examined the submachine gun, but dismissed appropriating it as a terrible idea. Instead, she simply relieved him of it, sure to remove the magazine. Using the dress, she tied his arms to the head of the bed and then crept outside, quietly closing the door.

A shout came from her left, sadly, in French. Checking on a colleague?

She dashed right, staying as light on her feet as she could. She reached the end of the corridor and was again faced with a choice of left or right. Behind her, the guard came into view. She pointed back towards the room at her old prison quarters before darting left. Her cover would be gone in seconds, but at least she would be away from him.

A bit of running took her close to another guard, but she pointed frantically behind her, just long enough for him to hesitate. She threw a fist into his face before he could respond, then swept him to the ground and straddled him, punching him out cold. Jennifer rolled off and pushed him into the wall, but there was nowhere to hide him, and after she heard the gunman at the room raise the alarm, no time either.

Only time to run. She bolted into a corridor: two more guards with rifles levelled. She pounced on the first guard on her way past and took him down with a smack to his booted ankle. Already inside the second guard's reach, she seized his leading wrist, then rolled her back into his body and slammed him to a wall once, then again, before smashing her head right back into his nose. She smacked her forearm into his chin several times until he slumped to the ground.

She took the weapon, but removed the magazine and the temptation to fire.

Onwards again. Another choice at the corridor, and a guard near the left side. She raised the weapon before he was aware. "Drop it. Now."

He looked around. Stalling. Her bluff was failing anyway; he knew where to look on her gun. But his hesitation provided the split second she needed. She swung the gun around and smacked the butt into his temple, and followed up with a high kick for good measure.

She moved with stealth through another corridor. The lack of windows or stairs narrowed her options greatly. But better to keep a move on and hope to avail herself of an escape route.

A staircase at last, leading upwards. That told her she was at the lowest possible floor. And heading up usually led to a point of escape. After a cursory check for hostile activity, she advanced.

The corridor up the flight of stairs was better illuminated. A large door stood at the end, solid but perhaps leading out. She ran away from the door and stopped to assess the obstruction in detail. Much as she wanted to escape, a sigil within a brass circle which looked recently defaced caught her eye. Within it stood out a stylistic letter 'W' and an equally ornate Omega emblem behind it.

Perilous as Jennifer's situation was, seeing it changed things.

That symbol struck a familiar chord. She'd seen it before, but associated it with a person rather than a building. She'd never learned what the symbol truly meant. But to her, it meant safety, security. Someone she could trust.

The only person she had ever seen with it:

Alice.

Everywhere she went, Alice wore a small brooch shaped as that symbol. Given the general circumstances under which they used to meet, though it was a curiosity, Jennifer had never asked about it. The woman was normally busy saving her life.

But what was it doing in this place? Up on that wall? Where the hell was she?

Is that why they haven't just offed me yet? Friends of Alice?

They certainly weren't friendly. There were better ways to express that than kicking her in the head. And whatever she did or didn't know about Alice, she wasn't a common thief. She wouldn't have kept such company either. It just wasn't her. So, whoever these people were, they *weren't* there to help in any way. Time to get out of there, then.

She listened for hostile movements, attempting to isolate footsteps, shouting. But her enemy was quiet, if they were around—more than the last lot, at least. She ran to the end of the corridor, which offered a left or right choice, but no signs of the *right* way.

She crouched and peered around the corner, both directions. All clear. But each had doors roughly equidistant at each end. There wasn't an obvious route to take.

Decision time. It was too exposed there for any real stealth, but there was plenty of room for trouble in either direction. Still, she wasn't going to work out an escape route by standing around.

Turn left.

She charged as fast as she could, making her way to the closed door.

There was a whistle through the air and a crack. Jennifer was on her back, staring at the ceiling by the time the sound registered. She spluttered and choked.

The blow had caught her right in the throat, but there was nobody in sight. She stood alone and frustrated in the empty corridor, with neither a door nor a convenient grate nearby.

Three deep breaths later, she returned to her feet. She couldn't see anyone . . . but sensed there was still someone around.

Concentrate.

Nobody was that damn good. Unless they were . . .

The slice through the wind caught her again, this blow straight under her chin. It knocked her backward and off her feet. She straightened herself up, then smacked the ground and cried out in frustration, knowing exactly who she was up against. Although she didn't, which just aggravated her more.

"Show yourself!" Her opponent did not oblige.

A different approach, then. She listened, even sniffed. She picked up that necrotic scent that she had become familiar with over the past year. Try as she might to deny it or escape the fact, she smelled the same stench that lingered around Grenshall Manor, around Mary.

And that was why it took time to pick up on; in the months in which she had barely moved from the bed, she had grown used to the presence of Mary and her Unresting world. But that knowledge gave her a hint of what she was now dealing with.

It probably wasn't a ghost. And not a mindless brain-eater or pumped-up brute like that Natalie or Thomas Barber, puppets of the deadly Violet. Living, then, just like Mary. Only whoever it was could fight—and exceptionally well.

Jennifer ran the other way and then stopped and sniffed. It was as good as she had. She caught the scent again, but almost too late as something cracked towards her. She raised an elbow and blocked the strike before lashing a jab forward. She caught something, but her opponent left her range again.

"You're a right pain, you know?" Jennifer snarled. She attempted to hold the scent, but the enemy was moving too quickly. She couldn't hold there; reinforcements could come at any moment. She headed back to the door, edging cautiously, not running this time. She continued to rely on her nose, but the putrid whiff surrounded her. The ghost walker could have been anywhere.

She reached for the door. As she got a hand on the grip, her unseen opponent seized her arm and wrenched it around. Jennifer leaned and twisted her body to keep her arm free. She got a punch in the face for her trouble, but at least got clear of an arm lock.

She launched another jab in front of her, but connected with nothing. A kick connected with her stomach, then two punches to the face and an elbow floored her again. She swept her leg, knowing where the opponent must have been—in front of her—but again, it was in vain.

"You really should yield, or someone will end up getting hurt." The voice echoed in the air around her.

"It's not going to be me," Jennifer countered. But she wasn't sure of the truth of that statement. She hadn't affected her opponent but had been floored three times, which not many had managed up to that point. And she couldn't even *see* who was hitting her.

She stretched her hands and felt a familiar tickling sensation within them. But they did not elongate into weapons as she desired. The ability to create those razor-like talons that had helped her in the past had deserted her.

She didn't want to lose. But she had bitten off far more than she could chew with her fearless foray into danger. It looked like she had entered the fray too soon, her own strength nothing like she had known it to be in the past.

She'd have foiled an ordinary robbery attempt, no problem. She could handle competent and well-armed guards quite comfortably. But that cloaked menace was another matter. She had no answer to that speed, that movement; the fact that she couldn't just engage in a straight fight.

"I'm not going back into that hole." She tried to get up again and leapt for the door, but another heel to the face put her right back down. It was only then that she realised what she had said. *I'm not going back into that hole.* That was what she had said in her early teens to that stepmother of hers. She hadn't felt that weak since those days.

To yield, to stay down, was not an option. It was escape—or die trying. And she knew full well if they wanted her dead by now, she would have been. *Whoever* they were.

"Fine," came the echo. "You'll just heal up again anyway." A rush of wind howled around Jennifer's ear and then the air rushed out of her lungs from a hard, unseen, kick to the gut. A flurry of punches and kicks connected, with her no closer to knowing where each blow was coming from. Her resistance ended as she hit the deck.

CHAPTER THREE

An overpowering fruity fragrance assaulted Jennifer's sense of smell and brought her 'round. She attempted to spring upward but found herself restrained by thick rope binding her to a chair. Anger flooded over her. To be knocked out once in the space of twenty-four hours was careless. Twice was just unheard of.

She stopped thrashing and took in her surroundings. She sat in a dining hall, very old in appearance, medieval almost, but somewhat run-down, deteriorating in places. Yet, the lengthy table before her appeared intact and rock solid. The spread on it most certainly resembled a banquet of times gone by; the only space left on it no doubt to accommodate plates.

As her vision cleared more, the only other individual present at the table caught her attention. Opposite from where she sat at one end, some distance away was a man with dark hair, neat and cut just above the shoulder. Piercing green eyes peered at her, striking even from that distance.

He wore a suit, clearly tailored to his build, athletic but not bulky. He stared at her, assessed, perhaps judged her, as her thoughts again turned to an escape plan. Had her razor fingers not deserted her at a critical juncture, she would already have been free. But then what?

He didn't look overly troubled by her presence, and probably rightly so, considering her latest performances. Her ghostly opponent was nowhere to be seen; a familiar problem. However, neither did any scent of death or decay linger in the air.

Though bound, Jennifer wasn't gagged. "So . . ." she drawled. "How come I'm still alive, then?"

The host laughed heartily, never taking his eyes off her. "Honestly. You have quite a low opinion of us after so short a meeting." He also spoke with an accent she couldn't quite place. Perhaps Italian. "Who do you think I am?"

"Gang boss, maybe?"

"Straight to the stereotypes, I see. Do you see any gangsters around here?"

Jennifer scanned the room. She could probably lose the ropes, but, assuming the ghost walker wasn't there, she wouldn't be far. The armed guards evenly spaced against the walls of the massive hall posed a more immediate threat.

A door stood at the back of the room behind the host, who she knew nothing about, but she saw no windows at all. She heard another door close behind her as well. Perhaps a changing of the guard? But, taken altogether, it meant too many X-factors, a maze of a place and all manner of other difficulties to contend with. It was hopeless.

To make matters worse, she couldn't pretend to be useful to them for much longer, intentionally or otherwise. "So you're not your typical organised crime outfit. But your boys were still trying to raid the British Museum. That makes you robbers—criminals. Stays in the category of organised crime, yes?"

The man twitched and shook his head. He looked disappointed in her. "The weak or dull mind would assume us common criminals. To dismiss my collective as merely lawless rabble, which we are not, would be a grave error.

"What happened to the dress I provided for you? I took a great deal of trouble and went to considerable expense to find something appropriate, and so well-tailored."

She shifted awkwardly in her seat. The idea of how total strangers could achieve a custom fit made her skin crawl. But she sat straight and glared defiance at her host. "You're right. It looked extremely fetching on the lackey you sent. I liked his attire better."

His pause told her that she'd succeeded in being suitably irksome. But his poker face at the least rivalled her own. "I liked mine on you better." She felt dirtier with each of his words. "It cannot be coincidence that we chanced upon such a competent vigilante. Or is it possible that you are simply too dense to realise who it is you chose to oppose?"

She did resent that. He *wanted* her to. "Which do you think it is?"

He denied her an immediate answer, preferring instead to keep staring at her. After a moment's analysis, he responded. "You know what I think? I think you're someone who went looking for trouble. A part of me hopes you do not find yourself short. However, I would like to know how you lasted as long as you did against my court."

"Court?" An unusual name for any gang, for certain. "In honesty with you, I don't know."

And if I'd been anywhere near my best, they wouldn't have lasted nearly as long against me.

She forced a grin. "You want to untie me? I'm not in any danger of escaping."

The host looked amused but soon afterwards nodded. One of the guards shouldered his weapon and advanced toward her, then released her from her binding.

She considered the escape opportunity: a clean chance to swiftly take out the guard and restrain him. But that would have meant taking a hostage—which wasn't an option—and would result in no advantage that she didn't already have. Also, in that room, whichever direction she faced, she had her back to someone. *And the ghost walker.*

And all this before she took into account the unknown quantity of the suited man at the other end of the table.

Meanwhile, the guard did not take his eyes off her for the duration of his chore. He had a soldier's eye, assessing her assessment. He returned to his post.

Her hands now free once more, she looked down at them and channelled the combative mentality she had such a firm grip on. That irritating tickle ran through her finger bones again, but not so much as a rapidly-growing fingernail sprouted. Thwarted before she started, her attention returned to the other end of the table.

"Thank you," she said, an air of sincerity about her. She examined her captor up and down, trying to work out what, if anything, had got him to the position in which he sat.

It pleased her to know that the ability to see chromatic auras hadn't deserted her entirely. She could extend her sight; sharpen her focus to such an extent as to see the essential energies of just about anything. When she said she had a bad vibe, she meant it like few others. And the skill contributed to her lack of illness in her teens.

From a brief snapshot, she confirmed that nobody was attempting to poison her, and that her captor displayed no obvious special powers or talent she could fathom.

"Well, you appear to have seen sense," the man replied, tucking a napkin into his collar. He snapped his fingers and one of the rearmost guards banged twice on the back door. Within seconds, unarmed staff in waiting attire rushed through and attended the pair at the table.

The table spread was quickly lifted, dish by dish, and they began to serve. Jennifer waved away a plate of prosciutto just as her staffer was about to serve. The waiter nodded and exchanged his plate for a fruit cocktail. His superior glared at Jennifer with some apparent disdain.

"*The Face of War* . . ." He let the words run across his tongue as he examined her further. "The Face of War." Repeating it did not add conviction to his tone. "A fruit cocktail person. Such a thought hardly strikes fear into the mortal heart, does it?"

"I've never called myself anything like that." She lightly rubbed her chin. "That's something to do with why I'm here though, isn't it? That name."

He grinned, folding a quantity of the meat around his fork before forcing every bit into his mouth. "You really have no idea, do you?" Without waiting until he had finished chewing, he continued. "Our organisation has quite recently acquired the services of a relative prophet, Vortext. When he speaks, we must listen, for he has always had something very useful to say on the rare occasions words leave his mouth."

Jennifer's eyes narrowed. She cut a piece of melon into a small chunk and scooped it into her mouth, sure to maintain eye contact. She made a point to finish chewing before answering. "Oh?"

He kept eating even as his servant continued to fill his plate. "He has been an exceptionally reliable find. Both of them were actually, him and that girlfriend of his. But you seem to have inconvenienced her somewhat."

I've no idea what he's talking about.

"Inconvenience is the story of my life. But tell me, what did I do?"

The host twitched, about to say something, but he restrained himself. "Nothing insurmountable."

She snapped with predatory speed. "Then why mention it? Is this something to do with me being the 'Chosen One'?"

He glared at her, ashen. "Do not mock that which you fail to understand."

She leaned forward on the table. "If I'm that important to you, I can mock freely. You already told me you're keeping me alive for a reason, so you can hardly force me to take your threats seriously."

The host relaxed, perhaps a show for her benefit. "You are only alive as long as it takes to exhaust my investigation, so enjoy your bravado while it lasts. If only you could see the painting I had back at my home. It carries the title, *The Face of War,* and I have it dated in origin from the sixteenth century."

"So?"

"So it looks exactly like you. That is no doubt why Vortext mentioned it. He is an impressive creature, I must say. At the moment, that painting is my most valuable treasure. And I believe it holds great secrets. If only we could unlock them."

Her eyes narrowed. "Not a gang boss but an art thief, then? One with serious resources, at that."

"Art?" he smirked. He took a moment to shovel some of his food down. "I—we—seek the world's truest treasures. Creations well beyond plebeian understanding."

"Like a painting with someone who bears a passing resemblance to me? Tell me, what did you get for your troubles in the end?"

He shook his head. "Nothing, thanks to your interference. We had spent weeks working out the logistics of that operation, and had a strict deadline. Your running loose disrupted our schedule beyond repair. Things mobilised rather quickly."

"And yet you had enough time to carry me."

"I told you: when Vortext speaks, my court listens."

"You keep saying that," Jennifer snorted. "What are you, some kind of prince or something?"

He grinned. "Yes. You have already met some of my court."

Jennifer leaned forward, and gnawed on the fruit in front of her. "*Whose* court?"

He stood and waved one of his guards towards the door, then gave a sweeping bow. "I, madame, am Gianfranco Manta. And in the places I walk, I am very much a prince. Please, let me introduce the Manta Court to you." His face dropped into a scowl. "So that you don't get any more ideas of running away."

Suits me. I'll get a better idea of what I'm up against.

"I would be honoured." She gave a mocking bow in return. He ignored the baiting. From the rear door, the ghost walker entered, fully corporeal. She remained wrapped in the grey cloak, which veiled the wearer exceptionally well. She walked close to Jennifer and gave a smug look, then took her place at the table some distance to the left of their guest.

Even though fully physical, the woman's movement was wraith-like, and she kept sheathed within her flowing robes a sword. Jennifer spotted its bejewelled hilt. It reminded her of that knife she had seen Mary with from time to time within Grenshall Manor.

Though not wishing to turn her back, her attention returned to the door as a tall, dark-skinned man walked in, slim but wiry. His head was shaven, imprinted with tattoos of a design she couldn't pick out. In contrast to the overconfidence she had seen in the woman, he looked distant, to the point of being elsewhere.

A striking young woman held his hand. She wore a bright red dress, with hair, boots, and lips to match. She held her forehead with her spare hand, and no sooner had Jennifer noticed the action than her own head bristled with a fierce itch.

Jennifer distinctly felt they had previously crossed paths, and she couldn't attribute it to the memory of Manta's recent words. But that couldn't have been right. And yet, something about her struck familiar, like perhaps they had been together for some purpose or other. She attuned her chromatic vision to sense whether any other tell-tale signs lingered.

Feelings of powerlessness, pain, and death all lashed against her in one sharp slam. The room swam and she seized the table for support. She blinked herself back to mundane eyes and it all vanished, as if it were nothing more than savage daydreaming.

Despite her surroundings, the red-haired woman exuded a sense of calm, trust, warmth, and a cute innocence free of any possible threat. But it seemed false, a trick of the mind. Jennifer's instincts screamed danger.

She attributed some of the malevolent presence to a knife-shaped shade she saw pulsing somewhere near the woman's thigh, a well-concealed weapon. However, the power Jennifer detected couldn't hide from her augmented sight. It reminded her in presence of the weapon Mary carried, only more like an evil twin. That made some sense.

The blade her friend, Mary, carried once held the soul-devouring sapphire which contributed to Jennifer's near-death. More infamously set into a necklace, it became the source of power that caused dozens of deaths and a reign of chaos which engulfed London, and brought a raft of undead, ghostly, and otherwise terrifying encounters. On Mary's knife, a hole gaped where the jewel was once embedded.

If that knife was anything like that, and in troublesome hands, then being trapped in this madhouse would be the least of Jennifer's worries.

"So that's what you meant by treasures you're after," she mumbled, looking around. The tattooed man and the redhead both took seats on the right hand side of the table. She reasoned that the ornate weapon of the cloaked woman was probably of some concern as well.

"Let's see." She was louder this time. "We have Vortext, the prophet. The cloaked warrior, over there. And you." She pointed at the woman in red, who clung to Vortext as if he was set to blow away. "What did you do to me?"

Her target looked over at Manta for a moment; not a pleasant look either. But Manta shrugged, gesturing back to her. "Yes, Cerise," he said, tapping his foot. "What did you do, exactly?"

Cerise stopped rubbing her head and cast Jennifer a murderous glance. "She's got something to hide," she said. "And she's very determined to do so. But her life has been far from boring."

"What do you mean by that?" Jennifer asked. Her head itched again.

"I witnessed you take a fall that should have, at the very least, stopped you ever walking again. And you caused us a great inconvenience before and after. Not possible from an ordinary person."

Jennifer reached for the nearest salad bowl but her designated servant intercepted and promptly loaded her plate. It was too much like those months holed up at Grenshall Manor. She could work her own spoon now more than capably. "No, thank you." She gently pushed the servant away. Manta nodded at the door. The servants departed at once. "You got me. I'm a freak of nature."

"Not a freak, no," Manta chimed in. "A special talent, certainly. Possibly even worthy of my Court. *The Face of War*? I should like to find out."

"She easily bested several of your guards," the cloaked woman stated. She sat back from the table, out of reach of the food. "Not me, though."

Jennifer felt the wounding taunt. "Off day," she hissed through gritted teeth.

"Which is why you are sitting here now." Manta poured two glasses of an old, wine, expensive by all appearances, from a nearby carafe, but Jennifer declined, preferring a glass of water.

"I—*we* would very much like to see what you can do on a good day." The three others nodded as one. "Still, it was useful to see the competence of my staff tested."

He took a sip of his drink before raising his glass at his court, one by one, and then at the spare seat on his right. His court each raised nearby glasses in reply. "There is always a place here for the right people. I hope you will be able to join us."

"Not interested in being a career thief, thanks. I had plenty of chances for that."

"For whom are you so principled?" Cerise asked. "Who do you truly fight for? What made you move against us?"

"Common decency." Jennifer rushed a glass of water down. "What's your deal? It can't be money."

"Why can't it be money?" Cerise said, looking intrigued. "What we are looking for is highly valuable. It would be a lot easier otherwise."

"Well, that's true. But it means more to you than just that. What's your game?"

"I simply believe in a better world,"

"Yeah right." Even as Jennifer spoke, Cerise's words seemed to take on an ironclad sincerity. Not enough to sway her own opinion, but she was beginning to see how Cerise had found her way into the court. It was all very subtle, but there was something about her contradictory to the effervescent young woman who seemed to be sitting there.

"So, a question for you: what's that symbol about—the one all around the place?"

The three looked at each other for a moment. Then, in unison, they gathered their glasses and refilled them before lifting them in the form of a toast. Manta gave Jennifer a moment to follow suit. She did not move. He shrugged. "To Winter's end!" he cried.

"Winter's end!" the others repeated.

"Yeah, I still don't know what you're talking about."

"Of course you don't." Manta drank heartily, then lowered his drink to the table. "Allow us to educate you. You see, there have been some dangerous threats to humanity running around for many years, threats which your politicians and law enforcement establishments have no understanding of. Like yourself, all at the Court have something which makes them exceptional by society standards. That doesn't make any of us 'freaks'. That makes us extraordinary. Which means we have certain . . . responsibilities to the world around us. You have seen for yourself what the Grey Lady here can do."

"That's an unusual name," Jennifer answered, her mouth thankfully moving faster than her mind on this occasion. She'd thought to mention this wasn't the first time she'd seen such powers manifest, but being as her current state of affairs was as a captive, with no guarantee of walking out of this establishment alive, the last thing she wanted to do was to drag her friends into it.

That said, she would have given anything to see Mary pit her mastery of the ghost realm against the Grey Lady's slippery talents. "If it's not too personal a question, what do you all do?" She was staring specifically at Cerise when she asked.

"I'm their best medic," Cerise answered.

"Uh-huh," Jennifer replied, remembering the hidden knife. She looked at Vortext. "I know what you do. But you haven't told them much about me, have you?"

Cerise leaned towards Jennifer, a most un-healer-like look on her face. "You are something of a mystery."

The detainee mirrored Cerise's actions. "Glad to hear it."

CHAPTER FOUR

Jennifer turned her attention back to Manta. She already knew all she cared to about this 'Grey Lady', too. "So. You were telling me about this sixteenth-century painting."

"There is little more to tell. Though I can easily picture you in the plate armour you—she wears in the painting. You have a warrior's eyes, just as I saw on the image."

"Where she is seen, there is always war."

Vortext blurted the words as if he had just woken up, then just as soon as he had, returned to a catatonic state—a disconcerting experience. "Cerise, shut him up before I do."

She shot Manta another glare but stood up and Vortext stood with her. The two left through the door behind Manta.

"Did he blab something he shouldn't have again?" Jennifer asked, suddenly grinning. "What's all this about starting wars?"

Manta, clearly infuriated, took another hefty swig of his wine. "Well, I am in no doubt about his talent even if you might be," he said through gritted teeth. "What he quoted was an inscription on the back of the painting. Again, I have never allowed anyone to see it, but there it is, word for word."

"Surely it's just another art piece worth a few quid you can shift on the black market?"

"It belonged to my grandfather!" he said, bashing his fists against the table. "I would never conceive of selling it, no matter how much it is worth." He slumped back into his chair and spoke in a far quieter voice. "It's all we had left of him. Of anything."

She was about to press him further, but she caught his sense of loss when he spoke. It was genuine; not possible to fake as one who had felt it as she had. Manta's 'grandfather' sounded as 'mother' did to her, or even 'Alice'.

Alice. That symbol. Had she been part of this?

"That business about the 'dawn of spring'," she said instead. "What are you talking about?"

He looked up at her. "Former residents of this place," he simply said. "We are only going to be here temporarily ourselves. Just long enough to accomplish our second . . . task."

"You're planning another robbery?" She didn't give him enough time to answer that. Too many other questions were burning at her. "Former residents? What happened to them?"

"They were very dangerous individuals. They tried to kill me, my court."

"So we had to act." The Grey Lady turned to face Jennifer, having sat motionless for some time. She looked more through Jennifer than at her, cold, utterly distant eyes in her otherwise pretty face.

Her mind refused to acknowledge the likelihood, but deep down, Jennifer knew exactly what they were getting at. The former residents had been eliminated. These were not people for messing around.

But neither was she. As against her as the odds were here, she had found herself not just amongst thieves, but murderers, too. That last day she had seen Alice Winter, she was eighteen years old. She had been officially adopted at fifteen, and hadn't looked back from then. When Alice had entered her life properly not long before that, her life had changed. No more bullying. No more injuries from home. None that lasted anyway.

Her adopted mother—the proper one, not the stepmother—wore that symbol; the one belonging to the former residents. And she did not have a callous bone in her body. At least, not that she had ever shown Jennifer.

And she wore *that* symbol. The one that persisted on the walls of this place, wherever that was, and reminded her of the one thing she just couldn't move on from. And her captors saw them as an enemy. She couldn't let them know that. She just couldn't.

"So, you lot, whoever you are, took out anyone who had anything to do with that sigil, because you thought they were a danger to you?"

"That order was a danger to everyone," Manta snapped. She found that rather difficult to believe but held her tongue. "Now, we can get on with our business without people trying to kill us."

Don't bet on it.

But as soon as she had the thought, she remembered she was no killer.

Remembered the worst night of her life.

"Now that we've worked all that out," she said, swallowing the lump in her throat, "what do you want with me?"

"If you're important enough to be part of a painting my grandfather treasured, then plenty."

"Blonde women who can throw a punch and look good in armour aren't that uncommon, you know."

"Matching your appearance so precisely, they are. He told me as much himself, an old war story."

"Your grandfather fought in a war then?"

"Never fought, no. His was a higher purpose. During the war, he kept a number of treasures safe from the careless bullets and bombs which were loose and everywhere. He had the good sense to move out of Milan, an increasingly dangerous place, and relocate to Berne. Quite a move, I know, but heading to the neutral Switzerland was good for business."

Manta sat up and puffed out his chest as he proudly told the tale. "Glauco Manta was an antiques dealer, which will come as no surprise to you in my field of work. He had many clients. The Nazis paid best and most frequently as they tasked him with finding such things, but Italian interest remained strong of course, even some French.

"He would take care to look only for those on a list given by Nazi experts on such matters, and actually became so good at it that they provided him the rank of *Oberst* and had him work permanently for them.

"But he found this painting, the only thing which survived a bombing in Berlin in 1944. He took it home, kept it from the other things by way of bribery and substitution. He treasured it and researched what he had known of the building beforehand. Just a house with a rich collector, but this was the only painting that remained intact."

"That's lovely, but that means the painting can't have been of me, doesn't it?"

"'She was seen in Constantinople in the eleventh century, Milan in the sixteenth, and others,' my grandfather told my father, who in turn told me. Father said that I should look for her, especially in battle, if I ever was. He was correct. I have been at war. But I still need to know what happens now."

"Clearly, I start a war with you all and fulfil some kind of strange self-fulfilling prophecy your mad self seems to have got into his head."

"See how far you get," the Grey Lady said, just loud enough to be heard, with just enough authority for all to listen. "You have clearly learned nothing from our last encounters."

"I learn all the time," Jennifer said, watching as her adversary rested a hand on her sword hilt. She knew that, even with a table obscuring her view. "And I learn fast."

"As do I," Manta said. "And I should thank you for reminding me why I allowed guests around my dinner table during this critical time." He snapped his fingers once at the Grey Lady who promptly stood, before vanishing in plain sight. "You see, I can afford no such failures tonight as I had last night. It took a lot of work to get out of there with little trace. But how do we improve if we do not learn from our mistakes, hmmm?"

Jennifer whirled round as she heard the door behind her click locked. Within seconds, the other did the same.

"It is a pity that some have failed to grasp this simple principle. And as such, they have proven themselves unworthy to both myself and those others whom they serve."

Manta reached under the table and produced a reinforced briefcase. He dropped it with no regard for the crockery below, and then reached into his inside suit pocket. He pulled out a set of small keys and turned them on locks first on one side, then the other, of the case.

Jennifer stood, alert for incoming trouble, but Manta waved her back to her seat. He moved without urgency, evidently in no hurry. "In this case is enough to pay each of you that which I agreed," he said, loudly and clearly addressing his guards. He gained the attention of each of them, holding and rotating the case so they could all see inside.

Then, he snapped it shut and dropped it on to the table, which scattered food all over the floor. "But I called each of you here because you *failed.*"

The guards stepped back, alert to Manta's sudden change of tone, and looked at each other, perhaps in the hope that his words were being directed somewhere specific.

"You had the simple task of stopping her from escaping. But she put each one of you down easily. And yet she insists she is not the Face of War, nor one of us. How can I trust you to guard me? How do I trust you to protect me when one unarmed woman embarrasses each of you?"

A mixture of reactions followed. Some guards hung their heads, others shook theirs, and a couple backed away in anticipation of treachery. Those few edged towards their weapons. Jennifer suspected they were probably the ones with the right idea. She lowered herself near the table, but, certain the focus of the others present lay elsewhere, she decided to keep it that way.

Manta returned to his seat, one hand on the case. "Seeing as I have set aside this money to pay you all, it shall remain that way—to whoever can walk out of here with it."

Immediately, one of the men readied his rifle in Manta's direction. But no sooner than he had found his aim, he began to gurgle. Jennifer saw no outer wound on him, but he coughed blood and collapsed to the ground, motionless.

The smell of death. It filled Jennifer's lungs again just as the guard next to him toppled forward, also coughing blood. He hung at a strange angle, as if leaning by the chest on something, but she saw nothing there. After a couple of seconds, he fell forward, just as the last.

One soldier ran for the door behind Manta. This time, she saw the ethereal figure thrust a shadowy blade straight through his back and out again. It left no hole in his armour, no marks at all, but he fell just as sure as if skewered.

The cloaked figure vanished again, and just as Jennifer worked out where she had gone, two more guards fell down dead. The remaining three armed themselves and dropped into a crouch, trying to pick a target. Two of their heads bounced away from their bodies as they dropped forward.

The Grey Lady appeared to Jennifer's left, central by the table with the blackened blade in her hands, bloodless. Her smile made Jennifer quite literally nauseous. It wasn't just the executions; something else had occurred beyond her sight. She could see its residue—a pale red glow around the killer that would have been lost to more natural eyes, but there was no mistake. Those murders had done something to her, given her strength. By taking theirs.

The cloaked assassin turned her attention to the last hireling, the only one not in body armour. Jennifer recognised him, now this punishment was going on, as the one outside her cell door. He shook his head before releasing a double tap in the Grey Lady's direction. She stood, untroubled by this attack which either missed, or more likely passed right through her ghostly form. She sheathed her sword and gestured to Manta.

Manta tapped the case. "Nobody else left," he said to the survivor. "Go on. Take it. Walk out of here. You've earned it, and as I say, I put the money aside for you all."

"B-but . . . she'll kill me," the guard babbled.

"No. Actually, I had other plans to see you dead. But I would have hoped, given your background checks, that you would have been more than capable of such a simple matter."

"You told us not to shoot her!" he protested.

"I also told you she was not to escape," Manta hissed. "But I'm giving you several options here. A chance to prove yourself. See? She's even put away her weapon. What possible danger could a man as tough as you be facing?"

"Enough!" she called out. "If you're doing this for my benefit, I've seen enough. Let him go."

The Grey Lady turned to her. "Weak," she said in a spectral whisper. "So soft of heart. You could never be the Face of War."

Manta threw his hands into a shrug. "Maybe not. But we have an hour before the next job. And so you know," he turned to Jennifer, "this was for my benefit, not yours. I can't surround myself with security which cannot do its job." He returned his attention to the sweating guard. "I am offering you an opportunity to prove yourself. I suggest you take it."

The guard squirmed, but looked around. Jennifer recognised the signs of one attempting to escape. Not long ago, it had been her. But they wanted her alive—at least for a time. Manta had just signed the guard's death warrant.

Manta calmly turned to Jennifer and held a hand toward the panicking guard. "The honour, Face of War, shall be yours." The guard raised his weapon and backed to the door, but no longer knew who to target. His gun point wavered between Manta and Jennifer, a fact that only seemed to augment the host's calm. "You should hurry up and kill him, brave warrior. He has a gun to you. It's you or him."

"What?" She couldn't work out what Manta had up his sleeve to protect him from gunfire, but his hand remained up. The guard's gun arm veered left and right, still trying to make his chosen shot count. "I'm not going to—"

"Look out!" Manta cried, and lowered his hand. The guard appeared to receive a sudden nudge off-balance and he stumbled, then fired an unsteady volley in Jennifer's direction. His shots missed both targets wildly.

Jennifer stood and vaulted on to the table, running straight for the guard. As she leapt off, an invisible force swiped her off-balance and she fell forward. She corrected herself against the wall and fell into a backward roll. As she returned to her feet, the invisible attacker grabbed her by the jacket collar and kicked at her hamstring, dropping her to her knees. As she tried to correct herself, she felt herself dragged back by the hands and took another series of punches to her chin. Before she could recover, the ghostly figure lashed her to the nearest table leg and then disappeared out of sight once more.

The guard seized his opportunity and tried the door handle, but it did not budge. Manta waited with a patient grin as he tried to force his way out with no success. Seconds into his struggle, he found himself suspended in mid-air, grabbed by his collar and thrown with some force back into the centre of the room. The ghost woman rematerialized close to him even as Jennifer thrashed to get free, but the binding, quick as it had been, held firm against her efforts. She did not stop trying.

"Disappointing," Manta proclaimed as he hung his head. "But very well."

The Grey Lady returned her attention to the mercenary. She lowered her hood and revealed a cold, resentful visage. She looked down on him in every sense. "Come on. All you have to do is defeat me, and you can go free."

He looked at the money still on the table and saw that he would still have to get past her to acquire it. He thought better of it and raised his rifle. He fired two rounds, but his target had once more become translucent and closed in on him.

With minimal effort, she drew her sword and sliced his weapon straps clear, then disarmed him and kicked the gun away. Her body solidified and she rehoused her blade. "Guns. Unsporting."

Jennifer slammed her hands against the table, drawing blood as she attempted to escape the rope. But she made little progress. She watched the desperate man draw a survival knife and charge the cloaked killer. She easily sidestepped his clumsy lunge, then grabbed his hair and rammed her knee into his face three times.

He dropped his knife, and it bounced right by Jennifer's feet. She reached for Fate's gift to her and seized it with her soles, then drew her knees upward. In her struggle, she noticed the Grey Lady turning back to face her, her opponent restrained in a brutal-looking arm lock.

"Now," she said to Jennifer, "*this* is for your benefit." She applied an instant and significant increase of pressure and snapped his arm, then dropped him limp to the ground and let him scream. Jennifer edged the knife a little closer to her, but still far from her bound hands.

Manta banged on the table. "We need to hurry this up," he told his henchperson. She nodded and zeroed on the mercenary. He dragged himself to his feet and made a dash for the door. The ghost walker grabbed his ankle and tripped him. She leapt forward and brought her feet neatly down on the base of his spine, to another painful-sounding snap.

She seized control of the howling man's head and stood, hauling him like a doll as he whimpered and thrashed with his remaining working limbs. She forced his head in front of the money case and shook it for him. She then wrenched it hard to the left and shoved him on to the money.

Though her victim already lay definitely dead, she drew her sword and pushed it straight through his spine. It did not pierce skin but appeared to pass straight through, as ethereal as Jennifer had seen its wielder.

As the killer stood proud, Jennifer flicked the knife upward just above her head and into her hand. She started to cut, but she could not miss the pale-red mist which encircled the killer, emanating from the onyx blade.

Once free, she went first for Manta. He did not even flinch. Just as she approached, she felt a deathly cold blade against her throat, ghostly by sight but razor-sharp to the touch. She stopped dead in her tracks.

Manta spoke without the merest change in his tone. "You have a great deal of fight in you," he said; "but too much mercy for those undeserving of it."

"Nobody deserves to be murdered like that," she responded. "That wasn't a fight; that was an execution."

"They were unworthy to call themselves my protectors." He waved the blade away, and it vanished. Jennifer knew that its wielder had done the same but probably wasn't far away. She had no control of her situation, and that irked her beyond belief.

"But very well. You have entertained me enough that I will offer you the same opportunity. Tomorrow, when we have what I came here for."

Jennifer felt relief that she had not been turned loose to be hunted down and slaughtered like an animal, as she had just witnessed. She had to hope another day would see her grow stronger. That morning, she had been feeling better than she had in many days.

But, a sense of hopelessness nagged at her, guilt that she had put the guards in that position in the first place and that she had failed to get them out of it. Unless she was feeling significantly stronger, an extra day's stay of execution would end up being just that.

"Indulge me," she asked, grabbing at anything she could. "Where is 'here', anyway?"

"You are in an old headquarters of our gravest enemy," Manta said, looking far too assured for Jennifer's own good. "We are in Gien."

That sounds French. How the hell did we end up in France?

"Why here?"

"It's a good base of operations to reach the Louvre." His lips upturned. "And this time, we shall be doing so without your interference. Put her back in her confinement, will you?"

"Turn around and head to the back door," said an echoing voice. She knew to whom it belonged. It had none of that force of terror that Mary was able to invoke about it, but even so, the disembodied nature of it still caused a little nervousness. Jennifer could not fight an opponent she couldn't track, or harm. No recourse other than obedience presented itself.

As she got to the door, Manta clapped twice. A lock clicked. The door opened and the red-clad Cerise sauntered in. She stared at the defeated Jennifer with an uncomfortable allure as she walked past. Though undoubtedly attractive, the situation did not lend to such a reaction and Jennifer knew it well. Other forces had to have been at work.

Jennifer settled herself, but Cerise already appeared satisfied with her reaction. The woman half-bowed to Manta, but with some noticeable grievance; not to having given deference, but something about the manner of delivery. It almost looked as if she'd made a mistake and was torturing herself over it.

"They're yours," Manta informed. "I still don't know what it is you do with them, but clear up the mess."

"Don't I always?" Cerise's lips upturned almost flirtatiously.

"And hurry up. We need everyone ready in forty-five minutes. I want the crown."

Crown?

"Keep moving." The echoing voice nudged her into action again. With one last look back, she observed Cerise dragging the two headless guards out of the other door with considerable strength, whistling a tune as she did so. She dumped the bodies through the door and then reached for the knife Jennifer had seen about her earlier. The door closed.

Jennifer wondered what they meant by all they had just said, whilst keeping an eye on her route back to the room in which she was being detained. She needed a means of escape before she, or anyone else, died for nothing. The heads on the floor taunted her, reminded her of failures there and in the past.

I'm so sorry.

CHAPTER FIVE

L ondon had scarcely seen a summer morning as pleasant in recent years. A warm, sunny day found itself in the perfect company of a coastal breeze, even though it was inland.

The lengthy, winding path to Grenshall Manor no longer festered with overgrown brambles, a superior condition to any it had seen in many decades. The once-constricting bushes had been cut back to their proper borders, trimmed meticulously into magnificent topiary, giving the path a stately look.

Kara's old car, the wrecked Mini Cooper, still adorned part of the Grenshall Manor fountain, though the mansion's new owner had creatively evolved the crash site into a contemporary construction; a permanent reminder of the liberation of the place from its deadly haunting, and the end of a lifetime's mental torture for a family as well as a new-found friend.

Kara chuckled as she stared at the piece, half-man, half-car, and remembered how the end of her previous car had come to be. They had used it as a weapon against a barely human opponent; a tricky one to explain to her insurer. Thankfully, her claim had been one of hundreds of bizarre accidents attributed to the 'freak weather' around London, just as her house had been subject to a 'gas explosion' at around the same time.

It meant the likelihood of a hike in all of her premiums in the next few years, but on the plus side, her expertise was in demand. And that meant decent compensation for her time. Amid off-the-record consultancy time in helping Inspector Hammond with his police reports, which no doubt contributed to his promotion to Detective Chief Inspector; taking lectures at University College London with the spike in admission enquiries for the course she could no longer lecture full-time; and marketing the carefully-edited book she released on the 'Great Storm of London', she was getting by.

Kara pulled up to the potholed driveway next to two more cars—a Mercedes she had recommended for the host to be chauffeured around in, and the battered Volvo 850 actually owned by her main driver. She grinned as she remembered one of her most treasured adventures, when she met Mary, a terrified and traumatised art student who became the last heir of a once-powerful noble house and a deity amongst mortals such as herself.

Grenshall Manor stood in a better state of repair than it had been in over a century, despite the additional damage it sustained the year before. Rapid renovation had taken place, but scaffolding remained over the damaged areas. They never anticipated a quick job.

On the construction, she spotted the grey-haired man she had first met working in a morgue those twelve months ago, hanging precariously in front of the clock tower. She gave a light shriek as he slid off the structure, but, held fast by a bungee, he stopped a very short distance from the scaffolding pole upon which he stood .

Kara leapt from her car, looking for the ladder. She could see none. "Crap!" she heard him cry as he swung dangerously, but he seemed more aggravated than panicked. Enough to convince her as to his safety. She saw steps built into the scaffolding, not much use as a rescue option, but she made her way over to the bottom rung all the same.

"It's okay," he called, and somehow found the balance to free a hand and wave her back. He then released a catch on his safety harness and rappelled down at speed. "Don't worry about me . . ." His feet hit the ground just in front of her. "Just helping with the renovations."

Kara gave a thumbs-up. "I'm sure, Ruthven. Need to see Mary."

"Lady Grenshall," Ruthven corrected. It was true now, following various legalities, but Kara wasn't in the mood for pedanticism.

"It's urgent." She had already turned towards the front door.

"Okay, okay, steady on! Bloody hell."

"I can't 'steady on', unless you can tell me Jen has called in the last few hours. Has she?"

"Miss Winter?"

She could hear Ruthven scampering behind her to catch up, and he overtook with deceptive speed. He gave his overalls a brush down, not that it made a difference to anything. He beckoned her closer and turned the handle.

"Yes. *Jen*. Has she called here today?"

"Nobody's called in at all. That's why I took an hour out to check the tiles."

"And Mary didn't think to call me?"

"I remember Lady Grenshall saying she thought she'd just gone over to yours for the night. But it does occur to me now that the gym's been pretty quiet lately."

They gave a push to the tall, solid door. An engraved silver sigil, an elaborate letter 'G', replaced the weathered and worn Grenshall crest of bygone eras. Inside, a mix of Georgian Regency and Victorian Gothic dominated the décor, something left primarily unchanged. However, necessary and highly expensive work had been done to bring the building kicking and screaming into the twenty-first century.

Kara marvelled at the significant improvements thus far carried out by the current resident. Bright cream and yellow colouring dominated throughout, with gold all across the knot-patterned skirting. Electricians and plumbers had brought the mansion up to modern living's high standards. One of the valuable Grenshall family tables stood defiant after the previous year's destruction, renewed and restored.

"So, where is she now? The lady of the manor?"

He took a step through the door and Kara followed suit. "Painting," he replied with a frown. "It's what she does to keep herself calm. I've seen her run to the art room and pick up a paintbrush the second she's got back from ghost-whispering, or whatever it is she does. I know better than to ask."

"And that's why she keeps you around." Kara smiled as she made her way into the reception area with the wire-haired man in tow. They turned left towards the art room. "Hey. I never *did* find out how it is you shake that creepy voice she does. However, I maintain my current theory of long-term exposure to the environmental conditions inuring you to its effects, given your background working at the sharp end of the public sector."

Ruthven, the current seneschal of the manor, stared at her as if she was speaking in another language and shrugged in apathy. "Ye-e-ah . . . and I still don't know what you're talking about."

"I wonder whether even members of the general public who deal with the dead on a day-to-day basis, have developed a natural resistance to the rigours of the '*Unresting*' environment."

"Nah," he said, chewing at his lip as he opened the door to the West Wing entrance. "It sounds a bit odd, but after you guys turned up, I saw something amazing. I know my stiffs pretty well, and I have *never* in my life seen anything like what happened with Jennifer. Lady Grenshall is a miracle worker."

"Runs in the family," Kara chuckled.

"She could do with remembering to eat before she sets to work, though."

"Aww, you're a sweetheart." She pecked him on the cheek whilst rubbing his head. He gave a resigned sigh as they entered the art room, once a study.

A speckled cloth covered the entire floor of the cavernous chamber, a room with no additional features other than a painting canvas and two chairs. To Kara's right, recently completed Grenshall family portraits leaned against the wall, tainted by Post-It notes which said, '*For Reception*'.

In the first, Lord Alphonse Grenshall had been reimagined by his artistic descendent, and proudly stood with the rest of his family. Proud and dignified in a military officer's dress jacket that he had rarely worn in service, Lord Augustine Grenshall stood to the left of his beautiful wife, Lady Arianna. His arms were around a dark haired, wide-eyed young girl looking somewhat awkward in a white, frilly dress. She represented the beginning of little Iris Brown's transformation from grubby urchin to sole heir of the Grenshall estate.

In the next completed painting, the waif had grown up. The eyes remained large, but her bearing had transformed from irresistible cuteness to upper-class beauty, which carried across to the painstakingly detailed curls of her black hair and every last blemish, of which there were few, portrayed on her features. Her smiling lips exuded self-confidence. Miss Brown had become the Lady Iris Grenshall that her descendant had come to know, and fully understand, before sending her to a final, peaceful rest. She had been painted as noble, heroic by her artist, the way she had intended for Tally Grenshall to be remembered. The truth of the tragedy that beset her in her final breathing days became a matter for none but family and close friends.

There were others there, work from Mary's old flat, including *Tooth*, *The Family Curse* and a revision of an old painting. It showed an image depicting the interior of Bolsover Castle, Derbyshire, which featured a young woman in a modern setting wearing a richly detailed black dress, her face obscured by darkness. Every one of the paintings had silver engraved annotations, miniature versions of the door sigil.

"Lady Grenshall will see you now," said Ruthven, in a mocking tone. Kara appreciated the humour, even in her current state. As they entered, the lady in question busily stroked a brush against a large canvas, her work unseen from Kara's position.

Lady Grenshall put down her brush a couple of seconds after hearing Ruthven speak. She was a slender figure, who sat cross-legged in blue and white striped tights and multi-coloured baggy clothing. Bright blue eyes stood out against her pale complexion, contrasting rich, raven black hair.

"Jennifer's not with you, then?" Lady Mary asked, her long, twitchy fingers now unoccupied.

Kara shook her head. "I was hoping she'd have got back here, but clearly not. I got a call from Detective Chief Inspector Hammond just before I left."

"She's been climbing the walls," Mary said. "Utterly restless since she could sit up and talk again." Mary's voice drifted and she stared at the ground. "I've done everything I can to make things as comfortable as I could. I really have."

"I know you have." Kara tried to sound as calm as possible. "She's never been one to sit still for long."

"But she's always come home." They both nodded in unison. "She didn't last night."

"Without wanting to sound like a concerned mother, I know she does. That's why I wanted to check with you first. Why don't you answer your phone, anyway?"

"Usually, it's a lack of signal across worlds," Mary told her. "But when I'm painting, I tell the staff not to disturb me for anything. I was only going to be another twenty minutes or so."

"Just for once, it's a bit more important than me chewing your ear about dead people."

Mary agreed, and then closed the distance between them. "What did Hammond have to say?"

"Something about a robbery last night. He didn't say much. Said he wanted to meet in person. I told him to be around here for about ten a.m."

"What time is it now?"

"About ten a.m.," Ruthven butted in.

Mary glared at Kara. "You need to give me a bit better notice than that," she grumbled. "The defences could have been up."

"Expecting company?" Kara asked, her eyebrows raised.

"That's exactly the point. This place still isn't officially on many maps, but it's useful to know if someone's coming over. If nothing else, I can tell Ruthven to put the kettle on." She turned to her employee. "R, either you or one of the others to the door please. Bring our guest straight in." Lady Mary turned back to Kara. "If you think *I'm* tough to get hold of whilst around here, Jen doesn't even *have* a mobile. Hates the things."

"Which is all well and good," Kara replied, "but when she runs off to go and take on something dangerous, she really needs to tell us."

"I know, right? I knew she'd do something like this one day. She went from just keeping up with her physical rehab exercises in the gym, to running around the estate, to a little further out. Got very into watching a few DVDs on various exercise types while she was bedridden. Mostly martial arts workouts, but she asked for a pile of *parkour* bits and pieces lately."

"Oh, joy," Kara winced. "Has she taken up freerunning for exercise?"

"Yeah—and she says she's far from back to full strength." Mary threw her hands into the air. "Given the one time I tried it with her, I nearly broke bones while she was bounding around like a basketball, I think she's got a very different idea of 'not in shape' to me."

A loud sequence of taps sounded on the door, immediately followed by two figures bursting through. Kara recognised another person Mary had taken on as staff, Karen Palmer, a flame-haired and lightly freckled young woman of a solid build and an enthusiastic smile and slightly older brother Lewis, similar of appearance and smart of attire. Both were direct descendants of a ghost Mary had dealt with a year past, who offered to help Mary's project after becoming fascinated with Mary's tale.

A bearded man she recognised, perhaps in his late thirties, with short ginger hair accompanied them. He wore a grey suit slightly too small for his stocky frame, and placed a set of round driving glasses into his breast pocket as Kara acknowledged them both. "Please tell me Jen's okay."

DCI Hammond shrugged. "We haven't seen anyone matching Jennifer's description, no. We found several other bodies, though."

Mary put her head in her hands, shaking. "Not again. Surely?"

"Huh?" Hammond asked.

"She's asking if we've got a repeat of last year," Kara said. "Like the Odeon incident."

"No." He looked up at her. "Not quite the same. Most of the bodies we found were dressed for a fight. Some security guards, too."

"Did they actually get in?" Kara asked. "Take anything?"

"It's clear *something* went on, but we had a blackout. All the cameras went down. The regular exhibits appear untouched, so we're not entirely sure."

"Well, we've got nothing better to work with at the moment," Mary said, sighing. "I say we go and look for ourselves."

Hammond raised a hand. "Out of the question. We can't just let the general public in and out of the area."

"Hate to say it," Mary answered, "but you couldn't stop me even if you wanted to. You wouldn't even know I was there if I went."

Kara quickly waved her arms. "Don't take that as a threat, by the way. I mean, you could save yourselves a lot of paperwork if you didn't even know we were there."

"Only, I *would* know." He frowned. "And even if I didn't, I'd always suspect that you were. And then I'd have to ask you to leave, or nick you for trespassing."

Mary was about to say something more, but Kara again interrupted. "Listen. Last time I saw you, you were in uniform and nobody was calling you 'Chief'. Not wanting to draw any rash conclusions, but I reckon you were one of a very short list of people who did pretty well out of all last year's chaos. And without Mary's help here, it's possible neither of us would have been alive to be having this discussion now. So, when we know our friend is missing and you confirm to us that her last known location was close to a crime scene you are still short half the details of—*again*—you'd do well to let us in the easy way."

64

Hammond rubbed his beard and looked away. Eventually, he shrugged. "This is more than my job's worth, you know. But you raise a good point. My claim to the Bond Street case, and that Barber lad confessing to a bunch of murders, helped out a bit. Could have all happened under better circumstances, but you've got some credit with me. If you're ready, I'll take you over."

"I'm ready now—" Kara started, but Mary grabbed her by the arm and dragged her out into the adjacent corridor. "Give us a minute," she called and shut the door behind them.

"What are you doing?" Kara asked. "He's just said we can go."

"Got something I've been working on for you." Ruthven waited outside, and on Mary's cue, removed a suit jacket from a coat hanger and handed it to Kara.

"It *should* fit you . . ." Mary said with a smile.

Kara took the jacket, a unique shade of matt black. As she touched it, she felt a clammy texture, well below expected temperature. In appearance, it bore a strong resemblance to an Armani she had in her wardrobe—other than being made of no material Kara recognised.

"Looks great," Kara said, eyeing the jacket suspiciously. "But what is it, and why couldn't it wait until after we've been to the crime scene?"

Mary pinched the arm on the coat. "If you travel anywhere with me from now on, and I have the slightest suspicion you're going to have to call on me to do something I specialise in—you wear this. Put it on."

Kara gave a light shrug, then removed her own suit jacket and replaced it with Mary's creation. As expected, it felt like clambering into cold jelly, but after a few initial shivers, she found it a comfortable enough fit. "I don't see what's special about it. Is it armoured or something?"

"Kind of. You know all that residue I was telling you about that I sometimes find in places of high ghost presence, such as the Gate

Chamber? Well, turns out you can kind of harvest the stuff. It happens, too, that it makes for pretty sturdy material. Sturdy, and most importantly, protection from the Unresting world, as you officially call it."

"Are we definitely going with that term now? You're the resident expert."

"Worked for people longer in the job than me."

Kara moved her arms in a stretching exercise, growing used to the coat. "How did you work this out?"

"I needed to do something other than ghost-bothering one day a few months ago. I started cleaning off this stuff in the Chamber because it'd been there so long. Then I started daydreaming on one of Tally's memories—the bit about the Guide and his cloak I told you about. It had to be made of something, right? I remembered something Lord Alphonse told her about it. So, I started mucking about, and a fortnight later, bang. I'm pretty sure it should offer some protection against dead stuff."

"Cool!" Kara squealed. "Does that mean protection against the world, too?"

Mary looked up for a second or two before returning her focus to Kara. "While I haven't been able to check for sure, as I get a free pass over there on that sort of thing, that's kind of what I was hoping, yeah. The woven death-cloth seemed pretty tough while I was waving it around over there, so my fingers are crossed."

"Death-cloth weave, eh?" Kara smirked. "You're like the Q-Branch of the dead, you are."

Mary chuckled. "I won't even tell you what *you* remind me of. Come on, let's go."

CHAPTER SIX

DCI Hammond cleared the pair for access to the area surrounding the British Museum. Mary had quickly got changed into darker clothing, or 'work clothes' as she put it, to prevent being dazzled by living energies, including her own, when travelling the lands of the dead. The three quickly cleared the cordons and, to avoid any awkwardness, Hammond quickly reassigned elsewhere the duty constables guarding the main entrance.

Kara watched Mary as inky darkness poured into her eyes, the *Guardian of the Gate* immediately checking the area for the presence of the dead. Mary bit her lip as she scanned the area in detail. Hammond had been distracted by junior officers asking questions and so argued for command with his nearest subordinate.

"What's up?" Kara asked, hoping she hadn't been the cause of a dangerous distraction.

Mary continued her survey for a moment, and then blinked several times. Her eyes returned to normal. "So, this is weird," she finally said. "This is *exactly* the kind of situation where I'd expect to see a couple of ghosts wandering about, but there's nobody home." She pointed to the chalk-circle body on the steps. "Something unusual definitely went down here. And I'm picking up rifts here."

"More portals?" Contemplating this possibility proved disturbing. Three large gateways to the deadly Unresting world sprouted across London and wrought havoc on the city. Only the intervention of Mary and her extraordinary abilities prevented greater damage. But if they faced an identical situation, Kara would have felt a deep fear from the pit of her subconscious, as would have most of the others on the crime scene. It would, in fact, have prevented an investigation at all.

Almost to Mary's relief, she shook her head. "Definitely no portals. Those I can spot a mile off now. But someone has been travelling the Unresting here, I can tell. Quickly. Pretty short distances."

"And Jen?"

"No sign. But give me a minute or two and I can check for certain. I can pick her out if she's been about."

Kara gave a thumbs-up. "Go for it, if you can."

"Weird thing with this gift: I can kind of pick up a scent on those I know pretty well."

"Handy."

"Isn't it, though?" With that, Mary crouched and reverted to her death sight, to attempt to sniff out Jennifer.

Hammond returned. He looked at Mary with some curiosity and made an uncomfortable sidestep as he made his way to Kara. "Has my investment in you two turned anything up so far?"

"Actually, yes," she replied, gritting her teeth. "It looks like it's a damn good thing you did call us in. I'm not sure what we're dealing with yet, but if *she's* seen something she's bothered about out here, then it should be squeaky bum time for us, too. Where did you find the other bodies?"

"Funny you should say that . . ." he answered. He pointed to a roof-top. "There was one there . . . and there . . . there, there, and there," he said, pointing in several directions. "We've just found those, I'm told."

"You have a body?" Kara said, inappropriately excited. "Whereabouts?"

"That one." He gestured to a building not far away from the entrance. "The beat constable said your friend appeared near that one. Looks like he fell off the roof."

Kara examined her surroundings. "It's a long drop. Can we get over there?"

"That's the most active part of the crime scene at the moment. But they're talking about moving the body soon."

Kara thought for a moment, then looked over at the meditating Mary. "Can you just keep them talking for a bit?"

"Won't be hard. They're trying to see if there's anything more to it."

"Lady Mary would be your best bet for that one. She's trying to find Jen, though."

One of Hammond's eyebrows raised as he watched the meditation with some puzzlement. "If you say so." He backed away. "Listen, I really don't know how you all got the results you did, but I know there's plenty more to it than I can see. So as a favour, I'll let you get on with it. It's going to be another high-profile case, and I've got credit from the last one I had, so that'll give me a bit of leeway here. Which means, as far as I'm concerned, so do you. But I'll have to stop and ask you how you do it this time, if you succeed again."

"And maybe this time you'll believe us when we tell you, too," Kara added, smirking.

"I did," Hammond said as he turned away. "But plenty of people don't, including my superiors. Even when things happen right in front of them. So, while I'm happy for you to do your thing, I need to know what you say so the paperwork is straight."

"That seems true," Kara replied, taking a long, pensive blink. "The interview subjects I had, despite exposure to severe and traumatic paranormal phenomena, defaulted to a state of subconscious blissful ignorance. In other words . . ." She opened her eyes. She had completely lost DCI Hammond, as intended, and chuckled. "The majority of people prefer to go on as if they haven't seen anything."

Mary's eyes flew open and closed like shutters several times, and she stood up in a giraffe-like manner. She staggered to Kara, placing her hands on her friend's shoulders. "She was up there, K," she said, pointing to several roofs. "She was running around up *there!*"

Kara looked around, assessing the damage to her surroundings. "He said that body over there fell from the roof." She freed herself from Mary and directed her eyes to the corpse.

"You don't think she—?"

"No!" Kara yelped. "I mean, she wouldn't—she doesn't *do* that sort of thing."

"You know, it might have come down to whoever that was or her, don't you think? If he was dangerous, she may have been left very little choice."

Kara's eyes thinned, an uncharacteristic aggression laced her tone. "Look, I told you, she wouldn't have, okay? That's not what she does."

"Didn't look that way when she was saving me from Barber. Not that I'm ungrateful or anything—but from what I've seen of her, she doesn't hold back. Remember that time I had the small possession issue with you? Because I do."

"Barber could take it, and I wouldn't have let anything happen to you. *She* wouldn't have let anything happen to you. Now, can we just leave it and get back to the job at hand please?"

Mary pulled a face. "Okay, fine. And by the way, she's definitely not here. Nor anywhere near. I'm more than a little worried that someone else is poking around the Unresting, though. And I'm guessing they won't have been friendly."

"Where did you see the ghost?"

"Wasn't a ghost. And to answer your question, just about everywhere up there." She swept her arms for panoramic emphasis.

"Pretty much where you said Jen was. So, either Jen chased her, or vice versa. We really need to find out what that was on the roof."

"I'm as interested in finding out more about that body. See, the thing is, even if there was no ghost, even if we're talking old age or other natural causes, I'd have seen *something* when I was looking. There was just nothing there."

Kara turned to the dead person in the distance. "That's not good, is it? Last time you mentioned something like that—"

"Was back in the Odeon, yes. And even then, I could see the reason for that right in front of me. This is different."

"Hmm." Kara scratched her head. "No portals, right?"

"Nope."

"So, we've not got a lot to go on. A ghost-botherer of some description, and did you say you can smell Jen?"

Mary drummed her fingers against her leg. "That's a thought. I know Tally did something similar before. I could give it a go." Within seconds, she returned to her death sight, and kept tapping. "Inside." She grabbed Kara's hand and pulled her through the entrance doors. "The strongest trace I had on her was inside."

The pair located a hole once occupied by a glass roof. Glass crunched under their feet as they looked around. Several police officers who were investigating nearby turned at the noise.

"Who the hell are you two?" one of them, a dour and weathered-looking sergeant, snapped. "You're not allowed in here." He pointed to his colleagues, a young woman in uniform and a smiling dark-haired male constable. "Nick 'em."

"Hammond sent us," Kara replied, holding hands in the air. "Dr. Mellencourt, resident historian. This is my associate, Lady Mary Grenshall."

The gruff sergeant glowered. "Lady, my arse."

"I'll put you on it if you hold me up any more," Lady Grenshall muttered, only fully audible to Kara. But the sergeant heard something.

"What was that?"

Kara moved her arm, gesturing for Mary to back down.

"Wait!" the female constable called. "You said Dr. Mellencourt, yes?"

Kara's eyes narrowed and she took a good look at the officer, checking for recognition. The young, mousy officer did not look familiar, but seemed confident the name meant something. "That's right."

"Do you know a woman, early twenties, blonde, kind of athletic?"

"Jen!" Kara and Mary blurted simultaneously.

The constable gave a tentative nod. "She never gave her name. Just yours."

Kara lowered her arms and moved quickly towards the officers, Mary following suit. "How was she? When did you see her last? What was happening?"

"Have you forgotten I just ordered you to nick these two?" the sergeant said, moving to do so himself.

"I'm on a DCI's orders, Sarge," the young officer answered, grabbing him. "I don't think we want to be getting in the way."

He simmered for a moment.

"He's actually on the scene if you want to check for yourself," Mary confirmed, pointing outside. The sergeant conceded and took a step back. PC Thorne, the female officer on scene, explained all about the sudden blackout as she was on patrol, the criminal gang and the courage of Jennifer as their friend sent her off to get help.

"So, you think this was a high-tech operation?" Kara asked.

"Must have been," Sergeant Cannon responded. "How else do you explain all the power outage and most of the electrics being broken within a quarter mile radius as happened last night?"

Kara turned to Mary. "See? This is exactly what I'm talking about." Mary shrugged.

"What *are* you talking about?"

"Oh, yeah. You were in Ghost World at the time. Never mind." She turned back to the police team. "So, nothing's been taken as far as you're aware, there's a load of damage to the museum roof and we have a missing person, several dead, but mostly the criminal gang? Bizarre."

"Very," the sergeant said. "But most importantly, we've got no knowledge of how they died so far. They didn't all fall off the roof." Mary looked over at Kara at this, but Kara cast a filthy stare back. "The strange thing was, there's a few of them we couldn't find a single mark on, so we're checking potential natural causes, but it seems a little unlikely. A call back on the first one said that internally there was a series of tears to major arteries consistent with stab wounds."

"What you're saying, is," Mary said, sounding confused, "that he looks like he had been stabbed to death, but no actual stabbing has taken place?"

Sergeant Cannon rolled his eyes. "That would be about the size of it, yes. Now do you see why I say it was strange?"

Kara shrugged. "As DCI Hammond will tell you, 'strange' is the reason he keeps us around. Now, I'll understand perfectly if you say no, but are you all right leaving us alone here a minute? We won't touch anything, I promise."

"I'm glad we have an understanding," the sergeant said, still glaring at the pair. "Because there's no way in hell I'll be abandoning a crime scene. I'm surprised you'd ask that of me."

Mary reached out and tugged at Kara's arm. "Yeah, I've got a trace. It's as good as I'll get from here. We should leave. If we're going to do this thing, we should go somewhere I can get hold of a bit more juice."

Kara bowed at Sergeant Cannon and backed away. "Are you thinking where I'm thinking?"

"There's only one place I know I can go and get this type of juice, K. Give Hammond a ring. We're going home."

~*~

Mary sharply raised a hand and made a pulling motion with her arms. The vault-like steel door of the Gate Chamber drew itself to a close. Kara gulped, try as she might to hide it, as it slammed shut. Previous conversation with Mary about that room provided the chilling reminder that there were very few ways out of it once the entrance had been sealed—and simply pushing the door to was not one of them. She started to speak, but Mary again waved her arms, this time in a wide arc to either side of her.

"I can't believe you talked me into this," Mary said.

"Look, we need to know if this thing works, don't we?" Kara replied. Her confident grin as she tugged at the death-cloth jacket was unbelievable, given the circumstances. "And besides, as you say, this is as strong as the trail to Jen gets."

"And that's the only reason I'm going ahead with this madness. She could be anywhere, Kara."

"I'm willing to stake she's not in Sydney."

"I'm not."

Kara grabbed Mary's hand. "Let's get on with it."

"Well, we've got somewhere to go . . ." Mary closed her blackened eyes. "I just don't know quite where yet."

On Mary's command, a surprisingly bright unnatural illumination washed over them. Within seconds, a series of tiny white and blue lights, decorative in appearance, mapped out a constellation on the wall. It was no standard constellation, however. Kara jumped back as soon as a number of the lights began to move around on the surface. At the same time, wisps of black smoke danced around the room and the two inhabitants, at great speed. Kara thought it both highly spectacular and incredibly disconcerting.

"What the hell—?" Kara said, and twitched at every smoke plume as if a swarm of wasps were flying around her head. Mary took no notice, and instead made her way calmly to the centre of the room and then dropped to one knee. A breeze which whispered in a thousand voices flew through the enclosure. Kara witnessed Mary's mouth moving in time with some of the whispers but could not hear her words, nor understand those on the wind. As Mary ceased, the movement of the black smoke did likewise, and stopped suitably clear of the pair.

The lights had also arrested their dance, and bathed the room in a pleasant pale blue tone. "When I said more juice, what I meant was, come and have a look at this! It's how I'm hoping we'll find Jen, with a little luck."

"You've managed to get the Gate Chamber to do this?" Kara asked, amazed.

Mary winked. "Kind of. I learned how to do this part myself. As I said, I can track people I know well pretty much anywhere. That's quite limited at the moment obviously, but if for any reason I need to find my house staff, you or Jen, I can do it. And it's a lot easier from the grounds of the mansion. I first found out I could do this with Lewis, with his permission of course, when he had a weekend away. I told him not to tell me where he'd gone. It took an hour or two, but I could kind of feel where he'd gone. So, I followed it through the Shadow Roads—like I did by accident last year at the hospital, and turned up about ten paces away from him at a party. Then, I just found my way back here—which is really easy now, by the way—and told him when he came back to work on the Monday."

"Click your heels three times and say, 'there's no place like home', eh?"

"Something like that. Look—that's where she was, at the British Museum, and that's where she's gone since." She pointed at the brightest of the lights, as it danced a certain distance, but suddenly vanished completely. "Oh, that's not good," she gasped. "That can't be good."

"Okay," Kara said, hesitantly. "She's just vanished from your sight. Does that mean something's happened to her?"

"Er," Mary said, biting her lip, "I . . . well . . ."

"Come on, Mary, answer me. This is serious!"

"I'm aware of that, Kara . . ." Mary said, flapping. "I've never seen this before. I-I don't know."

"Take us there. Take us wherever that was that just vanished, now."

"I-I can't." Mary held the temple of her head and tapped her feet on the floor, deep in thought.

"Whaddaya mean, you can't?"

"She just vanished, and I've no way of pinpointing that." She started to rapidly scratch her head. "When I've done it before, I usually just look for that light. That could be anywhere, K."

"No, it couldn't." Kara nudged Mary's hand away from her head and pointed her back at the wall. "That's a map of some kind. I can't read it, but you drew it—you must have a rough idea . . ."

"Yeah," Mary said angrily, "that's just it. I have a rough idea. I don't know how far out that could put us."

"Where does this part of the map correspond to?" Kara said, wandering up and pointing almost exactly to where the bright light once was. "City, county, country, continent—what have you got?"

Mary moved closer to the map and felt around it with her fingertips. "Well, it's definitely France . . ." she said, slightly calmer. "Looks a little like Paris from here actually." She stopped and looked at Kara, totally baffled. "What the hell is she doing in Paris?"

"Your guess is as good as mine." Kara looked at her expectantly. "Let's go and find out, shall we?"

Mary nodded, and then took Kara by the hand, turning back to the egg-like stone in the centre of the Chamber. The smoke swirled rapidly as the winds raised into a small cyclone.

"You know, I'm actually looking forward to this," Kara said. She was, though there was no doubt as to the butterflies in her stomach.

Within seconds, the rising black hurricane of the Unresting world carried the pair out of the Gate Chamber, out of the mansion and out of world of the living.

~*~

Kara travelled at sickening speed outside the normal conventions of time and space and into total darkness. At least, it looked to be at first. The multi-tiered gloom caused even the shadows to have shadows.

Cold, slimy vapours slopped at her face and set her heart rate racing tenfold. She gripped her hand tight to Mary, a stabilising anchor in the most mind-bending of environments.

The light from her face provided a flashlight for Kara to catch some of the sights, faceless entities she could hear whispering incomprehensible terrors. Her journey ensued for an indeterminate interval. She seemed to come to a sudden stop as soon as the light changed, her vision dragged only to a warm red glow in the sky from the setting sun. But it would not stop spinning. *Kara* would not cease spinning. She attempted to gain her footing with a step forward, but her foot came down on nothing.

The sun swirled around with dazzling brightness in the distance. In fact, *everything* spun—or just felt that way to Kara. Dazed and mildly nauseous, felt herself moving beyond her control and attempted to stop.

A freezing gust of wind blasted her forward. The soles of her feet pressed against nothing and she lurched forward with a shriek. She threw her arms out in an attempt to regain her balance and wobbled as she diverted her weight backwards, then fell into a sitting position. She established that they had emerged at the top of a flat building, and could see the unmistakeable frame of the Eiffel Tower from where she sat. Her nose gave her a mix of delicious coffee and roasting beef. They had reached Paris. And in so doing, they'd made the cross-world journey in one piece.

From across the rooftop, Kara saw Mary stagger like a drunk and teeter dangerously at the precipice. Kara lurched to her feet, then broke into a run. Mary overbalanced and flew forward. Kara snatched at her falling friend and caught her wrist, then yanked backwards with all the force she could muster.

She arrested Mary's momentum, but her weight pulled Kara off-balance. She wedged a foot against the end of the ledge and pulled backwards. The pair of them fell in a heap, but Mary rolled straight off and caught herself on the floor. She wavered, coughing and spluttering as if she was about to throw up. Her skin was almost grey. "Mary? You okay, Miss?"

Mary answered with more splutters, but eventually, spat a few times in a most undistinguished manner before rolling on to her back. "Okay . . ." she said when she finally got herself fit to speak again, "let's *never* do that blind again."

Kara looked at how close they had come to a pretty pointless freak death and exhaled deeply. "Agreed."

"Holy crap, I feel rough." Mary groaned. She sat up and held her head. "I know it takes a bit out of you when you know where you're going, but that? I feel like I've just had the shit kicked out of me. I could murder a plate of food right now."

Kara scrambled to her feet. She sighed, and offered Mary a hand up. "Well, you're kind of in luck," she said. "Unless you can see Jen from here, we're not far from back where we started. And you won't be able to do much in that state."

She squinted, trying to make out landmarks. The Eiffel Tower was easily visible; Paris it was. "Actually, I know a great restaurant about half a mile from here. But once you're back up and running, we're going to have to return to the case."

"I don't want to leave the case." Mary sniffed the air and let darkness wash over her eyes. She looked around, too, but wheezed after a few seconds.

"You're no good to us like that, girl. Whatever we're dealing with, if it's tying Jen up, we're going to need you at your best. And if that means a Royale with cheese, then—"

Mary put a finger to her mouth. "I've got a small trace."

"Was she here?"

"Not on the roof, but we can't be far."

"We're closer than we were."

"Definitely." Mary agreed. "First thing, though. Let's figure out how we're getting off this roof . . ."

Mary stopped talking and looked up to the sky, once again sniffing. She then shook her head and cocked an ear towards the stairwell entrance.

"What's up?" Kara asked.

After a few seconds, Mary shook her head and shrugged. "Eh, just hearing things I think. Still not quite straight after the ride, I reckon."

"Hmm . . ." Kara remained unconvinced. "Just check again, will you?"

"Why," Mary asked. "Did you hear something as well?"

"No, I'd just rather we didn't take chances. Please."

"Fine." Mary resumed her scouting. After a minute, she shook her head. "Nope, just a bit of ghost lag."

Kara gave a small nod before the two made their way to the roof access stairs and began the tedious traipse down to the building's exit. They eventually found their way to a main road and, after flagging down a taxi, to the restaurant in question.

The pair took time to recover from their recent exertions, and watched Paris go by with a tall drink and, in Mary's case, a huge pasta feast. Time flew quickly as they got their collective breaths back, and the food did not last long.

After her last mouthful, Mary burped, loud enough to attract the attention of the other patrons. "You're really not quite settled on this whole, 'Lady' thing, are you?" Kara teased.

Mary wiped her mouth with a napkin in the most deliberate and neat way possible, keeping an eye on Kara to make certain she was watching. When she had finished, she stretched like a satisfied cat. "I'm a *great* Lady Grenshall," she said with a grin. "And as it turns out, the *only* Lady Grenshall. Just because I've got a title and responsibility now, I won't let it change me. Besides, 1899 was *so* last year."

"The attempted possession in your head was definitely last year." Kara lightly tapped Mary's forehead with clenched knuckles. "Right, are you feeling better?"

"Fit as a fiddle," Mary replied.

"Then let's get back to the reason we're here before we end up on a weekend break. It's only Thursday."

"Okay."

But when Mary stood, she staggered, holding the dining table. Kara got up and grabbed her before she fell. "Oh, no, Lady. You're going to have to be able to stand on your own two feet before we move any further on this one. It might not be a weekend break, but certainly an overnight stay. Then breakfast, and back to it, bright and breezy in the morning."

"But Jen—"

"Is still out there somewhere, I know. But I can't do without the both of you at the moment. So, we rest and then tackle it fresh. Okay?"

Mary, groggy as she was, managed a feeble nod. "Fine. Turns out I'm a little lost for direction anyway." But the second she said the words, she looked up. Her eyes flushed with darkness and her head darted around.

"Something up?" Kara asked, watching intently.

Mary waved a hand in the air and Kara fell silent. "Someone's definitely been travelling the dead roads around here."

"Do you know where they went?"

Mary shook her head, finally having the presence of mind to shield her eyes from public observation, by way of using her hands as blinkers. "Not really. But there's a trace above me. Not far from here."

"Then we have a start point in the morrow."

CHAPTER SEVEN

Escape had not been a possibility the night before. Jennifer had bloodied her knuckles testing the integrity of the walls and of the door with a series of concentrated punches. The structures remained intact. The solid concrete floor offered no easy package either. Whoever had built the place, if it had been an intended detention area, it was a damned good one.

She decided to conserve her energy until she next encountered Manta and his dangerous, albeit self-depleting, squad. Whether the cull of mundane security had been as the ghost walker had said or just a measure to avoid paying them was the question of the evening. The question of the morning: whether she had enough juice to get out at the second time of asking.

On the matter of her energy, the night's sleep had actually been her most restful in a long time. She sat up, and immediately a jolt of energy coursed through her. She felt as strong as she ever did, her power returned with a vengeance. The last time she recalled such a surge, in fact, had been the very first day she truly felt her connection to the earth as she knew it.

Alice Winter had taught her how to access that link. Whilst given a night to contemplate her many regrets, one of her strongest related to the lack of time she had to understand the mysterious but incredible woman who had been a teacher, a guardian, and later on, a mother to her.

"It is a truly rare gift you have." The words stuck with her as if they had been spoken half an hour before. "You have had it since the day you were born." If only she'd known that since then, perhaps several years of her life would've been easier. But the easy life didn't like her one bit.

She had so much more to learn from Alice but never got the chance. She never did find out what had happened to her. Another regret. But somehow, Alice knew. The note she left said she probably wouldn't see her again, but it didn't tell Jennifer why. She remembered sobbing her eyes out that night, so vividly that she did the same in the cell.

Any wandering guard would have likely made the assumption her tears related to her detention, but the prospect of lengthy imprisonment did not bother her. She knew she would get her chance. But the loss of Alice impacted her hard. The only person who had offered her comfort as she grew up a freak left her too soon, with so much she never had time to explain. Jennifer's tears welled up even as she thought back to the first night she read the note. The words would never leave her.

I have to go. Stay safe, and go to the place I found for you. You'll be fine there.

Alice was right about that. Meeting Kara softened the blow ever so slightly. Sometimes, life came down to such inches and degrees. She had gone from having an adopted guardian to an adopted older sister, it seemed.

Her mind drowned in a tidal wave of thoughts and emotions. Every bad memory conspired to break her in the unfamiliar surroundings. Bitterness, anger, sorrow and creeping despair battered her at every turn. Though the inability to escape didn't bother her, thoughts of powerlessness tortured her. She perhaps hadn't been as powerless since the day Alice took her in, after the worst night of her life.

She couldn't control the flood of memories. It wasn't natural. But she'd fought to keep one of them truly suppressed: the memory of *that* night. It felt like someone had tried to force it out of her.

And then she realised. Someone *had* tried to force it out of her.

Cerise.

No wonder the woman in red had seemed so familiar. A powerful connection—but severed. Jennifer realised the woman had literally attempted to force her way inside her head! She could see it now—a hand pressed against her forehead, gentle but deliberate. She had clearly searched for something. She'd have found whatever she wanted, too, save for Jennifer not wanting to remember that crucial memory herself. Whilst conscious, she would have died before giving it up to someone else. She wondered if that knowledge provided her the will to resist, even while unconscious.

But that hadn't stopped the probe. Something else had—something considerably more recent. Whatever Cerise found, it had been great enough to expel her from Jennifer's mind. Jennifer had very little to speculate upon, her best guess the torment she relived from the London Underground battle. That would have slowed anyone. And one final result of the probe had been a flash of that 'Omega W' symbol she had seen in the building. She'd come across it somewhere else, and needed to know where and why.

Alice had always told her there was one important aspect to her talents—none of her power ever came for free. She had been given a solution, to donate some energy freely where she could back to the earth, and meditation worked as an effective conduit.

The previous year, to take Thomas Barber out of a fight, she had channelled a vast quantity of power from the electrical train line. The most powerful such request she had made. The energy surged through her, a wave of raw power. It felt incredible, but she never returned that power to its source.

The entity, Violet, denied her the opportunity when it ripped out almost every shred of Jennifer's life force with its attack. And for months afterward, she had nothing to give. Impossible whilst comatose; next to impossible when she awoke drained and half-dead. And so the situation remained unresolved.

In the mansion's surrounding grounds, she attempted to reconnect to the earth, kneeling and feeling the flow of energies around her. But the attempt failed her. No strength flowed to or from her there.

That link felt like another victim of the death and suffering that had been as much a part of the stately home's history as the family it had belonged to. Maybe Lady Mary Grenshall was just the latest chapter of that place of the damned. Or maybe the hit Jennifer had taken demanded a greater sacrifice of her personal power than she knew.

But there had to be more to it than that. Though a slow process, Jennifer had felt some of her strength returning with every run she had taken off the site. Mary had provided her an area as a gym, where she continued to rehabilitate herself, but only her excursions beyond the property saw her truly return to form, and not least her most recent exploits.

Jennifer sat cross-legged in the centre of the room and reached out with her gift of augmented senses. They initially blunted on contact with the reinforced floor, but she focused harder. Through a clearer mind, she recognised that the only noise she experienced originated from the traffic of her thoughts. An obstacle, just like the stone floor. She needed to put them aside to get to where she needed to go.

The stone floor did not provide the aura of desolation there had been at Grenshall Manor. The foundations of her temporary home, obscured by the champions of the dead, read as lifeless as volcanic ash. But she did not feel that interruption in the prison ground. *"Draw your strength from the earth . . ."* she whispered.

The earth responded in a way she had not expected.

Jennifer shuddered as a tingle of power rushed from her toes to the ends of her hair. She felt invigorated by an ancient force, one which stood long before the concrete, before the stone, before the chateau, before its ruin.

Chateau?

The land told her its story. The place had been purpose-built, at first to protect what was there from those who would just *take,* those who did not know what Alice had said to her. She could feel each individual stone of this place, the metal that still kept her in and intruders out.

More than that, she could feel, very close, a link to the very root of her own gift. She wondered if there had been some truth to the spurious prophecies her captors had spoken of. Nothing was impossible in her life.

. . . your whims from the air . . .

There were so many things she did not know about her own talents. So many questions that remained unanswered, down to the death of the one person she believed could have illuminated them. But the Consanguinity, the collective that held her captive—someone knew at least a little of what she sought. Someone *had* to.

The lock in the door clicked. Instinctively, Jennifer broke from her meditative state to battle-ready, from a relaxed posture she unravelled to one knee, arms stretched, ready to pounce.

She didn't even hear herself growling like a caged wolf as the armed guard, supported by another this time, backed up a step before he realised he had done so as she met his gaze. The previous day, the two would barely have caused her to break a sweat. Today, they were insignificant.

"Our king will see you now," he said. His voice shook with nerves, and she could see fear in both of their eyes. If they were all like these two, she could have walked out of there unchallenged.

But then how would I get any answers?

Every bone in her body tingled. It was a sorely missed sensation, welcomed upon its return, stronger than ever. Though she enjoyed the naturally earned increase in her muscle tone, the fluidity of shape was something she liked more. She stood, not blinking at her escorts, and watching as they gave her a clear path through the door.

"He could've at least laid on breakfast," she hissed, watching them continue to squirm. They had seemingly forgotten their guns.

Even though her communing had ceased, Jennifer had her exact bearings within the chateau ruins. The source she had tapped into chorally sang it loud in her mind. She knew every crack in the stone better than she did her own home.

Any hopes of breakfast died with the knowledge of her destination—not to the dining hall, but instead upwards, to a courtyard amidst ruined battlements. The place was reminiscent of a miniature coliseum, with square walls surrounding it, and the distinctive figures of the Manta Court sitting in a box amidst the broken seating. Manta and his closest minions seemed to enjoy their place in the lofty heights, royalty to which the rest of the world seemed oblivious. At least, until her capture, Jennifer had not been aware of that circus.

But, just to make matters even more absurd, she noticed an effort had been made to pull the damaged area into something beyond its former glory. Like a sham of an ancient gladiatorial function, it stood in all its anachronistic pomp. Each of the walls housed at least half a dozen of Manta's paid militia. Manta sat enveloped in a purple and gold cloak and though somewhat elegant, looked the most ridiculous of the lot of them.

But even from Jennifer's vantage, the Grey Lady shimmered as a translucent image, the same almost invulnerable threat she had always been. Cerise and Vortext remained an all but unknown quantity, which hampered Jennifer from making any plans. All, other than Vortext, appeared incredibly animated, apparently involved in heated conversation.

Her sight was either playing unwelcome tricks on her, or there were other sources of power surrounding them. Jennifer made no further attempt to see through her augmented chromatic vision. She instead focused her efforts on finding a way out. The high volume of firearms proved a serious complication. She had never been shot before but didn't want to find out the hard way how badly that would go for her.

"Nobody told you to stop!" The second guard had grown braver. Jennifer turned to him for a moment and contemplated knocking the courage out of him. She resisted the urge and turned back to Manta's court, wandering over to the motley band. Her escorts did not follow.

By the time she reached them, they had calmed down, apart from Manta himself, who stared daggers at Jennifer. In his hurried aggravation, he almost fell flat on his face when he tripped as he climbed out of the box to meet her. He stopped and loomed over her, but she stood her ground.

"This is *all* your doing," he spat. He prodded her hard at the shoulder. "I should have been wearing the crown right now had it not been for your interference."

She stared down at her shoulder, then back at him, but resisted the urge to react with violence. "What is this damn crown you keep going on about?"

Her captor clenched his fist, ready to lay hands on her again. Desired information or not, if he provoked her again, he was going to know about it. She eased back a step just to remove the temptation. He remained silent for a moment, his head bobbing as he considered matters. Eventually, he gave a disarming smile and returned, gracefully this time, to his box seat. He waved Jennifer across to join him. She moved to the front of the box and leaned into it. Sitting within the Court would have been a step too far.

She stretched her sight. It burned with rich colour, her will seemingly ignored on this occasion. A fiery, orange glow ran between Cerise and Vortext, though she could not determine how or why. Beyond that, weapons they possessed each carried similar auras, not all the burning orange, though.

A dark shadow surrounded the blade of the Grey Lady. That information came as little surprise. Jennifer could see Cerise's concealed knife as well, but only just against the woman's blood-red attire. A necklace she wore also exuded a sickly green colour. A golden light radiated from a silver sceptre which Manta sat next to, with something underneath his cloak that same foul shade as the necklace his colleague wore. Jennifer had no idea what any of it meant, but she recognised each as items of power.

Jennifer blinked, and her sight returned to normal.

"Are you okay?" asked Cerise. It seemed a less than sincere question. Her probing stare examined Jennifer with detached curiosity, not a sense of concern. She sat back, picked up and twirled a small first-aid kit.

"Fine, thank you," Jennifer replied. She kept Cerise a good distance from her. "So, why is this my doing, Mister Manta?"

She watched his calm evaporate in the space of that one question. But to his credit, he fought hard to hide it. "*La Corona De Reyes*. 'The Crown of Kings'."

"Nope," Jennifer said with a blank look. "Still never heard of it."

Manta gave a firm nod. "Of course you haven't. Why would you have?" He again offered her a seat, but she refused, determined to be no nearer the murderous mob than she had to be. "Very well. But you will know this is more than a mere inconvenience to me."

"Fine. Franco, tell me more about this crown of yours, then." She forced a defiant grin, made easier when she watched Manta frown at the informality. He really did like his appearances.

Pretentious prat.

"That's why we're even talking, right? Come on, where does a crown come into this?"

"She's delaying you," the Grey Lady said, staring coldly at the captive. "We should just kill her and move on. We have all we're getting here."

Manta stood and turned back to his Court. "Except for my crown."

"It's not here," Cerise replied calmly, "nor was it in the Louvre last night. We'll find it again, but right now, we cannot stay. They will locate us soon enough."

Manta considered for a moment but soon nodded. "Let us handle this last matter, and then I can keep looking."

"*We* can keep looking," Cerise said. "I want to see what all the fuss is about before this is all over."

"Know where it is . . ." Vortext muttered, but immediately returned to a distant stare.

Manta looked back at them all. "Fine." He left the box and threw off the cloak, revealing an old-looking suit of plate armour underneath. He turned to Jennifer. "It is interesting that I can put this on and it fits perfectly, but the suit I keep at home, the one I thought was important, nobody can get into. Hmph. If I'd been at my home, I might have invited you to try it. One last indulgence." He drew a sword from a scabbard at his side. "But as I can't, let's see what you have, Face of War."

"My king," sounded the whispered voice of the Grey Lady, "we should first proceed with the formalities. Our time is limited."

The fallen noble turned to glare for a moment at the one who had dared challenge his authority but soon conceded the point. "Indeed. The Consanguinity has not stood for all this time without structure."

"And your strength is assured through blood," Cerise added. "Haven't you always taught us this?"

"Indeed." He relaxed in stance, and threw his retrieved cloak loosely over his shoulders. "Despite being made to wait for the one thing I genuinely desired from this rather high-profile endeavour we have undertaken, we have several reasons for satisfaction. Prepare the rites."

Jennifer studied their conversation carefully, in an attempt to assess her enemy in full. Whilst she could normally identify physical weaknesses quickly, the court offered a greater challenge in that respect. She had only seen some of them in action, and possibly not at their full potential.

She wondered of what Manta was capable, given that the formidable Grey Lady took orders from him. She knew of his callous nature, of his vast amount of wealth and what he would do to get it. She knew of the bitter sense of self-entitlement and greed that drove him and made him dangerous to any who stood in his way. But no more.

The self-proclaimed king snapped his fingers. A couple of the guards dragged in a battered man, bound and gagged, wearing only his underwear. He writhed and fought to free himself, but they threw him at Manta's feet. Jennifer moved to aid him but soon found a familiar ethereal blade at her throat. She gave a frustrated snarl. Cerise knelt and reached for her barely concealed blade, handing it to Manta with a nod.

"Anywhere can be a temple with the right components," Vortext uttered.

"Indeed it may." Manta examined the curved knife with some concentration. "First, we must create one." He turned to the struggling male and hauled him to his knees by the hair, looking down with irritation. He then took the blade in a reverse grip and slashed just once across his victim's throat.

"Consider this a kindness," Manta told his prey, who clutched the wound, clawed for air. Jennifer gasped and tried to spin past, but the spectral assassin echoed and blocked her movement in perfect time. Manta continued. "Even a lighter cut across your arm with this weapon would have never healed. If I were without mercy, I might have allowed you to bleed out over hours, perhaps days."

"A pity, then, that we don't have days to spare," Cerise remarked.

The Grey Lady nodded. "Just time to do this rite, kill her, and go."

Jennifer looked at the man on the floor with her own attuned vision. It was true that even if they let her free shortly, she would be able to do nothing for him. The weapon's glow grew brighter. Instead of the blood gushing to the floor as it should have done, it clung to the blade and disappeared inside it. She watched in horror as the knife simply *drank* the gore.

Manta then squeezed the red jewel on the hilt of the weapon. Blood flowed around it. Not a drop escaped. He knelt away from the dying man, and pressed the tip of the knife against the floor. It scraped hideously on contact, but the blood flowed, and its wielder drew in red like a pen. He maintained contact as he moved in a large circle. She flinched as he wandered behind her, but the ghost walker kept her pinned.

When the circle of blood closed, a sickening feeling overwhelmed her. Though she felt no physical harm, her connection with the earth she had worked so hard to build suddenly severed. Her sight threw back to the mundane. She felt exposed, more vulnerable than ever.

Better that the enemy didn't know that.

She straightened up her stance and looked the Grey Lady straight in her eyes. The cold glare received came as no surprise. The two scrutinised each other for a moment, but as the rest of the court took their place within the circle, the pair disengaged. Manta handed the blade back to Cerise, who did not clean it before she returned it to its small sheath.

Jennifer took two weak steps backward and escaped the circle with no effort at resistance from Manta's court or the guards. Though dazed, she crouched in a fighting stance, hoping that was all it would be as she regained her strength.

Then Manta's court each stood an equal distance from each other within the circle. The guards closed in, but did not leave enough of a gap for Jennifer to easily exploit. Another squad behind the first put paid to any hopes of an easy break. Manta, still the closest to her, leaned forward and held out a hand to her. "You know," he said expectantly, "there is still a place for one of your talents within our circle. You need just say the word."

She thought about it, wondered what fate might have brought amongst those who may prove to be her own kind. But they *weren't* that. She had her failings, but did not belong amongst them.

The dead and bloodless sacrifice lay not far from her, one more innocent she could not save. Assimilation into the court boded little promise beyond further needless deaths, each offered up to a purpose she could not fathom. She could feel her equilibrium returning to normal, undamaged by the presence of their foul circle. Her judgement was final. "I'd rather die."

"Suit yourself."

Manta crouched, solemn, and touched the ground within the circle. "In ties of blood we are united." The words were repeated by the others in an echoing chorus.

"And united, our bonds cannot be broken," the Grey Lady finished.

"Good." The cult's leader gestured to the ghost walker, standing westernmost in the circle to Jennifer and directly opposite him. She withdrew her weapon, the incorporeal sword, and laid it in front of her. Then he pointed to Cerise, who did likewise with her own knife. Then to Vortext, who began to babble. His incomprehensible words buzzed around Jennifer's head like a hive of wasps. With every mumble, her balance broke more with scratching irritation. She needed to shut him up but couldn't move, crushed as he uttered more alien blasphemies. Then, just like that, he fell silent, but the sensation of cold insects continued to crawl across her body.

Finally, Manta stomped with his armour-plated foot from some distance away. The ground shook, and a shockwave rippled and felled her as she teetered. He appeared supremely satisfied with the result.

"The Armour of Earth belongs to *me*. Each of you, brothers and sisters, wields power that we have seized for our own. We can speak the words of this rite with meaning for the first time." The Grey Lady gave a distasteful look, but Jennifer noted she took pains to conceal it from Manta.

"And now, what was the recitation? Ah, yes. *Take the earth where others borrow. Call the storm where others blow away. Swim strong where others drown. Step into the fire without fear or regret.*"

Jennifer had never heard the words before. But they seemed so familiar. "Who the hell are you people?" she cursed. Only Cerise heeded her, and levelled a suspicious glance her way. But something about Manta's last words rang familiar.

"The armour I wear shakes the ground I walk upon. Earth's own strength at my feet." He smiled victoriously, but it swiftly dropped to a face of lament. "A fine recent acquisition. But still I do not have my crown. I must know its power for my own."

What did he just say?

Jennifer rose to her feet, but the act gained Manta's unwanted attention.

She focused, harnessing her enhanced vision. The ground had darkened around his feet, a sensation she recognised. She had done such an act in the past.

Draw your strength from the earth.

Where she borrowed, they took. The words he spoke a dark echo of the mantra Alice provided. Enemies, then, who didn't know who she was.

He pointed to the sword in front of the ghost woman, the blade curved like a katana, but the hilt more occidental in style. "The weapon we call the *Wraithbreaker* calls the storm of the dead. Every assault flies unchallenged, unstoppable, in worthy hands."

Free from either hands or a sheath, Jennifer noticed that the blackened blade bore a sapphire jewel in its hilt. She had seen a gem very much like it before. On a necklace. She'd heard the story from Kara. It, too, was originally housed in a weapon. The Grey Lady reached for the weapon and held it.

A strange feeling hit Jennifer, the discomfort she had felt around the Unresting world's influence in the past—just as with her early days with Mary. That unease washed over her in a wave, but she felt helpless to do anything about it. If the Wraithbreaker was anything like *Death's Teardrop* had been, it needed to be destroyed.

"The gift of words possessed by Vortext comes to us with the greatest force." The enigma spoke in an incomprehensible tongue again, though, Jennifer observed, not before his partner, Cerise, raised her hand to signal. Whilst Jennifer looked with her augmented eyes, she saw the aura surrounding the two strengthened. The link between them held stronger than first appeared.

But as he talked, Jennifer's dizziness returned. She fought it, determined to stay standing, determined to show strength. His voice—the power was overwhelming. She had to step into the circle, break this before it got out of hand. But the step forward dropped her to one knee.

As Jennifer stumbled, the voice ceased. She shook her head violently in an effort to recover, but the damage had been done.

"The last is the cruellest blade—the *Bloodsong*," Manta announced with relish. "Perhaps the one success of the British Museum operation was the Consanguinity's reunion with this. The most famed of our discoveries and our very symbol. By blood spilt, we have prevented the destruction of treasures more valuable than most are capable of comprehending. By blood spilt, we remain strong. Only by sacrifice and strife will we gain secrets of powers and places beyond measure. This is our symbol, the weapon whose wound will not be healed."

"I thank you for my gift, my lord." Cerise gave a sweeping bow, which might have looked mocking in other circumstances.

"No, thank *you*," he replied. "You brought the Consanguinity's greatest gift—the ability to imbue our tools with their true strength. I feared when the Consanguinity lost our dear Contessa D'Amato, that we, too, would be lost. But we know you, Cerise, as a healer, in more ways than simply our wounds. I do not believe it was by chance that you came to us, or your spoils."

"And your order has given my life meaning and purpose that I may have never known," she drawled, and turned back to Jennifer. "It is a shame that not all who are offered such opportunities are willing to take them."

"I don't need shiny toys to beat any of you."

They all turned to face Jennifer. Exactly what she wanted. "You couldn't touch me if you tried," the Grey Lady scoffed, and raised the Wraithbreaker. "I shall enjoy educating you."

"Good." Jennifer gave a satisfied grin at the challenge. "I've listened to you lot gabbing for long enough."

The robed killer vanished. She manifested again outside the circle, poised for combat.

"Wait!" Manta raised a hand and stepped towards the edge of the circle. He drew a sword of his own, no component of the recent rite. "You are right. It is time." He turned to Jennifer and raised his weapon. "But it is *I* who demand this challenge. You are not the Face of War. But you are an inconvenience. And you have wasted enough of my time. Clear the floor."

The court took comfortable seats in anticipation of the upcoming spectacle. The guards altered their positions, and ensured there would be no way out.

CHAPTER EIGHT

T he opponents could not have contrasted further. The unarmed, barely armoured Jennifer faced a man who appeared deadly, bulky, plated, and brandishing a glistening blade against a backdrop of ruins and destruction.

The chateau ruins. A means to an end. But they had all missed a trick. Jennifer's meditation from earlier told her the court were very close to a potent source of her own power, but their eagerness to leave after dealing with her—tying up the loose end—spoke volumes. If they actually knew what they were sitting on, the gang might have called off their next robbery. She was in no hurry to tell any of them. And that edge might prove critical to her survival.

Manta shook free of the cloak and readied his sword, controlling it with both hands. A low rumble travelled through the air. With quiet, detached focus, Jennifer felt the power boost run through her again, energy like she had not felt in many months. A sudden, quiet confidence steeled her as she prepared to wipe the arrogant grin from his face. But her special sight revealed that the armour he wore bolstered him more than by way of protection. Another disadvantage for her. And Manta hardly stood alone.

Perhaps attack would be the only way forward.

"Wanna prove yourself a big man in front of your mates, do you?" she taunted. "You look proper tough in that armour. Bet you feel really tough, too."

He dropped his stance and shrugged. "I do actually. I can have you brought a stab vest if you like?"

She rolled her eyes. "A weapon would be better."

"Some Face of War," he mocked.

"Yeah, we know. I'm a huge disappointment, wah, wah, wah. You're still looking for the real one. Now, are you going to give me the same chance you gave your boys?"

His face went red, and he hurled his sword at her feet. "Take it." He snapped his fingers and within seconds, he was thrown another by the Grey Lady. Jennifer watched, relieved that the blade wasn't the Wraithbreaker. She knew that weapon's capabilities, and had enough going against her as it was.

A terrible thought crossed her mind. She had never been involved in a sword duel, nor witnessed one. All technique she had gained came from movie viewing, and none of those were the useful ones. The little she had learned, it could have been as much of a hindrance to her as a help.

In his confidence—overconfidence, she hoped—he ordered that the stab vest be thrown to her as well. It wouldn't offer her that much protection against a proper sword, but with the energy coursing through her, it could tip the scales in her favour.

She gathered her focus, concentrated her thoughts into becoming that self-invented goddess she managed to call upon whenever in need of strength. She could feel her hair binding, tightening into that brambly mass she assumed when preparing for combat. Her drawn strength flowed like a waterfall, and as she outstretched her fingers, a wonderful, familiar tickling sensation ran through them, up and up until she satisfied the itch. They had sprouted into razor-like talons, deadly as the blade itself. It was her turn to grin, assured in the knowledge she felt something like her old self again. Perhaps better.

Murmurs ran through the court. But Manta simply sniggered and gave a polite golf clap. "Ah, good. There *is* more to you. Interesting to see your . . . *evolution.*"

Enough talk. She was ready to shove it down his throat. She indulged him a snarl and then closed in.

Something didn't sit right with her, though. The source of her strength felt as much a danger to her as an aid. How and why were unclear. But the time to sense was over. Now was the time to fight.

She got within the blade's reach of her opponent. He held his guard but circled, did not attack. She tried to step inside that range, but he held his distance, kept circling. "Come on, beast!" he taunted as she tried to find an opening, tried to forget about an easy escape route . . .

. . . *Distracted*! He lunged twice with deadly accuracy. It was as much as she could do to parry his assault. She backed off and retracted the talons in her sword hand, her right hand, but he allowed her no time to breathe. His strikes were lightning-fast, and only natural defensive instinct and a solid range of fighting skills helped her.

She barely retained her grip on the blade as he hit her again and again with an unrelenting salvo of attacks. She fell backward, but he pressed his assault, giving her an opening. She tried to sweep his legs from under him, but despite the weight of the armour he wore, he leapt back easily.

She rolled backward and flipped herself back to her feet, adjusting her footwork for another round. But this time, she let him come to her. After all, he was the one with the crowd to please, not her. She maintained her range, waiting for him to close in. But then, he simply lifted a foot and stomped it on the ground.

The ground rippled from under this shockwave, like jelly, not stone. The tremor threw her off her feet, back to the ground. He leapt at her with a cleaving thrust. She moved into a horizontal parry to block, but the ferocious blow instantly disarmed her. She dodged to her rear and winced as she felt the backlash in her wrist. She shook it a few times and extended her fingers for combat once more. Better than nothing.

"Knuckle-dragger," he mocked and came at her again, whirling the sword into a deadly barrier. She knew her talons would not protect against that, and moved in a crouch. She leapt away and to the side once, twice, three times as he drew close. The third time, he stomped again, but Jennifer was ready for him.

With some small momentum and strength, she leapt forward into a somersault, then shifted to her previous position. She retrieved the sword and closed the distance between them before he could fully steady himself. She mimicked his early flurry and landed true twice before the pain in her wrist weakened her effort. But both hits simply sparked off his armour, no sign that they had even slowed him.

"Hah!" He acted unimpressed. But he'd backed off long enough for her to focus and heal the injury. A minor one, but potentially costly. He raised his foot. She knew what was coming. She leapt to evade, but no ripples impacted the ground. Instead, he charged. She blocked as well as she could before landing with her wrecked balance.

Despite her defence, Manta struck with colossal power and speed. He smashed the front of her vest and grazed just above her rib with one blow. He disarmed her with a second. As she fell backward, she countered with an upward claw strike. Her hand danced across the front of his chest plate but drew four red grazes under his chin.

The attack quelled, she went on the offensive. Still supine, she pulled back both legs and jammed them as hard as she could manage into his chest. Manta staggered in retreat. She steadied herself on her knees and retrieved the sword, then thrust it right into the side of his chest plate. Her sword snapped in two as she connected. But the impact threw him back several paces, if still not off his feet.

Well, this isn't going well.

Jennifer didn't let up. She couldn't afford to. While he was off balance, she brought herself up like a sprinter, then burst forward and jabbed at him with the broken hilt. Though he staggered backward, he slammed his foot on to the ground and, fully committed to the attack, she tripped and fell forward. Before she could recover, he ran the remaining steps and brought his foot down over her.

Jennifer jumped clear, but not far enough. Shattering force crushed her ribs and she screamed in pain. Manta steadied himself and jammed his knee into the base of her spine, his full weight brought to bear. He grabbed her wiry hair and, pulling her head back, forced her to look up at the gloating Manta Court.

Manta rammed her head into the ground twice more. Blood ran down over her eyes. She hadn't stopped screaming. She could hear herself even as the pain told her to sleep, to let it all go. But she could heal. The power to do so still coursed through her. But to do so wouldn't save her. She did not have the strength to move.

"Remember. Not everything you do relies on raw force. You must learn more than that to defeat your enemies."

Those words had applied to her when she had been bullied at school. Her current situation was little different to her head being held over a toilet bowl all those years ago. Those now tormenting her were bigger and stronger—perhaps stronger than her. But she remembered thinking that at school, too, and she got through it just fine.

"My beautiful subjects," Manta's voice oozed, but carried well in the amphitheatre acoustics. "Is this here our so-called *Face of War*? See how easily I have her at my mercy. What do you say?" He drove his knee further into her back. She whimpered. He needed little more pressure to break it.

Vortext spoke, notably coherent. "Perhaps the words were not meant as that. It is possible that it was she who would prove *you* to be the one by that name?"

Jennifer could not see his expression, but was fairly sure by now that would have brought a smile to her opponent's face. "I-I can't cope with this brown-nosing anymore," she spluttered. "It's . . . making me sick." In truth, the nausea came partly from her injuries. "G-get it done with so I don't have to hear you all, will you?" It was a terrible gamble, but she had nothing left. Manta retracted his knee, then drove it into her back again by way of response. She cried out even through damaged lungs.

"I like your thinking, Vortext." Definitely glee in his voice. "It will be a worthy title."

"A king without a crown," Vortext muttered, then returned to silence.

"You've destroyed every enemy we've faced since my arrival," Cerise said in a silky, obsequious tone. "What reason have we not to believe you?" Jennifer hocked a gout of blood and attempted to spit it in their direction, but it barely landed a metre from her mouth.

"The thought will keep me going until I get what's mine. But for now, shall we let this one live in her pain? Or do I finish her now?"

The Grey Lady instantly raised her arm and raised her thumb, the sign of condemnation in that gladiatorial arena. Cerise feigned indecision for a few seconds and then followed her colleague. Finally, Vortext raised his arm in a puppet-like fashion and snapped his own thumb in the direction of the sky.

"It appears unanimous," Manta sang. "I shall make this quick for you."

He dropped his sword and placed his free hand under her chin.

~ * ~

Jennifer started to work on her escape the second she made her first jibe from the floor. By the time she spat the blood, she had already bought herself time for one last gambit.

She focused her chromatic vision hard and targeted the source of her great gift. Her best escape option. It had to be close. Very close. She touched the static ground with the tips of her extended fingers and summoned thoughts of rejuvenation.

The torturous knees boring into her back bludgeoned her concentration, but she only needed a little of the life force to regain some of her strength. The remaining pain would motivate her efforts. She reminded herself of the mental map she drew from her meditation whilst in confinement and, like a spiritual bloodhound, sniffed out the strongest point of the source—and the quickest way to it.

But Manta drew from that same source, although she but realised it. It flowed through him. She thought perhaps the plate he wore might have been the conduit.

Manta grabbed her head. She knew she would have just one chance, or be as dead as he promised. She flicked the shattered sword closer, seized the hilt with her elongated fingers. She lunged with the broken weapon—right through his lowest hand. He yelped, Jennifer's cue. She flipped over and threw him off, but grimaced as she caught her own chin with the tip of the shard.

She scuttled clear of stunned Manta, and exploded into a sprint. The ghost walker vanished in short order. The assassin wouldn't be playing this time, so Jennifer had to think fast.

Jennifer jinked left, straight at a row of guards. They took aim but seemed unsure, looking behind her for instruction. The element of surprise on her side, she leapt at one of the guards, and took him down in a flash. She rolled forward and retained her momentum. She sprang again, this time running three steps up the wall before her, and propelled herself backwards as the ghost assassin landed.

Jennifer regained her balance, took two steps forward and sailed over the court's viewing box to her right as if vaulting a gym horse. Another push took her up the next level of seating, then again and again until she had reached the fallen battlements.

A hail of gunfire opened up behind her, but she did not stop as she bounded, sure-footed, between stones. Bullets sparked with every step she took, but her balance was perfect, her movement swift and unerring. She aimed for the one intact corner of the fortification, the strongest scent of her target beyond it.

The Grey Lady appeared right in front of her, and swung *Wraithbreaker* high. Jennifer was moving too fast to stop or change direction. She threw herself down and in an attempt to tackle her suddenly vanished opponent. She roared as she smacked shoulder-first into a wall and tumbled back down several feet. Her sight blurred with agony, but the bullets hadn't stopped flying, with the ghost walker, ominous in her invisibility, no doubt closing for the kill.

Only adrenaline allowed Jennifer to ignore her pain as she pushed herself up with her good arm, only the promise of certain death with failure kept her on her path. A bullet grazed her left calf, and the already tender ribs nagged. She *had* to keep going.

She crouched, then flopped behind a damaged lump of wall large enough to hide behind. Holding her arm, without hesitation, she forced her injured shoulder upward against the wall, and back into place. Her eyes watered as her entire body throbbed, but she stood and moved. A whistle sounded in the air followed by a crunch—the spectral blade sliced straight through the stone as if it were butter.

With the little momentum she had, Jennifer leapt and spun in the air, landing just short of the tower wall. She jumped again and clung hard with the good arm, gritting her teeth as she yanked herself further up with the bad one. Pain was a luxury she could afford if she could stay alive to appreciate it.

More gunfire slammed into the tower wall as she hauled herself up it, grunting with the strain. Rivulets of sweat stung her back as they trickled over fresh cuts and grazes. Bits of debris slapped her in the leg, the face, everywhere, as the hail of bullets zeroed in on her position. But she gained the height she needed and climbed to the side of the castle, away from the ranged assault.

Her last enemy remained within sight. The Grey Lady replaced her sword in its scabbard, then took a running leap from the bottom of the tower. The killer's ability to cross worlds evidently helped little in scaling heights, but she climbed after Jennifer with practised speed. Jennifer made it across to the front of the castle, searching for that elusive power source. Her eyes attuned, she looked down. She felt it there, somewhere, but she couldn't quite see . . .

The Grey Lady grabbed her leg and hauled her with incredible force—

—but Jennifer needed to get down there anyway. She released her grip and pushed away from the tower, and took control of her fall. Her enemy chose to let go rather than follow. Perfect. Almost.

After a split second, Jennifer extended her hands and lunged at the wall. Her claws didn't stop her, but they did slow her significantly before the tips snapped. She screamed again with the agony, but kicked from the tower into a controlled somersault. Two, three, before coiling her legs to land, firm but safe, on the grass below. Her hands resumed their normal length, but the fingertips were bloodied, like someone had filed them.

"Ow, ow, ow, ow, ow!"

By the fifth cry, they had healed into cuts and scrapes, but had not resolved completely. Then she could see it. On the long grass ahead of her, stood a pair of twisted tree trunks, like vines, but bent into each other as an arch. A small gap could be seen at the top of the entanglement, something prominent missing, detected by Jennifer's enhanced sight.

However, as she stared at it, the static vines appeared to strangely unravel, just a little. Somehow, the grassland she could see through the arch looked greener, healthier, than that surrounding it. The long grass she stood on looked fine, but there was just something *better* about whatever awaited on the other side.

The left and right of the portal appeared normal. Inside, better. It made little sense, but little in her life did—even herself. If heading through that arch answered even one question, it would have made that entire sorry mess worth it. She collapsed as the rigours of her last few minutes caught up with her hard, but her enemy was still above her and looking down.

Jennifer still could not stop, could not rest. She crawled, each drag more arduous than the last, until eventually she forced herself to one knee, to a crouch. Another look up. Her would-be killer was no longer in sight. That wasn't a good thing. She needed to go faster. She staggered forth, her goal in sight, and pushed harder.

The relentless foe materialised in front of her again. Without thinking, she dropped into a backward roll, which spared her head as the barely visible blade flashed where she had just stood. Back on her feet, she ran for the lower wall, and heard the guards regrouped. Jennifer jumped at the wall, gripping with one hand.

She sprang away from the opposite side, over her pursuing opponent, who missed once more with a deadly swing. Jennifer's landing wasn't the best, but she recovered and sprinted for the wooden arches, her finish line.

She roared as she dived through, and felt every bone in her body tingle just as soon as she penetrated the vines. The sensation felt reminiscent of the tickle when she grew talons, only she felt it *everywhere*. Then, it intensified, a surge of fire coursing through her blood. She closed her eyes for a moment. Dared to take a small breather.

The noise of battle had become a distant memory.

~*~

Though it had been silent for a while, Jennifer still felt the need to look back. Just once, she turned her head to examine the archway she had come through to see if her killer had made it through, too.

The gate had vanished.

She stood alone against a backdrop of enormous evergreen trees and beautiful silence—though being a forest, it was never truly silent. Unseen birds chirped in the distance. Leaves shimmered in the breeze. Though unclear where she needed to go from there, it was quite the place to stop, regroup and gather her thoughts.

She shuffled over to the nearest of the trees and leaned against it. She inhaled the crisp, clean air around her. The best to ever fill her lungs. Her many aches and pains eased with every breath, which tempted her to relax, to sit and take in her surroundings. Just for a moment, she had found perfect solace.

But she couldn't enjoy it for any length of time. Manta and his crew were out there.

Just the other side of that gate. The one she couldn't find. She went back to the exact point where her environment changed, or so she thought, and found only lush, green forestry for her trouble. So, transported from death dancing around her at every turn to a relative paradise, in a matter of footsteps? It made little sense. Yet, her environment felt so natural to her, like she'd been there all her life.

Think about it. Where were you trying to go?

Anywhere, other than where you were.

Be sensible. You had somewhere in mind.

That power source. YOUR power source. That took you here. But this isn't it. It's closer. Much closer.

Now that she had worked so hard on getting in, Jennifer needed to formulate an escape plan. However, the absence of the gate which granted her entry told her everything she needed to know. From there in, going back wasn't an option. Forward or nothing. Otherwise, she'd sit there having a nice, relaxing break while Manta and his Consanguinity killed more innocent people.

He—they—seemed happy to extinguish life as readily as the monsters she had faced in the past, regardless of their apparent careful planning, whatever their ultimate goals. That made them even more dangerous. And she'd been away from home for . . . how long was it now? Not long in the grand scheme of things, yet long enough for her friends to grow concerned.

Actually, she felt better already. Must have been something in the air. But then, she had learned to love the forest long ago. Alice had taught her that.

There isn't time to feel sorry for yourself. Get a grip.

The forest felt vast, consuming. She could see no one else around. The breeze whispered through the trees, which seemed to lean away from the rising wind. Had it not sounded so ludicrous, she could have sworn they were peering down at her. Clouds gathered speed and darkened the entire scene. In the moments she took to catch her breath, the patter of water falling against the leaves resonated around her. The drops came slowly, and when a little caught her on the face, they felt far too warm. If she didn't know better, they might have reminded her of teardrops.

Within seconds, the dripping multiplied. The rain hit hard and heavy, drenched Jennifer before she had any chance of moving to a safe shelter.

Shelter. She didn't know where to go, how long it would take. But she had to act, whether she liked it or not. To sit out the storm—both the weather and Manta's machinations—was not an option. She propped herself up against one of the huge evergreen trees and leveraged herself back to standing. To her surprise and relief, nothing felt anywhere near as bad as it should have done. No echo of wounds, no fatigue. The forest greatly energised her, no doubt about it.

But in mere moments, it grew dark, constricting—almost as if the trees had closed in on her.

"Ow!"

She felt a sting in the palm of her hand. She pulled it away from the tree and examined the wound. Fresh blood dripped to the ground, distinct against the sudden shower. A thorn protruded from her flesh, an inch long. She plucked it out and threw it back at the tree. She watched it grow hundreds of them, as the lands around her mutated from comforting to treacherous even as she watched.

From miles away thunder rolled. The flash preceding the next rumble dazzled her. The forest could be a dangerous place for one alone and unprepared, and it had become dark, cold, wet. *Miserable*, just as she felt. The bracken snapped with every step. She revelled in one moment's tranquillity, only for it to be drowned out by—an ear-ripping howl?

That was new. The sound crawled down her spine, heralded danger. The call was soon joined by others, each closer than the last. Too close for comfort. She'd had little personal experience with wolves, given that they were nowhere to be found in Britain save for zoos. But she knew the unmistakeable sound . . . albeit it louder, in a deeper pitch.

A shadow loomed on the horizon. Then several more.

Footsteps followed, a rapid padding between ever-louder wails.

A pack closed in on her. She knew she couldn't stay there.

CHAPTER NINE

Although plagued by the emergency service sirens wailing through the Parisian night, Mary and Kara caught a few hours' sleep and breakfast on the run when daylight returned. Back to full strength, Mary transported them instantaneously to the rooftop above them, where she sensed the other Unresting traveller had passed.

They came to a stop amidst a deafening howl and an explosion of black wind. Kara shivered hard but soon recovered, with help from Mary's experience with the dead world, and the calming words she offered.

"Not quite a blind jump," Mary said, tapping her temple, "and one hell of a difference in distance. I couldn't see exactly what we'd be landing on up here, but I'm happy to settle for flat ground beneath our feet. Now then, let's see if I can get a better fix from here."

She sat and made herself comfortable before calling upon her power once more. Kara watched with the utmost approval at Mary's efforts and aided with scanning the area. For all of the mystic force thrown around, a good old-fashioned search for physical evidence was always worthwhile.

A cold wind picked up, nothing out of the ordinary around Mary. Kara ignored it and carried on her search, but found little more than dust and a carrier bag blowing on the breeze. She turned around to relay this to Mary, but her investigative partner shot back to her feet and into a battle posture. Her eyes darted around.

"Mary?" Kara said in a low voice. "Why so twitchy?"

Mary whirled around, looking behind her. "Incoming!"

Kara dashed to the roof entrance door, after her friend. Once close, Mary tackled her to the ground and spun her towards the door, but worked to ensure a gentle landing for them both. She stood up and primed her hands with light-devouring shadow.

A small, black cloud formed at a corner of the roof. The mass shifted in size and solidified from mere shade to a billowing black door. The roof became ice cold. The void shimmered, and from it stepped a tall, cloaked, figure, wearing a brimmed hat and carrying what looked like a staff.

Mary stood up, turned to the open door, and made a gripping motion into the air. "Sorry about this, K!"

Kara felt suddenly weightless. She flailed into the air as she rose from the ground and watched helplessly as Mary moved her arm sharply to the right, then opened her fist.

"Mary, wait—I—AAAARGH!"

Kara, unbalanced, fell through the open roof entrance door and crashed down the first flight of stairs. She braced for a collision but stopped dead just before she hit the bottom step. The door above her slammed shut. In the gap around it, she saw what looked like a flash of lightning—only, the dread-black lightning, a familiar sight a year past. Mary had protected her.

Kara growled, "Oh, I don't think so, little Miss Hoity-Toity. You're not leaving me out of this one after all we've been through." She ran back up the stairs and burst through the door.

On the rooftop, her friend and the cloaked figure stood locked in a standoff, the sky around them black as night. Mary wielded a knife, curved and reflecting brightly against an anomalous light. Mary's opponent held a staff, which appeared to be made of charred wood with a sculpted head. The details of the head were undetectable from where Kara stood. The tall figure appeared in no hurry to attack but looked calm, confident. Mary held her weapon more in hope than as a practised fighter. Kara knew that wasn't her area of expertise—hopefully the staff-wielder didn't.

Mary called upon her otherworldly connection. Horrific black lightning crackled from her fingertips and a black portal manifested behind the individual. "Not another step," she spat, "or I banish you to the arse-end of somewhere you *really* don't want to go."

"Interesting threat . . ." the figure replied, a male voice, Spanish, without a tinge of fear in his words. "But I think not." With a wave of his hand, he closed the portal and the surrounding darkness receded to its origins. Kara made muffled protests and started towards them both, but Mary swept the air in her direction with her shadowed hand, and a gust of the death winds pinned Kara where she stood.

Mary turned back to her new enemy and readied her other hand for attack. "Look, mate, you don't want to test me right now." For all of her power, Kara could see her friend trembled, and couldn't blame her.

The man threw back his head and laughed, his face obscured by the darkness of the Unresting world. "I sense you might be able to test me," he replied, shifting his weapon grip, "but you will not defeat me. Now, surrender and I may allow you to live."

"Surrender?" Mary spluttered. "Not while I've got a breath in my body, mate. You'll have to come through me before you get anywhere near killing my friend, you hear me?"

Time appeared frozen, a moment in which nobody moved. Then, the man with the staff crouched into a combat stance. "Whatever is necessary to stop your evil." He lowered his staff and pointed it in Mary's direction, and she, in response, aimed her buzzing, weaponised hand at him, primed for attack. The rooftop became a stormy battleground as the two closed in a few paces on each other. They circled slowly, each waiting for the other to make a move.

"Wait!" Kara called. "*Our* evil? You're the one running around terrorising folk. Do you know who you're dealing with there?"

That got his attention. Mary seized the opportunity and threw a wall of force that Kara could not see. He staggered back three paces, but regained his balance and pushed back, evidently with some power of his own.

A battle of wills took place between the two and the backlash knocked Kara to the ground. Mary gathered a small cyclone around herself, and pushed it towards her opponent. But he started to get the upper hand, and the summoning slowly but surely turned against her.

The shadow flame in Mary's hand extinguished, and a counter strike of Unresting energy knocked her off her feet and the knife out of her hand which skittered in Kara's direction. But Mary rallied and dragged some of the darkness into a focused ball, and unleashed it at her opponent. At the last second, he sidestepped the blast, which flew harmlessly into space.

Kara could not allow the battle to continue. She collected the loose blade and swiftly crept around the back of the cloaked figure. In a flash, she held the glistening weapon close to his throat. It grew strangely cold in her hand, though, and she felt a weight of resistance, as if she had been holding it there for far longer. She couldn't maintain her offense. Much quicker than she had intended, Kara lowered the weapon. To her great surprise, he, too, relaxed his staff, despite the advantage he had in the battle. Mary raised her hand and aimed another blast at him.

"Mary, stop!" Kara demanded, still looking down at the knife. She dropped it and backed away in disgust, without truly knowing why. Mary looked quizzically at her, but lowered her hand and allowed the dark energies surrounding them to dissipate safely.

The cloaked man vanished in a sudden breeze, and appeared instantaneously on the other side of the rooftop behind Mary. She whirled around to receive him. He raised his hands in surrender, holding the staff, yet not brandishing it in a hostile manner.

Mary turned to him as he slowly removed his hood. He had a weathered, albeit handsome, unshaven face, with unkempt black hair running down to his shoulder and blowing with the wind. His eyeballs fully blackened, just as Mary's Unresting sight did when activated—and Kara could not help but notice Mary give a small shiver as she stared at him.

Kara realised that this was probably the first time Mary had seen another living person match her extraordinary talent. Kara, too, found it disconcerting. More than that, she found it fascinating.

"I'm offering a halt to hostilities," he stated. "I do not believe you to be whom I first thought." He looked down at the dagger, while keeping an eye on the two women.

"Who did you think we were?" Mary asked.

"A problem has turned up in Paris. It seems the city has become very popular with our kind lately." He paused, examining the blade through darkened eyes. "Though, as I can see, not all of our kind are the same. May I?" He reached for the knife but stopped short of picking it up, quite aware of the tenuousness of his situation.

"Go ahead," Mary said, quite unexpectedly. "You won't be able to harm us with it, I'm certain of that." Given her recent experience with the blade, Kara found herself nodding in agreement. "Swap you, though."

He handed Mary the staff, an act of mutual trust as he gathered the knife. He poked his finger on the point of the dagger with his left hand, the hilt in his right, before looking up at Mary, apparently impressed. "Extraordinary," he said. "This knife. It is like nothing I have seen before. And it does not have the feel of a weapon intended to kill. Who *are* you?"

"Doctor Kara Mellencourt," Kara said, suddenly beaming. She strode towards him until blocked by Mary's arm.

"I am known as the *Guardian of the Gate*," she said in an uncharacteristically formal tone.

The man's eyes reverted to a more mundane brown colour. He carefully handed the blade back to Mary and relaxed his stance. "I am Cristobal Sergides, *Protecteur de la Porte Fantome Noir*. And this is a very special day. You are from London?"

"Yeah," Mary answered.

"I live and work there, but I was born in Didsbury," Kara interjected. Cristobal looked puzzled. There was something dramatic about his introduction which made her smirk. "*Protector of the Black Ghost Door?*" she translated. "Wow."

"Wow, indeed. I have not known of a Guardian of the Gate in many years. I had believed such a thing long gone."

"How many years, exactly?" Mary asked.

"Many more than you think," he replied, grinning with pearly white teeth. "Time seems less significant in the other world. Perhaps I spend a little too long speaking with ghosts."

Kara and Mary exchanged looks full of unasked questions. Eventually, Mary broke the silence. "So, how long have you been at this?" she asked. "Twenty years? Thirty?"

"At least a century more," Cristobal declared.

"Get outta here!" Kara squealed. "I had you pegged at forty, tops!"

"An occasionally useful trait."

Mary's eyes narrowed. "You look good for your age." She moved close to him and glared straight into his eyes. "A little too good, actually. And I'd like to know how. If I don't like what I hear, we're off for round two, got it?"

A chill shivered up Kara's spine as she considered the source of Mary's suspicions—Tally's greatest enemy, the ruthless Lady Raine and the life force of others she stole to attempt immortality. Cristobal looked taken aback by the accusation but eventually gave a nod of agreement. "I can't promise you'll like what you hear, but I will tell you what you want to know."

Mary shifted to the dark sight and examined him through extrasensory eyes. "Well, there's nothing bad riding around in you, nor any nearby demon shadows summoned to terrorise us, that I can see."

Kara's interest was piqued once more. "None of those 'spectres' you described from back at the Odeon, then?"

Mary continued to stare down their mystery guest. "He's not got a *Ready Brek* glow, no signs of possession." She reached for his cloak and rubbed that between her hands, too. "Nor anything weird about him, far as I can tell. Living being, perfectly healthy. This isn't deathcloth, either."

"*Deathcloth*?" He looked at Mary, puzzled. "What are you talking about? No, this is just . . . cloth."

Mary ignored him. "No knives or necklaces." She took a step back and folded her arms. "So who or what the hell are you?" A light breeze gathered around Mary, a preparation for hostilities, Kara inferred.

He gave a nod of assent. "I thought you might know at least what I am, *Guardian*, but of course, I have been here and you have been over there." He pointed north. "What I was? Lost. In my youth, I had a simple life, happy and happily married. I lost my wife to fever, and lost the will to do anything for many months. I just got up and walked one day. A long way from home. But I heard voices, including my wife's, and thought I had succumbed to madness. One of your predecessors, the seventeenth Lord Grenshall, as he introduced himself to me on a visit, told me otherwise."

"One of my predecessors?" Mary gave him a withering glance. "What was the name of this predecessor of mine."

"I shall never forget how Lord Alphonse calmed my concerns that day, when we sat at the dockyard and he simply told me I was not losing my mind. He spoke Spanish as if he had lived in my village all of his life."

Her eyes grew wide. "You met Lord Alphonse alive? In the eighteenth century?"

He gave a warm smile. "Indeed, I did. He seemed so determined that I should not worry about these voices, and that I should watch over the many ghosts I had seen, and would see. It looked as if he was setting matters in order before he himself passed on. But he seemed to be in perfect health."

Mary nodded just once, and Kara knew exactly why. They had spoken in great detail about the memories she gained from her immediate predecessor, Tally, of her own tutelage from Lord Alphonse. Mary explained that he had been in good health, and for the sake of preservation of the Grenshall Manor gate, voluntarily became an Unresting entity, a ghost, in order that he could pass on his knowledge. Sacrifice had often been an integral part of the mantle of Guardian of the Gate, something both Lord Alphonse and Lady Iris 'Tally' Grenshall, could attest to.

Cristobal bowed his head. "He told me of the remains of an old nunnery, *La Porte Fantome Noire.* He told me a tale of a gateway to the dead, which became present there, and of those who would abuse the dead for their own gain. When we got there, I heard more voices, saw more ghosts, than I ever had before. We spoke to them all night, and I heard so much anger, injustice, that it gave me a new purpose: to protect them as best I could, from others who might use them for harm, and when necessary, from themselves."

"There are some such cases," Mary conceded.

"He once said to me, 'Those who hold the gates—'"

"'—hold the world in their hands.' He used to say that to me—I mean, to Tally—all the time when he was training her." Mary gaped for a second, then thrust out her right hand. "I am Lady Rose Mary Grenshall. And you appear to be a counterpart of mine."

"*Protecteur. Guardian.*" He raised a hand and shook Mary's firmly. "Counterparts, indeed."

Mary abruptly freed her hand. "One question, how are you keeping yourself preserved all these years?"

"I had a feeling you would ask. But in no way that you'd have to put me down for. As *Protecteur,* I have taken a very binding vow to protect the dead."

"A vow to whom?" A steel edge lingered in her voice.

"To *them.*" His eyes flashed with the death sight and the chill breeze of the Unresting flapped around them. "I believe it is they who extend my health. I do not ask them to, but they know me well and would not see me join their ranks yet and will not let me simply walk away. I have been a shepherd to these spirits for as long as I can remember. I lost my wife far too many years ago now.

"I have watched governments rise and kingdoms crumble. I endured a civil war tear my native land apart. I kept violent spirits from tearing Europe apart during and after a so-called Great War. In the following war, someone came for me during a battle which almost threw the *Porte Noir* open permanently. And I'm *tired,* Lady Grenshall. I've stood at this side of the door for just enough lifetimes to wonder what is on the other side. Where my wife went. Nobody else has come for my job in many, many decades. Have you?" He looked at Mary expectantly.

Mary tilted her head. "You're deadly serious, aren't you?"

"Cross my heart and—"

"Don't you dare." Mary shoved him hard in the chest with one finger. "Besides, I've already got territory to protect, as you know."

Cristobal stared for a moment, silent. Then, he nodded. "I understand," he said solemnly. "But that raises two questions, what are you doing away from it, and what are you doing in mine?"

"We're looking for a friend of ours," Kara answered. "She's been gone from home for a little too long now after doing something extraordinarily foolish. We know she was close by recently."

"How do you know if you haven't seen her?" Cristobal asked.

"With these eyes, she stands out like you wouldn't believe," Mary answered. "If you know what to look for." Mary snorted. "She's pretty special. But she's something very different to me and thee."

"Hmm . . ." Cristobal rubbed his chin and tapped the staff along the ground several times in thought. "Different, you say? Tell me, this friend of yours. She does not see the shadow the way you can?"

"Nope," Mary answered. "Least, I don't think she does. She can definitely sense it a little, though."

"Can she travel freely through the dead world?"

"Definitely not."

"What makes her so different?" He squinted.

"Well," Kara interrupted, "I've known her to alter her physical appearance at will, so she gets very scary during a fight. Oh yeah, she can fight—I mean, really fight. She's a person of beyond normal human capability. Have you seen any tall and beautiful women capable of leaping tall buildings with a single bound? Or at least, across them?"

Cristobal fought it, but the emergence of a smirk ultimately defeated him. "You have such an interesting way of speaking, Doctor Mellencourt."

"And *you* haven't answered my question."

He shook his head. "Nobody matching that description, no. But someone or something has been running around. The black door that was opened up here earlier. I thought it was you." He looked at Mary.

"And I thought it was you," Mary agreed. "Shit. It wasn't Jen I saw up here at all. It was whatever I was looking at passing through the Unresting. I must've got focused on that after I'd eaten instead." She sniffed the air again before looking over to Cristobal. "And now that you mention it, it definitely wasn't you I was picking up either. But that does mean—"

"That there is another one with our talents, of our kind, wandering around here."

"A lovely little family reunion," Mary said with mock pleasantry. "Shame I don't actually have any family to speak of."

"So, this third ghost walker knows something we need to," Kara added. "And as we're pretty sure they were at the British Museum robbery a couple of nights ago, I reckon they know a lot."

"Wait—" Cristobal demanded, raising a hand. "Did you say that there was a robbery at the British Museum *two* nights ago? In London?"

"That's what I said, yes. Why?"

"Because there was a robbery over there just last night." He pointed into the distance at a massive building.

"The Louvre!" Kara and Mary cried in unison. But Kara pressed. "Do you know how they went about it?"

Cristobal grimaced. "I don't know much about it, but I was in Paris on other business when the area lost power. That happens all the time, so I ignored it at first, but some of the older ghosts in Paris told me of a living soul creating disturbance nearby. They spoke of deaths to souls before they reached the dead world."

"What do you think it was?" Kara probed.

"When I got here, I witnessed a flash which lit the city like daylight for a second. I know modern weaponry can do this, but the dead have no interest in such things. And a large weapon would have created a mass of restless souls. I have been in enough places at such times to know all of the signs."

"So, quite probably not an electromagnetic pulse," Kara said, "but part of the effect was almost identical."

"If he's telling the truth." Mary played with the knife in her hand and stared at him with a combination of suspicion and menace. "You seem to know an awful lot about all this business. How do we know this isn't some kind of trap?"

Cristobal shrugged. "What would be the point? If I meant you harm, I would have destroyed you when I had the chance." He took a step forward and stared down at Mary. "And how am I to know you are not trouble for me?"

A mischievous grin lifted Kara's face. "Now, that we can't promise to anyone. But you've got to understand, we don't know you. Our friend is missing, and you're the only link we've had to anything spooky since we got here. Mary insists that wasn't you on the roof last night, but that doesn't mean you're working alone."

"I never work alone," Cristobal said. But the two women remained tense, and a look in his eye told Kara that he may have realised such bravado to be inappropriate in the situation. He raised his hands and took a step back, then stared at Mary for a time.

"Lord Alphonse was proud of his family, wasn't he?"

Mary pulled a face at the question, but soon nodded. "Always."

He raised a smile. "Several generations later, and the Grenshall pride still burns in your eyes."

"As you are well aware, to be a custodian of the Unresting gates requires the most robust of wills. Oh, for f— I'm at it again, aren't I?"

Kara chuckled. "You are."

"What I meant to say was, am I correct in the assumption that —no, come on, less of the Tally speak. You knew him better than you like to let on, didn't you?

"He stopped me from believing myself to be insane. He gave to me freely, and as often as I needed. I owe him a debt for that. But I'm guessing as it is you I am speaking to and not him, my opportunity has passed."

Mary bowed her head. "I'm afraid so," she said solemnly. "I would not share his final fate with you, for fear you may find it too harrowing."

Kara eyed her friend for a moment. "You don't normally speak like that, Mary."

Mary looked up and blinked slowly several times. "My team back at the manor tell me this has actually happened a few times."

Cristobal dropped to one knee, his eyes focused on the ground. "Then I consider my debt to you now, Lady Rose Mary Grenshall, as his rightful heir."

The two looked at him for a moment, at first puzzled. But Kara spoke first. "Seems it's not just a big-ass house, a bank account, and a giant ghost rock you got in the will, then?"

Mary looked at her with disapproval, but then back to Cristobal. She snapped her fingers at him. "We haven't time for this. On your feet." It wasn't a request. "Have you any idea what they stole?"

"I'm afraid not. I tend to go to the Louvre once every two years. I keep a promise to one of King Louis XIV's house staff. But I pay less attention to the contents than perhaps I should."

"No highly dangerous mystical artefacts then?" Mary pressed.

Cristobal drummed his fingers against his staff in thought. "Hmm. That would explain plenty. But there was no way to tell. When the power went out, that was all I could sense."

Kara studied the area and drew patterns with her fingers as she tried to picture the scene. "Definitely more to it than E.M.P. Definitely something dangerous, of interest to people who should be of interest to us."

"And not in a good way." Mary added. "This knife here," she said, drawing attention to the item in question, "it was an old artefact, I'm told, whereby the original nasty bit, the sapphire, got transferred into a necklace. It was called, *The Grenshall Teardrop* or *Death's Teardrop* depending on who you spoke to, but whatever it was called, the thing was just bad news. So, we reckon there's more of these things around?"

His eyes widened. "*Death's Teardrop?* Lady Grenshall. Of course. I had heard of it from dangerous circles in London some time ago, but because I never saw it, I never paid it any real attention."

"Mistake," Mary grunted. "I've got a history with headline news not being what it says it is. Last year, I was dealing with 'terrorists', don't you know."

He held his hand to his chin for a moment. "I saw very little of that, other than a brief mention in *Le Monde* back at the time. I didn't think anything of it up until now."

"Yeah, that was me." Mary tried to sound as blasé as possible. To Kara, she still sounded like a celebrity trying to avoid publicity.

"The knife doesn't appear to be an object of evil," he stated. "And it does *feel* like a weapon."

Mary cast a serene look. "I call it, *Tally's Peace*. And what you feel is pretty deliberate. I used it as a bit of a focus to help lay the misguided ghost I was telling you about to rest. Tally was her name, in case you hadn't guessed."

"And you changed the very nature of the artefact with that act?"

"That's exactly what she did," Kara stated. "Nowadays, it'll calm a ghost down at fifty paces."

Cristobal looked at Mary with great respect. "I have met a number of my kind over time. But what you say you can do with the dead? Remarkable."

Mary looked puzzled. "You mean you can't? Well, what do you do with them?"

He sighed. "I cannot do much about the hundreds and thousands of souls I face. Wars and plagues have taken the people who have walked this ground. But not once have I seen any of them rest. They just linger, asking me for guidance. I do what I can to keep them away from trouble, but as they remain, whatever compels them to do so fades in whatever they call their minds. Some go mad, as you have seen, but the moment they become a danger to the public, I am left little choice but to destroy them. I hate it, but I cannot allow them to endanger the living. That is my task."

"That's . . . horrific. But if I couldn't make them rest, I'd—" Mary shuddered, her mouth wide open. "I'd have to do the same." Her voice trailed off, but Kara remembered her current priority— Mary's, too.

"Right," she said, trying to remain detached, despite her desire to dig deeper into how his history contrasted with Mary's. "We've concluded that these robbers are not leftovers from Tally's mess—"

Those last words made Mary twitch, and attempt to interrupt, but Kara continued. ". . . but all we know about them is that they were hitting museums, have a really nasty trick up their sleeves, and a ghost walker running about. Which means they're not bothered by locked doors either. So, what's the link? And what the hell have they done with Jen?"

Mary looked up in agreement. "What I'd like to know is where they are. We'll get the rest if we can find that out."

Kara returned her attention to Cristobal. "What did you do once the alarm went off?"

He grinned. "Actually, I went out to see what the trouble was."

"Did you see much? Where they went, maybe?"

"Yes," he said, his face grave, his eyes distant. "I saw their numbers. There's quite a few of them. Well-armed, well-equipped armour. But I didn't see who had the blackout attack, nor the 'ghost walker' as you put it. I would have got closer, but someone who can follow me and keep up even where I go made further investigation too great a risk."

"Well, consider us reinforcements," Mary declared.

"It's currently our best lead on Jen," Kara agreed. "Mary, can you get any of the ghost walker's trail from here?"

Mary's eyes washed over with darkness. "Actually, up here? Easy. Our walker hasn't exactly left rifts wide open like Violet, but the bouncing about still left a rough trail."

"This is true," Cristobal added. "Whoever it was didn't care about how they were moving. They just did it."

Kara raised an eyebrow. "Is it possible they don't *know* how their travel works?"

"What do you mean?" Mary turned to her. "I can see the gears in your huge brain grinding, but I'm not following."

Kara tapped at her clammy suit jacket. "Could they just be moving around with something like this? Maybe this is an artefact-based endeavour, too?"

"Like *The Guide?*"

"The Guide?" Cristobal queried.

"Yeah, he wore a cloak a bit like yours," Mary answered. She reached out and pinched a roll of his cloak. "Not quite like yours. Made of the deathcloth."

"Deathcloth?"

She explained the residue and Kara's new jacket. "But, of course, that was over a century ago."

Kara chuckled. "And you remember it like it was yesterday, you'll be telling me next?"

"Actually . . ."

"Never mind. Cloak. Just like his, yes. Now, that trail . . ."

"Actually, I have an idea which way they went." The two women looked expectantly at Cristobal after these words. "There were vehicles along this road. They went that way." He pointed at a main road on the opposite side of the roof to where they could see the museum.

"You might've told us this before," Mary complained.

"I had no reason to a moment ago," he retorted. "Also, I ran into a problem with it, in that—"

"In that the trail stops after a while for no reason?" Mary interrupted. "Just like when I was looking for Jen."

"Just that," he answered. "Though I have a theory. There is only one place in all of France I have trouble looking at properly, not far from here, in fact. There has been some kind of repulsive force over the place for many years, so it is very dangerous for me to get in and look. I could probably get *in,* but maybe I don't get out again, as I don't know what I'm going into, or how many."

Kara perked up as she remembered knowledge she had read up on some time ago. "A repulsion ward. A defensive blocking of, I'm gathering, people from just being able to walk in from the Shadow world or suchlike?"

"Exactly that," Cristobal confirmed with a nod. "Alarm bells. In my own backyard."

Mary tapped her feet. "Do you know where it is, then?"

"I do, yes. I wanted a better look, but I thought about it, and decided it was not a visit to make alone. And I have not had many upon whom I could call for help."

"Let's have that chat another time. It sounds like you have a lead to me. Will you take us there?"

"An offer of backup to this intriguing place? Gladly." Cristobal gave a sweeping bow. He then turned around and made a circular motion with his staff, until a tearing sound could be heard in the air. A shadowy gate opened behind him. He gestured the others forth.

"Well," Mary said, looking cautiously at the travel method. "Getting into strange portals creates its own troubles. But I've done much worse of late."

"I kind of wish we were better prepped for trouble," Kara said with a shrug. "But it's all we've got." She seized both of the others by the arm and stepped forth.

"Ah, sod it. In for a penny . . ."

CHAPER TEN

As the howling intensified, so did the pace of Jennifer's heartbeat. They grew closer, approaching from several directions. Though she could still not see the creatures, their shadows flitted between the giant trees. They loomed over her, stared down and judged her as they bent in the wind.

The forest continued to change. Twigs on the floor were now mostly covered in thorns. Vines danced underneath her feet and all around as she worked out her next move. Everything moved with one purpose—to hit Jennifer with everything it had. The harder she worked, the harder it pushed back. She couldn't miss it. The sky was barely visible under a dense canopy overhead. She listened, in an attempt to track the closest wolf. Each of their cries shattered her concentration and foiled her efforts.

She identified the closest shadow and broke for freedom in the opposite direction.

Vines sprang from the ground, coiled around her ankle, and yanked her, face-first, to the dirt. Jennifer yelped as she took the brunt of the landing on her right arm. The impact reverberated through her shoulder, wounded back at the chateau, and reopened her ripped fingertips.

That shouldn't have been anywhere near as painful, especially for someone who regularly recovered so quickly.

That injury. It felt better before. It hasn't gone away. Why?

The vine tightened. Her leg throbbed, and still it grew tighter. If this kept up, she'd be crushed. She morphed her fingers into their battle mode and felt a terrible tearing on her right hand, like someone was drawing knives down each finger, with every inch. She winced, but it was that or the leg.

Claws extended, she hacked and slashed at the vine until it flew apart, shredding holes in her trousers and scratching her leg. Though she heard the pacing paws, she spotted the leap half a second too late. A massive, furred beast bowled her backwards and pinned her arms to the ground.

Twice the size of the biggest dog she had ever seen, she struggled in vain to throw the bulky thing's weight off her. She jerked her head out of the way just in time each time it snapped its jaws, once, twice, thrice. The creature had her pinned, and she sensed the rest of the pack moving in for the kill.

Desperate, she stretched her wrist back as far as it would go, as hard as she could manage and slashed the back of the beast's restrictive leg. It yipped in pain and reared, which threw half its weight clear from her. Enough. She slashed again at its belly—to sting, not to kill—and knocked it further sideways. She then swung her leg back and straight into the large wolf's gut. She rolled with the momentum into a crouch and bashed the animal hard on the roof of its nose with her knuckles. She stood, and stomped it unconscious, then turned tail and broke into a run.

Still she had not healed. She'd never reach full speed in this condition. Running remained better than dealing with the other wolves. She pushed through the cramp building within oxygen-starved muscles, built up her speed. Every time her foot pounded the ground, she felt it jabbing at her nerves. The howls, the shuffling of paws, the threat of death breathing down her neck, continued to provide ample motivation to keep moving. She looked back, just to see how close they were.

Her legs went out from under her as a second wolf slammed into her from the front. One lapse of concentration put her down again. She recovered and rolled just in time as vicious jaws almost snapped her head off. She danced in a zig-zag pattern out of the way as its relentless attacks continued and kept her off balance. The warrior soon fell backwards, and split her legs far back to avoid its deadly bite.

The wolf closed in. Close enough for her to seize the initiative. Jennifer threw her legs around its neck and quickly crossed them, and arched her back and twisted, squeezing hard as she turned. She kept out of range of its teeth as she leaned on its immobile body and maintained her hold until the wolf stopped thrashing. She could see the rest of the pack closing in. She had to let go, to run again. The restrained wolf wasn't quite out of the fight yet.

"Sorry, mate."

She shifted her weight with all the force she could manage and felt the crunch as the wolf's constricted neck snapped under her hold. Then, she took a mental snapshot of her surroundings—approaching wolves, treacherous ground, trees.

Trees.

That was her best chance.

Ignore the pain.

Easier said than done as she bolted. The pack was seconds away from tearing her apart. She used her momentum and took a running leap at a tree in front of her, to the left, then sprang to the right. Another tree. Then forward and left, another, and again. Once more, each time gathering height, distance, maintaining momentum. Finally branches were in reach.

She grabbed as she bounded and swung, continuing her ascent. The howls grew quieter, more distant. All she could hear was the sound of her own breathing which grew heavy.

With her last jump, she misjudged the height and winded herself as she missed her connection and crashed, stomach first, into a particularly thick branch. Which proved fortunate. She slid. She wedged the tips of her claws into it and dangled for a moment. It wasn't comfortable, but allowed her to breathe a sigh of relief as the pack of wolves stalked below, frustrated. Retracting her right talon, she threw her loose arm upward and grasped the top of the branch. She shifted her weight for support before retracting the left claw. Her shoulder throbbed as she pulled herself up.

Jennifer pondered how long she would have to remain there before her pursuers grew bored and left. Yet, the entire pack stared up at her. She looked back and couldn't miss the unison in their movement. Though five sat poised under the tree, she sensed just one presence. And it burned with disappointment at her hiding away. She also wondered why her preternatural powers of recuperation had failed her again. She wasn't anywhere near the Unresting lands now, so that couldn't have been it.

Come on, Jen, think. You got this far, didn't you? Escaped the ghost walker before the wolves were even a problem. Just ran through that weird set of trees without a clue where you were going other than to follow that source of power.

Of course!

Despite the failure to heal, her special sight had to be worth a try. She closed her eyes and shut out all the sounds around her, the calls of the wolves a distant memory. After a moment, she could only hear the rush of breeze between the trees, the sounds of strangled warbling, from the local birds. No, that damaged her concentration again. She had to keep her thoughts on track.

Her mind was clear, the noise now gone. She had shut out the pain from her injuries, too, but now just wanted to see around her, as she knew she could.

Jennifer opened her eyes. Amidst the dullness of much of the forest, a trail appeared more colourful than most. Hardly a yellow brick road, however she plainly detected the leaves on the trees were a brighter green along one line than anywhere else within sight. The trunks along that same aspect were a richer brown than the grey-brown of the rest of the area. The thorny vines lined either side of the path, rather than on it. Once the wolves had gone, she could climb down, her path quite clear. Until that time, she remained stuck with only the company of her own mind.

~*~

The unpolluted air Jennifer breathed in that strange place reminded her of days both better and darker. Better, because they brought back her escape from everything other than sitting in the forest, enjoying the peace unmolested. Darker, because of how she had ended up in the forest in the first place. Driven there because the rest of her world had forced her away. Some things never changed.

Gary Stone, her father, had moved them out of their quiet home near Cardigan Bay into the bustle and pace of Cardiff city life. He just couldn't get himself straight, never managed to come to terms with the loss of his wife, her mother, Katherine. With nobody else around he really spoke to, it made growing up in the area awkward at best.

Jennifer did her best. She tucked him into bed on those days which proved too much for him. She kept him busy with days out walking the beach or just out at night when neither of them could sleep. She even sang a song or two for him when he really looked like he couldn't carry on that day. She never left him alone until she managed to force at least one smile out of him each day. She knew then that he would be okay.

Within days of her starting at the school, the new girl who had grown up out of town was the talk of her class for all the wrong reasons. She had the misfortune of telling her past to exactly the wrong person and before she knew it, rumour spread like wildfire that she had killed her mother. Other kids rounded on her, called her names like 'Killer Jenny, 'Jenny No-Mum' and even 'Death'. Before too long, things got rough physically. She came home on many a day with cuts and bruises, and her clothing in no better a state.

A week before the end of her first term, her worst antagonists followed her home. She didn't make it back to the house before they kicked, punched and spat at her until they'd put her on the floor, sobbing, shredded and too hurt to walk home.

It turned out to be one of the most important days of her life.

After they all ran away, laughing and chanting familiar taunts, she sat, unwilling to move for several minutes before she considered picking herself up and struggling home. The already patched-up uniform was practically ruined. She had no idea how she was going to explain it all to her father. That was the least of her worries. When she got up, she almost fell back down, unable to support her own weight. She attempted to hobble home. It would give her plenty of time to think about what she was going to say.

Jennifer collapsed four times just getting to the end of the long street, and four times she pulled herself back up. Although she didn't want to go home, few alternatives presented themselves. Tears streaming, she resolved to keep going. Maybe her father could even help—if he was in any fit state.

"Someone looks like they could use a hand."

A radiant woman in a bright green, flowery dress hovered over the fallen schoolgirl and offered her one. The glowing lady crouched and examined her thoroughly. "Hmm, that doesn't look good at all. Cuts and bruises in the main; however, your leg's more serious. Nasty sprain—and a fracture on your left index finger. Also nasty. Can't have you going home like that."

"Are you a doctor?"

"Better."

Jennifer found herself drawn to this mystery woman straightaway. She was tall, blonde and simply beautiful, perhaps in her thirties.

Jennifer shrugged, and instantly regretted the excruciating experience. Everything about this woman soothed and reassured—her touch, her smile, which exposed perfect teeth and a gentle manner. Already it felt as if several of those bruises had just gone away. To her great surprise, she felt as if she could walk quite comfortably with the woman's aid. Jennifer grabbed her hand again and pulled herself back to her feet, wincing as she dusted herself down. "My dad's going to kill me," she lamented, unable to look her healer in the eye.

"Shouldn't get into fights then, should you?"

The words were uttered in a jocular manner, which caught Jennifer's attention. She looked up, greeted with a wink. Jennifer let go of her hand. Immediately, she yowled as every punch, kick and claw she took burned with a vengeance. "Was hardly a fight. I just took a kicking."

"You didn't *have* to."

Jennifer stepped back and glared at the tall healer. "What? Were you watching or something?"

She received an inappropriate chuckle for her trouble. "Me? Goodness, no. I've only just arrived here."

"What makes you think I could've got out of that? There was a whole bunch of them just after me. I had no chance."

"Well, this wasn't your first time dealing with them, was it? This has been building for a while."

Jennifer folded her arms, ignoring how painful that was. "How did you know that?"

The healer winked, a glint in her eye. "I didn't say I was far away."

Jennifer staggered a step back, and her injured leg failed her. She instead fell. "You're not a doctor, you're not a teacher, and you're not a neighbour. So, who are you?"

"My name is Alice Winter." Alice shone brightly against a dull, grey street. "And I want to help you, but only if you wish me to."

Regardless of her level of trust, there was something about that woman which Jennifer found wholly compelling. When she once more offered a hand, Jennifer took it without hesitation or question. Immediately, the anaesthetic calm returned.

"Got a spare uniform?"

Alice chuckled. "That bothers you far more than your wounds, doesn't it? Your pride. That's good. You should be proud of yourself, always. And, no, I don't have a spare uniform. I have no children of my own, and I have long since been rid of mine. I'm sure your father will be all right once you explain things. He might even give you a hand. Have a word with the teaching staff at your school and see if they can do something about the dreadful bullying. But remember, whatever he says, you're still going to have to handle this yourself."

"That's what I'm afraid of."

"I thought it might be." Alice smiled. Her temperament and confidence kept Jennifer's spirits high. She felt a tingle over each of her wounds, a surge of energy like she never had before. She felt certain that she could have dealt with each and every one of her bullies, had they still been there. Alice had clearly noticed. The blonde goddess's eyes lit up as she processed this sensation. "You have nothing to fear. Not now, not ever. Not from the likes of *them*, at the very least."

Alice released her hand. The tingling continued. "I shall be seeing you again, young lady."

She didn't doubt it for a moment.

"Jennifer." Alice started to walk away, then turned back. "You'll be fine for now. I'm sure I'll see you again when you're not."

What that was supposed to mean, the schoolgirl did not know. Nonetheless, she felt much better than she did before they had spoken. And she continued to feel sprightly, could not work out why. She had just come through quite an ordeal, after all, and just moments ago, she could barely stand. Now she walked with a spring in her step, even. And the bruises—well, she couldn't see any. She rushed home, to check properly and clean up. The uniform was a different problem. But nothing felt insurmountable.

"Hi, Dad! I'm back!"

Her father was in the kitchen. Not alone.

"Jennifer, I'd like you to meet Ann."

"Um . . . hi." He hadn't even noticed the damaged blazer.

The woman, short and broad-shouldered with neat brown hair down to her shoulders, looked Jennifer up and down before she spoke, not a hint of warmth or welcome in her eyes. "You must be Jennifer. Heard a lot about you." Nor in her voice.

"Really?"

"Your father told me a lot about you."

That was something. Before allowing anything to ruin it, she made a run for her bedroom. That said, whoever this 'Ann' was, something about her did not sit right with her, a suspicious look given that went beyond a damaged school uniform.

Jennifer skipped school for a few days, in order to keep her miraculous recovery to herself. It remained a mystery she had to unravel. The healing process should have taken weeks. Yet, she could feel that buzz with every move, confidence, swagger, and unwavering strength. She changed into her gym kit and ran for hours, never seeming to tire. It was a beautiful thing.

On the third day of her involuntary holiday, she came home for lunch, and unexpectedly bumped into Ann in the kitchen. Her father hadn't returned from the factory yet, and wasn't due for a few more hours—she'd counted on that. The acting stepmother glared, and slapped a piece of paper hard on the kitchen surface. The inevitable truancy letter had arrived. "So," Ann asked, "where were you today?"

"I-I couldn't go into school." She gave a true and accurate account, painful, but surely worthwhile.

The powerfully built woman scowled at her and leaned forward. "Don't give me that, girl. There's not a scratch on you. Nothing wrong with you. Other than that you're a liar. You've been skipping school, mucking about and lying to your father. Don't think you'll get away with it with me."

Jennifer stood agape for a moment, realising no sympathy awaited her. She understood how her condition and story would not be consistent to an outside point of view and cursed an impossible job. "I'm not trying to get away with anything," she answered, as she backed away.

"Giving me lip as well, I see. Well, I don't like fibbers, and I don't like chancers." Ann stepped into the eleven-year-old's personal space and loomed over her. "Now, I'm going to ask you again. Where *were* you?"

~✳~

The forest had grown dark, caused by trees closing in and blocking out the sun as much as the time of day. The wolves had grown tired of waiting for a tricky meal, Jennifer's existence becoming a distant memory to them, allowing her to clamber down from her safe spot. She hoped they were long gone, with the ground so dry that any attempts at stealth were lost to snapping twigs. That quickly changed.

The eyes of the pack had gone. Despite knowing this, she couldn't shake the sensation that the forest continued to observe, to judge. Shadows bent unnaturally against the light in her peripheral vision, flitting away every time she attempted to catch them head-on. Leaves blew towards her, not with the wind. She moved across the branch to test it and the leaves followed, the foliage below her still, but pointed upward.

A deluge hammered down through the branches, soaking her thoroughly. Though it left her unprotected from the near flood, it had the saving grace of cleaning the blood from her. The wounds had slowed her, though had not stopped her. She had to decipher the mystery before it proved seriously harmful, or even fatal.

That energy source was her only lead to figuring out who or what she was. Maybe it was somewhere dry too, if she was lucky. She could still feel the rigours of the day. None of her attempts to heal herself had proven effective.

As she thought about it, she realised she hadn't eaten in some time and it was obvious after a strenuous day. She scanned either side of the path ahead of her and found very little, other than grass. Her hunger had distracted her from focusing on her journey. The path she followed led her to a cliff edge. A wooden branch the size of most trees grew outward from it, just a few feet down, which her magnificent sight still marked as the path. She shook her head, blew rain off her drenched face, and lowered herself down.

Through the mist accompanying the deluge, she couldn't see very far at all. She walked in a crouch, arms outstretched to keep her centre of gravity low. With the mist soaking it, the limb grew more slippery by the second.

As she traversed the branch, other trees appeared in the valley, past the cliff face, through the haze. From those, other branches, stable footing, availed itself before her eyes. She stopped, looked carefully for her designated path. Even as she pondered, the wood beneath her feet creaked, then snapped, plunging downward.

Without thinking, she leapt for the next nearest tree, and a higher branch. She latched her arms around it quickly. The soaked wood provided no secure grip. She slid until holding on by her fingertips. Ignoring the resultant pain, she dug in hard, willing the points to be razor-sharp as they could be.

Part of the bark disintegrated, throwing one hand of her grip free. With her other, she quickly snatched at the remainder. She retracted the claws and slapped her other arm on board, wobbling as her hands bore the entirety of her weight.

She heard a hissing below and looked down. Rapids. Water crashed against rock as her hold continued to fail. Below her instead was nothing but a sheer drop. She looked up; putting everything she had into remaining upright. Her soaked palms slipped. She was back to her fingertips. She'd plummet into the torrent in seconds unless she found a better way.

Jennifer searched frantically. Other branches lay ahead, part of one gigantic tree. She took a gamble and released a hand, the other pressed in so hard she could feel the tree taking root on her. Then with the flailing hand she threw herself into a more solid grip of the branch and pulled, hard.

Her biceps cramped as she hauled herself higher, remembering all the while what the alternative brought below was more than enough incentive to succeed. With some extra effort, she swung a leg up and coiled herself around. Gritting her teeth, she pulled herself to the top of the branch and took a breath, let the cramp ease . . .

The branch splintered. No time for anything other than to pull herself up to all fours and seek the nearest part of the tree. She stood with bent knees and spread her hands wide. As her footing fell through the sky, she got just enough purchase to leap, flailing for a hand hold. She caught it, but there was no stopping this time. She used her momentum and swung straight to the next part of the tree, lower. She adjusted her balance through the air and landed feet first, then bounced, not allowing her footing to slip.

Jennifer had the motion now. It reminded her of bounding across London rooftops, only much trickier. She changed direction on the next branch, moved across it, and built up a run. With little time to think, she followed the line and leapt to a lower rung of the skyscraper-sized tree. Three quick steps. A leap forward. The next branch.

Two more steps taken—a jump left. Then she twisted her body and shifted all of her weight right and sprang again. The flight lasted for a long time to her mind, with not enough speed. She was falling short of the next connection. She threw her arms out and reached. Fingers on the wood! Jennifer clutched the merciful salvation with all she had, cradling the tree, one hand over another.

The tenacious young woman clawed for breath, pondered her next move. She checked the integrity of the branch. It appeared in no danger of breakage as the others had. Good start. Though still in a perilous position, there wasn't a better time to figure out where she was going.

According to the illumination gained from her path, straight down.

"This is *no* time to be a leaf on the wind, Jen," she grumbled to herself as she sought a safer alternative. Something she had observed about this place—there never seemed to be a safer alternative when she looked for one. *Nothing new there, then.*

Other branches were a distance away now; no momentum, too high. The trunk was nowhere in sight through the mist. And if it was anywhere near as slippery as the rest of the tree, even if she reached it, the result would have been the same: downward. Perhaps it was time for a leap of faith, after all. She looked down, just on the off chance she could see ground, but it was impossible through the drizzly mist.

"All or nothing," she told herself as she released her grip. She threw herself down, unable to resist thinking that was the story of her life.

CHAPTER ELEVEN

Cristobal's portal had led them to a small hilltop. In the distance, castle ruins stood with a relative hive of activity. No sooner had they landed than their guide immediately shepherded them to a better vantage point around the other side of the hill. But a figure, masked and armed with an assault rifle, was close by.

"Down!" Kara whispered, half shoving the others as they each threw themselves prone on the ground. She fumbled around her jacket pocket for a small pair of binoculars. She opened them and scanned the area ahead of the armed individual.

Cristobal pointed to the unassuming half fortress which stood in front of him. "There."

Kara took a closer look. The initial scouting revealed a large shuttered ramp to the side, from which with careful examination, she could see tyre tracks on the road. She followed them across the road for as long was as visible from the angle, and relayed the information in whispers to her accomplices.

"So?" Mary asked.

"There's nothing else around here for some way," Kara replied. She was about to continue, but the presence of the nearby guard silenced her temporarily. He wandered past and pressed on with his patrol.

A look of intense concentration formed on Mary's face as Kara turned to her. Her Unresting eyes were at full width. But she suddenly recoiled, her face scrunched hard.

"You found Jen, then?" Kara concluded.

"Urrgh, no." Mary rubbed her eyes, almost clawing at them, until they reverted to blue. "There's something *really* weird here, though."

Kara checked again for nearby guards, and pulled a sour face at Mary. "That, coming from you, is something to worry about. Cristobal, what have you got?"

"Probably the same as the Lady," he said, looking pensive. "Very bright around here, usually suggests high levels of living energy. I normally see it with heavy concentrations of people, sometimes from one gifted differently to either of us." He lifted a finger in Mary's direction.

"Yep," Kara acknowledged, though remaining vigilant, "that's how Jen looks to Mary in the Unresting world. But you've said that definitely wasn't Jen. So, someone else?"

"Try some*thing*," Mary answered. "I know exactly how Jen looks, but whatever I picked up on was off the fricking scale as that goes. My sight's still not straight after that."

"Okay, individual or source, do you think?" Kara rolled on to her back, scanning past the others, checking there was nothing they'd missed behind them.

"Well, I didn't get a long look, but whatever it was didn't move. At all."

"What you see has been here a long time," Cristobal added. "When I check the area map, it is as Lady Mary says, a high concentration of power. It has never seemed a threat to my charges though."

"Hmm," Kara said, rolling back to her front. "Sounds crazy and highly dangerous, just like usual, but we're no closer to finding Jen.

Is there anything we can do other than poke at it? I'd like to go have a nose around."

Mary snorted. "Well, at least I know you haven't been replaced by some strange clone since we last saw each other."

"Check again when we're done here."

Kara raised the binoculars and swept further around the area. Closer to the damaged building, she discovered two more of the armed patrol, keeping close to the ramp. She checked the fallen turrets at the top of the ruin, but found nothing other than a small gathering of pigeons. "So that's three armed guards, half a dozen sky rodents. I reckon you two can handle that."

"Right up until we get shot," Mary grumbled.

"I'll keep checking."

Kara spent a moment attempting to ascertain patrol routes of the guards. When the first of them wandered close by, but failed to see them behind their ridge, she was comfortable they were on the edge of their range and lowered the binoculars. She turned back to the others. "Other than those three, nothing's moved the whole time we've been here. I'm actually wondering if anyone's home at all."

"I think we're just in the bit where nothing's happening. The gate's where it's at, right now." Mary's eyes betrayed evidence of a return to the shadow sight, as did Cristobal.

"I thought that was painful?" Kara asked, looking at their eyes. She forgave herself for feeling slightly left out. But then, she looked down at her binoculars with a perhaps unjustifiably smug grin.

"I've spent a long time practicing filtering my sight," Mary responded.

"And I longer," Cristobal added with a grin. His smile quickly vanished though. "This place. It has seen much death and trauma not long ago. I have been close to this area at times, but never had this sense."

"It's quiet because everyone we might have met is dead, you think?" Kara asked.

"It's definitely possible."

"Yeah." Mary bit her lip. "That makes it even more worrying that I can't tag Jen anywhere."

"We know this is a place of a certain power," Cristobal offered. "Our ability to see through the dead world is disrupted. So far, more has been seen with plain eyes than special ones." With these words, he blinked, the inky black in his eyes replaced with dark brown pupils, a sincere look.

"This is the back of the place," he continued. "The sides of this fortress are mostly blocked by hills. The front looked the most intact last time I was here."

"Definitely worth a look," Kara said, gaining Mary's agreement. "But so is the giant thing of power. Still, they're both over there."

"Kara—wait!" Mary protested, but Kara was already up into a speedy leopard crawl behind the nearest guard and moving far faster than she had any right to.

Once clear of the guard, she found cover behind a wrecked stone, then got up and prepared to advance. She took a wide arc around the castle in case of unexpected extras. The others were nowhere to be seen, but that could have meant one of a few things. She scanned the area with every sneaked step, crouched low as she moved forward.

It took Kara several minutes to draw close to the front of the chateau. Her meandering movement had taken her further out than she had thought. When she made it around the side of the hill, a huge steel door greeted her in the distance, over a heavy metal drawbridge, currently lowered, still unattended. Tyre marks lay at the side of the bridge nearest her. Everything pointed to a hasty exit, either previous, or imminent.

Curiosity overriding caution, she edged rapidly towards the drawbridge, seeing nothing but clear space ahead of her, which granted rapid access to a courtyard area. She could see on the ground something glistening in the light, and as she got closer, two or three such instances. She decided to press on to the drawbridge itself. She reached out and tapped lightly with her foot; a sound check. Comfortable, flat rubber soles weren't too noisy against it.

She stopped halfway across the bridge to check the portcullis ceiling. Nothing out of the ordinary there. She crept over to the courtyard entrance and leaned in, tentative, stealthy. At either edge of the space stood two massive and heavy steel doors, both closed. She spotted an observation box, a cross between Roman culture and medieval design mostly laid to ruin. The gleaming reflections became clear now; three swords scattered on the ground and in excellent condition.

Several tiny pieces of stone fell to the ground just in front of her. With it, footsteps echoed in slow rhythm inside. Kara listened carefully. The movement sounded as if directly above her. A moment later, she heard a clatter behind the door to her left. She instantly pulled back. As she moved away, she tripped, but caught her hand on a side rail to stay on her feet. She winced at the stubbed toe.

A small placard, a coat of arms, though not of mundane heraldry, lay in her path: a simple shield with an Omega symbol almost cradling a letter 'W' in a most stylised manner at its heart. Under the placard, an obelisk-like object imprinted firm on the wall, a brown wood texture protruding against a faded green painted background. She could also just about make out an icy blue patch with a few strange yellow coils on the bottom of the same wall before the rest was scratched out or rusted over.

"That looks familiar . . ." she mumbled, for a second forgetting where she was. "Can't quite place it though . . ." She attempted to pick it up on the move, but it was still attached to a piece of rock, too heavy to carry on the run. Turning on her heels, she moved away quickly and into a decent hiding spot. She shook her head, irritated at her failure to remember, her inability to locate the others.

Just like that, they appeared in front of her. Kara stifled a shriek.

"Much as I've seen you guys do that before," she said, calming herself, "it never gets any less disconcerting."

"I won't tell you how closely I was following you when you went on the little recce then," Mary smirked. Kara twitched. "So what's with the swords, you think? And what was so interesting on the floor?"

"Not sure on either," Kara answered. "I've seen that symbol before though. At Grenshall Manor, I think."

"You saw my coat of arms?"

"No—the other symbol. By what Jen uses as a gym these days. The one we couldn't identify."

"So that's weird." Mary replied, a perplexed look on her face. "Did you see anyone else?"

"And just as importantly," Cristobal added, "did anyone see you?"

"No on both counts," Kara replied, shaking her head, "but I did hear movement. Directly above me."

"That's not the same location as the power source," Mary said.

Kara mused for a moment. "Settled, then. I check around here while it's quiet. You have a look at that light. Cristobal, if you wouldn't mind, ease my path, please?"

"I'm not sure about us splitting up," Mary protested.

"You can find me easily enough. And if it all goes horribly wrong, don't hesitate to."

Mary and Cristobal turned to each other, staring as if in psychic conversation. Without saying anything to each other, the two soon nodded and turned back to Kara. "We have the chance to look around the place," Cristobal said to the both of them. "Let us take it. It may not come again. The more ground we cover, the better chance we have of finding your friend. And even if we don't—"

". . . we know we can at least have another look for her on the old GPS."

"GPS?" Kara challenged. "Jen hasn't even got a phone on her."

"*Ghost-world Positioning Search*," Mary said with a grin.

"So it's half a plan," Kara said, turning back to face the fallen fortress. "I take it you're some good in a fight, Cristobal?"

"I haven't lost yet," he said with a grin. "And what about you two?"

"Kara will tell you I'm not easy to kill," Mary answered.

"What about her?"

"Don't worry about me," Kara replied.

"Famous last bloody words," Mary spat.

"Try stopping me." Kara folded her arms.

Mary glowered at her for a moment, then gave a grunt. "I wouldn't dare. Shall we do this?"

They all nodded. Cristobal's eyes washed over with the inky shadow. Mary followed suit, and gestured that they should hold their position for now.

"Okay," Mary whispered, "Vision's much better filtered in here. I'm picking up three life signs—one above, two through that door. Do you agree, Cris?" He appeared to look around for a moment, and then eventually nodded. "*Si. Tres.*"

"All yours, Cristobal," Kara offered. "Sort 'em out, ghost through that big steel door, and, once you're done, let me in so we can work out the next bit. There's a good chap."

"I can work with that," Cristobal agreed.

"That's settled, then." Kara raised a hand. "On my mark: one, two—"

"Hold on!" Mary held a blocking hand to Kara. "Movement outside confirmed. Not normal. One of us outside." She pointed at herself and Cristobal. "Also, other nasties I can't put my finger on."

Kara clenched her teeth. "There's not one part of this I don't want to know about. Mary, you're up."

"And at 'em." With that, the three swept into action.

~ ✲ ~

Mary moved swiftly to the source of her sensory alert. It proved difficult to ignore other activity she picked up in the chateau, but her designated task required her full attention. Mostly in the Unresting world, she knew herself to be practically undetectable to the mundane eye. She remained all too wary of the fact that her targets were unlikely to be anywhere near mundane.

Already, she knew of the one who walked in her world as capably as she; and, on arrival at the scene, discovered a section of ruins with a number of guards evidently licking their wounds from a recent encounter. A small army hustled, preparing to leave in a precise military manner, but she couldn't help but notice that they looked as if their noses had been recently bloodied. It encouraged her. In her heart, she recognised Jennifer's work.

And then she saw the bullet holes around the crumbled stone. Lots of missed rounds. No blood. She followed the visual trail across the overgrown lawn neatly to the small gathering of non-uniformed types who stood in front of a tall stone archway that burned her death sight. With a minor effort of will, she dampened her senses to survey, and could see the gathered individuals left signatures of their own. Not anywhere near as luminescent as the strange gate, possessed of entirely different energies to those she knew, but each individual and singular.

One man—or more precisely, his armour—exuded a similar, but considerably weaker, brightness. The other two looked entirely unique. Not to each other, but to her death sight. It had none of the blinding brightness of Jennifer, the gate, or the figure the others seemed to be gathered around, but their scent proved repugnant in an entirely different way.

Much as she wanted to theorise about it with Kara, the other anomaly bothered her the most. The ghost walker wasn't gathered with them. And that meant that she could have been anywhere. The priority threat at all times as far as Mary was concerned, fortunately happened to be the easiest for her expert eye to detect.

Her deadly counterpart turned out to be close to the others after all. A frustrated figure stared down at the gate while standing on the damaged battlements. Bearing a blade which shone silver white against her death sight, strange in itself, the cloaked individual did not stand sentry. More, there appeared to be a specific fixation with the gate itself. Mary gave a victorious smile.

She tuned into the heated conversation taking place at the arch. The man in the attuned armour directed the nearby soldiers, and an off-road vehicle pulled up for him. He waved in a command for the driver to hold. "Cerise, I am disappointed. All of this and still she got away? She is tough, but not immortal. What happened?"

Cerise shuffled away from the armoured man. "She is also quick, my lord."

He put a hand around her throat but appeared to apply no pressure. "Is this going to be a problem for us?"

The blood-red woman sighed. "She is in a dangerous place. She is unfamiliar with it."

He released his hold. "You seem familiar with the perils she will face. Do you believe she will survive them?"

The blood-red woman sighed. "She survived all of this . . ." The woman swept her arm over the scene and Mary ducked behind a slab of stone even though she was fairly sure she couldn't be seen.

The armoured commander nodded. "Then ensure the job is done. Grey Lady, I'm sure you would be all too pleased to finally put her out of my misery?"

The cloaked figure traversed the Unresting world and covered the distance between her vantage point and the gathering around the gate instantaneously. Mary watched with some curiosity but plenty of caution. The Grey Lady was a completely different proposition to Cristobal. Even as she unveiled her hood, she moved with deadly poise.

But Mary also noticed the tiniest of movements from Cerise, an inconspicuous hand gesture directing the ghost walker to stop. She did just that.

"Apologies, my Lord Manta." Cerise bowed with total deference. "I would not like to see you short of your best bodyguard."

Manta scoffed. "Did you see what I can do now? I do not *need* a bodyguard. But you are correct; we may face trouble soon. It would be useful to have a reliable hand. Do you fancy you could deal with her?"

Cerise held up her hands and looked away from her lord. "I am the court physician, no hunter." She turned back to Manta, and to the one near the gate who hadn't spoken, a wiry, dark-skinned and tattooed man. He looked back with a grin.

"The oracle?" Manta queried.

Cerise nodded. "The *hunter*. He said so himself earlier. It is a good sign."

"I will hunt alone. But I do not hunt *her* alone. She has friends." His eyes widened and he looked around. Mary took that as her cue to leave, and backed away. The oracle locked on to her, but he stared, vacantly for a moment, and then nodded. "I will see them later."

He stepped through the gate, and Mary turned away from a blinding surge of light as the oracle vanished into the archway without trace. Also from behind her, she overheard one of the court yelling something about 'response times' as she traced a route to Kara and Cristobal. With the other traveller of the Unresting nearby, Mary only hoped that she managed to avoid pursuit, or they were each in for a great deal of trouble.

CHAPTER TWELVE

The cry of "ALARM!" roared against Kara's ears, and for a moment, she wondered what she had done wrong. But as she moved quietly through the courtyard, she could see that no hostile activity rushed her way. On the contrary, the alert took any potential threats away from her. It had to have been one of the others.

The door on her left hand side started to rumble open. She backed into the portcullis and crouched, hoping she hadn't been spotted. No sooner had the door finished opening, than Cristobal blinked into sight directly in front of her.

"Trouble!" He disappeared as quickly as he arrived.

"Great."

Automatic gunfire echoed around the courtyard from a lone guard. The next moment, Kara saw him crumple to the ground.

"Okay," Cristobal said, more quietly but still within Kara's hearing. "All clear." Kara got up and ran inside, straight for the open door. Two unconscious guards lay at their feet, one lying flat on his back and looking peaceful, the other slumped against a wall as if thrown there. A ghostly Mary gave her a cheesy thumbs-up while Cristobal looked more relieved than pleased.

Kara shrugged and relieved the floored guard of his assault rifle and his body armour, adjusting it over her existing coat of differing protection. She first checked the safety catch was on and then rapidly removed, examined, and reloaded the magazine.

Mary looked at her with some surprise. "You know how to use one of those?"

Kara nodded. "Thought I'd better learn after last year. Pulled a favour with a mate of mine in the Army. Total last resort, but all things considered, probably not the world's worst idea."

Cristobal made an uneasy face. "Much as I hate the things, the source Mary investigated blinds us elsewhere. We seem to be up against much more than we thought."

"We really are," Mary said, nodding. "But I know where Jen is."

"Great!" Kara answered. "Can you lead the way there?"

An antechamber to a labyrinthine series of corridors, each un-marked and poorly lit, beckoned them. The door had been operated by a large but assisted lever. The room lay in an archaic arrangement that could have led anywhere, a place which could have been the downfall of many an invader up to now.

Mary nodded. "Won't be easy. Someone mumbled something about response times while I was nosing around."

Kara strapped the rifle over her shoulder. "As in police response times?" Kara chomped her bottom lip. "Hmph. Explains why they're in such a hurry to clear out."

"Yes. Not helped by the fact that a bunch of them started shooting at Jen earlier."

Kara gave her a questioning look, but Mary's grin answered. "No chance. Looks like Jen was way too quick for them. But they've sent one of their big hitters in after her."

"Big hitters?"

"Some oracle-hunter-type guy. Don't know what he's got, but I think he saw me. He went straight after Jen, though."

Kara grimaced. "We're going to have to time this really well. They don't want to hang around for police, but even though they're on the run, we can't just go up and take them all on. Anywhere we can sneak past?"

"No. Their ghost walker's carrying something incredibly nasty, and won't worry about being spotted by anyone. If she doesn't have us, she'll shout loud to the others. Either way, it won't help."

"In that case, we're mostly stuck here until the authorities get here. It won't do us much good to get picked up either. So, we are going to have to time our run to that gate." She gave her trademark look of impending mischief. "The way I see it, we may as well use the time productively. Let's have a look around while we have the chance."

Cristobal smiled. "I like this plan."

Mary rolled her eyes. "I don't. Also, I'm not even sure how we're going to follow Jen and the other guy. If everyone went to Narnia just by running through that arch, everyone probably would have."

"You see many civilians wandering about since we got here?" Kara said. But after Mary's filthy look, she led the three of them quietly down the corridor. Through Cristobal and Mary's extrasensory guidance, they made it two floors down without challenge, or, unfortunately for them, anything of interest. But when they reached a door at the end, they heard voices. "Something's in here," Cristobal whispered. "Whatever I saw."

Mary squinted through inky black eyes. "Yep, picked up on that. But I can hear folk in there, and my French isn't up to being nosey." Kara gently pushed her out of the way and cupped an ear against the wall.

"All right," she heard a male voice utter. A loud clash, which sounded like wood on wood from the other side of the door, repelled her for a second, but she stubbornly returned. "I'm taking the Porsche. We agreed I won yesterday's bet, did we not?"

"Yeah, you did . . ." said the second voice, also male, chuckling. "But, I wanted to say double or quits on that."

"You can't!" his colleague replied. "I already won the drive. What else is there to bet on?"

A third guard spoke. "Whether or not the boss' new bitch turns up dead in a ditch. Reckon that's worth a bet, no?"

Kara's heart pounded, though she resisted the urge to kick in the door and spray the room with bullets. She had gained crucial information. She lifted a hand, raising three fingers.

"No more bets, man. I'm taking the Porsche."

Kara turned to Mary and mouthed, "Open the door." She released the safety catch on her rifle and crouched down, braced.

"Stay cool," Mary commanded, a hand on Kara's shoulder. "We've got this."

"Fine. Leave one of them upright."

Kara's team disappeared and after a few seconds, the door clicked open. Behind it, a panicked guard held a clipboard rather than the weapon he had put down. Three crates lay open around him. He dropped his clipboard and raised his hands high in the air. Kara took a split second to admire the way Mary and Cristobal worked together, considering the brief time they had known each other. And that they hadn't reappeared.

The two guards least central to the door were unconscious, leaving the easiest target for her directly at the other end of her rifle barrel. She readjusted her grip and pointed the business end at him, who was halfway across to aiding with the final crate.

"So, about your latest bet. Where may I find her?" She matched their native French. "Why would I know—"

"Guys!"

She watched the horror on his face as the other two appeared from nowhere on either side of him, remaining translucent. Mary held a flickering hand up. A whip-like crackle of the shadow lightning arced and surged around it.

"I'll ask again," Kara said with extreme force. "Where is my friend?"

Cristobal gave a nod, and he and Mary advanced on him two steps.

"I don't know!" he whimpered. Under that kind of stress, Kara suspected that much was true.

"Right. Where is everybody else going? I assume you were meant to join them?"

"Back-back to our the boss' base of oper—"

He never got to finish his sentence. Three shots rang out. Two hit him directly in the forehead, almost on top of each other. Kara wheeled on one of the floored guards who had her in his sights, but he fired first.

They went wild, struck as he was by a mighty burst of dark energy Mary unleashed, which jolted out of her fingertips like black lightning. It slammed into the target and he let out a howl of agony before thrashing around, darkened veins swelling. After a few seconds, he stopped moving altogether.

Mary gaped at the results of her attack and dropped to her knees. "Oh, shit!" she squealed. "I-I didn't mean to—"

Kara, shaking, looked first at her friend and then a few inches to her left. The smoking wall caught her eye. It dawned on her how close the hole was to her head.

"You just saved my life, Mary," she mumbled. Mary shuddered, staring at her still-crackling fingertips. "I didn't mean to—"

"Look." Kara pointed at the dead guard. "That was someone he worked with. Shot him twice in the head without blinking." She moved her pointing arm, and changed Mary's focus, to the recent wall damage. "That was where I was standing. Two inches that way. He wouldn't have missed. Him or me. If you hadn't have done that, I'd have been lying there, just as dead. And if it had been him taking a pop at you, I'd have done exactly the same."

Mary nodded.

Cristobal peered into the closest open box. "Over here."

Mary moved to where he had indicated and strained to lift a heavy stone slab. Kara looked over. She was well aware that with the aid of her connection with the Unresting world, Mary could have drawn upon considerable strength to ease her burden. But she also knew that raising the option at that time would have been foolish, given her last use of it.

Instead, Kara took hold of half the slab, made of stone but about the size of a large book, and had a look at it. Carved into the stone was the Omega-W symbol again, with an elaborate design about the wording. Blood had desiccated liberally across the stone, too dry to have been any residue from the recent shooting, and green vine-like weed as strong as wire wrapped around it. She turned to the third guard, the last still living, and then to Cristobal.

"It's this again," she said, gesturing at the recent acquisition. "It'd be really useful to know what it is. Can you wake him up so we can ask him?"

Cristobal moved to shake him, but then looked surprised, leaning over both sides of him. "I'm afraid not," he said with a bowed head. "I think I know where that third shot went." Kara shuddered, even more grateful for Mary's intervention. But her friend wasn't going to like her next request. Kara eased control of the slab into Cristobal's arms despite its awkward weight. "Hold this. Mary?"

Mary faced Kara.

"Dead as he is, he might know something useful." She checked her watch. "We've a minute to use wisely. Find out what you can."

Cristobal raised a blocking arm towards Mary, but she took a step forward, almost daring him to do something. "You can't just go wrestling souls like this. That makes you nothing more than a common necromancer."

Mary lifted her head with an air of cool superiority. "I am nothing like a common necromancer," she declared. For a moment though, Kara didn't see Mary there. She witnessed the actions of a far older presence. But the detail was unimportant. She shrugged and let Mary get on with it, though for a second, Mary herself looked puzzled. She soon regained her focus.

"Listen. The New Musketeers are one member down. We need to get her back. And right now, I need to see more D'Artagnan from you than Cardinal Richelieu. Okay?"

"What has Dumas got to do with this?"

Kara grinned. "Long story, love. I'll tell you if we get out of this in one piece. Trust her." He shook his head, overloaded with bafflement.

The room darkened and grew cold. Kara pulled her jacket tighter, but knew it would protect her from the imminent change of environment. Mary went straight over to the body of the shot guard Kara had been interrogating and spoke in a chilling voice which carried around the space. "SHOW YOURSELF."

It was in English. The command called upon the depths of an alien place. The language would not have mattered.

An apparition resembling the fallen guard manifested just over the body. It immediately cowered, reaching for a sidearm it did not have.

The next few seconds of the life he no longer had played out. He soon realised things were not going as according to plan and panicked. As soon as he saw Mary, he froze, petrified. She raised her hands calmly.

"Look, we don't mean you any more trouble. I—"

"Fuck you!" He lunged at Mary with pointed fingers, but she calmly sidestepped and, with a flick of her wrist, forced him back with a compelling gust of death wind.

The Guardian of the Gate pulled up her skirt and reached for the knife she had put away earlier. Kara spotted a cold aura around it, like frosty breath but from a blade. It was disconcerting but impressive at the same time. More remarkably, the ghost visibly relaxed when he saw the erstwhile weapon.

"Tell her what she wants to know and I'll help you quickly."

He nodded, understanding her every word.

"All I need to know is where our friend, Jennifer, ended up," Kara enquired.

The ghost shook for a second or two, then shrugged. "She couldn't find her. She was seriously annoyed. Said something like, 'the bitch just vanished'."

"Wait a minute," Mary asked. "Who couldn't find Jen?"

The ghost shivered. "She disappears and walks through walls, just like you two." He pointed to both Mary and Cristobal. "But she kills like nobody I've ever seen. Her sword is ghostly like her. Nothing can stop it."

Mary looked at Kara. "What did I say about that toy of hers? She's totally going to be a problem."

"Yeah." Kara gave a nod. "But one problem at a time. Where did they see her last?"

"Outside the castle. She leapt off the side. Don't know how she got away."

"And you've *no* idea where she is?"

"I couldn't see where she could have gone. I got told it must have been that gate, but it's just a stone arch."

"Mate, you're a ghost, and even when you weren't, you saw someone act like one. You need to broaden your horizons, son."

Mary shuddered as soon as she stopped speaking, a similar reaction to the necromancer jibe. Again, Kara let it go. "Right, next question. I want to know—"

The sounds of sirens echoed even at that level of the ruins. Kara roared in frustration. "We have to wrap this up."

"Done," Mary acknowledged. Though the cellar grew bitterly cold, none of the living shivered.

The ghosts of the other two guards manifested. The shooter shrieked in horror at the sight of Mary, who turned to him and raised the knife.

The noble looked a foot taller in the shadowy settings as it was. She stood by the first ghost and started to glow a silvery blue, she morphed into a staggering presence, a paragon of calm against the greatest fear. Kara noted that Cristobal looked on in even more fascination than herself.

The light grew blinding, Mary's voice soothed as running water in the distance, but echoed like an orchestra. "REST NOW. LEAVE THIS PLACE IN PEACE." The light flashed, but then dimmed slightly as Kara witnessed Mary's silhouette move to the next. "REST," Mary commanded again, and a second flash of light burst over the room.

"Incredible!" Cristobal squealed as if punched in the stomach. His mouth hung wide open.

"I know, right?" Kara said, grinning like a proud mother. "She's getting so much better at this!"

"I've never *seen* this before," he said, somewhere in the dazzling shower of illumination. "I have seen many things. But nothing like this."

"Sssh!" Mary hissed. "One left."

Kara realised the remaining guard was the one Mary killed. She gently put the stone on the floor and stood again, then placed the back of her hand on Cristobal's sternum, giving a gentle nudge. He took the hint and gave Mary as much space as he could.

The light reverted to a pale mist, mostly emanating from *Tally's Peace*. Mary's own halo was dimmed as she closed in on the shuddering apparition. The room fell silent. Kara looked on, chewing her bottom lip as they watched, waiting to see what Mary had in mind. She couldn't see her friend's face from where she stood, but Mary's hand trembled as she held up the knife—then dropped it as she shakily lifted her hand.

Kara moved quickly to retrieve it. No sooner than she had placed a hand on it, she felt an icy chill, even wearing the protection she was. But it wasn't the clammy chill of the dead she had expected. This was a cool, soothing ripple that washed over her. She placed the knife back in the hands of its owner, steadying the trembling arm with her own free hand.

"You can do it, Mary," she said in a low voice, staring into Mary's glossy onyx eyes. "You've dealt with much tougher."

Mary blinked twice and her shuddering ceased, her grip tightening on the blade. "These guys have seen all sorts, Kara," she said, distant. "Nothing like the others I've seen before. Murderers for hire. All that's kept these two going has been the money."

Kara pondered the words briefly, but then acknowledged with a nod. "Mercenaries. Makes some sense. Though that one shot the other two while I was talking, to shut them up. That isn't the act of someone who has the chance to take the money and run."

"What if they hadn't been paid yet, Doctor?" Cristobal mentioned.

"Still no reason at least one of them couldn't go back for his money. They might not all have made it, but we know they weren't acting out of the kindness of their hearts. Honesty goes out of the window on such things."

"Better ask him then, hadn't we?" Mary brought her blade hand to bear and thrust it directly into the incorporeal chest of the remaining ghost. "Cover your eyes a second." Kara obeyed immediately and could see even through that a blinding flash. She heard Mary utter the words, "I'm sorry," before the light returned to normal. Kara opened her eyes in time to see Mary drop the knife and herself collapse to the floor. She caught her just in time.

"What did you just do?" Cristobal asked, but Kara shook her head.

"Not now."

She had forgotten. Every time she had seen Mary perform this powerful act, it had come at the price of immense physical exertion. Mary had just done it three times in a row. She was bound to be exhausted. That was not to mention the fact that she had likely just seen fragmented memories of three murderous individuals, too. She held her friend tight, but was soon pushed away, the healer looking somewhat enraged.

"*What the hell*?" Mary stared quizzically at the pale corpse.

"What?" Kara asked, still holding a hand out. "What did you see?"

"Do you know why he just killed them?" Mary snarled. "This one wasn't working for money. He was obsessed. By some woman."

"Romance?" Kara matched Mary's expression. "Him?"

"Not exactly. Bright red hair. Would have literally done anything for her. It was stuck firmly in his head that if anything went wrong, he was to kill the others, deal with the threat, then kill himself. No witnesses. Just . . . burnt onto his brain." She slumped backward, now heavier in Kara's supporting arms.

"Take some time, get your strength back," Kara said calmly. "We're going to need you up to strength as soon as we can."

To her great surprise, Mary reached for her knife and stood upright like a shot. "Then let's get on with it." She returned the weapon to its concealed sheath.

"You need to rest. That looked more exhausting than normal."

"It was. But it gets easier to handle with a little practice."

Cristobal grabbed Mary by the shoulders and spun her around. "How?" he asked, eyes wide as saucers. "How did you *do* that?"

Mary shrugged. "It's just a thing. I've kind of been able to do it since I got any of these powers. I just kind of *do*."

Kara cleared her throat and straightened her posture. "I believe a state of meditative calm and compassionate thoughts were one of the things we picked up on in my interview. If you exude calm, certainly to that level, then the ghosts essentially go with it. This then gets somewhat amplified and the result induces an effect of 'final rest' for the subject. Naturally, the only conclusion that we have drawn is that the non-living entities leave through this, to our knowledge never to return."

Cristobal scratched his chin. "Is it the knife?"

"No," Mary replied without hesitation. "I could do it before I got hold of *Tally's Peace*. It just makes things a heck of a lot easier. Less concentration required. Which is probably why I don't tire so easily, or at least for so long, afterwards."

"She's a walking thesis, this one," Kara said, rubbing the top of Mary's head. "It was due to her actions that as far as we can tell, the properties of the artefact altered drastically. The alteration, we suspect, took place when she dealt with a particularly difficult and accomplished spectre, the previous official incumbent of Grenshall Manor. Hence the virtual impossibility of using it as a conventional weapon."

Cristobal sneered. "I can tell you come from academic roots. You make everything sound so . . . interesting."

"It is." Kara reacquired the engraved stone. "But time to leave. Heavy gunfire leads to police sirens."

~ ✷ ~

The three friends headed to the side of the castle ruins they had not previously seen. They remained out of sight of the emergency services by retaining a ghostly presence, even Kara, whose hand Mary clung to grimly. In any case, the authorities remained too focused on blood and bullet holes to have their eyes everywhere.

The trio worked out a route, with the help of Mary's earlier reconnaissance, to the anomalous archway of bent branches standing in the centre of plain grassland.

Kara whispered as she examined the construction in a visual and tactile fashion. "Amazing. To me, it looks like nothing more than a bunch of twigs tied together. I suppose another half dozen and the place would be camped out by hippies once a year, but it just seems like a thing around the back of this castle. And where, oh, where is the souvenir shop? I'm amazed this place isn't listed and attracting tourists."

She walked straight through the archway, and emerged from the other side. Kara was somewhat disappointed when she turned to face the others.

"I know of at least three tourists at the moment," Cristobal commented.

"And even though I can't find any bookmarks, I've got a paperweight right here." Mary tapped her foot on the neatly carved rock they had retrieved earlier, resting by her foot. When she did so, she gave a squeak and jumped backwards.

"Something up?" Kara asked. "That rock actually do something?"

"Yes!" Mary nodded. "Yeah. It changed colour and the grass moved around it—kind of . . . weird."

"Oh, is that all? I thought you were going to tell me that it sprang legs and started to run."

Carefully, Kara gave the stone wedge a prod with her foot. Sure enough, the rock altered from a dull grey to a lighter brown in front of her eyes. At the same time, small vines shot from it and appeared to fumble around the grass, trying to latch on to something. It made for freakish viewing. She pulled a face and took a step back. "Right," she said, sounding purposeful. "I suppose if I were to ask you to use your sight around here, it'd blind you?"

"I figured it out," Mary answered.

"That's not good. I need to know how this works, and I was hoping we could figure it out the safe way." She pointed to the stone. "Still, that thing's got some power, so . . ." Her gaze returned to the gate. "Somehow, either the twain shall meet and do something, or we're horribly crossing the streams, so to speak. But if these little vines are reaching out and trying to grab something *and* covered in blood—urgh!"

With a concerted effort, Mary lifted the stone and carried it close to the gate. "If it wanted to eat us, it would've done so by now, I'm sure."

Kara watched from a distance, trying to work out the link. Mary stepped into the gap underneath the branches. The grassland behind the arch appeared to shimmer very briefly, as if a television set not quite functioning correctly. Mary turned around and placed it in the centre of the gate, no doubt prepared to move faster than most if things started to go wrong, as inevitably they would.

Kara walked to the archway. "Leave it leaning at the foot of the arch and give it another prod," she suggested. Mary nodded and did exactly that. There was a ripple in the air, once more, the light within the gate disrupted and the miniature vines reached out. They touched the side of the gate and the twisted branches wriggled an inch or two, but that was it. Kara placed her hand within the centre, but nothing else happened. "Hmm . . ."

"Well, it didn't blow us all up as you feared. That's a good start."

At this, Cristobal ran towards them, looking concerned. He pointed behind him. "There are two vehicles heading in to the castle."

Kara sighed. "Well, yeah. The police would hardly be able to miss all this. If we're doing something, we need to do it now."

Cristobal nodded. "Let me keep them busy for a moment," he said. Before either of the others could respond, he disappeared from sight.

Mary twitched. "Why couldn't it just be a door we could open with a key or a code or something?"

Kara looked at the stone and then gave a victorious squeal. "Mary, you're an utter genius!" She grabbed her friend and gave her a peck on the cheek. "That's *exactly* what it is. A keystone." She pointed at the gap, not much bigger than the engraved artefact, at the top of the configuration of branches. "We need to get *this*," she started to lift the stone as she spoke before looking directly up at the top of the archway, "up *there*."

"Yeah, but how? You know how heavy it is." But Kara was already lifting, keeping the stone close to the branches. The vines had not vanished. Rather, they continued to cling as it moved upwards, almost scuttling as she moved it.

"Maybe with two of us on it?" Mary nodded, getting both hands under the rock. Between the object and their combined strength, they were able to move the stone up to the top of the arch at a tiptoed stretch. Their arms wavered and wobbled, strength giving out just as they got it underneath the desired position.

"Can't . . . hold it . . ." Kara grunted. The two struggled to keep it steady. But just as they were about to give up, the vines tightened and dragged the stone the few inches it had to get into place.

As the keystone settled, the rest of the woven branches danced and unravelled, locking around the new addition. Considerably larger vines grew from the centrepiece and ensnared themselves around the rest of the construction. Finally, although the scenery in the gap under the branches did not change, that clear water shimmer that Kara glimpsed before became far more prominent.

She flopped her arms, with Mary doing likewise, both exhausted from their exertions. "Well, this had better be worth it," she said. She took one more look around and then reached inside. There was no feeling at all to differentiate waving a hand through air. But it disappeared from her sight. "Okay. That's worth it. Coming?"

Mary grimaced. "Because travelling through bizarre supernatural gates has done me so much good in the past." She shrugged. "But you're going in anyway, and that's still our best chance at finding Jen. Sod it. What's the worst that could happen?"

"Horrible and painful death?"

"Or several years in a foreign prison. That'd be boring, wouldn't it?"

"Touché."

Mary bent her arm and raised it in offer. "Shall we?

Kara accepted, latching her hand through the loop. "Let's."

Whistling their theme song, the chorus to *Always Look On The Bright Side of Life,* they stepped into their newest challenge.

Kara felt a strange mist-laden sensation, much like walking through one of London's famous pea-soup fogs at night. But she also felt a minor jolt in her hand. The one in which she held Mary's arm.

Mary no longer stood by her side. Or anywhere around her.

"Oh, crap."

CHAPTER THIRTEEN

The temperature dropped as rapidly as Jennifer did, the soggy mist transitioning into freezing fog as she lost her breath through the air. After a long drop, she finally spotted a blanket of cloud—no, the ground! About to bend her knees, but before having the chance, she plopped straight through a cold, white mound—probably snow—before it all went very dark.

Darkness, the least of her worries. Air, a greater priority. It *was* snow. She could feel its full force dragging her under. She had to escape, quickly, before she suffocated. Straight back up, her only hope.

There was nothing wrong with relying on old tricks. Especially when the old tricks were reliable.

She shook out her hands as the mounds on either side began to crumble and fall in. A familiar tickle ran up her wrists and shot all the way to her extending fingertips. With additional effort, she curved the tips into rake-like appendages and swallowed a mouthful of snow as she looked up to work out her escape. She turned her head aside and spat out the choking ice water, then threw her left arm upward and thrust into the facing side.

Though the sky was falling on her, she held her grip firm and pushed up with both legs before extending her right arm and penetrating the white wall in front of her. She shifted her body weight to the left and lifted and jabbed her left arm with legs bent, putting everything on her considerable upper body strength.

Then she went right and up. Left and up. Into a rhythm. Soon she scuttled upward with assurance and pace, swatting the falling tumult away with her head as she fought against the slide . . .

. . . and out. Her body straight as a plank, she took care to drag herself out and then shifted her mass on to palms and shins. She looked ahead. Her senses provided a light show in front of her, which could equally have been snow blindness hampering her efforts she supposed, but the way remained clear. The stability of the ground was another matter entirely. Still, the options were very limited. It was ahead, or under. Jennifer began to detect a theme within the treacherous lands she had blundered into.

But no matter what my odds here, half a chance is better than being mown down in a hail of bullets.

Forward, then. And fast. She launched herself ahead, like a monstrous toad pounding across lily pads. After a few bounds, she hit her stride and practically flew through the air, her pace relentless. Soon the soft snow hardened to drifts in an icy, mighty sea. But her path was clearly defined, both in stable ground and mystical tracking.

Jennifer was pretty certain she had never moved that fast on her own power in her life. And the freezing air was merely fresh, bracing to her. It was still pure and clear, just like the forest, purer than anything she had inhaled in the past. She felt *alive*. Inexplicably and inexorably alive. It was a beautiful feeling. And she never wanted to stop.

Eventually, she reached stable ground and slowed to catch her breath. She gave a shout of exhilaration and punched the air, but then took time to stop and take stock. Not in the best condition in the first place, the stolen flak jacket was ruined, and her trousers weren't doing a whole lot better. She also knew that none of that had put her out of the fight.

~*~

Trudging through torrential conditions, tattered and battered was not a new experience, little different to back when she wore the school uniform. Back then, however, her headmaster insisted that the uniform should always be worn neatly, in order to breed the strong sense of community the school prided itself in. Every day led to either a beating, being spat on, or slapped. Getting home was no help, either. All that meant was the new self-proclaimed matriarch of the house, her father's partner, questioned why she had destroyed yet another uniform whilst pissing about or why she'd been giving her teaching staff lip. It just led to more of the same.

Night after night, she would lock herself in her bedroom, or be locked in there, to avoid further hassle. And even that didn't always work. Many a night met with the pair wailing and battering on her door as the couple stopped enjoying their drugs.

One particular day, she unfurled herself from being placed head-first into a dustbin by Charlotte Williams and her gang. Reeking of rotten food and covered in other rubbish, she went home following a shower and spare gym kit she had been loaned by the school after turning up at the staff changing room in that state. She protested for quite some time about how she was not involved in a prank, or for that matter, larking around. After a lecture about standing up for herself better, she went away in a strange combination of the spare kit and her school shoes. Once she had cleaned herself up, she noticed that the bully had inflicted further cuts and bruises, but nobody cared who wasn't Jennifer Stone. In fact, even Jennifer Stone wasn't certain she cared anymore.

On the way home, she called into an electrical store, to kill some more time. After a good twenty minutes of browsing, not once asked by anyone if they could assist, she made a realisation: everyone had her down as a loser or a good-for-nothing anyway. It wouldn't exactly discredit her if she got something for herself out of that reputation, for once.

She headed to the personal audio section and, having checked nobody was looking, removed a small personal stereo system from its home on the shelf and walked out with it. Following suit with some batteries from a nearby corner shop, she took a very scenic route home, switching on the radio.

Jennifer ate before she got home, fish and chips. She remembered clearly. Probably more so for her stomach trying to think for her at this time. But the food and the comfort items did the trick of making her feel better. She returned to the exact reception expected—her father and Ann both staring daggers on the couch, and shouting over each other to ask where she'd been. She'd told the truth, at least about ending up in the bin as she threw her clothes straight into the washing machine. They both pulled her away from the machine and just got in her face.

". . . nobody has money for new uniforms . . . you need to stop getting into fights . . . don't know what we're going to say to your teacher . . ."

Then the perennial killer.

Let me deal with her.

Her father protested on her behalf a number of times, but his health had grown steadily worse with every passing year. It exhausted him even to put up a verbal fight most days, leaving him little more than a minor hindrance to his fit and healthy, squat and strong wife. And not enough of one to aid his daughter.

Ann grabbed her by an already bruised arm and attempted to hold her secure, but she wriggled free and battled her way out of the kitchen.

Her stepmother tripped her on her way past, and she crashed into a chair, breaking it. Ann then gave a shriek as she recovered. "I'm sorry!" she said as she took hold of Jennifer and ushered her out to the staircase. "I didn't mean to—let me check if she's okay."

What she had meant was, *let me check I've finished the job.* Dazed as she was, escape was always going to be difficult for the teenager. But her guardian wasn't done with her, and all her father would have heard from downstairs was a fight. Things were a little one-sided, but she kicked and screamed in that room, both of them did. And it was always her word against Ann's as to what was happening. She never came out on top of that exchange, as Ann harried and chipped away at Mr. Stone's energy with every snipe. He often ended up too tired even to finish listening.

The following days at school were no better. It was time to work out a way out of this. Her only thought was to finish her exams and then move on. Very far on. She considered running away from home every morning she left, but there was nowhere to go. The mysterious Alice hadn't turned up again. She should have known better than to have placed her hopes in anyone other than herself.

But the fact was, that next day, she had got up and walked out feeling just fine. Barely a scratch on her. She never knew how that kept happening. All she knew was that every time she wanted to protest about her life at home, she could never prove it. Every morning, she was simply better. It was the same with her bullies. They just came at her again and again, assuming they hadn't done her any proper harm.

Jennifer may have been too young to have remembered the first time around, but she was born fighting. That run of painful days reminded her to fight back. She found herself cornered after school yet again, but this time, weeks, months of frustration took over her. She charged at

Charlotte with a savage cry and grabbed her by the hair as she bundled her backward. Having fallen well, she smashed her forehead directly into her tormentor's nose, hearing a squishy crunch as she landed the blow.

The ringleader yelped in pain, but the red mist had descended. She smashed her elbow into the girl's cheek as payback for the bin drop. Then another for being spat on. And another proper smack for reminding her that her bitch stepmother was just going to back them up later on. But she wanted to finish this. Hurt her so bad that she'd never do it again.

As she pulled her fist back, her arms were grabbed from behind by two of the others. She flailed as if she'd been possessed, but couldn't break their grip and was held in place. Charlotte was a bloody mess on the ground and bawled so loudly, it could have been heard from the other side of Cardiff.

Despite the obvious pain she must have been in, she stood up and stomped towards Jennifer who struggled to escape her heavy restraint, though her face, which had been pounded like so much raw meat, nagged her with pain. Her rage dropped into shakes as she looked on, horrified at what she'd just done, but her victim showed no such delay.

Charlotte pulled back her fist, but trembled as she held it back. Eventually, she lowered her fist and spat a gout of blood into Jennifer's face before returning to hold her own. "Fuck her up," she mumbled, glaring at her held enemy. "I don't want that bitch back at my school." So much for the theory of taking the biggest one down.

That was the worst beating she had ever endured up to that point. They punched and kicked and stamped and bit until on this occasion, she failed to remain conscious, let alone standing. She had woken up in all kinds of pain perhaps ten minutes later, still aching like hell, but after a moment or so, able to get to her feet. She hobbled home, feeling every step.

By the time she reached home, physically, there was no evidence of her ordeal. Again. Psychologically, it took everything she had not to run away when she turned the key. But when she stepped over the threshold that time, it felt different. There was nothing to fear at home anymore. None of them could do what she did. That made them weaker. That made them nothing to be hiding away in her bedroom from.

"Where the bloody hell have you been?" her so-called stepmother asked. "Out causing trouble again? I ought to turn you in."

"I ought to turn *you* in," Jennifer snarled. "But as you've been getting away with, I can't prove anything, so you're fine there. But you can't hurt me either. So, you should stop trying, for your sake."

Ann stood statue-like for a moment, stuck for words or reaction. Then her lower lip quivered. "Are you threatening me, girl?"

Jennifer shot her a glance of disdain. Then, she stood and went to her room. Ann went to follow, but Jennifer spun around on her heels, stopping the troublemaking woman dead in her tracks. "I wouldn't bother. I'm actually up for a fight tonight. And it doesn't matter what you do to me, I always get better. Makes me a stupid person to pick on, right?"

Her father emerged from the kitchen, bleary-eyed and off-balance. Jennifer bounced to the lowest step on the staircase, her anger high and her pain low. "And you can leave me alone tonight, too. Unless you're bringing me food."

He wavered but did not argue. And that was her whole problem with him. It hurt so much to watch him struggle in his ever-deteriorating state. He wasn't much use, but he was still her dad. He still *tried*. It wasn't a perfect solution, but as soon as she got her exam results, it was time to go. For everybody's sake.

The next day, she went to school wearing a perfectly patched school uniform and with a smile on her face. Charlotte and her gang had made one big mistake—they told her that they didn't want her walking in the next day. So, that was exactly the plan. Wander in, head up high, hopefully not get any more bother from that lot again. Because they would not be impressed by her turning up fit as a fiddle.

Unfortunately, that ended up being the greatest problem. She made her way to her classroom, five minutes later than she probably should have, only to be greeted by a heavily bandaged Charlotte pointing her out to an older woman bearing some resemblance to the bully. She assumed it to be her mother. Next to them stood her form tutor and the headmaster. The rest of the class were all pressed against the windows, waiting for the inevitable activity.

Jennifer considered running, for all of a second. But then she remembered there was no reason to. She just had to explain the story that Williams and her mob had been picking on her since she turned up at the school. That was just a little bit of self-defence she'd engaged in there.

"... and I'm afraid, Jennifer Stone, that this not only falls far short of the behaviour we expect of our pupils," Mr Walters, the headmaster said, barely looking at her. "But this level of mindless violence, whether in school hours or not, is completely unacceptable for most civil human beings, never mind those wearing the uniform of St David's. You leave me no choice but to expel you with immediate effect, as well as to inform the police. What you have perpetrated is nothing short of an assault."

"What do you mean, you're expelling me?" she cried. She did herself no favours by slamming her fists on the desk in front of her. "You can't do that! She started it!"

And then she remembered the flaw in her statement, at least from the point of view of an outsider. Like some kind of walking miracle, no evidence of the cracked ribs or other fractured bones lingered, no sign of a single bruise, not a drop of blood anywhere other than on the soiled clothes remained.

Just like at home, it had rendered her an easy, repeat target. No evidence showed that the person who *should* have been remanded had done a thing to trouble her. And that same person had turned up, having been smacked almost senseless in her fit of fury, pleading victim. She didn't have a leg to stand on.

The frustration was so great that she'd nearly gone for Mr Walters out of spite. But the situation was already lost. She stood up and opened the door out of his office, but found herself obstructed by two police constables, looking down at her.

"Is this her?" they asked the head. She turned to him with a look of horror.

His solemn nod just made matters worse. "I'm sorry, Jennifer, but Mrs Williams wishes to press charges, and I couldn't risk you causing any further trouble as you left."

"What? I—"

He stood up and came to the door as they slapped a set of handcuffs on her. "Please escort her off the premises." She turned back to the police, incredulous as they nodded.

The walk of shame through the corridor and out of the school was more brutal than any fist to the face. Though she had made no real friends there, there was quiet applause and nodding from some of the pupils who ignored the efforts of teachers to usher them back into their classrooms. Her archenemy and her accomplices had also turned up to gloat, the smile on Charlotte's face clear even through the mashed face.

The image remained with her as she was bundled into the back of the police car, remained with her every day following. It had been by some way the worst day of her life.

And that was not even the worst of it.

~*~

Her breath came back to her quickly, cuts and bruises remained, though nothing to slow her down. However, it seemed there was only snow for as far as the eye could see, leaving her no closer to true safety.

But then she remembered, she didn't have to be looking at this through human eyes. In fact, it was much better that she didn't. This whole damn thing started with a look for that mysterious energy source. It would be truly beneficial to locate that before proceeding.

The other thing she had only just noticed, now that she'd stopped for a while, was her own shivering. Unsurprising really, given her rough guess on the temperature put it much colder than anything London could manage on its worst year. And she was hardly attired for such an expedition.

She bowed her head in disappointment. Nobody would see her but that wasn't the point. Treacherous terrain couldn't kill her, yet a lack of a proper coat just might.

She supposed that she could have been in there for a whole lot longer than she originally thought. Also, she hadn't dealt with her growing hunger. There just hadn't been time, given everything going on. The chill increased. A blizzard also beset her, reducing her vision ahead of her, on top of everything else. This was no way to go, and nobody would find her if she did. Not her first choice of routes at all.

The source showed no signs of getting closer. It all seemed so pointless. She dropped to her knees and beat at the snow with her fists.

She tried to remember she had not voluntarily embarked on this expedition, other than that the alternative had been to face a firing squad. Given her current circumstances, the next stage was to make this trip worthwhile. To survive.

She could sense her thoughts rambling. The day had definitely caught up with her, but it hadn't finished with her either. Through bleary eyes, she gathered what little concentration remained and willed a chromatic enhancement upon her sight. Through such eyes, a glowing path still burned in the snow like scorching fire, yet still appeared to have no end in sight. Her talent showed her that the snow would not poison her if she required water, but, then, neither would it alleviate her hunger.

In addition, she had gone numb as soon as she stood still. Another problem with the biting climate. She moved but couldn't feel the steps she had taken.

She scrunched her face and followed the glow through her squint. Onward—her only real chance. She waddled and shook herself in a determined effort to keep the circulation flowing. The hope of *something* at the end of this, some treasure at the end of the rainbow, staved any thoughts of stopping. She kept running. Every splash through the snow gave her rhythm. Every beat channelled her mind, cleared it of distractions. Uphill, unstable ground, it didn't matter anymore. Soon, all she could hear was the regular pad, pad, padding of her own feet against the soft ground, her mind lost within a steady trance of the quiet noise on the steady trail.

The snow exploded from below. The blast sent Jennifer high into the air before she returned to earth, face-first and then rolled left, sky and snow alternating enough times for her to forget which was which. She stopped, sprawled on her back with the air around her muffled, as her ears were buried in the endless white stuff. She tried to sit up and winced from the strain on her neck. But that was soon forgotten when she looked left, found the source of the disruption.

A polar bear crashed towards her, probably twice the size of any she had seen on television or in books. Maybe it was just that she hadn't seen one in the flesh before. Still, it was hostile and coming for the only food source around. Her. She rolled away with a yowl and scrambled straight to her feet, a staggered bounce left and right as she regained just enough of her footing to assert control of her movement.

She looked back, just once. The giant bear had closed in and pulled back a paw for another mighty swipe. Ready for it this time, Jennifer threw herself right instead, straight into a roll. It stomped with its right foot. She wasn't going to outrun the creature, that was for sure. Which left only one option, and frankly, a stupid one.

Stupid was better than nothing.

Out came the claws again. It would be on her terms. She crouched into a fighting stance, waiting for the beast to attack. It raised a paw and pounded the ground, smashing a mist of snow her way. She protected her eyes, but the bear pressed its advantage and advanced, repeating with the other paw. Jennifer withdrew as it pushed forward, bashing and blinding as it moved, gaining ground with every step. Constant retreat wasn't helpful. It was time to turn this around.

Listening as much as watching, she gained the measure of the time between each bash, and waited for the bear to get closer. When the force of the sledgehammer-like paw alone was enough to stagger her, she slashed up-wards and across with her opposite hand and cut deep into the fur of its arm.

The beast roared, deafening her with its pain, but it swung at her anyway with the good paw. She moved just in time as its own claws shredded what remained of the body armour she wore, and grazed her back. It was still powerful enough to disrupt her balance.

She landed face-first but picked herself straight back up, just as the creature leapt on the ground on which she had fallen. A white shockwave slammed her onto her backside. She watched as the giant creature lurched forward, and stretched her legs wide to dodge another attack.

Jennifer flipped backward into a roll, then into a crouched attack stance. Leverage finally with her once again, she launched herself straight at the beast and let loose a barrage of clawed attacks, stabbing it again and again. It gave a final roar, but soon crashed to the ground on its belly.

Jennifer looked down at her vanquished opponent. A pond of red grew against the white as she took stock. She hadn't meant to kill this thing, just slow it down enough to get clear.

That isn't an excuse and you know it. You've been here before. You could have pulled back. Stopped yourself.

Face it, you WANTED to kill it, didn't you?

"NO!"

She punched the snow in disgust and let out a roar. She knew the creature had no such thoughts whilst it lived. And attempts to punch the thing unconscious wouldn't have gone well. It came down to one or other of them walking away. And she hadn't come that far for it to not be her. She crouched, looked at the mess and shook her head. But wherever she was going, she wasn't there yet. The fight had at least warmed her up a little.

Warmth.

Food.

She examined the mystical path again. Her route was clear, but for all she knew, she could be days in that place. It was far from an ideal arrangement. She looked back down and then crouched.

Warmth and food.

She decided she might need it for whatever was next.

CHAPTER FOURTEEN

Kara had been left no time to formulate a plan to find Mary before arriving at a clearing at the edge of a cliff. The rapid shift of terrain from the grounds of the chateau took her aback and required her immediate attention.

She steadied herself as she looked carefully over the precipice and breathed a sigh of relief that her path there had been relatively controlled. A proper look around showed an environment the likes of which she had never before seen. She gaped at the immense, vibrant green trees surrounding her, taking in the untainted air of the place, its freshness almost reducing her to a state of ecstasy. "Well, this is a very different experience to Planet Unresting, I'd say, M—huh?"

Her words hadn't conjured her friend either. She turned back to the spot she had stepped out of and watched as a wild flux of red and blue energy cumulated in a patch of air approximately the size of the gate. Each colour jostled for supremacy, a rich visual battle unfolding in front of Kara's eyes.

Behind the light show, a terrible image flashed in shadow, a winged demon. Kara gave a shriek and jumped back. Another discharge showed the silhouette lingering, though the creature appeared to force its way through the electrical cage and forward—towards Kara. She whipped her rifle from her shoulder, only for it to instantly burn hot in her hands.

She threw it away just in time to see it burst into flame, then *become* pure flame. It flared before her eyes, and vanished into a scorching gout of bright yellow heat. That caused a second scream in short order. Especially as the creature kept coming towards her.

She backed away a few steps, but soon remembered that a direct retreat would result in a fall to her doom. She gritted her teeth and prepared to receive the attack, cringing all the while. The creature in front of her, with reflective but dark-blue skin, stood perhaps nine feet tall, and over half as wide. It had a bat-like face and stared at Kara through huge, yellow eyes, spine-like teeth in a jaw that opened wide enough to swallow anything close by. The stuff of nightmares—at least, until it spoke. "Whoa! How did you do that?"

Kara would have recognised that voice anywhere. Mary's voice often sounded surprisingly deep considering her slight frame, but it sounded like a squeak coming from the monstrous form.

"Do what?"

"The thing with the fire."

Kara stood agape for a moment but then just shrugged. "Never mind that—who are you and why have you eaten my friend?"

The creature closed in to loom over her as Kara fell backward. "Kara, what the hell have you been smoking? I'm right here. Took me a bit of effort to get through that gate, almost as if it didn't like me or something. But I kept telling myself, I wasn't leaving you alone, and that I was coming through the gate, same as you. I just walked through the gate in exactly the same . . ." Her voice faded as she looked away, downwards. Kara noted that the beast was staring at its own shadow.

". . . way."

A look of confusion fell upon Monstrous Mary's face. She waved her hands in front of her face, then stomped around, which caused the ground to shake. Kara cowered, but the beast looked equally horrified.

"Holy shit! That's really me, isn't it? With the huge hands and the shadow and the teeth. And the wings."

Kara slowly evaluated her friend and her new form. It may have been a different look for her, but the mannerisms, the voice, the movement, evoked everything about her friend.

Kara returned to her scrutiny of the place.

"Fascinating," she said, in a way that could easily have been a Spock impersonation. "A hyper-natural environment with, as far as I can tell, perfectly breathable oxygen seemingly clear of any of the usual pollutants, intact, but mutated forestry, a complete intolerance to contemporary firearms, and . . ." She turned to face the spot the gate had been. Only calm but oversized forest remained.

"*Wings,* Kara! Massive *wings!*" Mary reached for her additional appendages before giggling as if tickled. After several half-successful efforts, she eventually managed to spread them. The wingspan extended almost twice as long as her new form was tall. Kara had to admit, it was quite an impressive sight.

"And indeed, alterations of appearance which are evidently a result of the environment, but are various depending upon—what? Mary, how do I look just now?"

It took a moment before she stopped playing with her wings, but the bestial Mary retracted them and stooped to stare Kara up and down in a truly intimidating manner. The form was likely a contributing factor, but another was the sheer glee that her friend seemed to be taking moving around.

Soon though, the huge creature rose and took a step back, the rack of boned teeth forming into a cheesy grin. "Kara," she said, once more spreading her wings wide, "you look the same as you always do. Slightly stiffer posture maybe, but even your clothes are the same." The grin dropped. "Aw, crap. I hope this isn't going to be one of those awkward things you see on TV when the person who has mutated changes back to normal and forgets their clothes when they do."

Kara snorted. It was definitely Mary in there. "Well, I don't see a pile of ripped clothes anywhere, so we'll just have to hope for the best." Her friend shrugged. That ended up looking quite absurd on a creature of Mary's current size and appearance.

"Actually, as I was about to say, there is the possibility that what we are experiencing is simply sensory illusion. But if it is, it's a damn good one. I take it when you first spoke, you were referring to the fact that my rifle quite literally just exploded into fire and vanished. What I will say is, that's better than you or I doing so. And also, I still actually breathe from wandering blindly into another strange, alien world."

"Yeah. Didn't we say we weren't ever doing that again?"

"Different this time. On that occasion, we knew where we were going. We just didn't know how to steer once we were there. Which reminds me, does your normal trick work here?"

"Haven't tried." Mary squinted and held up a mitt of a hand. "I'm already finding it ridiculously bright in here. Reckon I'd blind myself if I even peeked."

"Oh, yeah," Kara replied with a nod. "Strange, alien world. Probably wise. But that does raise a question: how are we getting anywhere if we don't know where we're going?"

"We came here to look for Jen. No other reason. So, we just need to figure out which way she's gone and we're off to a good start."

Kara gave a sour look. "Even if we knew which way we were going, I can't see any bloody tracks, nor am I an expert in such things. Say, whose dumbass idea was it to wander into somewhere weird without any prior knowledge or at the very least, a travel map, anyway?"

"Yours, I believe. We really are the worst investigators ever, aren't we?"

"Or the most intrepid . . ."

"I'll go with the craziest." Mary unleashed a sigh which sounded like a bestial hiss. It was no coincidence that an entire flock of birds took to immediate flight before she had finished. "What's the plan, Professor?"

Kara could feel herself twitching. "It's *Doctor,* as well you know, *Lady* Mary. And my original plan was along the lines of, keep walking, get to Mount Doom, and deposit the ring with the minimum of fuss before anyone notices it's gone. Small snag being that we left the ring back at the mansion. And it probably wasn't even the same one the bad guys are after this time. So that one's out. Don't suppose she left any breadcrumbs lying around in a convenient trail, did she? Or am I mixing up my stories now?"

Mary lifted a hand as if to slap Kara around the back of the head. But she stopped short, acutely aware that with those hands, she'd stand a good chance of taking the inquisitive doctor's head off. The threat nonetheless remained. "So, in your year without any trouble from the pair of us, did any of your studies turn up any truth to some of these fairy tales? Because that really would be interesting."

"Wouldn't it, though?" Kara smirked. "Believe me when I tell you, I haven't got enough time or research funding to look into half the things I want to. This place is going right up my list, with the usual proviso that I get out in one piece. Now then, where's a Mister Tumnus when you need him?"

"Are you still on the sodding kids' stories?" Mary said with a frown which really did look quite threatening in that form.

"Maybe."

"You'll be looking for something labelled, 'EAT ME' next."

Kara tapped her foot for a moment. "I'd be all over that if I thought there was half a chance. But there's got to be something I haven't considered. Don't suppose you can hear anything extra with those big bat ears, can you?"

"Not over you gabbing, no."

Kara didn't answer, by way of challenge to that last statement. Mary knew her well enough to take up on it, cupping her huge hands to equally large ears in an absurd scene. They both remained perfectly still for a minute or two, leaving Mary to respond properly.

Eventually, she shook her head. "I know which way the birds flew, but I don't think that's any good for us. There are things in there I can hear moving about," she said, pointing to the forest, "but that could be anything."

"Best we've got at the moment. Ready to fly?"

"I don't know if I actually can."

"It was a figure of speech—" she started, but already, she could see Mary willing her wings into action. Such was the force behind their beating that she found herself blown backward. It wasn't a dissimilar feeling to being stood by a busy helipad just before take-off. And to their great surprise, Mary found herself airborne in short order.

"YAHOOOO!" She flew a ponderous but steady circle above and around Kara. "See how long I can keep this up, shall we?"

"I really don't think this is . . . WHOA!"

Mary swooped and grabbed her, the two climbing above the trees before she could catch a breath. It was hard to know whether to be whooping with excitement or terrified, but in Kara's case, terror rarely won that particular battle. The wings reached a regular rhythm, slow, but reassuringly regular—just like their flight. The frequent thumping was, however, all the passenger could hear.

"This plan, then," she shouted over the wind and the flapping. "Can you hear where we're going?"

"Not anymore!" Mary replied. "Wind and wing noises are too loud!"

"So, how the hell do you know where we're going?"

"Ah, you see!" Mary said, a cheerful tone in her bellow. "It's not just my ears that are big. My nose is doing well, too!"

"Well, I wasn't going to say anything, but—"

"Seriously. Once I'm past the smell of all that Chanel No. 5 you use, you're quite distinct. I didn't even realise it until now, but that's true of the Unresting world, too. It's kind of part of how I track in there. It's also probably why meat turns my stomach these days. It all smells rotten to me. Ooh—I've got a faint trace of Jen. She went this way." She pointed ahead. "One not so good thing, though."

"What's that, then?"

"I'm not used to this flying business yet. Hence this is knackering. Less intense than a blind jump through my place, but I'll wear out pretty soon."

"I've got legs. We can walk for a bit. Unless you're really close?"

"I'm not."

"So, set us down, then. We may need your creature features later on."

Mary gave a nod and slowly began her descent into the heart of the forest. She released Kara and the two of them walked, with Mary sniffing loudly every few minutes or so.

After a while, the bat-like aristocrat twitched and stopped. Kara followed suit. "What?" she asked.

"You smell that?"

The minute an olfactory prod was given, she couldn't miss it. "Yeah," she replied, her nostrils twitching as she raised her head and sniffed. "Rotting meat. Really quite strong, actually. Disgustingly so."

"I thought that was just me. I told you, most meat smells like it's rotting to me these days."

"But this is really strong," Kara said, covering her mouth with her sleeve. Mary's bulky frame started to shudder, her giant hands also flying to her face. Kara could hear the buzzing of flies. She could only begin to imagine how bad this was for Mary and her augmented senses. "Terrible plan, I know, but not the first we've had today. We should look into that."

"You're right," Mary mumbled. "That is a bloody stupid idea. But seeing as that smell has overpowered every other that I've got just now, we better had. Just in case."

"Just in case?" Though a question was asked, Kara had reached the same worst-case conclusion. The thought made her shudder. She was as much up for going to eliminate the possibility as to face it. "Lead the way, Batsie." Mary glared, baring her hideous teeth. Kara simply gestured her forth.

They walked for several minutes, braving the clouds of insects. But even those dispersed almost as soon as they were anywhere near Mary. It was an interesting pattern which struck true any time they came into contact with any wildlife.

As they grew closer, they could see specks of blood on the shorter, thinner trees beside them on their path. Specks became lines, until eventually they reached a group of trees which looked as if they were bleeding themselves. Mary's reaction after giving one of them a gentle poke suggested it was more than mere appearance.

In the interests of inquisitive research, Kara did likewise. The bark was as soft as a bunch of grapes. It trickled red. Kara grimaced and backed away slowly.

"This is seriously grim," Mary said, looking around with her mouth still covered.

"Agreed. And that, coming from you after everything you've seen, is quite an endorsement." Kara had made a firm chronicle of Mary's ordeal the previous year, from the London Underground amnesia, right up to the inheritance of vast power which she received for her troubles. Kara figured that setting foot in a different strange realm would have side-effects for Mary dissimilar to her interaction with her own world, distinct again from her influence on the Unresting.

Whereas the place appeared to be a real paragon of nature, Mary's domain was death. Or at least, that which was no longer considered living. Forces in direct opposition to one another.

"No wonder everything's running away from you in here. I remember what you told me about that time Jen grabbed you and how she reacted. Imagine an entire place made of Jen!"

The giant cleared her throat. This time, bats fled the scene. "Not the best choice of words just now, Kara."

Kara realised her error quickly and held a hand to the bridge of her nose, her head bowed. "Sorry." She returned her gaze to Mary, whose eyes were wide once more. "You've stopped squinting. Has it grown darker in here?" She looked up and around herself as she asked. It had a little, but the overgrown, tangled branches above would have done that.

Mary mimicked her movements. "I have. There's something different about this area. It feels more like my place, only not."

"Yep. I can breathe here, for a start. Though that could be the magic suit jacket you gave me." Mary gave a scornful look. "So, what else is different?"

"The Unresting place just *is*. This glade? It feels corrupt somehow. Kind of reminds me of when I came into contact with the blue jewel of doom when I got it off Violet. Something is just *wrong* here."

"Then let's find out what."

They got into the centre of the glade. The surrounding trees dripped like a red waterfall. Kara closed tightly towards Mary, who herself looked unnerved, even within her current appearance. But bodies had been strung up at the far edge of the glade, which Kara did not see immediately as they were the same shade as the gruesome trees from which they hung.

Most likely, because none of them wore their original skins.

Kara thrust a hand to her mouth as she looked at the assortment of flayed corpses and dropped to her knees. All of her will went into steeling herself against the grotesque sight.

She found herself moving upwards. The bodies disappeared from her immediate vision as the giant Mary smothered her. There were muffled words which could have been an attempt at comfort, but even with her eyes closed, she could only see one thing.

"Easy, Kara. You've done so well up to now." Mary sounded remarkably calm. But then, she had seen scenes, memories, that were on a par with the worst this glade had to offer. It was interesting how the human mind learned to cope with various traumas, something she had dabbled with in study as a side project on the paranormal research. Mary, of course, was an exemplary subject for all of the above.

She released herself from Mary's secure grip and looked her friend straight in the eye. "So what do you believe caused such an anomaly within this unexplored realm?"

Mary advanced straight to the bodies and untethered one of the ropes from the blood trees. She examined the corpse in her giant hand. The yellow eyes blackened, as she poked at the flesh. Then, she lowered the body to the ground and turned back to Kara. "Well, that's . . . kind of horrific. No skin. No soul, either. I-I can't do a lot for them."

Kara pondered this for a moment. "Do you suppose this could just be a part of where we are? A broken part, as you say, but an element of it anyway?"

"Could be, but it's very, very different. And the body I picked up? Male, clearly, but I had the faintest trace of Jen's scent here. And this other one that seems familiar, too. Can't put my finger on why, though."

"But you could see with your death sight here?"

"Yeah, but again, it was weird. I've at least managed to pick up Jen's trail again. We need to go that way." She pointed past the dump of bodies. "And we're flying. At least for a while."

Kara nodded. "The farther away from here we are, the better, if you ask me."

"Totally." Mary scooped Kara from the ground and spread her wings.

She didn't voice this to Mary, but Dr. Mellencourt secretly hoped that no worse fate had befallen Jennifer. She would encourage Mary to fly for as long as she could. She hoped they wouldn't be too late.

CHAPTER FIFTEEN

Since getting the better of the bear, Jennifer successfully avoided further trouble on what turned out to be an incredibly long walk. She'd managed to count to 20,000 on her route before getting bored and losing concentration, especially with nothing but brilliant white terrain to be seen for miles.

Her new makeshift cloak smelt disgusting every time she caught a whiff against the rising winds, but it stopped her from freezing to death. As she took a second to consider that unhealthy alternative, the uncomfortable gale escalated into a proper blizzard—a slap in the face, of sorts, from the environment. The snowdrift ruined her counting, and left her even more lost.

What was left of the flak jacket acted as a handy bag for a hefty chunk of the now-frozen meat she had no ability to cook. She slung it over her shoulder and clung on to it for dear life. Some of the snow provided a hydration stopgap, but frankly, a canteen would have been nice. Just moments later, she felt herself growing colder still as the ice water leeched what little heat she had managed to retain. She tugged the cloak tighter around her.

While she retained a certain level of self-pity, Jennifer considered it a shame she hadn't had time for proper planning for her extreme camping trip. Other lamentable oversights: a lack of good company, a toasting fork for all the mushrooms and marshmallows she hadn't encountered thus far, and maybe a bottle of vodka to pass around.

Not that she drank, of course, but even though Mary had cut down considerably since they first met, she occasionally liked the odd shot or two when she'd come back from the more traumatic excursions to the ghost world. It was always nice to provide hospitality.

She tittered at the thoughts, an attempt to keep her mind ticking over, rather than losing it to the sapping cold. To keep herself awake. Just a few minutes' sleep and she could wake up fresh. Perhaps the numbness in her fingers and toes would get back to a torturous burning.

No. If she dozed off now, she wouldn't wake up again. She'd just be there, frozen in time, in a place out of time, with nobody knowing where she was. Kara and Mary would think she ran away. And the reason she retreated in the first place, Manta and his little cult, would still be out there.

She couldn't give them the satisfaction.

Jennifer kept up her mental exercise. A distraction from the duration itself, Kara swore by counting, and Jen had learnt well. Besides, the storm had lightened considerably. Her last dozen steps saw the snow coverage decrease to about an inch underfoot, muddier, more patchy. She would not freeze to death this day.

She felt warmer, too. Warm enough, in fact, to consider removing the stinking, blood-soaked and heavier-with-every-step fur patch. The precipitation transitioned and diminished to occasional falling flecks, but then each fell faster, heavier, harder. First sleet, then drizzle.

The sound of thunder rolled in the distance. With every step, the plain white became less so. Patches of green and small shrubs cropped up within her line of sight. A second roar of thunder deafened her. But the environment at least took some shape, and a little colour. Her walk felt like she had crossed continents, but having stepped from what felt like the worst Siberian winter to the Amazon at the height of rainy season compounded the feeling.

Jennifer had reached the end of the road. The undergrowth thickened exponentially, green life hugging her ankles and demanding her full attention as she hacked through it. It reached a sudden end, a cliff face, discovered as she almost walked off the edge of it. Which would have been a stupid way to go after everything that had been overcome up until now.

She scouted around, looking for a safe way down, but saw nothing except a long drop. An attempt at proper communication had to be worth a try. "Okay, you've got me."

Rocky steps leading below manifested before her as she blinked, much to her surprise. Though the possibility of another trap occurred to her, it was better than a treacherous fall. A flash of her chromatic sense showed her a brightly lit path and just one route to the source of her quest. Jennifer threw up her hands, sighed, then carried on with her journey.

The steps provided a route into what appeared to be a large lake. Yet the water frothed as a stretch of rapids might, which gave her pause. And when she held her path, it settled a little. A sense hit Jennifer that as she watched the lake, she had the nagging feeling that it was looking back.

She clutched the bag of meat to her stomach with her life. Then, she did as she always had in life. She pressed on.

Her feet dipped into the bubbling foam, and with the next step, Jennifer suddenly plunged into a deep expanse of the moving, warm water. As she thrashed through the blackness, she attempted to rise and swim back to the surface.

Darkness clouded her vision as she found herself rushing along a cave. Her hands tapped solid rock, which she was certain hadn't been there before. Jennifer looked around, got the measure of her surroundings. Just as the steps had manifested, so had a roof of stone. Bubbles of air shot through Jennifer's mouth as she failed to stop herself cursing her luck. And immediately following the expulsion of vital oxygen, she concluded luck had nothing to do with it. The place was actively trying to kill her.

Fine. If that's how it is, that's how it is. But I'm going to make you work for it.

She fumbled around for a clear end to the rock, but with no luck. Less air. Running out of time. Time to find another way. She checked down and around, switching her sight to more augmented eyes. Though dark, the light changed below, and the obvious place to swim toward. She discovered a chasm at the bottom about big enough for her to go through, but not a lot else. Options were thin on the ground, her air expiring. She swam straight through the gap.

Stuck. Her arm caught on a rock enclosure as she looked through the other side of the tiny pass. Her bag strap had snagged on the surrounding stone. She jammed her legs against the rock and yanked hard several times, but to no avail. Air. Time. Both problems. It was her or the bag. No real option. She called upon her razor fingers, decided to slice in, grab as much of the meat as possible and then continue out into new water.

No sooner had Jennifer got into the bag than she heard further movement behind her. She turned, caught sight of a school of jagged-toothed fish rapidly closing in. She abandoned the trapped bag and the contents before everything and darted through the crevice, then out and upwards with the speed and ease of one of the fish herself. Looking up, the waters had a clear run to daylight. She moved her arms and legs in steady synchronisation and pushed all the way to the surface.

Limbs aching and stiff from exertion, she breathed out, hard and fast. Even with this short experience of it, the air around her felt muggy, sweltering. A rocky ledge presented itself, and she thrashed for the cliff face, grabbed as hard as she could and pulled up and clear of the water. One of the fish leapt clear of the pool with a wide open mouth. It found her left leg and clamped hard.

Her scream should have been heard for miles. Jennifer shook her leg, but the fish stuck fast. She shifted her grip and closed her eyes as she kicked the wall as hard as she could. She screamed again, then felt a small crunch as the wretched thing ceased thrashing, but its death throes did not release its agonising grip.

Through hyperventilating yelps and narrowed eyes, Jennifer cast about for more stable ground, still worried about the droplets of blood falling into the water. She threw her arms upward and pulled for additional clearance, but had seen one of those things leap. Another launched from the pool, but its frenzied snapping was nowhere near her. Such luck wouldn't hold.

The ledge to her right offered a chance at safety, but there was precious little leverage from her current position, and her grip was weakening. The third springing fish gnashed much closer than the last. Too close for comfort. She was sure that her generous donation of bear meat served as a satisfying distraction, the only reason she hadn't been pulled in by the entire school. But it wouldn't keep them for long. She crawled up the wall, howling with every second step, and aimed for the ledge, hoping for a clean run.

The pool below her frothed and bubbled, tiny specks of black appearing near its surface. They'd had their starter. There was only going to be one chance, or the main course was coming up soon. Jennifer shoved with arms and legs to full extension, leapt through the air, and hoped.

From her angle, she approached almost head-first and shifted her weight into a forward roll for a successful landing. On to the next job. She plucked apart the jaws of the dead fish attached to her and threw it back into the pool. They little cared what they ate, judging by the explosion of flesh and bone as soon as the corpse touched the water's edge.

The rapid healing to which she had grown accustomed had yet to help her wounded leg. It probably wasn't about to drop off, but if the fish were that unfriendly at the chance of fresh meat, whatever was on the surface was unlikely to be any better. She sat and ripped off the shredded rags of her trouser leg and then wrung them dry before assembling an improvised bandage, tying it tight onto the bleeding leg.

The minute's rest hadn't done any harm either. She sat on a protrusion of flat rock, heavily overgrown with a thick series of vines which stretched across and over the ledge. The difference in temperature from the last place to her current environment couldn't have been any more extreme. The muggy, sweltering heat roasted sweat out of her when she already lacked hydration. The fact that a pool lay immediately below with only the issue of a small horde of deadly flesh-eating creatures between her and relief was simply a taunt too far.

She cast another enhanced gaze over the area. It truly was the land that kept on giving, as the as-yet unknown destination appeared brighter and stronger than before, past the thick vines and beyond. She didn't know how far it reached or how long it would last, but the vines provided a climbing rope, of a sort.

Just as she complained to herself about being thirsty, the heavens opened. Hard. She gave a wry smile as she looked up and let the cool water wash against her, clean off a little of her recent filth. Her tongue was hanging out of her mouth long before she realised she was even doing it as she drank in the droplets of rain. Better than nothing. And then, her brain nudged another concern forward—those vines would become incredibly slippery soon.

She forced herself back upright and took her time with the climb now that she was high enough up to not worry as much about what was below. Claws for grip were not an option there; the twisted plants did not feel strong enough to take any strain beyond her actual weight.

She clenched her teeth every time she hauled herself up a foot or so. Her wounded leg hadn't improved. But she was not going to fall, which was something. And at least with the rain, she could stop for a mouthful every now and again. The last few feet of climb proved incredibly treacherous, her footing lost several times—to more howls every time she whacked her calf against the wall of rugged stone—and some last-minute changes of grip. She roared her relief when she finally hoisted herself up to the summit.

Jennifer hauled herself to her feet, holding her wounded leg, but triumphantly taking in the view. It was such a beautiful valley, the risk of evisceration aside. She was soaked through, the rain incessant and relentless, her hair lank and sodden, as was her clothing. But, at least she was warm. She trudged on, following the trail of energy, hoping that it would be a nice straight walk from there to whatever her goal was.

She could hear the sounds of nature all around her. She heard a thrum, as if she stood under power lines, which changed pitch and circled around her entire hearing range. Cicadas, perhaps. The hair on the back of her neck stood on end, like a cold, thin hand tickling her.

Huge birds flew overhead, and a cloud of flies revved nearby. As soon as she laid eyes on them, they gathered, a swarm of suitable size to obscure her vision of everything in their direction. And now that she could hear the collective, it became the only sound audible to her.

Jennifer gave a smile and walked, with a mind to give the cloud a wide berth. It wasn't going to be anything good. But, then, the undergrowth grew thicker with every step she took. Tall palm trees withered above, giving the appearance of throttling each other with their branches. Tiny movement darted around everywhere, and she wiped her drenched face clear, checking for more immediate danger, ready for anything. She took a moment to confirm her route, and advanced.

The droning grew louder. She indulged herself a quick look behind and could see the black swarm gathering, swirling. No doubt, the insects in the cloud retained an unhealthy interest in her. Time to pick up the pace. Her leg still stung, more than before perhaps, but the thrumming bass of the swarm had to be a worry.

Jennifer checked her footing ahead, plotted a route, and broke into a sprint. Good timing. She looked behind her. The low moan corrupted into a scraping whine, a sound similar to circular saws, and she watched as the thick forest behind her disintegrated into a cloud of wood chippings. They effortlessly cleared a path to her and kept coming.

Even at such incredible speed, she had little chance of outrunning them all. Nonetheless, she bounded through the terrain, leaping over vast tracts as her momentum carried her through the air as much as on land. Not long into her burst of speed, her ear rattled with the sound of one of the insect's near proximity. It resembled a locust, but one closer to the size of a rat, and considerably uglier.

She ducked her head just as a blade of bone swung at her from its abdomen, and only just missed. It was a second or two ahead of its companions. Taking care to avoid the sharp end, she batted it with the back of her hand and sent it careering into a nearby tree. However, the attack hadn't done wonders for her balance. She threw herself flat to the ground as the swarm strafed past in a cacophonous dirge.

They slowed and prepared to circle round, but Jennifer didn't wait on them. She pushed herself upwards and jolted in the counter direction to their collective turn, then grabbed a nearby vine. She shimmied up it with the ease of a crawling rat, ran to the edge of the tree branch, and threw herself forward and to the right with all the strength she had. It took her to another branch, from which she swung with her arms. It felt good, but she would feel better getting clear of the deadly cloud.

Another two got ahead of the swarm, but she met one with a jab to its eyes and the other with a swift, firm kick. For every two, though, there were at least a dozen more. Jennifer needed a more definitive solution, and quickly.

She surveyed the area from her hanging position. A swamp laid a short leap away; not her greatest plan, but nothing better presented itself. She released her hold on the vine with a destination in mind, and landed just as the cloud gained ground. Staggered steps, but motion in the right direction was all she needed. She took one deep breath and shut her eyes, and then hurled herself straight into the grey, hot mud. Then, she stopped dead. Counted. Hoped that they'd just go away before she needed more air. Tried not to think about how deep the bog was and how much trouble it would be to escape. One problem at a time.

Seven. Eight. Nine. Ten. Surely those things had had enough by now? She swam upwards. As she feared, the morass proved five times more resistant than that of normal water. Fortunately, Jennifer Winter could call upon strength to match. She stopped thrashing and concentrated, felt the strength of the swamp around her, and willed herself the power to match. To get out of it alive.

Though her natural healing had failed to hear her call, something must have admired her fighting spirit. She felt raw force coursing through every muscle, and wriggled into a breaststroke a salmon would have been proud of. She thrashed with rhythm, with might, with a total refusal to fail.

Up she came, back into the light and air, with the murderous winged creatures nowhere in sight. She could still hear them, though. Again, one problem at a time. She finished thrashing her way through the mud and planted herself on solid ground. When it finally cooled, she saw that it soothed her wounded leg as it dried. Spontaneous action carried the occasional advantage.

More than the mud though, that brief summoning meditation did more than she had first asked of it. Strength manifested in other ways. The mud on her hardened, but caused no pain. Instead, it merged with tougher skin. Her hair had become the brambled, wire-like knot that she gained in what she liked to call her battle form. She suspected her eyes were a yellow shade of feral as well. Naturally, her hands were now the trusty weapons which had benefited her so much in that testing territory.

The swarm charged at her.

She stood ready. Unafraid.

Jennifer shifted into a combative crouch, an adapted kata. Through the monstrous rumble, she stepped forward and whirled with her claws. With every step, she danced, certain of her footing, more certain still of her accuracy. With every move, at least two of the buzzing terrors were sliced in half. She stepped into a run, and then leapt, a pirouette through the air. A mist of red surrounded her as she punched a hole of destruction into the black cloud.

But the enemy continued relentless, without any instinct to retreat. That suited just fine. She hacked and sliced with expert precision, and whittled the horde to a few lone attackers in moments.

As she drove her fingers through the last of them, breaking it in two, the realisation dawned on her that she had not defeated them cleanly. She felt a fierce sting, reached behind her, and discovered several of the bone blades protruding from her back.

She staggered, her movement suddenly considerably less certain, driven by just one thought: to keep going, to reach her goal. But things became blurred, wobbly. She couldn't focus, couldn't stand, couldn't see anymore. An attempt to redirect her will just led to imbalance, a drop to her knees.

Just keep going.

She couldn't, try as she might. But she returned to her feet and advanced, not entirely in control.

She fell forward, her strength entirely spent.

CHAPTER SIXTEEN

This is the most beautiful place!" The altered Mary squealed her words between slow poundings of her newly grown wings. "Seriously, I can breathe here, there are no insane dead things trying to kill us or haunt my dreams, and everything's in full high-def colour. I love it!"

Kara clung to her back as they flew high above the forest below, her winged friend now seemingly adjusted to flying as second nature, not far from walking. "Stunning scenery, beautiful camping country—oh, and the small issue of some disgusting valley of skinless corpses. It kind of creates a problem with the tour brochure I'm putting together in my head."

She could feel the frown Mary pulled even though she couldn't see it. "I mightn't have been here long, but that felt out of place, even for here. I dunno, like a desert in the North Pole."

"Well, I haven't seen two of them since I got here, thankfully." Kara made a mental note to look into it if they ever got out of there. "Also, has it ever occurred to you that when we get home, you might stay like that? Don't you find dating awkward enough as it is with the whole ghost whispering, scary eyes, and death touch thing?"

They flew in silence for a moment, other than the flapping.

"Not that I've had time for anything other than 'ghost whispering' as you incorrectly call it, but you know, forgive me if I get to compare notes between now and the last time I unwittingly threw myself into a life of action, adventure, and necromancy. Unlike what I was doing then, this is pretty friggin' cool."

"Well, yes, you have me there, I suppose. But given that you are the 'Guardian of the Gate', you can breathe just fine even when wandering around dead lands. I can't. Still, I'm wearing your handiwork, remember, so that might be keeping me going here just as well as it would at your place. Much as I'd love to see if you're actually right, I'm not taking it off any time soon.

"Also, if it's so great here, why haven't we just found Jen yet, on a beach somewhere, holding up a cocktail and telling us to come on in 'cos the water's lovely? Also, was that a pterodactyl I saw over there a minute or two ago? No, you might be finding it cushy over here, but for pity's sake whatever you do, don't drop me, okay?"

They banked right and descended a little as the temperature dropped sharply. The green scenery below faded into a plain white and their path became obscured by a wintry fog. "We're getting closer," Mary yelled. It sounded muffled in the obfuscating mist. "The scent's kind of faded though. I'm worried we're about to get lost."

Kara gritted her teeth. "Paradise Island, my arse. All right. That it's getting silly cold up here is probably something to do with that. Giving me a small problem—" She shivered by way of demonstration. "Your jacket helps with death winds, but not so much against plain and simple Arctic temperatures. I'm about to have a problem, too."

Mary attempted to turn her head to face Kara, but it just wasn't possible. "Crap. I haven't got anything to help either."

"That's okay. Have you lost Jen's trail completely?"

"I'm about to."

"Right." Kara clung on tighter. "Then just keep going in the direction you already are. How are you holding up?"

"I'm fine. Not even tired actually."

"Good. Because I'm going to be in serious trouble if it stays like this. Where's a flask full of soup when you need one, eh?"

"Okay, this place isn't as good. Hang in there, K."

"I intend to." With a shiver, she tapped Mary's neck with her left hand. "Now, mush!"

Mary gave a nervous chuckle, then drew her knees in slowly and then kicked out, beating her wings at increased pace. Kara's grip slipped, and she realised this had occurred only after she slid. She could no longer see far past her arm, such was the freezing fog.

"Didn't I just tell you to hang in there?" Mary said, jitters in her voice.

"Doing my best . . ." Kara's words were feeble, her breath freezing in front of her. Though the increased speed was appreciated, the wind just bit harder.

"No, you're not. Talk to me."

"I-I can't." She shivered. Icicles grew on the end of her nostrils.

"Now I know something's wrong," Mary grumbled. "Come on, tell me something. Anything. Just keep talking."

Kara managed half a smile. "I preferred it when you didn't know me so well," she answered, barely above a mutter.

"Yeah, well. Okay, what did you want to do before you became a permanent student?"

Kara managed a scowl. "Thought about being a pilot."

"Never knew you had an interest in flying. And you're doing a good job of it just now."

"Comes of growing up around planes."

"You did?"

"Yep. It was quite funny, actually. Mum was never too polite about pilots . . . said they were never grateful about her keeping them in the air."

"Why? What did she do?"

Kara opened her mouth to answer, but croaked instead. She wheezed and then tried again. "Engineer. RAF. Decent rank. Barking mad, but you'd love—" She slumped, her grip around Mary's shoulders slipping.

Mary slowed her flight to a careful glide. "Is that why you decided against being a pilot in the end?" There was no answer. Mary tried again, more forceful this time. "Kara. Answer me. Why did you get a Ph.D. instead of a pilot's licence?"

Kara reaffirmed her grip on Mary's shoulders. "Because . . . when it came down to it, I wanted to study . . . history and psychology . . . more than I did maths . . . and physics."

"I can understand that."

". . . Could've gone either way . . . but it's what happens when you get . . . a good teacher. They just . . . sell you on to . . . a course. I also . . . got . . . ribbed for being . . . a daddy's . . . girl . . . But . . . that was . . . hardly . . . true." Kara's eyes clouded. She finally noticed herself shaking uncontrollably. She slid upward, tried to regain control of her body, but it seemed to be ignoring her efforts.

"Daddy's girl?" Mary asked. "What's that about?"

"Archaeologist," Kara blurted. Her blinks were slow; her vision alternated from pure white to pure black in cycles.

"And you've become Indiana Jones. You're just missing a trilby and a bullwhip and you're well away."

Kara could hear herself chuckling inside. But externally, she could not vocalise anything else of use. She attempted to pull herself back to a steady grip, but just slipped further. She closed her eyes. Mary's desperate cries seemed a great distance away.

When she opened them, she was falling. She could see only white as she flapped, flailed, grasped at nothing. There wasn't much she could do but hope the landing was soft.

Her descent came to an abrupt stop. A pair of massive, scaly hands seized her by the torso and clutched her close to their chest. "Keep talking to me, Kara!" she heard. She felt her lips move, attempted to comply, but nothing came through.

Kara closed her eyes.

~*~

Mary kept her wings flapping and hence kept the pair of them airborne, but Kara showed no signs of returning to consciousness. Mary shook her, though, and stared in horror as her friend remained insensible.

Mary's attempts to hold Kara upright caused problems with her flying, with too much to think about besides staying in the air. She stayed focused on Kara and, at a point in which the blanket of snow reached an end, and merged with rock and greenery, made a slow descent.

Mary also noticed an increase in the temperature. She almost dared to consider that good news, but after a moment, she recognised that they had gone from one extreme to another. The climate now proved humid, stifling.

She found a clearing in the greenery and set down gently, doing the same for Kara as she tried to revive her. "Kara! Kara, wake up! We can't stay here."

Mary didn't know why they couldn't stay there. The nagging feeling that someone or something tried to prevent her crossing into that world wouldn't go away. It coupled poorly with the thought that if she had failed to get in, Kara would have had to alone face everything they had thus far.

A light cough and a splutter warmed her though, as Dr. Mellencourt blinked rapidly and looked at her with blurry eyes. "Fortune and glory, kid," she mumbled with her customary grin. "Fortune and glory."

Mary caught herself growling. "Are you quoting Indy at me?"

Kara rubbed her eyes and gingerly sat up. "Would I?"

Before Mary could think of a decent retort, something slammed into her chest at high speed and stung hard. She lurched forward and crouched over Kara, spreading her wings wide to make herself the only likely target for their attacker. She attempted to draw on her death sight, but stopped immediately when the brilliance of the place almost burned out her natural eyes in the attempt.

A distant imprint seared into her cornea like a shadow on a negative, though it gave her a flash of another human being. She remembered—he had been despatched to kill Jennifer. She growled again, unrestrained and guttural this time, and she felt Kara shudder against the back of her wing.

It hadn't fazed her attacker though, who stood at a distance and leaned upon what looked like a longbow against his leg. She saw him apparently pluck a flying creature of some kind from the air and in a clean move, twisted its head off. He then nocked its body onto the bow and pulled back, taking aim at her again.

Mary glanced at the projectile that had already hit her and lodged into the chitinous outer skin. It looked like a stinger but about the size of a throwing dart. He hit her again. The body of the projectile exploded into a red pulp, but the stinger jammed into her, just like the first.

However, neither shot had truly penetrated her tough, reinforced skin. She plucked one out and an acidic black liquid hissed and dripped onto the ground. She could take these, though wouldn't risk one to less plated areas, but Kara probably couldn't. She glared at the hunter, enraged, and moved Kara into cover. She spread her wings and threw herself at him.

He looked up, but his expression remained blank. A mob of giant insects dispersed, but not before he had plucked two of them from their flight with great speed and accuracy. As nasty as they looked, they seemed to fail to notice his presence at all. Once more, he killed them with ease and turned the stingers towards Mary.

As she went at him, he jabbed them both into her stomach, but once more, they wedged before causing any real harm. She responded with a back-fist to his face, which sent him flying backwards. Still furious, she flew at him again, but he muttered something. The incomprehensible words echoed around her and, as she heard them, she landed as if drunk and staggered away from him. He kept talking, but, although she still couldn't understand him, she moved toward him—or tried to, and ended up moving in the opposite direction. She moved herself left, and travelled right. As she tried to control her erratic motion, she walked head-first into a tree.

The echoing voice continued to bore into her brain as her balance failed her. Nothing she tried could get her anything as basic as standing upright and moving as she desired. Instead, the tattooed, chanting figure walked towards her and raised his hands as she fought to stand.

Mary heard a *whomp* through the wind and then a crack, similar to bamboo against skin. The chanting assailant fell silent—and crumpled to the ground. She shook her head, and then looked around to see what had happened. Kara stood, holding his longbow like a club.

"You all right?" Kara asked.

Mary plucked the projectiles from herself and nodded. "Just my pride wounded," she answered. "Did you see any of that?"

"Not a thing." Kara smirked. "Now, shall we get back to looking for Jen?"

Mary grinned. "Only if you've finished your nap."

They both looked down at the downed hunter and then back at each other. "We can't be far off," Kara said. "It looks like we got lucky finding him before Jen did."

"I dunno. I think she might have run into a problem similar to mine. Say, didn't that voice of his cause you bother as well?"

Kara looked bemused. "Dunno what you're talking about. Were these things you got stabbed by laced with any hallucinogens, do you reckon?"

"Not impossible, I suppose. But it doesn't seem likely."

Kara shrugged. "Guess we'll never know, then. Be a dear and grab him if you can, though. May as well ask him a few questions when he wakes up. See if you can find an apple and some long grass, too. Better sort him out a ball-gag, just to be sure."

Mary scratched her head. She wasn't sure whether to baulk at Kara's bossiness or be delighted that they had the same idea about interrogating their attacker. *After* they had found Jennifer. In the end, she chose the latter. She hoisted the limp body onto her shoulder and pointed ahead. "She's that way. I can smell her."

"You'd be able to smell anything with that snout."

"I'm gonna slap you."

"Jen first. Slaps later."

The two proceeded to follow Mary's nose.

CHAPTER SEVENTEEN

Jennifer pondered her situation from the comfort of the police cell, the conclusion of a humiliating and frankly false arrest in front of the entire school. A spell in a young offender's institute might not have been the worst option. At least she wouldn't have to deal with that shrew of a stepmother for a few months.

She had no worries about handling herself in Borstal. Once they found out why she was in there, some of them would leave her alone. If that didn't work, they'd just have to find out the hard way what it would take to put her down.

The thought put a smile on her face for half a second, until she considered the many other issues it raised. It would have meant leaving her father alone with, and unprotected from, that nasty piece of work. She'd actually started to enjoy school, too, mostly down to her exponential improvement in sports activities in the last year.

Mrs. Jenkins, one of her P.E. staff, informed her on good authority that she was well on course for the Wales Under-18 women's rugby squad, and that scouts from Great Britain and Wales had come to watch her play hockey a few times as well. One sniff of that kerfuffle and any chance for an athletic career all went up in smoke.

She butted her head against the wall a few times as she reflected. *Stupid, stupid girl. That's your ticket out of here well and truly buggered.*

She'd dealt with her interrogation about as well as someone with such an implausible explanation was ever going to. It gave her half a chance of skipping the detention centre and instead making it to a madhouse. No. Hardly an improvement. It was a nightmare and no mistake.

The door clicked open and a particularly grumpy constable ordered her onto her feet. She wondered what fresh hell she was about to walk into that time. Surely they weren't going to ask her the same lot of questions all over again?

A surprising sight greeted her.

"Dad?"

It *was* him. In deep conversation with the desk sergeant. Stranger still was the fact that he was wearing a suit. He'd even shaved. She barely recognised him in that mysterious shell. For the first time that day, she had something proper to smile about. She had thrown herself at him in a huge hug before she had even realised. "Oh, thank you, thank you!"

He pushed her off after a couple of seconds and examined her up and down, then shook her by the shoulders. "Oh, Jen, love," he said in a broader Welsh lilt than she had ever developed. "What's happened to you? You're not a bully. I know you better than that."

She looked back at him. He was as clean as she'd seen him in some time. Instead, she gave him the warmest of grins. "I'm so glad you came, Dad."

"Yes, well, who else was going to?"

"I know but . . . I wasn't expecting—oh, never mind. It's just great that you're here."

He had already reverted in part to his more default state of scruffy. But Jennifer didn't care. "We obviously have a lot to talk about. But first of all, let's get you out of here."

"How?" Jennifer frowned. "They obviously think I did it, think I'm some sort of psycho."

"I got a call from the school. They told me it was Charlotte Williams said you battered her?"

"That's what she said, yes."

"Helen Williams' daughter?"

"I wouldn't know."

He chuckled. "Oh, it was her, all right. Helen Williams. I checked. Your mother talked about her all the time, back in the day. They went to school together, too. Used to be at each other's throats all the bloody time, you know. Some things never change."

Jennifer grinned. But she thought carefully about what he'd said. They *never* talked about her mother. Ann wouldn't have it. Even besides that, she'd enquired a few times before and he'd just change the subject, tell her to leave it alone, or head straight to the drinks cabinet. He never had a laugh talking about her. Not once. She squeezed his arm and beamed at him. "So, she used to fight a lot, huh?"

"Your mother? She was a walking riot if you were on the wrong side of her. If you were someone she cared about, though, there wasn't anything she wouldn't do for you." His voice trailed off as he spoke. He gave her a warm stare. "You remind me so much of her sometimes." He turned away quickly.

Jennifer had so much she wanted to ask him. But even though there had been precious few opportunities like this one, they were still in a police station. She was still in big trouble. There was only one question possible. "So, how are you planning to get me out of here?"

"Oh, I already told you, love. Some things never change."

"What?"

"Well, Charlotte, like her mother, is not exactly a model citizen herself. I spoke with Mr Walters for a while. Turns out there were a couple of other girls who came forward about Charlotte. So, we can't get you back at Cardiff High, but pressing charges, shall we say, is in nobody's best interests. Now, let's talk more on the way home, shall we?"

It was late afternoon by the time they left, and early evening by the time they approached their home road. They had a good couple of miles in which to chat and catch up, to explain how much the gang had provoked her. And for the duration of the trip, he'd *listened* to her. She'd listened to him. "This has been really good, Dad," she said as they approached the house. "We should do this more often."

"What, escape police stations and basically blackmail folk?"

"No, silly." She gave his arm a gentle punch. "I meant actually spend time together. I hardly see you these days."

"Well I'm always at home, you know."

"Yeah, but so's *she*." Jennifer pulled a sour face she reserved solely for the mention of the woman. "And I don't want to be rude, but you have to admit, you're not often in a fit state to talk."

A look of lament trickled onto his face. "I know, love. It's—I—" He bowed his head, eyes closed. "I'm sorry. It's just since your—"

They stopped. Jennifer seized his hands and gripped hard. "Everything I know about her is what you told me. And like I said, that hasn't been much."

"I've just . . ." He shook, then broke into sobs. "There was nobody like her, you know. Every day I remember at least one thing she said or did that made me smile. Today, I got really lucky. Plenty of good memories. But it's been really hard. All I have left to show for our ten years together is you. And you're going to be a superstar, with or without me. It's not your fault I've had so much trouble coping."

"It's my fault she's not here though, right?" Jennifer pulled away and turned from him. But he grabbed her hand this time.

"Don't you say that," he insisted, shaking her. "Don't you *ever* think that. There was nothing anyone could have done, or they'd have done it. Given what I saw, it was a bloody miracle *you* made it that day." He squeezed her tight. Her eyes welled. "Look at you. My little miracle."

The house door opened. "I don't know what you're hugging *her* for." Ann Malone. The one thing standing between her and fixing her life with her father. "What school's going to take her now? Waste of fucking space."

She felt her father tremble again just before he released her and turned to face his partner. "Leave us a minute, Jen. We need to talk." It wasn't the browbeaten look he had normally when he 'needed to speak with her', though. The red flush on his skin and the clenched fists suggested that was going to be a different conversation.

"I'm coming with you," Jennifer offered defiantly.

"No. This needs to be me. Give us an hour." He started walking towards the house. His command wasn't negotiable.

"Just don't hurt her."

She's not worth it.

"I wasn't going to. Just ask her to leave." She watched her father—her *real* father—head to war. In an hour, she'd finally be rid of that bitch plaguing her every breath.

~*~

She had blown the hour sitting on a wall several streets away, staring at a bottle of vinegar-like cider and a couple of cigarettes she'd managed to acquire from other truants, in exchange for the personal stereo. It hadn't cost her anything, and if she was going to make good on a fresh start with her father, harbouring stolen goods probably wasn't the best start to it.

Granted, cigs and alcohol wasn't either, but he told her to stay away and so she complied as best as she could. She'd never smoked before, and quickly came to the conclusion she wasn't missing much. It was just something to *do*. The bottle went into the nearest bin. Regardless of anything else that happened that day, a drink to celebrate or to drown her sorrows would have destroyed her greatest victory and so was never on the cards.

She stubbed out her last smoke at the exact point she'd left her dad. It was incredibly quiet. *Must've been a quick conversation.* She shrugged, then let herself in.

There was a strong smell of bleach filling the house. Something else, too, but she couldn't place it over the chlorine. Or the pungent aroma of nicotine and tar. Actually, that was *incredibly* strong. Nauseatingly so. Like her sense of smell had sharpened of late.

"Hello?"

Then, she heard a repeated scratching sound. Rubbing. *Scrubbing.* Had her father been so eager to rid them of all traces of Ann Malone that the first thing he decided to do was to clean?

After her call, the sound stopped. Instead, a low mutter, over and over again. She stopped in the corridor and listened. That was Ann's voice, not her dad's. The words were the same every time. "Not leaving this house . . . not leaving this house . . . not leaving this house . . ."

Something small and metal clattered to the floor against the linoleum surface of the kitchen. Anxious, Jennifer crept forward, around the staircase and into view of the scene.

The sight etched into her brain would last forever. A blood-soaked floor which had been fruitlessly assaulted with a mop and bucket. Ann's bulky frame on hands and knees, with a lump of steel wool. A knife lay in front of her, soaked in red. Shoved in a corner, folded up like so much rolled carpet, the motionless, perforated body Jennifer only just recognised as her father.

Trembling like a leaf, Jennifer took a step back. Her life's ruiner looked up at her with cold, determined eyes. "I am not leaving this house." It was not a mumble this time, instead clear, comprehensive speech. "Not for you, not for him, not for anyone."

~*~

Jennifer opened her eyes. Her body moved backwards at a slow walking pace, though horizontal, and evidently not on her own power. Her right cheek scraped against the grass, gathered occasional scratches from contact with thorny vines. She tried first to turn her head, to figure out exactly how and why she was moving, but nothing happened. She forced her eyes downwards, but her view was blurred, limited by the constraints of regular human anatomy.

With a little effort, she finally managed to turn her head, but it felt like it had been chained to a lump of lead. She could tell something dragged her, but not any creature she could see. Her instinctive escape attempt went badly, on account of not being able to feel anything to fight against. The knife-like bones still in her back must have been venomous. Had they punctured anything major, she probably wouldn't have woken up.

Half a chance it would've been a small mercy, where I'm going.

Being dropped and dragged rarely ended well, from all accounts. In those surroundings, she logically concluded she had become another food source. She didn't have time to eat, let alone to be eaten. But, until she could move again . . .

She tried her legs but couldn't feel them at all. Then her body. Nothing. Then her arms. Still no luck. But, as her head bashed into a small stone in its path, she yelled. At least that pain centre was working. Small comfort.

She channelled her mind, attempted to summon some vestige of strength from anywhere in order to move of her own free will. Her vision tuned to the bright path that had got her into that mess in the first place. As it happened, whatever it was pulled her in the correct direction. It was tempting to just let it run, see where it took her, but if it was like everything else in there, standing on her feet would give her a distinct advantage.

She turned her head from side to side, slowly at first but then faster with all she had.

And all she ended up with was a sore neck as a result. Her body had stopped moving, however. Another clearing in the middle of the drenched, muggy undergrowth, was the end of the road. She ground her teeth, staring at her flopped arm. If she couldn't move her hands, the addition of sharp appendages probably wouldn't help. But focusing there rarely let her down when she needed to channel power. With an effort of will, she tried to let the tickle grow through her palm, as it always did. But that wasn't happening either.

Somewhere ahead of her, she heard a rustling in the bushes. Jennifer was running out of time. She had to move, but, to do that she had to shake the paralysis. She had a talent for sensing poisons and pollutions to herself and others as developed as her ability to fight, but prevention was always better than cure for such matters. What to do when poisoned . . .

That's it. I've been going about this all wrong.

She surmised the venom to be the source of her condition, so the solution was to expel the danger. She still had the use of her head. Maybe she could vomit it out? As she had the thought, another occurred to her. One she could just *feel*.

She lay perfectly still, her focus holding on her own body, nothing else. Though she continued in a state of numb paralysis, after a few seconds, the sense that her body remained mostly intact became reassurance in itself. She couldn't feel its continued wounds, but she knew they were still there.

As she looked within, the contamination grew clear. It hadn't gone further than her shoulders, in itself a partial relief. And better, she could feel her own blood flowing, the pollution with it, separate entities. With that clarity, anything was possible.

Her body lay still, calm. She envisioned the toxins seeping clear, out of her pores, envisioned a return to movement, a return to strength. As she did so, she watched her skin take on a rotten jaundice, nasty, but all for the greater good. Black ichor grew on her fingertips and freshly grown fangs produced a disgusting taste somewhere between sour milk and strong vinegar tapping her tongue.

But she continued her focus, let it go. She could see it falling from her mouth, feel it dripping from her fingertips. But actually, that was great news. She could *feel* it dripping from her fingertips. Could feel her fingers, her palms, and eventually her arms. A couple more minutes, she guessed, and she'd have expelled the lot.

Partially detoxed, she could at least feel her arms again. She continued to jerk forward with great speed, but started to claw at the ground in an effort at resistance.

An ear-splitting hiss got her full attention as the creature it belonged to, a slithering reptile perhaps twice her size, hurled toward her. She sat up, ready to defend herself. She pushed herself out of the way as it snapped at her with dagger-sized fangs. A vine definitely held her leg, but she couldn't reach it from her current angle. With sublime effort, she reached for the neck of the snake, and clutched it with all her strength.

"If you bite me, I probably have had it. So, let's stop you doing that, shall we?" It kept going, and to an extent, her with it until the vine offered stubborn resistance, stretching her between opposing forces.

She tightly clung to the snake, which stopped it in its tracks, too. Something eventually had to give. She hoped that either the reptile or the detaining plant would fail, rather than her arms.

She still lacked leg movement. There hadn't been time to expel all of the venom, just enough to stop her being completely immobilised. Under the circumstances, Jennifer was pretty grateful for that. But the creature was powerful, and to top it all, its cold, flawless scales slipped in her grasp. It slapped itself against the ground, thrashing itself clear of her diminishing grip, and after a few seconds, it wriggled free.

Suddenly, Jennifer found herself a few feet above the ground, where the snake had once been, and only just caught herself from a firm face plant into greenery.

It turned sharply. Jennifer pressed herself up to her senseless knees, and prepared to receive the return charge. She just prayed the green manacle didn't add to her concerns by dragging again.

As the snake opened its maw and leapt, she clenched a fist. She swung it hard upward, then straight down at an acute angle at one of the mutant fangs. It hissed as she caught the tusk-like tooth just below halfway down. The impact was like hitting a wall, and she flapped her hand accordingly, but before the thing was out of reach, she lurched forward with both hands at the target.

As she latched on, she pulled and twisted. The loosened fang snapped outward, providing a much-needed weapon. As a bonus, the snake retreated in a shriek of agony. It would be back, but that bought her valuable time.

She clambered back and flipped herself around to face the vine coiled around her ankle. Then, she shuffled forward and slashed at a connecting joint of her restraint. It frayed, but was as tough as old leather. Several inelegant hacks and stabs finally severed it.

She cleared the remaining piece with a few slaps. She scoped the area, checking which of her adversaries would first return for her. And she had yet to completely expel the venom. A cursory detection revealed a return of the slow spread. She was genuinely uncertain what was going to kill her first.

But according to that exact same glance, whatever she was looking for was right where she was. In this area somewhere. She attempted to focus more accurately, to no avail. It could have been anywhere. It could have been the damn snake for all she knew.

"Right," she snarled. "Whatever you are, if you're here to help, now's a good time. If you're here to help, come on out!"

The response was another hiss. The undergrowth moved in two separate places. From one, the snake came crashing toward her, back for another go. Whatever the second disturbance was would have to wait. As the reptile lunged once more, Jennifer slashed wildly at its head with its own fang. The monstrous creature evaded by slithering around, but stayed close.

With incredible speed, it circled her. All too late, she realised what it was doing. It was all around her, ready to constrict. With its size and likely strength, it would crush her bones to powder. She couldn't let it get a full grip.

Her eyes followed the swirling path of its head and she held her arms high into the air, looking for her one chance.

In a split second, it pulled in tight. With no time to waste, she drove the fang into its head with both hands, but held fast and plucked it out. The snake hadn't run off that time. Instead, it attempted to lock in its deadly crush. It blasted the wind out of her lungs, and already she could feel her ribs pop.

Desperate, she brought the improvised dagger down on its head again. The grip grew no tighter. She repeated her assault four more times before her strength, her breath, failed her. She dropped the weapon and slumped forward. Her vision blurred. She had nothing left.

Just before darkness descended, the hold loosened. The coils, thick as tree trunks, fell forward and her limp body followed suit. She had barely enough strength left to gather her breath.

Blood leaked from Jennifer's mouth as she wheezed. Whether the poison had finally gotten to her, or other injuries had taken their toll, the body had given up.

"... where ... are ... you ...?"

It was the strangest thing. Jennifer could sense the jungle, that place, *laughing*. There was just no other way to describe it. But her instinct told her it wasn't laughing at her. There was a feel of satisfaction, of contentment.

Whether that was true or she was just hallucinating was uncertain. But that was what she felt. So, she smiled, content that she'd given the whole ordeal her best shot.

The jungle whispered, but she could not see any movement. Then, she felt a horrific pain around her ribs. A gout of blood flew from her mouth where she tried to scream, but to no avail. She could feel herself moving. Not dragged this time, but lifted, gripped from her stomach. Her head flopped downward, allowed her to see the carrier. Another of the house-sized vines.

It could have finished her with ease, but instead, it straightened her up. When it relaxed its grip, she was sat on a mound of itself. It supported her back as well, seating her as if she was in a chair. A vine even rested under her chin and kept her facing ahead. She felt as if something was trying to make her comfortable after her ordeal.

Around her, the jungle moved. *All* of it. The undergrowth shifted and reshaped, forming a living wall in front of her. Behind it, further motion. Branches and leaves tightened and wrapped around each other, but parted in the centre, leaving a twisted dais and a facsimile of a throne in the centre. From the throne, a bulge appeared. It warped into a female humanoid form.

The plant life continued to shape itself into more defined constructs. The leaves on the humanoid head faded from summer jungle to a more autumnal red, then yellow . . . blonde, strands of *hair*. The body underneath became smoother to look at, softer, and lightened, gradually taking a more recognisable appearance.

A pretty face formed underneath from the tree and smiled warmly at her. Smaller branches swirled in a mesmerising fashion around the arms and legs, like living tattoos. The leafy figure moved, no longer like an animated creation, but an incredibly graceful human being. Eventually the form on the throne dais appeared entirely human. And one Jennifer recognised immediately.

"Alice?" Jennifer forced from her broken lungs in exceptional discomfort. "Is that *you?*"

The jungle smiled.

CHAPTER EIGHTEEN

Why has it taken you so long to come and see me?" Alice asked.

"I can't believe—you've been *here* all this time?" Still dangerously wounded and numb from the venom, every word Jennifer uttered sapped her strength. But she needed answers. She faded.

Alice uncurled herself from her living throne, the coiled branches around her twisted, every one of their movements mesmerising to watch. She moved with the grace of a goddess, flowed with the living jungle, which cleared a path for every step she took. Jennifer's chair rippled and pulled her closer to her host.

A look of realisation crossed Alice's face. "Ah. No, I am not her."

"Th-then who are you and why do you look like . . . like—" She wheezed where she should have uttered the rest of her words. Even the energy to finish her protest ebbed away.

"I took the form best suited to you."

Jennifer spluttered, at first unable to form words. Then, she summoned a reserve from the deepest pits of her rage. "You thought *that* would be good for me? Whatever you are, you don't know me at all!"

Not-Alice raised an eyebrow. "I know you better than you know yourself." The words were quiet, low, but said with an unswerving authority that left no room for doubt or question. From that, her face instantly shifted to a grin. "Interesting though, that *you* chose *that* form."

"What are you talking about?"

"Jennifer *Winter*," it started. Any pretence at a human voice blew away with a gentle breeze. Instead, every leaf rattled in unison, leaving an echo when the being moved its lips. It should have been disconcerting, but Jennifer had heard this voice speaking to her for many years. Or at least, that was how it felt. "Once Jennifer Stone. You altered your appearance because you—"

"DON'T say it!" She had almost forgotten, herself. That night changed everything. Including her own outward appearance. The Alice facsimile smirked, then took a step back and examined her broken form.

"My, my. The image of the one they called The Face of War. Certainly the spirit of war from what I've seen of you. As much of a test for me as I have proven for you."

Sore, exhausted, wounded and still not recovered from the sting, the only thing to do was to sit back and endure whatever was next. Quite bothersome was that she was as comfortable as she had managed in quite some time. "So, you *were* trying to kill me."

"No. Not kill you. See you. The real you."

Jennifer's anger showed no signs of abating. "Who the hell are you? And who or what is this 'Face of War' everyone keeps going on about?"

"I have no name. Or perhaps I have a million names. But Alice Winter knew me as one. She would call me, *The Primal Essence*."

"Really? Did she ever say why?"

It spoke in Alice's smooth and comforting voice. Jennifer believed the words to be a direct quote from the mentor that never was. "*The spirit of a sentient realm, lost to the memories of most.*"

In her mind, Jennifer shrugged. Her body proved incapable. "Back to the attempts on my life. Why? Did this 'Face of War' offend you?"

"Not at all. You bear the likeness of one who aided me as a champion of the realm." The Essence's eyes rolled back in its head. Images scrolled, too fast for Jennifer to truly see, but they looked like archives of many memories. Thousands, perhaps. It was all too much of a blur.

"Sixteenth century, in your record of time. She came to me, survived my tests as you have, and asked for help. A great beast, she claimed, plagued her home. When she left this place, she proved greater than the beast. A true champion."

"You said you were waiting for me?"

The Essence tapped its own shoulder. "Alice saw you worthy of being marked from birth. Though unusual, she felt there was something that bore keeping an eye on. Less time has passed than when I last saw your likeness. More time has passed than when I last saw Alice. It appears she was correct. She was a rare talent."

Jennifer's head nodded, her eyes closed. But it was not long before a gentle hand rested upon her neck. A soothing touch revived her. It reminded her of a time that the real Alice had healed her after one of her school incidents, but so much more concentrated, more potent. Within seconds, she felt as if she had just woken up with a shot of caffeine, adrenaline and rocket fuel all at once.

"I wish to extend my apologies. I had not realised you to be in such a dire predicament."

"Yeah. I—um . . . it really isn't a problem." Jennifer sat up straight in her chair and plucked the bone daggers from her back. Each removal hurt like hell, but she grinned through her grimace every time. She stretched her limbs, wiggled and flexed, satisfied and rejuvenated. She could feel again. "Do you know what happened to Alice?"

"Yes. I can show you."

Jennifer was torn. On the one hand, she wanted her question answered the best way possible. On the other, it could tip her over the edge. But as she looked down, tested each of her limbs, and felt better than she ever had, she felt it worth the risk. "Please."

An image froze on the eyes of the Essence. A snapshot of a terrified Alice Winter. But then the embodied Essence blinked. With it, the still image vanished, leaving just blue pupils in their place. "Before I can give you the answer you seek," it spoke, once more through wind which rushed through the trees, "I must ask you one final question."

"Fire away."

The entity beamed. "A question of *yourself*. The one you *truly* came here to answer."

"What do you mean by—?"

Her words died. Because, in truth, she knew. "No." Jennifer attempted to bolt from the chair, but branches in the arms seized her faster than she could move and held her fast. "Don't make me see that again! Don't!"

The makeshift chair she sat upon uncoiled back into thick roots and disappeared into the ground. Those holding her grew longer and suspended her from the ground. Below her, leaves skittered in several directions before the earth itself bristled and turned.

A circle of etchings formed where she looked, and from inside, a mound of dirt grew, before blowing away in the wind. This continued with a rumble, until, in seconds, there was a deep hole where previously there had been flat ground swathed in green.

Jennifer struggled against her restraints, but with no leverage and no latitude of movement in her arms, she may as well have been encased in a tree.

"Let us see what it is you really want." The voice of the Essence came through as a deafening echo, the mouth of the marionette not even bothering to move this time. The branches released her as she screamed, and she had nowhere to go but down.

Jennifer landed safely in the pit trap. But no sooner had she established this and looked up, she could hear the sound of sliding land above. She crouched, preparing to leap, but darkness descended before she could move farther.

With nowhere to go, no air and no hope, she had survived that far only to get stuck with one last thought—the one she had most endeavoured to bury in recent years. Now, it had buried her.

~*~

The young Jennifer leaned up against the wall. Her legs had turned to jelly, the wall the only thing keeping her upright. All her hopes of a brighter future lay dead, still bleeding on the floor. One person—one callous, self-centred, violent, abusive excuse for a human being—had ripped it away from her. She had nowhere to go, no life and no future. It all started and ended there.

"What did you do?" she whimpered, clinging to the unrealistic hope that there might be some plausible explanation for the woman kneeling on the floor, other than she had just murdered him.

"WHAT DID YOU DO?" Jennifer seized clumps of her hair and started to sob herself breathless. She wailed at the world and thumped the wall that held her upright.

"He tried to kick me out, Jennifer." That was the first time Ann had voluntarily called her by name. Usually, she used something else. Always derogatory, always unpleasant and demeaning.

"Why did he try to kick me out?" Ann surreptitiously reached for the murder weapon, but not discreetly enough to escape Jennifer's notice. She stood, her face sour as she dropped any pretence at surrender.

"Oh, I know why. He got some mad idea that his troublemaker daughter was actually going to make something of herself and said I was holding you both back. So, we had a little disagreement, and, well, here we are. Really, as usual, this is all your fault. I mean, look at you. You're not going anywhere now you've been kicked out of school for beating the shit out of that poor girl. You have form now. And all in the same *day*? Priceless."

She had a point. Things went from ruined to hopelessly lost in one trip home. But that was still no reason for Ann's disturbing smile. *All in the same day*. What did she mean by that? She couldn't have planned things any better from her point of view. She was enjoying every moment of Jennifer's ordeal. Her father was in a corner on the ground, with too many stab wounds for it to have possibly been an accident.

"Oh, that's right. You did *that* today, didn't you? You're out of control. Your dad got you home to spare you from any more embarrassment with the police, but you couldn't handle him dealing you some discipline of his own. You went ballistic. Wouldn't be long before you started on me as well. Oh, this is delicious!"

Jennifer ignored the attempts to goad her, and shook her head out of disbelief. She examined the scene, try as she might to get away from it. One crucial flaw in her adversary's plan lay right in front of her. "Your fingerprints—all over that knife."

Ann's eyes burned through her, but still a trace of a smirk remained on her face. "I had to defend myself from you somehow. You'd gone berserk." She brought her weapon hand into clear view. Jennifer backed away, but the bulky woman moved with practiced speed and closed on her just as she got to the door.

Ann took a swipe with the blade as Jennifer reached for the handle. She yelped as it grazed her arm, but rolled away from the next attack.

Ann now blocked that escape. Her father's body lay in front of the back door. Stairs.

Jennifer sprinted upwards and narrowly avoided the weapon being lodged into the back of her heel. She heard the woman in hot pursuit behind. Time to lock herself in her room and maybe climb out of the window.

Too late. Ann threw a hand forward at the top of the stairs and tripped her. Jennifer crashed headfirst into the bathroom's skirting. Dazed, she rolled over and parried a direct thrust, just in time. She grabbed Ann's weapon hand and wedged her foot against the bannister for extra leverage as the two struggled.

Jennifer forced herself back on to her front and pushed up from her knees. She slammed Ann's arm to the floor. Ann jabbed her in the ribs again and again, but Jennifer maintained her grip.

Ann shuffled herself around and leaned all her weight against the teenager. Pressed between her and the staircase wall, Jennifer battled for control of the knife. Her grip slid, and Ann bashed repeatedly with her spare hand until she got free. She sent another elbow straight into Jennifer's chin.

Dazed, Jennifer tried to break, but Ann chopped her in the throat and sent her flying backwards.

Her stepmother hadn't finished with her yet. She stamped on her out-turned right foot. Jennifer screamed and rolled backward, sprawled face-down on the floor. Jennifer swiped at the back of Ann's ankle. On contact, she grabbed it and pulled. Now they were both off their feet.

She received a kick for her trouble. She had made it close enough to the door to scramble for it and turn the knob . . . locked! Jennifer fumbled for her keys. Ann closed in. Jennifer threw a solid jab straight into Ann's nose.

"You little bitch!" Ann cried, holding her nose with her free hand. "I should have smothered you with a pillow when I had the chance." Jennifer punched her again, this time square in the gut, which bent her enemy forward and shut her up at the same time. She grabbed Ann's hair and back of her neck and rammed her head into the corridor wall twice. She then seized the knife for herself and pushed the sharp end to Ann's throat.

"Sit there. SIT THERE!" Jennifer spat. The knife wobbled in her hand as she held it. Her enemy flinched with each twitch. "You killed my dad! I'm calling the police."

"Coward."

Jennifer leaned forward. "What did you say?"

Ann slowly wiped a trickle of blood from her mouth. "I said, you're a coward. Perfect chance to get rid of me and you ask me to sit here while you call the police. Look at the state of me. And the one thing you had on me is in your hands. Covered in your dad's blood. It's just your word against mine. And I'll plead self-defence all day long against the known junior maniac. You silly girl."

No, no, no!

"Don't try and scare me," Jennifer protested, but her voice wavered as she reached for the telephone handset on the table behind her.

"I already have, haven't I?" Ann grinned triumphantly. "Make the call. I dare you. See how much worse this gets for you. What will you do, eh? Tell them I did it? I'll just tell them how you meant to finish the job with Charlotte earlier. I'll tell them how you lost your temper with your dad. Then with me. You won't end up in Borstal by the time they're done. You'll end up somewhere you'll never see the light of day. And it couldn't happen to a nicer girl."

"Why do you have it in for me so much?" Jennifer's hand wobbled, her control over the weapon minimal. She did not get her answer. Ann lunged at her in an attempt to rearm herself. Without thinking, Jennifer dodged sideways and thrust the knife directly into the centre of her stepmother's chest. She leapt back with a squeal as Ann fell backward and cracked the back of her head against the wall, and then slumped forward, driving the knife deeper.

"Ann? ANN!" No response.

Trembling, Jennifer crouched to check Ann's breathing. Blood ran from both sides of the body. But she raced to her father in the kitchen, desperate for a pulse, for life, for anything. There had to still be some hope.

But not one. That woman had seen to that. His final expression was one of struggle, perhaps fitting, but no help to Jennifer, no comfort whatsoever. Her eyes glazed as tears fell, and didn't stop falling. She could hear herself wailing, but it sounded miles away.

She didn't know how long she had been there by the time she composed herself again. But her first action was to straighten her father's face. She couldn't leave him like that, she just couldn't.

This wasn't the plan. Not at all. Things just got worse with every step. She glanced at her arm and twitched. The knife wound had gone. She suddenly felt nauseous as the whole, nasty mess just rendered itself incredibly difficult to explain.

As for the rest of this mess, where to start? Someone nearby must have heard at least some of what had taken place in the house. It was just a matter of time before they caught up with her. And though Ann Malone would never bother her again, she was absolutely right. Given the earlier events of the day, blame would only be attributed to one person—the only one still breathing.

She stood up, still sobbing, and went back to the front door. With unsteady hands she unlocked it, took a good look around and then stepped out, sure to close and lock it again behind her. She wandered, head down, until she cleared the street, and then ran.

She would not stop running any time before she reached the one place she could go safely. The one person she could talk to. Prayed she could trust.

~*~

Jennifer had cleared town and reached the nearest remaining forest. That was where she'd been told to seek out her enigmatic ally. If she had followed a false trail, she was doomed. "Alice?" she cried, in the hope the one person she needed to could hear her. "Alice, are you there?" But to no avail. No answer came.

When she stopped calling, she stood alone for some time, surrounded by silence—other than the wildlife and the distant sounds of passing traffic in the night.

Now what?

With nowhere to go, she sat, legs crossed, in the middle of the small wood and rocked back and forth.

And then, the trees rustled without the slightest breeze. She felt a tap on her shoulder. She turned around, but nobody stood behind her. She checked both sides, in case someone was playing tricks. Not that she was in the mood.

But when she turned back, Alice stood in front of her, and reached down to stroke her head. "Lovely to see you, Jennifer."

Jennifer stood up and threw her arms around Alice, sobbing uncontrollably. Alice held her and squeezed tight. "Something wrong?"

"I don't know what to do, Alice, I-I-I—"

"Tell me what's happened. Whatever it is, we'll fix it."

"You can't!"

"Then why did you come to me?" Alice sounded surprisingly cold. "You must have thought I'd be able to do something . . ."

"I-I've nowhere else to go," she blubbered. "Not now."

Alice drew Jennifer off her, but held the top of her arms. "Look at me." Jennifer obliged through tear-glazed eyes. "That sounds serious. Tell me what happened. Leave nothing out."

Though initially reluctant, there seemed little option. For some reason, she had a feeling lying to Alice would be ineffective at best. At worst, she risked losing the trust of the one person she could. But on the other hand, Alice would probably find her actions so reprehensible that she would have turned her in herself. She had already started to blub the truth even as she thought about it, though.

When she had finished, she went to run, but Alice raised a hand and she stopped still. Alice looked blank, distant, but Jennifer dared not move. After a moment, Alice rose, and then turned to face her once more, calm as could be. Jennifer shuddered in fear of her anticipated words.

"I'm sorry about your father," she said in a quiet, level voice. "Though I am pleased to see you finally broke free of your cycle."

"What?"

"You recognised wrong in your life and chose to do something about it."

"I didn't *mean* to kill her!" Jennifer screamed. Then she realised how loudly and looked around.

"Nonetheless, it's true that this won't look good for you. You shall have to permanently disappear."

Jennifer looked at her in horror. She gave a slow nod in acknowledgement. "Jennifer, you are protected from harm in ways you probably don't understand. When we have managed the situation, I will help you to utilise that same talent in other ways."

She still didn't understand. "You-you're telling me I have to go back? To that house?"

Alice contemplated for a moment. "On the contrary, it is time to leave. For good. The authorities find the recently deceased problematic. You will never need to revisit your old life again. I promise you that."

Jennifer of course agreed with little hesitation. "Thank you!"

Alice gave a thin smile. "Oh, do not thank me. You may not like my price. But I suppose it won't be your worst option, all things considered."

CHAPTER NINETEEN

Jennifer had no light around her, no air to breathe, no freedom of movement. The taste of dirt trickled into her lips. The memory, as vivid as if it had just happened, receded and her attention returned in full to her immediate issue—being buried alive. Though she couldn't breathe, she could feel her fingers, stinging at the tips. She retained some movement, however minimal. A few waggles and she could also feel dry dirt scrabbling away. Nothing else moved. She kept moving her hands, clawed at the dirt, *fought for her life.*

Because that was all she knew.

She started at the shoulders, pushed and pushed until the mound around her arms loosened. She inhaled dirt and choked it back out, the earth sliding back into place to hold her still. Her eyes watered as specks rained down on her face. No air. Little time. She forced her will into shaping her hands, still low from her suspended crouch, into familiar razor fingers. *No, digging is better.* She made them thicker, tougher, more crab-like and then clamped and scraped until dirt began to give way. With more movement available, she began to batter her arms clear, then eventually, her way out.

Her lungs begged for air, as did her limbs. She continued to wrestle with the soil until enough of it came loose to allow for full torso movement. With free arms came a gap above her head. She took a huge breath, then seized upon blessed leverage. She retracted her reinforced appendages and pushed down, shoved herself upwards out of the earth. Finally, she could see the surface.

The sweltering jungle awaited her. There stood the lifelike construct of Alice, the Primal Essence. It offered a nod of acknowledgement, and then walked over. It lifted a foot and wedged it on Jennifer's fingers, to pin but not to crush. Instead, it looked down at her. "That day made you what you are. And yet, that day holds you back even now."

"I-I could have saved him . . ." Jennifer whimpered. Her eyes welled just as they had when she'd been fifteen years old. "I left him alone for an hour and she murdered him."

"Did you anticipate that happening?" The foot pressed down with crushing force.

"No!" Jennifer protested. "She was violent, sure, but I didn't think she'd kill anyone."

"But she did. And not only that, she tried to kill you. She even considered doing it sooner. You weren't to know any of that until you forced her to reveal it."

"That's no reason for me to kill her."

"You had *every* reason." The foot pressed harder. Jennifer winced. If the pressure continued, bone would pop soon enough. "She murdered your father, then attacked you."

"I'm not a murderer!" Jennifer grasped the attacking leg with her free hand, but it would not budge.

"Nobody is calling you one." The Essence reached down and slapped her weak grip away. "Except you. And you continue to blame yourself for an act of self-defence against a threat more immediate to you than any others you faced up until then. This is unworthy of you.

"You acted on instinct. You saved yourself and rid your world of one who would have undoubtedly killed again and again had she got away with your murder. Had you died, think what good would not have been accomplished because you weren't there to do it.

"And *still* you hold back, even when you oppose those who have destroyed dozens, and if you allow them, will destroy a great many more. Think on your good deeds and stop punishing yourself for circumstances beyond your control.

"*Think*! Who lives today because you were around to protect them?"

She thought. *Kara. Mary.* And with those two, thousands of London's denizens, unaware of the peril they faced in the summer of 2012. Jennifer's mind moved to answer the Essence's question before she had time to deny herself more. That police constable she told to run for help. Several other innocent bystanders to increasing evil in the world. She hadn't been a dead loss at all. As she stopped crying and looked up, the Essence removed the offending foot. Jennifer flapped her hand and winced. It smiled.

"Good. Then you understand. I cannot afford a cold-blooded murderer acting for me. However, by necessity, you may find yourself required to kill once more. I need neither a callous soul nor one shackled by needless guilt. Jennifer Winter, you could be as great as the Face of War whose image you chose. As I said, I find it interesting that you opted for that form."

"I changed my face so I could avoid justice. Nothing more."

"You haven't avoided justice. The burdens you bear are penance enough. Mortal authorities, just as Alice spoke of when you first turned to her, are not adequate. Not for you. But maintain your healthy respect for them. Rise, Jennifer Winter. Take what you came here for."

"I came here to escape bad people trying to kill me. It was looking pretty rough out there."

"Do you plan to stay in here and wait until they go away, then?"

"'Course not. I just needed to regroup so I can deal with them on my terms."

The Essence nodded in approval. "Good. A warrior of the mind as well as of the body. I need the services of the likes of you. Will you accept?"

Jennifer raised her eyebrows. "Depends. What am I accepting, exactly? Am I taking Alice's place?"

The Essence shook its head. It looked somewhat sad. "She wanted you to act alongside her. It is unfortunate that the opportunity no longer exists."

"So, what was she, if not a Champion?"

The construct frowned, and then raised its hands. As it did, roots and vines emerged and twisted, until two new seats formed. It sat upon one and beckoned for Jennifer to sit on the other. Though she didn't trust the opportunity for further tests or assaults, she felt the entity had learned everything it was going to about her and indulged it by making herself comfortable. Looking satisfied, it continued.

"In the past, mortals have chosen, for their own ease, to borrow power from this place in one of two basic methods. One such as you, who cannot help but fight, can do so with my blessing. Your most suitable path is one more of instinct and less of study. Alice wanted to know everything about the Primal world and was prepared to dedicate time to doing so—time, which you no doubt feel you do not have. However, you have earned the right to choose her path instead, should you so desire."

Jennifer looked pensive. She'd seen Alice do so *little,* but never doubted the power behind that approachable exterior. Alice had made her a promise: that she would help her to learn of herself and her powers, but spent a lot of time away. That raised a mental note: she never actually said where. "What did she do for you, exactly?"

"She called herself a 'Primal Traveller', as had some who stood before her. She told me she was no Champion."

"But what's the difference between the two?"

The Essence shrugged. "I claim no responsibility for these names. It is your kind who insist upon labels for everything."

Jennifer immediately thought of Kara, who very much fitted that profile. She did have legitimate research reasons and knowing potential allies and enemies, and their talents had undoubted appeal. But for Jennifer, a long way out of her comfort zone, more practical information took priority.

"I take it that all the weird things Alice showed me I could do came from here?" she asked.

"Weird?" The Essence looked confused.

"Sorry. I meant . . ." She raised her hands and stared at them, felt the tickle as she summoned their razor-like form. With only a fraction of the effort that she had ever exerted, she shifted the remainder of her body into a more golden, bark-like protective skin covering. Though she couldn't see it, she knew her eyes became a cat-like yellow and her hair shortened and bobbled until it became a knot of brambles. "This is not usual for most *mortals*, as you put it. None of this. From what you said, it was Alice who brought it out of me."

The Alice avatar smiled, and spread its arms wide. The tattoo-like coils swirled and shifted once more, and then the construct itself emulated Jennifer's body alterations as if a mystic mirror. It retained Alice's face, however.

"Ah. I see. You wish to know how you can alter your form so. Well, from your birth, Alice knew of you. A friend of hers died just moments before she arrived, and Alice could not save him. She overheard some others speaking of your survival. It impressed her so much, she chose to watch you. To see how you developed. She had hopes for you, but insisted that she would not interfere. rather, she would wait until you grew mature enough to make difficult decisions for yourself.

"She sensed that trouble constantly gathered around you. I agreed. It seemed a waste that you had come so far only to run into mishap. Hence, I agreed with Alice that the endurance you demonstrated reflected accurately of you. I heard you say that if you were to fall, someone would have to work for it. So, I made them do so. Just as the talents that I have only bestowed upon a Primal Champion before, other gifts lay latent within you, too. The skills of many mortal warriors over their lifetimes became yours to learn, or more truthfully, remember."

Jennifer froze as she took in everything the Primal Essence had said. It made as much sense as if she had always known. "So, is that how I've been able to fight since . . . well, the time I first got into a proper fight?"

"Yes. The gift Alice asked me to grant you ensures you are in a position of strength when dealing with your kind. She survived long enough to teach you how to communicate with me, too, from your own lands."

"Yeah, she said she meant to teach me a lot more, but I had to wait until my eighteenth birthday or something. Oh. That's what you were telling me, wasn't it? Oh, I should have paid more attention to what she was saying to me. She said on that birthday, she was going to take me to—oh, of course. *Now* that all makes sense. She never did come back after the note . . ."

Her head bowed, her thoughts focused on all Alice's promises and learning. Though she had long ago formed a guess on the answer to what remained on her mind, the question remained necessary. "Essence, exactly what happened to Alice?"

"The best way for me to answer your question is through her eyes." The Essence reverted to the less armed and armoured form it had when Jennifer first witnessed the avatar. Its eyes rolled and spun like fruit machine reels, until they stopped once more on one image: that of Alice cowering from an unseen person or thing.

"I will show you the last thing she witnessed. From what she has told me of such, your experience may feel stronger than memory. It may closer resemble . . . experience."

The image of Alice froze, and as Jennifer stared at it, the petrified snapshot grew larger, closer, tried to swallow her. She had nowhere to go. The clearing around her blurred as if rushing towards her, then vanished entirely into a dizzying spectrum of light and colour.

~ * ~

Jennifer found herself back in the vast Primal Forest. She looked back and could see nothing, but knew something which did not belong to that world shifted in the bushes. She ran, left with little choice. She could've probably handled one of them. Two were a dangerous proposition. Certainly these two, anyway.

She turned forward to watch her footing as she fled through her planned escape route. They were quick, the both of them, much quicker than she had hoped. She hadn't even time to summon a trap in the ground or call one of the dwellers of the territory to her aid. There hadn't been time for anything that day, not even to give a proper explanation to the girl.

They'd found her, had tracked her for some time. She had to stay at least long enough to be sure they were focused on their target, nobody else. But there just hadn't been *time*. There'd barely been enough time to scrawl the note for the girl.

If she lived long enough, she'd at least check in on the contact she'd been given. This 'Kara Mellencourt' person who knew nothing of her soon-to-be ward. Things were safer for the both of them that way. Oh, she was loathe to leave the girl with a total stranger she'd met all of once, but there had been no choice. No *time.*

A blade which could cut through anything on the mortal plane. Another she knew to be equally dangerous, but not why. Her pursuers were armed with both of these things. And her? A pointless bit of wood in comparison. At least the ghost walker could not live up to that title in these lands. But it meant little when dealing with decades of martial practice and other unknown talents.

So, Alice ran, fast and hard, and used the one other advantage she had: the territory. Answering her will, the leaves and vines below skittered across the ground behind her and bound together, reformed and repositioned in an effort to confound, to trip and to tangle. She indulged herself another look behind.

The assassin in the grey cloak hewed and hacked her way through every trap she laid. The other one, the brunette, too exquisitely attired for deadly pursuit, appeared to walk briskly behind the bludgeon in front of her. Alice's improvised traps simply turned aside for that lady. The cloaked assassin leapt and made short work of the distance between them. No point running now. She'd have to stop and make her stand.

She shifted forward and ferociously twirled the quarterstaff in an effort to force her opponent on the defensive. Against another opponent the move may have gained her a few steps, but the killer remembered her crucial advantage. The onyx blade sliced through the wood as if it wasn't there, and Alice, no fighter herself, had no chance against the lightning-fast roundhouse kick which followed.

Though floored and dazed, she still had a few tricks left. She scooped up a handful of dirt and called upon the Primal Essence in one of its more common names to mortals. She flung the contents at her enemy and the debris multiplied in content and speed. It was as if she had launched a boulder from a siege engine as the blast threw her opponent backward, but not off-balance. The sword fighter rolled away from them and stopped on one knee, poised for another attack.

Before Alice could prepare to receive the charge, a deafening high-pitched whistle assaulted her eardrums, and the air itself seemed to hit her as if she'd been hit by a swung brick. She fell flat on her face.

Alice rolled on to her back. No sooner had she done so, when a jagged heel rammed straight through her windpipe. The well-dressed brunette smirked through pretty lips as she removed her boot and watched Alice choke on her own blood. She gasped for air which did not come. As her vision blurred, she attempted to channel her mind into one last effort of healing, a little more fight.

She felt a sensation in her stomach colder than any she had experienced in her 103 years of life. The cold ran through the rest of her body and seized everything, almost agony enough to make her forget about her other wound. A spasm jerked her head involuntarily forward. It allowed her to see the faceless killer squeeze a blood red jewel on the hilt of the blackened blade.

She let out an ear-shredding scream as she felt herself pulled closer to the sword. It rapidly went dark and with a pain such that death would have been preferable. Death happened anyway. It just took so very long.

~*~

Jennifer lunged forward until on all-fours and felt the same agonising, inhuman chill she had experienced when the entity calling itself Violet forced those needle-like fingers into her. She knew what it was that Alice had felt before her death at the hands of the Grey Lady and this *other*, but lived it again nonetheless. Her veins, crackled black, shot to the forefront of her skin, now reverted to its most fragile form. She felt a void in her stomach, a fresh, agonising wound. She reached to check. It felt intact. She fell to the ground and tried to scream, but only foam escaped her mouth.

Then, Alice—no, the Primal Essence—reached out and touched her with a warm, medicinal hand. The veins receded, the stomach eased, the pain, gone. What she had seen though, would remain with her forever. Now she had some idea of what Mary had endured. "Don't ever make me do that again." She took rapid, shallow breaths.

"I never *made* you do anything," the Essence retorted. But then it pulled Jennifer by the hand until she stood next to the construct. It looked about to say something, but instead snapped its head to the right and stared. Jennifer found she had done likewise before she really thought about it.

The ground shook. Jennifer saw the tips of trees shudder and fall. A series of sickening shrieks followed.

"That's not her. . ."

"That's not *who*?" Jennifer asked. The rapid pounding continued, a stampede perhaps. She could not see the cause.

The construct looked fearful. "One mortal has gained power enough to enter and travel my land freely, no matter what I use to oppose. But something else threatens us. An ancient force of destruction."

Jennifer looked at the Essence, then back to the disrupted jungle. "I'm guessing you're a few years older than me. And that anything you call ancient has to be something to worry about."

"It's fortunate, then, that there is a Champion to defend my territory, yes?"

Jennifer gave a loud sigh.

CHAPTER TWENTY

Jennifer ventured into the heart of the jungle, the hopes of the Primal Essence seemingly pinned on her success. She thought it might have been yet another test, but given the power she knew the entity to possess, and the fact she sensed genuine terror from it, she braced herself for a tough gig.

"Invasion!" it had cried, whilst ushering her toward the source. Another treacherous mission, then, but she did agree to take the Primal Queen's shilling, figuratively speaking, and had been doing so for quite some time without ever knowing what it had all been about. *Time to earn your pay.*

She shimmied up the tallest palm tree she could find along the path of destruction, careful to steady herself every time the ground shook. She assumed it related to enemy movement.

First impressions: flat ground and stumps where dense jungle forestry once stood. An awful reek of death, sulphur and burnt flesh. Plumes of heavy smoke. The place looked like a war zone, quite literally as if a bomb had just hit it. But that was impossible. Nothing about that matched anything she had seen. And then there were the screams. High-pitched shrieks, to be sure, but no evidence of where they originated. Even with that vantage, little seemed clear.

Another shriek. She listened and turned to triangulate the origins of the noise. *Over there.*

There came a *whoomph,* followed by more screams as she saw a dark cloud ahead in the undergrowth—not of smoke but a strange fire. The shriek grew louder, the beat of heavy stomps faster. The enemy was running.

Jennifer crouched, armed with two bone blades she had pulled from her own back, and poised to leap just as soon as the wretch came into sight. A hideous shadow scuttled across the ground, humanoid, barely. Monstrous, certainly. It carried a short, sharp pointed weapon as it bashed its way into her visual range.

The beast writhed and staggered. It appeared to struggle, its movement aggravated. It clawed at its eyes, as if they had been attacked and damaged. As it came through the smoke, she spotted something slung over its shoulder. Or *someone.*

She leapt down at the creature. It moved with surprising agility and took a defensive swipe with a club-like fist. The beast stamped on the ground, but Jennifer, well-prepared, threw herself into a flying back-flip.

To her surprise, the creature didn't press its attack. Instead, it placed its captive down and spread its wings. Thick, black smoke escaped its wide nostrils, and the beast snarled. It opened its mouth and launched a blast of pure black fire at her.

Still light on her feet, Jennifer leapt into a roll to her right and ran forward. She leapt toward a tree, shoved it with her foot and launched into a flying whirlwind of spinning talons. It blocked her assaults with reflective, chitinous arms, and shoved her backward and to the ground.

She rolled back to her feet on impact. The beast flapped its wings and leapt with power at her. She evaded just in time as its leading foot came down with a thunderous crunch. It swung with claws of its own. She ducked to avoid instant decapitation.

"Hey!"

Kara's voice came through the smoke behind them. Her silhouette emerged just a second later. "Stay away from my friend!"

"Your *friend?*" Jennifer backed off, her gaze remaining firmly upon the creature. "Kara, when did you have time to make a friend out of *him?* Also, monster here to deal with." A thought nagged her. She had just heard Kara's voice. Inside the realm.

"How did you—? Essence, if this is another trick, we're having words."

"Essence?" the creature grumbled. "What are you—wait a minute . . . Jen?"

It gaped at Jennifer. She managed to discern a look of real surprise on its face. But she doubted it compared to her own surprise when she realised she recognised the creature's voice. "*Mary?* What the hell?"

It retracted its wings. "*Jen?*" The creature took a step back and stood next to Kara. Jennifer leaned forward, but held her ground, hesitant. "My, but you look different."

Jennifer relaxed entirely, then shot Mary a quizzical glance. "Says you." The flesh around Mary's pointed teeth curved into a grin. Jennifer shuddered. "What are you two doing here? And how did you find me?"

"Thought we'd come looking for you," Mary answered. "You've been gone a while."

Jennifer acknowledged the statement with a nod, but then her attention turned to the unconscious figure on the ground. She snarled and sheathed her bone knives with the aid of a broken vine, then marched across to him. She lifted him by his chin.

"Why is this scumbag with you?" she demanded.

"You know him?" Kara stepped closer.

"They sent him through to kill you," Mary added.

Jennifer blinked her chromatic vision active. Vortext appeared almost as an outline, only the glow around him that she noticed when he was in the presence of Cerise made him visible at all. Disconcerting as that seemed, she also couldn't help but notice that Mary appeared as an imposing shadow. The land she stood upon appeared ailed, dry and dying. Nearby trees rotted from the inside. It was little wonder that Mary proved able to bash them aside with such ease.

She returned to her conventional sight, bewildered and uncertain which question to ask first. She slapped Vortext around the face. As he stirred, she transformed the same hand into a weapon.

"Start talking, and fast," she growled. "You're an oracle; tell me who or what I'm dealing with."

"*We* are dealing with," Kara imposed. Jennifer ignored her.

Vortext squirmed in her hand. He stopped when she drew him closer to her razor talons. "Don't hurt me!" he pleaded. "Who are you talking about?"

She examined him, saw abject terror in his eyes. "Your chums in Manta's court."

"Manta?" Kara intervened.

"Shut up, Kara!" Mary snapped.

"Who's Manta?" Vortext asked, almost an echo of Kara.

Jennifer glared at him for a moment, then let him drop to the ground. She still led with her taloned hand. "How could you not know that?"

His face contorted, his eyes darting all around. "I do know—I did know . . . I-I don't know, I can't even think straight. Where am I?"

A more reasonable query, but still not consistent with Mary's earlier warning. "Okay. Let's start with something simple. *Who* are you?"

His face once more stretched in many directions. He scratched his head and then bashed at it with his hand. "Damn it! How can I not remember my own name?"

"You have until I count to three."

"Wait, Jen." Mary's mighty form cast a shadow over her and held a hand in front of her. "I'm fairly sure he's telling the truth. When we first met, I couldn't remember my own name. I know the signs."

"It's taking me all the concentration I have just to talk right now," Vortext said, through narrowed eyes. "My name. It's Antoine." He tapped his head for several seconds. "Antoine Vincent."

"So, why did they call you Vortext?"

He tilted his head and looked upward. "An old online name I had. Ugh, this is so strange. I feel like I've been looking at everything through smoked glass since . . . I don't even know when." His eyes widened and he scrambled backward, sobbing. "What the hell happened to me?"

Kara stared down at him. "Now, I'm sure he's telling the truth as well. That or he's the greatest actor I've ever met. And if he is, we can just set Mary on him and she'll have the truth out of him in a jiffy."

"I'm telling you the truth!" he screamed. "What I, what I, wh—I can't even speak." He took a deep breath and started again. "What I know, I'll tell you. Know . . . what I know, I knew lots. All the time. Didn't even know what half of what I knew was most of the time."

"You're babbling," Jennifer scowled.

"Yes, I am! And it's wonderful! My own words. Not someone or something else's."

Jennifer retracted her talons. She thought back to her initial observations at Manta's stolen chateau. The aura that surrounded him encircled the redheaded woman who clearly wasn't his partner. "She was controlling you, wasn't she?" Jennifer asked, her voice more gentle than it had been in a while. "This Cerise person."

Antoine looked pensive. "Her name was Cerise Favager. She was a nurse I met in a nightclub, I remember now. I had a DJ slot for a couple of hours that night and I saw her dancing with her friends. I couldn't take my eyes off her. I went to talk to her for a while, but she wasn't too interested, so I went back to my set. But a week later, she turned up at my apartment door. The last thing I remember was that she had red hair that time. It was blue when I first saw her."

"People like a change from time to time," Kara remarked. "But a bottle of hair dye isn't usually also life-changing. Especially not for someone else."

"Manta's the name of the guy she worked for," Jennifer stated. "They all worked for him. The ghost walker, you, Vortex—I mean, Antoine—and Cerise. And a small, heavily armed squad of mercenaries. He had a 'court' around him. You were part of it." She looked at Antoine. "Actually, you kind of saved my life. 'The Face of War' mean anything to you?"

He picked himself up. "I have no idea what you're ta—" But then he stopped. "Wait a minute—yes, I do. They fear you, the Consanguinity. There's something big planned." He blinked several times. "Consanguinity? Who? How do I know all this?"

Kara frowned. "So, she's had you under the thumb in a literal and unnatural sense all this time? And Jen, you said something about a link between the two of them."

"You're wondering if it goes both ways?" Mary concluded. "Like myself and Tally, kind of?"

"That's exactly what I was thinking," Kara replied.

Jennifer nodded. "It's possible. That can't have been an overnight trick Cerise tried to pull." She thought back on her last words and twitched. "She tried to get a hold of me while I was out cold, too. I caught a trace. I'm not exactly sure what stopped her, but I think she saw what took me out of action last year."

"Your fight with Violet?" Mary's ears tweaked upwards. "Her attempt to devour you from the soul outwards? Yep—that'd traumatise any poor sod unlucky enough to relive it. Good to see you looking so much better, by the way."

Jennifer opened her mouth to answer, but at the same time, the ground shuddered. From a point behind them, the land warped and scenery shifted and rose into a familiar-looking dais—the throne of the Primal Essence. From a mound of jungle in the centre, the construct reformed into the Alice shape. It sat, looking apprehensive, on the living throne. On either side of the throne stood two columns, both a hybrid of wood and vine. At the top of each, maws resembling Venus flytraps stood open, watching as the two marched in, Kara in tow.

"Why haven't you destroyed the threat?" the construct asked, an air of desperation in the voice.

Jennifer stopped and examined the expanded throne and the construct's expression, confused for a moment, but quickly remembered why she had been sent.

"I believe the threat you were talking about . . . isn't," Jennifer answered. "The real problem lies elsewhere." She turned to Antoine and tapped at the makeshift hilts of her bone blades. "Don't move, or do anything stupid. It'll go really badly for you." She then looked over to the Essence, who raised her hand. Vines shuffled around him. Mary stared down at him, too. The look on his face told Jennifer that he believed her.

She turned to Mary and whispered. "Follow my lead." The giant gave a small shrug, but then an equally discreet nod. Jennifer slowly advanced three steps, bent to one knee, and lowered her head. Mary immediately did likewise. Without looking, Jennifer could already sense confusion from the source of her powers. She took a deep, calm breath and placed a palm firmly on the ground. "Primal Essence, you are in no danger here." She pointed at Mary, who gave a low growl. Jennifer remained unsure as to whether it was intentional. "This is Lady Mary Grenshall, Guardian of the Unresting Gate."

"Then what is she doing so far away from her lands?" demanded the construct.

"She stands at my side, Primal Essence. And has done every day since I met her."

A moment of silence passed before the construct spoke once more. "What do you mean?"

Jennifer looked up and faced the puppet. "The creature you see before you does not appear so on my world. Mary, and Kara with her, are the bravest human beings I've ever met. Kara rescued me long before I knew who I was. And Mary?" She turned to her friend with a tearful eye and placed a hand on her snout.

"When I fought alongside her, I fell. But she refused to abandon me. She sat with me daily, told me stories, sang songs, made clothes, did anything she could to keep me company, keep me from giving up. She did this for almost a year. That's a long time for one of my kind. And she—*they*—came in here, not to make war, but because they thought I might be in trouble. They came to rescue me.

"They risked everything in here to do so. Kara hasn't got a Primal Gift, nor the protection of the Unresting. She's just a regular human. And she came for me."

The construct looked pensive, but after a moment stood and spread its arms out wide, then lowered its hands. At this, the columns rumbled, then descended back into the ground, unravelling as they did. The throne also slowly came apart, curling into the ground like roots of trees. Then the facsimile took languid steps off the dais and stopped just in front of Mary.

The construct looked over to Kara, who smiled back. "Just a regular human?" it repeated. "Don't be so sure." The construct became as one with the branches and dissipated, returning to the earth from whence they rose.

Jennifer reached for Kara and gave her a warm hug. "Right," she replied before they separated. "Now, I'd like to know what you two crazy idiots were thinking, coming in here after me."

In perfect synchronisation, Mary and Kara looked at each other and broke into the familiar refrain of the song they whistled when they first stepped through the gate. Then Kara stopped and glared at Jennifer. "What were *you* thinking running off into certain danger nowhere near fully fit without us?"

"I knew what I was doing."

"Sure looks like it," Mary muttered. "Okay, then, smartarse, how are we getting out of here?"

Jennifer scratched her head. "Same way we came in, I imagine."

The ground crackled nearby, once more roots and branches taking form. The familiar creation of the Alice facsimile came together in seconds. Behind it, an archway, much like the one Jennifer came through to get to that treacherous world in the first place. She stood upright, chest puffed outwards. "See?"

"So, we haven't been introduced," Kara called to Jennifer, pointing to the artificial human.

"Kara, this is Al—" She stopped herself with a shudder. "Kara, this is the Primal Essence. At least, a part of it." She swept her arms around, spinning herself in a full circle. "*This* is the Primal Essence. It's just trying to be accommodating."

"Aww, how sweet—" Kara started, but Mary spoke over her.

"Ah, good. Maybe you can tell me what was going on with the flayed bodies in the glade."

The Essence frowned. "You don't know?"

"I wouldn't have asked if I did, would I?" Mary snarled, extending her wings. The construct took a hasty step back, which raised Jennifer's eyebrows.

"Easy, Mary," she said. "I don't know what you're talking about, but the Essence is definitely telling the truth."

Mary gave a begrudging nod and retreated to a crouch. "I'm sorry. Look, I believe you. It's just what I saw was nothing short of grim. It felt like something from my world."

"As I thought," it said.

"Hence your reaction," Kara inferred.

"I take it that is as much a blight on your lands as it appears to me?" Mary asked.

"A disease," it answered. "I have had an invader. She carries powerful tools, and even I cannot stop her. Him—" It pointed back at Antoine. "—I could not see him, until you slowed him. Does he work for her?"

"Couldn't see him?"

The construct nodded. "Your friend, Mary, I can sense anywhere. As easily as you. Your friend, Kara, I can see, as a traveller from your lands. I can see him now, but I could not before."

"I couldn't see myself before," Antoine hollered. Jennifer turned to deal with a potential threat, but the other three all nodded.

"That'll have been about the time he wasn't running off his own steam, right?" Kara observed.

Jennifer agreed. "It will have been. So, tell us—this invader. Red hair, shorter than me, necklace, and a nasty knife?"

The facsimile of Alice looked blank, then contorted its face. "Not all the time. The last few times. Before, she looked very different. And different again the time before."

Jennifer held her hands to her face. "So, it sounds like Cerise, but either there's more than one of them, or—" Her recent memory prompted her again. "You said you can see Mary anywhere in here. The Grey Lady, the cloaked person you showed me in your memory. You can see her easily, too, yes?"

The construct nodded firmly enough that Jennifer thought its head would snap off. "Yes, I cannot miss her. More than anyone who has stepped through the gate."

"And the dark-haired woman with her when they murdered Alice."

"The same invader."

Jennifer sighed, almost a hiss. "Then she can change her appearance. Great."

Mary pounded a fist into her palm. "Well, she's screwing around with business on my turf. So, Primal Essence, even if Jen hadn't been here, you'd have my help. I made a promise. I'm keeping to it, no matter where that takes me."

The construct sat, legs crossed, and rocked forward in a nod. "The being comes here to dump the bodies. Whatever has been done to them has happened before they are placed here."

"I saw them. They had no souls about them, as far as I could tell," Mary added. "But then, I've had trouble with that sight since I've been here." Mary flapped her wings in protest. "Maybe it's this form. Hey, why do I appear like this here anyway?"

"You will forgive me," it responded, "but I have met none from the world which you protect. That world in which nothing lives. Only some of those who have travelled there. Tell me: how is it you, mortal, have survived that place?"

"There are certain perks to becoming a Guardian," Mary said with a worried look. "But I can normally stand between worlds, if you know what I mean. 'Ghost walking', we've called it."

"No ghosts walk here," the Essence stated absolutely. "This is no place for the dead."

"Then you've answered half of my question," Mary said with a nod. "The Unresting world is comprised of billions of them. Ghosts and undead, I mean. Some of them retain their sentience, others are just basically dust. They are the usual source of my power, as you are Jen's, but if they're not here . . ."

". . . that would suggest that you have been powered some other way . . ." Kara chimed in. "So, am I correct in hypothesising that Mary has been powered by Primal realm energies as opposed to Unresting here, if the connection is limited, or even severed?"

The Primal Essence once more looked blank.

Mary's eyes widened. "Well, that kind of explains something. See, some of the stuff I've been doing here, like the extra strength and that death fire—usually stuff I avoid doing like the plague. I had to defend myself, Kara, with everything I had. Not exactly fine control on that kind of attack, so I'm afraid I broke a few more things without meaning to. I only blasted those monster flies with that flame in the first place by accident. What I was trying to do was make us both vanish. But of course, I found out the hard way that I can't sidestep like that here. So, *that* happened instead.

"Also, the super-strength thing? Usually powered by souls. Found this out way before I went full-time." She turned to Kara. "About when

I accidentally almost ate you, actually. And it usually drains the hell out of me. Here, I can do it all day."

"You basically hit battle mode the minute you got here," Jennifer concluded.

"Maybe, but why do I look like this, with the wings and all?"

"I thought all of your dead were like this?" the Essence queried. "Somewhere within you or your memories, the image came to me."

"*My* memories?" Mary looked horrified. But she soon scratched her head. "Ah. If you were rooting around my brain, you'll have seen quite a few that don't belong to me. Like Tally's." She put a huge hand to her mouth. "Every day, I learn more about how my inheritance works. And every day, I remember what this inheritance means.

"It's quite cool running around like this here, but I can't back home. I can't look like this, and more to the point I can't *be* this. Because the moment I forget is the moment I have a chance of being one of those people who plague the existence of others. And then I really would be as dangerous as you assumed, Primal Essence. It mustn't happen; not now, not ever."

The construct stood and moved slowly towards Mary. Then it stretched. Its legs extended to match Mary's height. It leaned forward and pressed its lips to Mary's snout, before reverting to its original size. It then moved to Kara and kissed her on the forehead. "Lady Mary Grenshall, Guardian of the Gate, it appears I have misjudged you. Should you come again, you shall pass through my domain without challenge. I will recognise your presence. And you may choose the form, Guardian, in which you choose to manifest."

She turned to Jennifer and smiled. "And Jennifer, you have always had that welcome. You chose your skin once, chose a battle form, but you limited yourself. You are capable of so much more." It pointed at

Mary. Within seconds, Mary shrank, her mass reduced significantly and her armoured chitin altered to the pale tones more familiar to her.

"Oh, that's better!" Mary remarked as she stretched. "I might hang on to the wings, though." Even as she said it, the wings on her back did not vanish; they instead shrank in proportion to their owner. "And if I catch the bastards wrecking your place, I promise you they'll live to regret it."

The Alice resemblance appeared satisfied. "I'm sure they will."

"Assuming that is our gate home," Kara said, pointing, "we should be on our way. If nothing else, I'm hoping twenty-five years haven't passed back on our world while we've been away."

"Kara," Jennifer glowered. "We're not in Narnia."

"You're sure about that?" Kara retorted. "How do we know C.S. Lewis didn't come here as a writing retreat?"

Mary sighed. "We don't. But if we've been away for *that* long, the consequences don't bear thinking about. Shall we?"

The others nodded. Mary scooped up Antoine and hoisted him on to her shoulder with Jennifer-like strength. She then stepped forward and led the way. Nothing more than a shimmering ripple occurred when she drew near, and eventually vanished through the underside of the archway. Jennifer insisted Kara go through next, with identical results. Jennifer turned round and waved at the Alice-a-like, which waved back. She hoped that if it chose to manifest for her again—that *when* she came back to the Primal Realm rather than *if*—it would opt for another form. If she never saw an animate Alice again, it would be too soon.

That part of her life had gone. She finally felt ready to move on.

On that thought, she stepped back through the gate.

CHAPTER TWENTY-ONE

The few seconds Jennifer took to step through the arch gave a cool, refreshing sensation. She had no time for such analysis on the way in.

On the other side, though, back in a green area of France, it seemed faded and dull in comparison to the Primal Realm. And this through normal vision, too. Mary dumped Antoine on the floor and patted her back where bat wings once stood, and looked almost disappointed for their absence.

Jennifer eyed Kara as she took a drag of a cigar and stared at a cloaked male in a large brimmed hat. All a considerably less dull sight. The man in the hat sat on a pile of unconscious bodies attired as Manta's guards—she switched to her Primal sight for a few seconds to confirm they remained alive. He took what she assumed to be his own cigar back from Kara to finish it off. The castle ruins looked exactly as she had left them.

She wandered over to the three of them. "Since when did you start smoking, Kara?"

Her friend turned round to her, calm but amused. "Since I got out of that place in one piece and decided to celebrate." She took a deep breath. "Anyway, fun time's over. There's a hell of a lot to catch up on, I think."

Jennifer looked at the stranger, who gave a nod of acknowledgement, which she returned. "You don't say. Who's *this*, for a start?"

The stranger stood from the pile and offered a hand. "My name is Cristobal Sergides. I have something in common with the Lady Mary here." The instant she took his hand, she understood what he meant by that. The uneasy aura of death surrounded him. She'd grown almost used to it on Mary, but someone new brought back all the unease.

Still, he had evidently done good work, and the other two weren't in a fight with him, so she took that as non-hostile at least. She took the hand and shook it firmly anyway, failing to suppress a wince as she did so. "Jennifer Winter. I'm with these two."

"I know," he said, a reassuring glint in his pale grey eyes. "They insisted on finding you, whatever the risks of stepping through there." He pointed at the archway, where Kara had gone to pluck a keystone from the top of the arch which Jennifer had not seen on the way in.

"They're like that," she replied. "I can't decide whether they're the bravest folk I've ever met or the least sane."

"A little from column 'A', a little from column 'B'," Mary interjected. "But you've done the same for me, Jen, and would again, so we were always going to look for you."

"Good friends are an invaluable commodity," said Cristobal, "as they might be some means of handling these people."

"I'm working on it," Kara grumbled, phone cupped to her ear. She then wandered away. "Hello? DCI Hammond, please. Tell him to drop whatever he was doing. It's urgent. Dr Mellencourt. Yes, he'll know who I am."

"Problem," Mary said. "They need to be picked up by the local authorities. But we need to not be here when they are."

"Agreed," Jennifer answered. "Too many awkward questions as it is."

"What about him?" Mary asked, pointing to Antoine. "We can't hand him over to the authorities. There's no telling where he'll end up, probably lost in the system."

"And if we let him go and anyone finds out, he's as good as dead." Jennifer had not forgotten the price of failure within Manta's court. And Antoine, stripped of any control mechanisms, might still have served as a useful oracle for them, but the odds seemed slim.

"I can look after him for a while," Cristobal said, stubbing out his cigar before walking several steps further away from the gate. "Perhaps you have further questions for him, too. I can create a travel gate straight back to my place, which will get us there in little time."

Mary raised a hand. "No. Three of us can travel just fine, but Jen's got no protection in our place. As for him, no idea, but I'm going with unlikely."

He paused, then soon took the smallest of bows in acknowledgement and stood down. "Then what?"

Kara returned to the others and tucked her phone carefully into her breast pocket. "Hammond has been on standby," she announced, "wondering where the hell we got to, in his own words, and has been waiting to hear from us, in case we found anything out."

"Paris sounds possible," Jennifer agreed.

Cristobal raised a hand to speak. "My place is in Caen. It would take a little longer to get there, but is the safest place I could name in France."

"Safe sounds better," Jennifer answered, "Though we might have to thumb a lift from the sounds of things."

Kara turned back to face the chateau ruins with a grin. "Oh, I think we can do better than that."

~*~

Kara used the trip to ask Jennifer just about everything about her time away from Grenshall Manor, and as such, gained information on the Consanguinity, their sadistic leader, and the others she'd heard about. She wanted to pester Antoine further, but his recent ordeal saw him unconscious throughout the lengthy drive.

Mary and Jennifer both checked he hadn't died on them, but together reached the conclusion that he had endured many months of mental strain, not just their recent conflict.

"I'll say one thing for that Manta bloke," Kara quipped. "Terrible, greedy, obsessive thief he may be, but I can't knock his taste in cars. I mean, it was awfully good of him to lend us his Merc, wasn't it?"

"If by 'lend', you mean, 'pinch', then yeah." Mary finally let go of the door when they entered Caen. "How we didn't get pulled for having your toe down as far as you did all journey, I'll never know. Also, didn't you tell me when I bought my Mercedes that they kind of just quietly waft along? This thing sounds like the bleedin' 1812 Overture."

"I suspect they've been a little busy with the business we just ran from. Considering the heavy firearms discharge there, speeding fines are probably the least of our worries if the rozzers do pull us. Also, this is an E36 AMG model. It's what happens when you give a Merc an overdose of gamma rays and slap it around the face until it gets angry and turns green."

"Two hours, thirty five minutes, the satnav told us," Jennifer mused. "You lopped almost an hour off that. And now, if you'll excuse me, I'm going to throw up."

Kara gave a tut. "Honestly. You both charge headlong through inter-dimensional gates and neither of you bat an eyelid. I drive a car like the manufacturer intended and you all have kittens. I've never known whining like it. You're with me, right, Cris?"

Cristobal remained silent for a moment, but after being pressed by the driver, pulled back his cloak hood. "You know, next time, I might just take the portal."

"Meh. Everyone's a critic."

Kara parked the Mercedes on a main street, exactly as instructed, and they made their way along an obscure path and into what appeared on the outside like a rectory. Inside, darkness consumed their sight until Cristobal clapped twice. After a short delay from the time of his signal, candlelight flooded the room. Although the exterior seemed very traditional, the inside much resembled a more contemporary apartment setup, right down to a minimalist design.

Though Kara's grin hadn't faded since she initially started the vehicle to a deafening snarl, Mary looked around with her blackened eyes, examining her new surroundings with suspicious curiosity. That Mary seemed so ill-at-ease put Jennifer on the highest of alerts.

"How did you do that?" Mary asked the host, twirling as she walked, looking up.

"A simple parlour trick," he answered casually. "I had no time to extinguish the candles before I set out. But instead, I called upon a veil of the dead world to sit around them, much like a curtain drape. To the casual eye, the room is simply too dark for mortal sight, thick enough to dull the other senses as well. Though I have very little to rob, it prevents people browsing at will."

"I like it," Mary said with an approving gesture. "Low enough level that nobody flees screaming, too."

"Exactly," he replied. "I don't know about you, but when I was learning how to master my responsibilities, I found calling on power far less difficult than refining my hand."

Mary snorted. "You got that right."

"So, bit of a personal question, but where'd you keep the gate in here?" Kara asked. Jennifer understood Kara's curiosity. What she had seen of the place thus far could have been held in half of any one wing of Grenshall Manor. But he pointed to a cellar, a door only partially revealed from under a table.

"The house was built around what was left of an abbey," he answered. "As I understand it, the original keepers of the gate were part of a nunnery, but I was told that a long time ago, and even then, my source lacked proof."

"So, how did you get into all this then?" Mary asked. "Anyone attempt to try and kill you and take over your body as their own, perchance?"

He looked at Mary, puzzled, then shook his head. "Nothing like that." He pulled up an uncomfortable-looking chair and sat upon it, bidding his guests to do likewise.

"I don't know why you'd think something so ridiculous. It all seems long enough ago now that I can barely remember. In my youth, I used to fish in Santander. I met Yvette there, a French merchant, who became my wife." He looked as if recounting someone else's story, until the last word. "Fever took her, not long after we talked about children. I spent many nights restless, which was to be expected, but still, it grew too much. And I remember that I just got up and left my home after that. There was nothing to stay for. I set sail, heading north, hoping to forget, to find something new.

"Then, I heard her. It couldn't have been, I thought, but I definitely heard Yvette's voice calling me. And others. They sounded so lost. I thought it foolish, but I spoke to them and they answered. Somehow, I seemed to calm them. When they were calm, I felt restful at night, could sleep again.

"After some time, I made port at Le Havre, and something about those I spoke to guided me along the coast to the old nunnery. Though the structure had fallen to ruin decades before I arrived, I could hear the place as clearly as if it were still taking novices. And then, I found *La Porte Fantome Noire*, as they told me over and over again."

"You just turned up and moved in, then?" Mary queried with some disbelief.

"Not exactly." He reached for a lighter and ignited his cigar, inhaling its fumes deeply before continuing. Though a relatively pleasant aroma, Jennifer didn't care for it and shuffled away from the direction of the smoke. His house, his rules, she supposed.

"I stayed for some weeks and tried to find peace here as they did. But I did not, and at the end of it all, neither did they. What we found with one another was company. They kept me from madness. Still do. But before long, I had a visit from a dangerous man who showed me the true hazards of the place. He had a plan to raise a small army, using corpses and ghosts. He got a few together and threw me out, barely with my life. When he did so, the voices grew quiet. I could only hear Yvette's.

"I knew this could not be allowed to go on. I returned to Spain—Toledo—and sold my old residence to buy a sword. I knew nothing of it, but Yvette had acquired friends. Great warriors, in their lifetime. They taught me much, in my days and in my dreams. But it took me some years before I dared return here.

"When I did, I found my old rival, who had grown strong from commanding these spirits, these souls, as I eventually discovered. I also learned of the true strength of Toledo steel. He threw the full force of the dead at me, but I survived, with help from the weapon and from Yvette. I could not see her protection, but I could feel it—against some of the most dangerous of the dead."

"Spectres," Mary stated. "I ran into some of those last year at a cinema. They took some beating."

"Yvette was like an angel to me. I could just feel her, giving me strength as she stood by my side when I defeated my enemy. Without the spirits at his command, he weakened greatly. Without his power, he was no match for me. I stayed here. Then Yvette introduced me to her father. He had been dead before we ever met, but I could see him, clear to me as you are now. I had defeated a long-standing enemy of his, and he asked me to stand watch over this place and all that came with it. Over many years, I learned what he truly asked of me."

"Many years?" Mary queried.

"Too many."

"More than fifty, then?"

"Much."

"And how is it you look so good for your age?" Mary asked. "And for that matter, are still going?"

He shrugged, smoking some more. "I do not know exactly. All I know is that a number of the restless dead I have encountered wish me to continue talking, looking after them. I have made many good friends. Not all are so friendly of course. But I can handle them."

Mary frowned at him. "Have you destroyed souls to preserve your life?"

Quickly, he shook his head with great vigour. "I have destroyed only the truly dangerous souls," he said. "And I absorb nothing of them. Too dangerous. But the more friendly spirits halt my ageing. I did not ask for it; they just *do*."

"Hmmm," Jennifer grunted, aware of what she had seen and heard of Mary's ordeal the previous year. It sounded nothing like the man's tale. Thus far, he had proven himself helpful by her friends. Mary picked up on the questioning glance Jennifer cast her, and nodded.

Jennifer's throat went dry as she considered the dead in her life, everything Mary had told her about the area with hanging, soulless bodies in the Primal Realm and the information the Primal Essence had given her about her mentor.

"I saw what happened to Alice."

Kara shuffled in her seat and glared at Jennifer. "Come again?"

"I saw who did it. A ghost walker. And someone else."

"What did you see, exactly?" Kara demanded.

Jennifer then explained the vision, that the ghost walker was probably the same one going by the name of the Grey Lady. "And as for the one with the dark hair, I've no idea who that was."

"That 'Grey Lady'—" Mary said, staring at the floor in a pensive manner. "From the way you described her cloak, she reminds me of the Guide."

"Who?"

Mary pulled a face. "Nobody I've met. A ghost walker going back to Tally's time. It's a distant memory for me, now, but everything you said sounded like what he was wearing."

"If that's the case," Kara added, "she's perhaps wearing that 'death-cloth' you work with."

"Well, she may not be a proper ghost walker then," Mary said. "Unless it's purely for show, there's no reason to wear one if you can do what I do, unless you can't travel to the Unresting world without it, or you're still new at the whole thing."

"Oh, I don't think she's new at this," Jennifer said, looking with slight suspicion at Cristobal. "Come to think of it, I don't think she's *new* at anything. She reeked of death, I mean, literally, it was the only tell I had when she was hiding in that other place. I could *smell* her." She sniffed at the air.

"You, Cristobal, are like a regular bather compared to her, but I can barely scent Mary at all these days."

Cristobal turned to Mary and lifted his hands into the air. "Should we take that as a compliment?"

Mary winked at him. "From her? Abso-bloody-lutely." She returned her attention to Jennifer. "So, you reckon she's old?"

Jennifer scratched her head. "Well, from what Cristobal's told me, anything's possible, I suppose. But the other thing is, I've noticed how she moves. You don't fight like she can without practice, and a lot of it. She got the better of me twice already. I'm only still here because, both times, someone told her not to off me."

Mary and Kara looked taken aback by that revelation. Kara composed herself quickly, though. "She's taking orders then?"

"Yep. The first call came from Antoine. The second from Manta himself. And yet Antoine wasn't exactly in charge of himself, let alone anything else. Manta on the other hand? He seemed to be at the top of it all."

"Except that if he listened to Vortext, as he was then," pondered Kara, "and Vortext was being driven by this Cerise woman, then I've got to wonder who's really on top of that crr-azy love triangle."

CHAPTER TWENTY-TWO

The four, lacking any better knowledge as to how to track their enemy, ordered food for collection and littered a table with notepads and blank paper. Takeout in hand, their thoughts turned to the captive they had taken, unconscious in an adjacent room.

Mary pensively stared at the door as she attacked a slice of pizza. "So, two problems with our boy there: first off, he's out cold, and second, even if we do bring him round, the guy can't actually remember anything about what he did."

Jennifer rolled her eyes. "Nothing's ever straightforward with us, is it? But seeing as he's our only lead, we're just going to have to try and wake him up, aren't we?"

"Yep," Kara agreed, "but I think it's going to take a little more than smelling salts to bring him round."

Jennifer grabbed a jug of water from the table and stood up. "I've got a method, and a serious lack of patience right now. Let me at him."

The door they stared at flew open with a loud crash, and Antoine stumbled through it, still shirtless. "Where am I? What the hell have you done to me?"

"What are you talking about?" Kara challenged, but he continued his stagger toward a way out. He made the mistake of leaning on Jennifer on his way past though, and she promptly threw him over her shoulder and left him flat on his back. She crouched, a hand to his throat, and bared teeth.

He seemed to ignore her physical threat. "These tattoos. Which of you did this to me?"

Kara stood over them both and stared at him, puzzled. "You mean you didn't get those done on a stag do in Ibiza after one too many sangrias one night?"

"That still happens?" Cristobal interrupted. Their peculiar line of questioning confused the detainee into relaxing a little.

"This isn't the chateau . . ." he mumbled.

"You know that," Jennifer snarled. "We've spoken to you since."

"Who are you?"

Kara sighed. "This is going to be more difficult than first suspected. Okay, Antoine, what's the last thing you do remember?"

"Tattoos. We were talking about tattoos."

"Not just now, you idiot," Jennifer hissed.

"Shhh!" Kara lightly pushed Jennifer away from Antoine. "Go on."

He tapped at his right wrist. "I got this one, my nickname of Vortext, just before my birthday. It was the only one I had, too. I mean, what are all these others? How many are there?"

Jennifer pulled him upright by the same wrist and checked for herself. "Can't say I'd really been looking before. Two big ones up each arm, one across your chest, and a huge one covering your back. Nobody gets *that* drunk."

"So, it's a reasonable guess you've had them all done since you became part of the Consanguinity," Kara noted, "whether you knew about them or not. But I can't think of why they'd just want you decorated. Jen, did any of the other members have any tats?"

Jennifer thought back to her experiences, going back to the more sedate. One or two of the guards may have had some mundane designs, but she recalled none within the Manta Court, other than the ones on Antoine. "Nope. Not as far as I could tell. They were all better clothed than Antoine here, but I seriously doubt they were marked with anything much."

Kara examined each of the tattoos for herself. "Don't know much about you, Antoine, but given you sound more local than ex-pat, and that I don't recognise any of these from any Russian gangster movies, I'd hazard a guess that you haven't done time in a Moscow detention facility in recent years?"

"What? No!" He had a horrified expression on his face. "Or at least, if I did, I don't remember it, but then I wouldn't be with—never mind. Why ask me that, anyway?"

"Because I wanted to rule out other 'club' memberships. So, these are all to do with something else."

"I don't recognise a single one of those in modern popular tattoo art." Mary moved the others from crowding him and examined each in detail, poking at them. "The ones on the arms just look like tree roots. The one on your right pec—hmmm, that knife looks a lot like *Tally's Peace*."

"Yep. Cerise has one almost just like it," Jennifer reminded her.

"Only with a red jewel in it where a blue one's missing on mine. That's right. But what's it doing on his chest, I wonder?"

"What's any of it doing here?" Antoine griped. "Why would anyone just . . . *brand* me like this?"

"I think that might be it." Kara looked at Jennifer with a frown. "If you're the only one marked, there has to be something behind them all. Had any premonitions lately, Antoine?"

The confusion on his face gave them the answer.

Jennifer examined him with her full enhanced vision. At such close range, and without immediately dangerous distractions, she could still see traces of the faint aura she had seen surrounding him, burning from the blade tattoo and the roots on the arms. Primal power, faded, but not gone. It looked every bit as much a poison as tainted food and drink she had the ability to detect. "Mister Vortext, I do not believe Cerise has been a good partner for you at all. Pretty controlling, I'd say."

"Got that right. Are you saying it was her who did this to me?"

"Seems likely. Some medic, she is."

"That's what she told you?" Mary glared at Jennifer in disbelief. Jennifer gave a nod, equally unconvinced. Mary's eyes flashed black, and then she leaned in to Antoine and scrutinised the etchings on him with her own death sight. "Hmmm. Perhaps not a medic. But a surgeon, certainly. That's not ink. That's scarring. But that's the work of an extremely steady hand."

As Jennifer nodded, Antoine adjusted his seating position. He leaned back on his palms, wrists facing forward, and as he did so, she noticed animation on the arm markings. She blinked to double check, but the markings on his arms looked as if they were attempting to take root into the ground. Antoine relaxed in his position and his attention appeared to be some distance away. The red glow grew all around him. Without thinking, she gave him a swift kick, directly on his knife etching. He yelped in pain.

"What the hell?"

Kara also leaned in, but Mary moved her away. "I saw that, too. I'm not sure *what* I saw. His arms looked chained to the ground. Like something was about to . . ." Mary's eyes widened, and her mouth dropped open. "It isn't the same, but last time I saw anything like that was around Barber. When I took a proper look at him and saw chains. I can't see any now, but as I said, this isn't that."

"But we do know he was bound to Cerise somehow . . ." Kara noted.

"And it's clearly related to the tats," Jennifer concluded.

"Bindings, chains and roots," Cristobal reiterated. "And what you saw only happened—"

". . . when his roots almost plugged themselves into the ground," Kara completed.

"*Draw your strength from the earth . . .*" both Mary and Jennifer recited simultaneously but then stopped and looked at each other in recognition. Jennifer shook her head. "The Consanguinity said it differently. But it seemed close enough to remember. What was it now? *Take the earth where others borrow.*"

"Ah." Kara nibbled her lip. "The proverbial 'playing a record backwards' trick. But all roads lead to earth, right?"

"Earth," Antoine mumbled, "connects lands of restless dead and shadow to most vital of light and life."

Jennifer turned to him. "What did you say?" she demanded.

"Four elements, five worlds. Some stronger together, but none bound to the other. Master of the Crown masters all."

"What are you talking about? What does that mean?"

Antoine blinked. "You just kicked me. Why?"

"What were you talking about before?"

"I just said you kicked me and I don't know why."

The red aura Jennifer saw around him grew brighter and she saw his arms touch the ground once again. She gritted her teeth in irritation and stooped, then clenched a fist. She slammed it into his jaw and knocked him out cold, then lifted him and placed him face-down on the nearest table. As she checked that none of his limbs directly touched the ground, she felt a tug on her sleeve.

"What are you doing?" Kara's eyes narrowed and her teeth ground. "He was telling us stuff."

"Yeah, and he didn't remember a word he just said. Again."

"So? We did."

"So, I just saw him lighting up the same way he did when I first saw him. I don't think he's completely free of the hold on him. But I've seen Manta at work. He hasn't seen Antoine since we nabbed him. So, if Manta even thinks we've been told anything, he's a dead man."

"He had more to say," Kara protested.

"I'll bet. But if there's any link between him and Cerise . . ."

"Quiet a minute, you two!" Mary looked carefully at Antoine's back, specifically the etching which adorned most of it. She poked and examined, and then beckoned the others to her, pointing to the centre of it. A circlet-style crown took pride of place in the centre of his back, itself surrounded by a small ring.

"From that, several spokes led out to a larger circle, containing four further symbols located on four compass points, each in an arched trapezoid form, longest edge facing outward. At the North point, a breeze-like swirl. At the East point, a small image of flame. At the South point, a series of roots, similar to the larger designs on his arms. On the final West area, waves and droplets predominated.

"You see that? They look like elements to me. That's one's Fire. Got to be Air, that one. Clearly water. Meaning that one's got to be Earth." She tapped the south-located symbol.

Jennifer took a closer look, but soon nodded. "Yep – what he was just yapping about."

"So, what's with the outer ring?" Kara queried. Another set of spokes did indeed lead to a ring further outwards and another four wedges, containing different symbols. These four lay northwest, southwest, southeast and northeast.

Mary drew into the air above his back with her finger. "Four elements, five worlds, he said. But I can only see four symbols here."

Jennifer held her chin. "And *five* worlds? Unresting, Primal, and another three. One of them isn't even here."

"Have we counted the one we're on?" Kara noted.

"Have now," Jennifer replied. "Now, elements are easy pics. What do these mean?"

Kara sought a nearby notepad and started scribbling frantically. "Okay, judging by the fact that you two have that one thing in common about the earth, let's start at the south. Between earth and fire, that's a clump of dark shadow mostly."

"The texture on that is unbelievable," Mary observed as she felt the darkened segment. "That has to be the Unresting. Shadow and void. But I thought the winds would have related to air, too."

"Interesting." Kara continued to scrawl notes. "If that's right, there's what looks like a fang there between earth and water."

"So, that would be my place," Jennifer said.

"Leaving just the crown and the beast," Cristobal added.

Mary turned to Jennifer. "Couldn't the beast be your place then?"

"Good question." Jennifer tapped the circlet in the centre. "It's guesswork, just like there being two crowns there. The only thing is that this one's in the middle of everything else."

"I assume this is the one Manta wants?" Mary pointed at the crown in the centre of Antoine's back. "If he gets it, we have an awful lot of not good to deal with."

"Like we haven't already." Jennifer shook her head.

"Yet another question," Kara asked nobody in particular. "If those three tattoos are all control mechanisms for Antoine here, what's this one all about?"

Antoine groaned and tried to push himself upright. Jennifer took aim to hit him again, but Kara made herself a real obstruction. It wouldn't have stopped Jennifer had she not spotted that the controlling aura had faded back down. She stayed her hand.

"I think they said 'ritual circle,'" he groaned. "Manta wanted a copy somewhere they could never lose it. She used the knife. It took her hours. What have they done to me?" he screamed.

Mary bowed her head. "Bad things."

Jennifer pulled Antoine back up to a comfortable seating position on the table and gave his cheeks a light pull and a couple of taps. "So, we have a very interesting map here. Unfortunately, it doesn't come with a convenient timetable as to where the Consanguinity are going to be next."

Antoine dropped his head. "I'm really sorry. I just don't know. I don't even know what I've been saying."

Kara frowned. "Seeing as you're still our best lead, we'll have to keep trying to jog your memory."

Jennifer gave Antoine a little personal space. "If that's our only plan, I'd like to know what they meant by the 'Death of Winter' that they were on about."

"They weren't just saying that when they decided to kill you, were they?" Mary asked. "But I'll bet you didn't even tell them your name."

Jennifer scowled. "Alice Winter. I took her name. Jennifer Winter. That's no more her real name than it is mine, is it?"

Antoine's eyes grew bloodshot and distant. Jennifer spotted the field of light around the tattoos grow stronger and he started to repeat words, first inaudibly, then eventually very clearly. "To the death of Winter! To the death of their Order!"

"Settle down, will you?" Mary commanded. Jennifer had heard Mary when she was truly making an effort to assert her will, but Jennifer could feel none of the force, none of the dead world chill that usually came when she called upon such power. Yet, he slumped immediately to a relaxed position.

"Huh?" Mary stared at him, baffled. "I didn't even . . ." She snapped her fingers. "Hmmm. Stand up." He complied instantly. "Walk over to that chair." He obeyed once more. "Sit on it." Three out of three. She turned to Jennifer, looking almost ill. "That's really quite horrible."

Jennifer looked at Mary, then over to the marionette that was Antoine, then back to Mary. "It is. Don't do it again."

"That's just it—I didn't really do anything. Not like I can. This guy is in serious trouble."

"I've noticed." Jennifer nibbled a fingernail as she considered the situation. "But we're not doing great ourselves. It occurs to me that the link is still there between him and Cerise. Means he can't exactly hide from her. Rotten news when she's got a friend like the Grey Lady who can turn up anywhere."

"Lucky this isn't a good place for the Grey Lady to come, isn't it?" Cristobal rose from his seat and clenched a fist, and as he did so, the lights faded, a reminder of his own power. Jennifer wasn't certain it would be enough, but other than forcing them to negotiate the Gate Chamber inside Grenshall Manor, she couldn't immediately think of any safer sanctuary for him. As she said herself, he was a dead man if they got hold of him again. The four of them would have to make sure they didn't.

"Cristobal, are you okay with him staying here?"

"As okay as I am with you all being here." He gave a roguish grin, but Jennifer didn't know which way to interpret that statement. "Intruders will not find it easy here."

"I agree." Mary nodded. "We can't really take him anywhere without him being a liability to us and himself. And we've all got enough trouble as it is."

Kara broke her silence. "'The death of Winter,' he said." She stopped and watched Antoine very carefully. Jennifer suspected it might have been just to check he didn't babble further on her repeated words. After a few seconds, she carried on.

"Now, we know he wasn't talking about you from what you've told me, because otherwise, why would they have wasted time trying to get you on board? And I doubt that they meant Alice, unless they were all solely dedicated to destroying her, which seems unlikely. That means there must be more to this Winter business than we know. Jen, did Alice say anything to you ever about her surname?"

"She never really mentioned it. And I didn't really think to ask about it."

"All things considered, I can't think of any reason you would have."

"*Omega W.*" Antoine muttered. "Omega W."

"Now what are you on abo—" Jennifer muttered, but she already knew the answer. *Winter's End. The death of Winter. Former residents of the chateau.* "Omega W. The 'W' is for Winter. That was the name of their enemies, the Consanguinity. Winter."

"Omega Winter?" Kara said, but Jennifer could see already that her highly attuned mind was working hard to ascertain truth. "No, just there for show. Replacement letter 'O'. Organisation? Office? *Ordo* . . . Order. Winter Order?"

"*Order of Winter*," Mary stated. "It's definitely the Order of Winter. I know that name . . . Because Lord Alphonse Grenshall knew that name. He knew it very well. He was a member of it, after all. It's a third-hand memory through Tally and her . . . unfortunate act."

Jennifer's face dropped, and she felt numb. "Alice wore that brooch on her every time I can remember seeing her. She never left without it. Even when she—"

She'd wished for the knowledge of what happened to Alice Winter. Now that she had it, it scarred her mind as if she had experienced her last moments directly.

"*The Consanguinity of Enlightenment* had an enemy. An enemy who used that symbol and I *have* seen that symbol before and I remember where now, it was on Alice and oh, how have I been so stupid?" She slumped forward, head in her hands. "Alice worked for them, didn't she? That's why she disappeared. Why they came for her. Why they killed her. Why she never came back. The Grey Lady and someone else. In the Primal Realm. And you're telling me Lord Alphonse was a member? How long has this been going on?"

Mary shrugged. "There wasn't anything about a Consanguinity I remember. Nor Tally, nor Lord Alphonse."

"I might suspect the Consanguinity hasn't been around for as long as the Order of Winter," Kara mentioned. "But it seems they've made their mark."

"Made their mark . . ." Jennifer repeated, distant. A low, grinding sound crunched in the room whilst everyone sat in silence, looking at Jennifer. It was only when she made the realisation that the sound was her clawing the table that she stopped. "I'm sorry."

"It's okay," Kara said, gently placing an arm around Kara. "We understand."

"Other than the damage to the table." Cristobal glared at her, but then took a step back. "I can get it repaired."

Jennifer recovered herself and stood upright. She turned to face Kara, looking stern. "You understand. That's nice. One question, though. How did Alice know to send me to you, Kara?"

Kara adjusted her collar. Jennifer could count on the back of a thumb the number of times she had seen Kara socially uncomfortable. "It wasn't a random place in London at all. You knew that I wasn't exactly 'normal'. That's fine. But you must have met her in advance. Must have known that she wasn't coming back. You knew that much, but you never said. Just let me believe she'd gone missing. Might come back one day. She was going to her death and you *knew*, Kara. You must have."

"Now, wait a minute."

Jennifer's fingers sprouted into talons and shot into the table. Antoine leapt away and on to the floor. Mary and Cristobal each flanked Kara, but once in position, stood firm. "I've waited years, Kara. My best friend in the world and you can't tell me that Alice left you with me because she was being hunted down like a damn dog? You, of all people, lied to me?"

Kara stared at the floor. "She made me promise," she mumbled.

"What?"

"She made me promise not to say anything."

"Why?" Jennifer spat. "Because I'd have followed her?"

"Well, are you telling me you wouldn't have?" Kara looked straight up at her in challenge.

Jennifer stepped forward and got right in Kara's face. "Of course I would have. She was my *mother*. Or as good as I had until they took her from me." Jennifer could hear a guttural growl.

She knew it was her. She didn't care. Kara took a step back, but Mary and Cristobal stood their ground. Mary's eyes flooded with darkness and halted any further pursuit.

"And if you had, you'd have died with her." Mary's words were spoken quietly, but with absolute sincerity. Though furious, Jennifer thought twice about pressing the matter. "Alice knew you well enough to get you away from the situation. You'd have gone with her, no matter what. And where would that have got you?"

"I could have saved . . ."

She thought back to her father, just lying there.

No, you couldn't.

"I could've done *something*."

Kara gulped but spoke. "You could have been killed, is what you'd have done." Kara plucked up the courage to say, "I'll tell you exactly what she said to me. *'I need her somewhere that no one will get to her. That only the right people talk to her. I can't tell you where I'm going, but I'm not sure I'll be coming back. If I do, I'll tell her everything. If I don't, help her. Any way you can.'* That was all she said to me. I started to ask her a question, but she ran away. I'm sorry, really sorry I didn't tell you before, but you were doing fine until—"

"Until what?" The fire remained in her heart. But that kept her alive, too. It was okay. "Until Mary showed up? Until I was too weak to move? Until it was safe?"

Kara looked Jennifer straight in the eye. Aggression gripped her words. "Until you were ready to hear it. Listen, Jennifer, you've kept me in one piece for a long time now, you've kept a bunch of people safe from harm and you've made sure that despite anything thrown at you, you're still here. Your ordeal in the Primal world included. But if you'd gone with Alice and faced her enemies, would you have been around for this conversation? Or if you survived, would you have lost it and ended up as one of the people we had to hunt down?

"I am sorry, Jen, and no amount of times I tell you will do how sorry

I am justice, but I'd ask you to remember one thing just now. I'm not the bastard who locked you up and tried to have you killed. And I need you at your best right now. Remember why we're all standing here at this exact moment in time."

Jennifer exhaled heavily enough to be heard anywhere in the room. "I do." She retracted her talons. "We need to finish what we started." She looked directly at Kara. "And I'll put this on hold for now. But we're far from finished."

"That's all I can ask for." Kara bowed her head once more.

"The Consanguinity," Jennifer spat. "They murdered my mother. They held me prisoner, and then they tried to kill me. They have my full attention."

Mary pulled a sour face. "Seems they've got mine, too. I cite family business."

"And I'm just nosey," Kara added. "So, radical idea, I know, but how about we get a step ahead of the bad guys for once?"

Jennifer, Cristobal, Mary, and Kara looked at each other and nodded as one. Antoine looked up at them all and gave a sheepish smile. "Well, you've got my vote."

CHAPTER TWENTY-THREE

Jennifer, Kara and Mary left the broken Antoine under the protection of Cristobal and his Unresting domain. Though the oracle remained far from safe, they had no better alternative to offer.

Intrigued by Kara's mention of a plan, the other two chose to indulge her and let her explain as they returned to the stolen Mercedes. Jennifer walked just ahead of the others, the keystone slung over her shoulder in a hessian sack. She considered herself on high alert, given the sensory warnings she had seen around Antoine.

"Mobile phone signal in his house is worse than at yours, Mary," she complained. "And how in this day and age does a man live alone with no computer and no Internet connection?"

"That's just it," Mary remarked. "He's not of this day and age. Not really. Also, I'll have you know the connection speed at my place is hard to beat anywhere."

"It's true," Jennifer added. "Gave me plenty to watch, at least. Anyway, you had a plan, Kara?"

"Thought it might be worth getting the police to assist us with our enquiries."

"Isn't that what we citizens do for them?" Mary asked.

"They won't be able to crack this case on their own, as well you know. Besides, we—" Jennifer stopped dead, and pushed the others back, too.

"What is it?" Kara asked. Mary's eyes immediately flooded inky black, and she looked around for herself.

"There's some folk poking around the car."

"Manta wouldn't have reported it stolen, would he?" Kara put her head into her hands. "Oh, shit."

"What?" the other two asked.

"He wouldn't have had to. Car like that's going to have a tracking system. Oh, Kara, you idiot!" Kara clamped her hand over her mouth immediately after the outburst.

"I'm saying nothing," Jennifer muttered under her breath. She sized up the hostiles, checked their clothing, carried items, and posture. They could easily have passed for a law enforcement unit to the casual eye, but quite apart from anything, one of them had opened the vehicle without the use of force of any kind and started to root through it. It suggested he had a key, not the usual order of the day for an armed response unit.

"All that while being paranoid about Antoine, and they find us by something that basic. Good thing we did park around the corner or—"

". . . or they'd be right on our doorstep," Kara hissed. "They haven't actually seen us yet."

"What are we going to do?" Mary whispered. "Act natural?"

"Nope." Jennifer bared her teeth in a fierce grin. "The other thing. Mary, you see anything over *there*?"

Mary shook her head. "Nothing special."

"Good. We could do without unwanted ghost walkers."

"We could just take them out?"

"We don't actually know how many of them there are around here. And they aren't sympathetic to bystanders."

"True. And that means I can't just order them away either. That could get out of hand pretty fast."

"That leaves us with not getting spotted," Kara answered. "We could do with another car."

Two almost identical vehicles emerged from other streets and stopped. Jennifer examined one of them and saw the front passenger reach for a set of binoculars. She started to address Kara, but her friend nodded vigorously and crossed the street. Within seconds, she had got into a taxi, and beckoned the others over. The taxi driver barely waited for it to close before moving, as per Kara's instructions, in the opposite direction.

Manta's team fanned out. Though the streets of Caen appeared to bear none of the bustle of Paris, a number of startled passers-by littered the streets but stayed out of the way of the official-looking squad. Kara geed up the taxi driver in French as if she were jockeying a racehorse. He nervously followed her instructions until they were clear of the search.

"So, what was your plan anyway?" Mary asked Kara.

"Ironically enough," Kara chuckled, "I was hoping to figure out a way to track them down. Well, they've just given me an idea."

"Go on," Jennifer ordered.

"I'm hoping that, given the circumstances, Interpol might be able to help. At the moment, that takes us back to Paris."

"I hope you're not expecting me to get the taxi fare," Mary grumbled.

~*~

Mary did pay for the taxi but only to the local train station. They returned to Paris within a couple of hours and went straight to the police headquarters. Mary and Jennifer were happy for Kara to do the talking, and Kara was more than happy to oblige. On the way, she had contacted DCI Hammond, in the hope that he would smooth their path somewhat.

He met them outside the Paris Police Headquarters, looking dishevelled and less than pleased. "Last-minute Eurostar bookings are seriously expensive. I hope you weren't lying when you said Lady Grenshall was covering this." Mary gave Kara a killing glare.

"You know, I'd like to say that I'm full of righteous indignation that you've buggered up my holiday with the wife and kids, but it turns out you've just buggered up my holiday. The morning I turned up at your manor was my first day's leave since before Christmas, and I spent it reading up on the biggest case I've dealt with since some shenanigans down at Bond Street Station."

"In other words," Kara noted, "we're great for your career and you need us to call you more often?"

He looked up at the massive elevation of the building. "You're about to end it for me, I don't doubt. I've next to no pull here, you know, right?"

"'Next to' is still an improvement on what we have," Jennifer grouched.

"Damn right," Mary muttered.

They made their way to the reception desk and Hammond flashed his badge. Several minutes of telephone calls ensued, with New Scotland Yard confirming Hammond's identity and him looking sheepish as he attempted to explain his position to his superior. It turned out to be the biggest laugh Jennifer had all day. Eventually, the desk officer relented and directed them to an interview room.

A fresh-faced and athletically built young male officer with a crew cut and in tactical gear entered the room. He waved them all to sit down. A tall, plain-clothed woman with dark hair and in a navy blue suit, carrying a tablet, entered, and stood in the corner of the room. "Detective Chief Inspector Hammond?" the uniformed officer asked.

Hammond responded in the affirmative.

"You have orders from your superintendent to return home immediately."

He shook his head. "I'm on leave."

"Which is why you have orders to stay off the case." The plain-clothed woman stepped forward and showed him the tablet screen. He examined it studiously and returned it to her, grave-faced. He muttered something uncomplimentary under his breath.

"I'm sorry, Kara. Interpol *are* involved already. And they've made it clear I either lay off or I get laid off."

Kara sighed. "You can't just leave, Eric. This is important."

The female officer opened the door and waved him through. "He has no choice. And his leave has been cancelled effective tomorrow."

"Then we've no business here either." Mary stood and spun toward the door, but Kara yanked her back down.

"I came here to ask some questions. And I'm not leaving until I have some answers."

Jennifer spotted the plain-clothed woman's eyes dart around at every one of the visitors, and she tapped rapidly at the screen.

"You seem hostile." The male officer tilted his head. "Not a good idea, Miss—?"

"*Doctor* Mellencourt. And if you have any interest in solving the museum robberies at all, you'll spend less time threatening me and more time listening to what we've got to say."

His colleague ushered Hammond out of the room, and immediately followed. He shut the door and then glared at Kara. "Do not speak to me about my interest in solving the Louvre robbery. I lost eight of my friends that night. So, if you know something about it . . ."

"How did you survive?" Jennifer placed herself between the towering officer and Kara. She looked at him closely. After her question, he stopped, stunned.

"What?"

"How. Did. You. Survive?"

After a lengthy pause, he bowed his head. "They were a different team to mine. As soon as we heard about the British Museum, we ordered a security increase, just in case. Eight of them. Eight highly trained, well-armed men. And I still don't know what happened to them. None of us do. We have released none of this. How did you know?"

"British Museum." She took a step back from him and moved her shadow from Kara. "But I'm not easy to kill." She closed her eyes. "Never have been."

He studied Jennifer carefully, and she in return appraised him. His movement, his poise, despite the recent tests to his morale, showed her a more than capable warrior within his field. It also showed her an officer who had been forced out of it. His head, first lowered in shame, now bowed slightly. Mutual recognition between the battle-scarred.

"Sous-Lieutenant Luc Debussy." He offered a hand, which she shook firmly. "Did you get a look at the bastards?"

"I can give you a full description of the ringleaders, if you want. But we want to know their next move. And we need a little more from you guys to be able to do that."

He scratched his head. "I shouldn't even be here. And you know, as we're in the police headquarters, I could just make you tell me what you know.

"I wouldn't advise that." Mary's words were spoken quietly and without menace. But Jennifer felt the hairs on her spine raise. It came with knowing what potentially came next. She remembered herself and gave Mary a knowing look. Her friend winked.

Kara clasped her hands together and leaned forward across the table. "Look. We just want to help solve this." She reached into her pocket and thrust the keys to the Mercedes she acquired on the table. "Black E63 AMG model. I know the licence plate, too. There were a bunch of vehicles over at a wrecked chateau in Gien."

"If you were to check the place now," Jennifer added, "you'd probably find bullet holes and casings all over the place. But by the time you've done that, the royal wannabe Manta will probably already have hit his next place. That means more people dead. So, you don't have time."

Debussy considered her words for a moment, but then grabbed the keys and opened the door. In French, he shouted outside.

Kara started to translate aloud for the benefit of everyone else, but he returned to the room with haste. "Follow me."

~*~

Debussy and the others huddled around a computer terminal with the aid of an administrative staff member. "According to our check," the admin confirmed, "this vehicle, and all these others you confirmed, Doctor Mellencourt, belong to a Contessa Valeria D'Amato."

"Does she know they're stolen?" Kara asked. "Or did we miss a member of the Manta Court somewhere?"

The admin navigated his computer pages with rapid mastery. "The contessa hasn't been seen in public in at least three years, maybe more."

Jennifer leaned in just as soon as she saw the photo image. The woman, a glossy-haired brunette with full lips and shiny, dark brown eyes perhaps in her early thirties, had an air of elegance and glamour about her, even from the digital capture. It looked like a portrait pose. "That's her!"

"Who?" Mary asked.

"The woman the Primal Essence showed me. With the Grey Lady. They killed Alice."

Kara jabbed her in the rib, but Jennifer simply growled in response. She blinked slowly several times. "Where was she last seen?" she asked the admin.

"On CCTV footage in a Parisian nightclub. She had previously been seen in the company of one Gianfranco Manta."

"That's our man!" Kara practically cheered. "Have you got anything on him?"

The admin drew up a photo of a man, perhaps in his late thirties, with a charming smile. The top of a stylish suit and cravat could be seen from the crop.

"The profile says he is the grandson of Glauco Manta. Ah, *oui*. His family are the reason we have anything on him at all. Glauco Manta: Swiss-Italian, held rank in the Nazi military. Antiques broker. He headed up one of their occult artefact search teams."

Kara snapped her fingers. "That makes a lot of sense. I studied that era but couldn't find anywhere near as much as I would have hoped. Hadn't thought to tackle it again since everything last year. I really should. I might discover some fresh insights."

Mary frowned. "So, is he really just keeping up a family business?"

Debussy scanned the open file. "Glauco was killed in 1945, a warehouse explosion in Brussels just weeks before the war ended."

The admin continued. "His son, Enzo, inherited everything from him directly, but a war crimes investigation followed. For a number of reasons, including residence in neutral territory, it took longer than average to process. In the 1970s, the majority of Enzo Manta's inherited assets were seized, most of which were held in indefinite quarantine. Enzo died in poverty in 1974."

Jennifer took a moment to absorb the information she had been provided. "So, where does Gianfranco come into this?"

"Long-term daddy and government issues," Kara said, reading over the admin's shoulder. "He was an only child. His mother raised him, but it looks like everything got sold off around him as he grew up. Apparently they lived in a chateau up there, but even that got auctioned and they were cleaned out of their whole, quite extensive collection. The stuff went worldwide, but a crown they had only got as far as Berne. He got taken to see that crown almost every day by his mother."

"A reminder of past glories," Mary mused. "She never let him forget."

"The Crown of Kings?" Jennifer recited.

With permission, Kara ran an Internet search on an adjacent terminal. "I've checked and cross-referenced this in a few languages. Its primary title isn't in English."

"Try Spanish," Jennifer offered. "Manta did at first."

Kara did as advised. "Ah, yes, *La Corona de Reyes*. There's a record of that being held in Berne for the last eighteen years."

"If he wanted it so badly, why didn't he hit the place earlier?"

"The recent attacks have been very coordinated. But that's a very good question. It can't have been just that. Hmmm, says here that the senior curator for the last twenty years died earlier this year. 'Famed for getting together a collection of quite obscure artefacts and never once sent any of it out on loan, despite several requests.

"'Considered obstinate by a number of his peers, the last act of Holger Winter's life before his untimely death was to arrange a number of loans, providing much-needed further exposition for a collection rarely seen by the rest of the world'."

"Hold on," Jennifer interjected. "You said, Holger Winter. . . They've been hunted down, one by one, and he wasn't even hiding."

Mary leaned over her shoulder and looked closer at the monitor. "Doesn't happen to say what he died of, does it?"

"According to this, internal bleeding. Unknown origin."

"I think we know the origin," Jennifer muttered. "Very specific stab wound."

"I was thinking that," Mary agreed.

Debussy turned to her. "Thinking what?"

"That he didn't die of natural causes."

"There aren't any records of suspicious death."

"If you look at the autopsies of your team, I guarantee you'll see something very similar."

"Meanwhile, it's interesting to see how few of the artefacts were photographed in this day and age." Kara clicked frantically and found only grainy images and vague descriptions. "This entire collection remained behind closed doors that entire time."

Jennifer nodded. "Someone didn't *want* the rest of the world to see it. Someone was protecting everything here."

"And I think he gave his life for the cause," Mary added. "Why would he send them out of his protection, however he did it, rather than leave them there?"

Jennifer pressed her hands against the table and drew scratch marks. "He must have known someone was on to him."

The lighting and power dropped. Fire alarms rang deafening everywhere in the building. As Jennifer processed that information, a waft of stale, dead air drifted under her nose for a fleeting moment. She looked up, chromatic vision active, and saw Mary twitch and darken eyes at the same moment.

"Did you—?"

"Yes."

"She's here."

~*~

Through the darkness, Jennifer called on her augmented senses and inhaled the rotting stench, to find the Grey Lady before she found her target. The scent faded quickly, but Mary wasted no time in summoning her death sight. "I'm going after her," Mary declared.

Kara made to protest, but Jennifer spoke first, clear and loud over the chaos. "*Do not* get close to her," she ordered.

"I don't plan to." A gale rushed across the room, blowing paperwork everywhere, and Mary vanished.

Debussy stopped for a moment to look around, but he reached into his flak jacket pocket and pulled out a torch before once more barking orders. He swept the torch around, but Jennifer again intervened. "Get everyone out of the building. You're sitting ducks in here."

"Numbers? Tactics? Weapons?"

"One. The other two things, nothing you can handle. Kara, stay close."

Kara shook her head. "You catch up with Mary. I can't keep up with you, definitely not in this."

Jennifer ground her teeth. "Find some armour and stay in a corner, then." Debussy made a small effort to stop her, but Jennifer bolted out of the door and barged through the police crowd on high alert. She sniffed the air in order to catch the faintest trace of her unseen foe, but caught nothing. She remembered Mary's more familiar scent, and attempted to catch that instead. The trace remained faint, but she knew Mary wouldn't have gone far, as she wouldn't 'blind jump'.

Jennifer cleared a path like an unstoppable juggernaut through to the top floor. Her strength, speed, and unhampered sight in the station allowed her to catch up with Mary in short order. Scent became unnecessary as soon as she got close to the interview room in which she detected her friend, a sure giveaway being the three bodies that lay outside. She scanned through chromatic eyes and found not one showing any external injuries.

Jennifer smelled blood from inside. She put her foot through the door.

"Where is she?"

"Jen." Mary crouched in the corner of the room, above a prone and bleeding figure. Jennifer crouched beside Mary, who tried to keep a sliced throat together.

"Keep both kinds of eyes peeled." She looked for life signs. Faint. Seconds left. She crouched and called upon her Primal connection, and closed her mind from all around her. She felt the familiar flow of energy surge into her fingertips, and touched the severed throat. His heartbeat pulsed in time with the rapid remaking of flesh, and within five of them, he gave a heavy wheeze. Another second later and there wouldn't have been a sixth.

"He'll live."

Only then did she take a proper look at his face. DCI Hammond.

"Mary—wasn't Hammond meant to be leaving immediately? And if so, why is he on the top floor and not heading out?"

"He was. And I had exactly the same thought. All I can think of is that somewhere down the line—"

". . . this was a smokescreen for something else."

Jennifer slumped. "Oh, how could I have been so stupid?"

"What?"

"The keystone. That's what she was after. She must have picked up on one of us two when we got back to Paris."

"Why, though? It's not like you need it to get to your place."

She thought it through. "There's a chance they don't *know* that."

"How? Didn't they see you run through the arch without it?"

"Who knows? They didn't see you either, obviously. Speaking of which . . ."

"She's gone. Didn't stay long."

Jennifer examined the recovering Hammond. Remembered the blood. All so untidy. "Now why wouldn't she have used Wraithbreaker on him?"

"No reason whatsoever."

They both looked at each other, the same thought forming in their minds at the same time, the same words uttered. "Unless it wasn't her."

"Then who?"

"Her." Hammond spluttered and attempted to sit up, with little success. "Officer with Debussy." He closed his eyes and fell back prone.

"She was in on it the whole time." Jennifer stood up and inhaled the air. "Why else are we up here?"

"We've got to find Kara."

"You do that. I'll look for our rogue detective." Mary disappeared into the Unresting.

Jennifer started to make her way out of the room just as several armed officers turned up at the open door and trained a number of guns on her. She heard loud orders barked at her and slowly raised her hands. They had her bound and in cuffs within seconds, but Kara sprinted up behind them.

"Eric!" Kara attempted to force her way closer, but the team blocked her path.

"Hands in the air!" the commanding officer ordered in English. Jennifer got the measure of them in a glance. She could have taken them out, but not without risking Kara. Their commander spoke again. "You're under arrest."

"Don't be stupid. It wasn't me."

The emergency power activated. She heard another command from behind the squad. After a brief argument, Debussy ordered the others to back down and they each took positions in the corner.

Jennifer looked at him. "Debussy. We need to find your colleague. She's in on this."

He pursed his lips as he considered, but then nodded and waved the armed squad aside and released her. "Kara," she demanded, "I don't suppose you have the keystone, do you?"

"Got evacuated by this lot. Couldn't go back."

"Be right back." She burst through the door and back to the last place she had it, the computer room, before the power went out. No bag. She roared and swiped a screen off the table. It sparked and shattered on impact with the floor. "Dammit!"

A minute later, Mary turned up at the door with Debussy's former colleague being dragged in by her hair. "Would've preferred another way," she grumbled, "but she doesn't take orders easily and, as you know, I have to be careful when I resort to violence." She threw her at Jennifer, who let her fall at her feet, and then stood lightly on her hand.

Jennifer leaned in and spoke quietly but clearly. "Where's Manta?"

No answer. Jennifer lifted her by the shoulders and met her gaze. "I'll ask again. Where is he?"

The suited officer laughed briefly, and then spat in Jennifer's face. Jennifer cleaned herself, then replied instantly with a head-butt that knocked her on to her back. She sharpened her fingertips and held them to her throat. "Last. Chance."

"Or what?" She finally spoke, a grin as she wiped the blood from her face. "You'll kill me? You wouldn't. And you have nothing for me to fear."

"Don't bet on that." She stepped off the murderer and turned to Mary.

Kara walked through the door and stared coldly at the captive. Her attention shifted to Debussy, and her eyes lingered on his holstered pistol. She closed her eyes for several seconds, then stood next to Jennifer. "Have you checked she is not under the influence of any other power?" she asked both her friends.

Jennifer hadn't thought about it, her attention consumed by the pursuit. Examination through enhanced sight bore no fruit, however. Mary, death sight active, also shook her head. Kara crouched down by their prisoner, who laughed at her. She just waited until she stopped, never breaking her stare. And then she spoke, quietly. "You nearly killed a friend of mine."

"I'll have to try harder next time," the woman hissed.

Kara rolled her eyes. "The longer we don't find Manta and his little cult, the more people will die. And I will not allow that to happen. So, you tell me where to find them, and you tell me now."

Their enemy did not break. "I do not fear your friends. I have even less reason to fear you. And I welcome more deaths. Take revenge. Kill me if it will make you feel better."

Kara twitched. "You won't get off that lightly. Have you ever been to the Unresting world?"

"Unresting?"

"The name refers to the dead, who haven't yet found their peace. From experience, for someone like you or me, it's not a nice place to be." She removed the deathcloth jacket from herself and threw it over her face.

"Kara?" Mary interrupted. "What are you doing?"

Kara ignored her and watched for a moment as the woman attempt to throw it off, but then hindered her escape effort.

"Kara!"

Kara released her hold on the jacket and let her victim throw it off. The escapee gasped for air as she got clear. Then Kara grabbed the woman under her chin and forced her attention once more. "That's just a touch from the place. Mary, here, can take you there."

"The Eternal Darkness," she muttered, looking at Mary.

"That's what the Manta Court call it, then?" Jennifer mused.

"Then you know what I'm talking about," Kara said. "Have you heard of an oubliette?" Her enemy seemed baffled by the question. "The tiniest of dungeons that could only be accessed from a ceiling hatch. Like the name suggests, it's a place in which one can easily be left and forgotten. One word to the lady here, and that's it. You go somewhere no one will ever find you. You don't want to spend ten seconds over there. You really don't want to spend so long there that time will mean nothing to you."

Mary looked over to Jennifer, wide-eyed and whispered. "Okay. She's scaring *me* now."

Jennifer raised a hand. "She's up to something. Go with it." She had no doubt that Mary could have made good on the threat Kara offered. She also knew full well she wouldn't.

"I've never heard of the Manta Court."

"Liar," Jennifer snarled. "You helped the Grey Lady. I know she was here."

"Ah. The Right Hand. She had use for those souls. If only she had time for your friend, too."

Kara ground her teeth. "You'd better hope somebody still has use for yours." She stood and walked to the door. "Wait a minute. You're saying you don't know who the Manta Court is, but do know the Grey Lady? What about the Consanguinity of Enlightenment. Mean anything to you, sister?"

She looked at Kara as if she had asked the most ridiculous question, and then sat up straight.

"You think the Consanguinity and this Manta Court are one and the same? That is not *my* court. All those threats. And you know nothing about what you see. I have nothing to concern myself about."

Mary outstretched her arms, and with an effort of will, gathered an icy wind around herself. Jennifer shivered as she felt the edge of it. Behind the rogue officer, a high but thin black rift formed in the air. She raised her right arm higher and the door slammed open. "Sorry, Monsieur Debussy, but this matter needs to be private. What goes on within these four walls, stays within these four walls."

Through the bitter cold, Debussy trembled as he shifted past Kara and out. Kara retrieved her protective jacket and wrapped it around herself. Once sure Kara was safe, Mary continued. "And as for you, you have every reason to fear us. My friend here wasn't lying about the oubliette. Remember your place."

"You're too late." The woman looked up, her eyes burned with conviction. "*Winterstorm* is underway."

"What are you talking about?" Jennifer asked, but the officer simply grinned as she sprang back to her feet and ran for the portal.

"*To Winter's End!*" she yelled, and then dived straight through. Mary gasped, then leapt in after her. The rift instantly closed.

"What are we up against?" Kara asked as they both stared at the space.

Jennifer threw her arms up and wide. "I've got nothing."

The portal reopened. Mary stepped out with the Consanguinity fanatic in her arms, pale grey of skin and with protruding black veins. "A few more seconds and she'd have been done for. And she won't be talking any time soon."

Jennifer sighed. "So, that's our trail cold again then."

"Not quite." Kara looked down at the unconscious body. "I may have a plan."

CHAPTER TWENTY-FOUR

Debussy returned to the room, flanked by two members of his own team. "I don't know what just happened in here, but I want answers."

Kara glared at him. "Even if we had them, we have a friend who needs medical attention. Have you taken care of that yet?"

"I'm asking the questions here."

"And all the while you do," Jennifer interrupted, "more people will die. Friends and colleagues of yours. We'd like this problem to go away as much as you would. But we could use your help."

Kara spoke, low and measured. "See how well you go catching them without it. If I need to waste time explaining to you what just happened, then neither yourself, nor any squad you throw at them will have any idea what you're dealing with. And that means you aren't ready for it. And if you aren't ready, you won't last until morning. So, your decision, but I suggest you either get on board or get out of our way."

Debussy hesitated. "I'm in charge."

Jennifer shook her head. "You don't even know if your superiors will give you this gig. But in charge of us? You wouldn't know where to start."

"And currently, neither do you. So, you need me."

Kara's eyes remained locked on his for a moment, but she eventually conceded. "I wouldn't go as far as to say *need* you."

"What did you have in mind, anyway?" Jennifer asked.

Kara sat back at a computer terminal and pointed at the screen. "Before we arrived at the station, Manta's lot found us by tracking the car we, ahem, borrowed from him. So, we know we can track his cars. And if they're all registered to the Contessa D'Amato, that ought to give you a list to work with. Speaking of vehicles, is the driver of this computer nearby?"

Debussy raised a smile. "Good idea. We have a means of finding the thieves. Thank you for your suggestion. Now, you have until I count to five before I have you all arrested for being in my way. One."

Jennifer bashed the desk with a clenched fist. "I'm telling you, this'll go badly for everyone."

"Two."

"If we walk out of here and you try and stop them, you and your men are as good as dead."

"Three."

Kara grabbed Jennifer by the wrist and shook her head at her, then turned back to the officer. "You're scared, aren't you?"

He paused long enough for Jennifer to gauge his answer. "He looks terrified. Quite right, too. The police haven't done well at all against this gang so far. I don't think he's sure he can do better."

"Four."

At four, the armed officers inched forward, ready to move them by force if necessary. Jennifer sized them up and rated they'd be on the floor as soon as they touched her sleeve, but thought better of escalating the situation further.

"Have it your way." Jennifer signalled the others to the door as she made her own way out. "Don't say we didn't warn you."

~*~

"Had to open my big mouth, didn't I?" Kara fumed. "They were so busy running around like headless chickens they hadn't even thought of that basic thing."

"They would have done soon enough," Jennifer calmly replied. "And they've got the resources to throw at the problem."

"You're probably right. And they got Hammond into an ambulance. Considering what you told me, he's looking well."

"He's getting better by the minute. He'll probably want to join us in an hour's time."

"He's got my number. If only we knew where we were going."

Mary raised a hand as if still in school. "I may be able to help with that."

Kara shook her head and waved her down. "We are not doing that again."

"No, we aren't. We don't have to. I've got a very strong link to the Black Ghost Door, as Cristobal calls it, and it won't exhaust me to do it, either."

"Won't that be guarded," Jennifer enquired, "like the Gate Chamber?"

Mary nodded. "Absolutely. But while you were chatting, I called ahead."

Jennifer frowned. "Thought you got a dead signal over there?"

"I didn't mean literally. One useful thing about Cristobal having so many friends around is that, well, they're around. Certainly in Paris, anyway."

Jennifer grinned. "And what's our plan back there?"

Mary wagged a finger. "Just me on this one, unless you want to risk the dead roads as well. You'll have to give me an hour or so, but I should at least be able to run a trace on 'Miss Grey's' rifts, now that I've had a bit of personal contact. As you say, she reeks of it. And can't close a rift neatly for toffee."

Kara hugged her hard. "You're a genius, Mary!"

"You're the genius," she replied. "I'm just the one crazy enough to leap into oblivion on a regular basis."

Jennifer ran her tongue over sharpened fangs. "You got that right. Don't be too long. They won't."

~ * ~

True to her word, Mary returned to the original rooftop she initially entered Paris on. She had Cristobal with her, the two arriving hand-in-hand.

"Much as I approve of the extra backup," Jennifer said, "what have you done with Antoine?"

"Left him with a large TV and a fridge full of snacks," Mary said. "Oh, and a pretty strong ward. He won't be wandering to the shops, and nothing's wandering in there, either, without jumping through some very nasty hoops."

Jennifer gave a thumbs-up. "So, where are we going?"

Mary cleared her throat. "You're going to love this. I think they're in Italy."

Kara nodded to herself. "I can well believe it."

"It was easier than I thought it would be. There's quite a bit of Unresting juice gathered around there. Not like a gate, though. Something else."

"It is just as Mary says." Cristobal adjusted his hat. "Just collecting energy. Even here, my flock seems disturbed."

"I'm feeling every beat of it, too."

Now that Mary and Cristobal had drawn her attention to it, Jennifer noticed something as well. A sense of agitation in the air. She had thought nothing of it, with car horns and loud shouting; nothing out of the ordinary in a capital city. She assumed it to be tension as she awaited Mary's return. But in the hour she waited, she had witnessed fights on the streets, and a series of car crashes that hadn't looked entirely accidental.

Cristobal reached under his cloak and revealed that he was carrying two swords. He unclipped a scabbard from his belt and handed it to Jennifer. "I understand Manta is a strong swordsman." Jennifer nodded. "I should like to see if I can offer a few tips. And first, I must ensure you have a strong sword. Blades from Toledo are well-known, of course. Their strength and quality is legendary. Some rare weapons even have the strength to stand against more mystical opposition."

Jennifer examined it through her chromatic vision. "It looks like it hasn't aged a day, but I can't see any special power about it."

"Nor have I been able to, all this time. I like to think that some ordinary human beings possess extraordinary talents." He unsheathed a similar blade and assumed a combative stance. "Now, let's see what you have."

They sparred for half an hour on the rooftop while Kara fielded a phone call from DCI Hammond, apparently quite miraculously back on his feet. He asked them to meet him outside Charles de Gaulle Airport before he flew home. Mary sat eating and recovering her strength from the Unresting travel.

Jennifer twirled her blade through her fingers with perfect poise and fluid movement. Then she returned it to its scabbard. Cristobal signed off with a sweeping bow. "What you have learned in minutes, others cannot master in years or decades."

She reciprocated. "I shall let you into a little secret: it's a gift of mine, just as you can speak with the dead. But I'm new to this thing."

He smiled. "Not new, I gather. Just newly aware."

She considered his words, and reminded herself of her target. "When I last fought him, he wore some tough-as-hell brown plate armour. And he enjoyed stomping as well. Kept throwing me off my feet when he did."

"*The Armour of Earth.*" Cristobal exhaled. "That alone would have been a challenge for you."

"You know what that was?" Jennifer asked.

"That was definitely part of someone's trophy collection back in the Second World War. I remember having to deal with an incident in Tours. Part of a unit of SS testing; that, and other artefacts, like the shadow cage."

"You think it might have been Glauco Manta's work?" asked Kara, looking thoughtful.

Cristobal straightened his clothing following his sparring exploits as he thought about it. "Now that you mention it, there is every possibility. All I know is that I intervened to stop them murdering most of the town to just see what it did."

"What happened?" Mary asked.

"I summoned a black portal and threw most of the unit through it. The SS officer in the armour escaped, but the town was clear. Well, a little."

"Still under Nazi occupation at the time," Kara stated. Cristobal nodded in confirmation.

"So, what do you know about it?" Jennifer asked. "The more we know about what we're dealing with, the better."

"Probably very little you don't already know," the Spaniard responded, unsatisfied with his answer. "The SS officer inside the armour came under no gunfire from me, so I do not know its tolerance to that, and you know of the crushing strength it provides."

"Bit like what I had when I was wandering around your turf?" Mary suggested. "Only without the added hideous?"

Jennifer arched an eyebrow, then snapped her fingers. "It was almost exactly like that! It could well be a Primal set of powers. That would explain what I felt during the duel. I thought it was just me being off-kilter, but now that you mention it, Manta matches skill with some nasty tricks that armour offers him. Still, things will be different when I see him next."

"They certainly will." Cristobal threw on his hat and whirled the dark cloak over his shoulders.

~*~

Hammond stood, propped by a short wooden cane and greeted them all warmly. "You're right about everything," he said, looking at Kara. "They're completely clueless. Debussy's actually here with his squad. Five, including him, tac gear all round. Not one of 'em under six foot."

"It won't do them any good," Jennifer griped.

"So I gather." He steadied his weight against the cane. "I caught a few details, but my French isn't great. They're thinking the next place to get hit is the *Musei Capitolini*, so they're letting Italy take the lead. But it's officially an Interpol operation, so these five clowns are getting in on it. *If* they get there before it's all been robbed."

"Wouldn't happen to know if there's a crown there, would you?" Kara asked.

"No clue. Why?"

"Because if there is, that's what they're targeting."

"Wouldn't know. I didn't get to earwig that much about it. Scotland Yard is aware, but I'm waiting for them to call me back. I don't fancy my chances of getting the nod, though."

"Stupid decision," Mary reiterated. "You'd think they'd want to be seen bringing the robbers of the British Museum to justice."

"Well, I certainly do."

"Good decision," Jennifer countered. "You're not fully fit. Anything less with this lot and you won't be going home anyway. Just not in the way you thought."

The chief inspector's phone rang. He stepped away from the others for a couple of minutes, then slammed the phone to the ground and stormed back. "Bastards," he spat. "What's wrong with them? Gilt-edged opportunity to get in on a big one and they *don't* want anything to do with it? 'Leave it to the Italians', they said."

The DCI waved his flight ticket home at the others, as he handed Kara a note. "Look," he said, "I've been threatened with severe disciplinary consequences if I go. Apparently, the nation is to have nothing to do with it. So naturally, that extends to you three, too."

"Actually," Kara objected, "you'll find that we're not here on any kind of official business, so we're not quite governed under the same rules as you."

"Besides which, I'd *love* to see anyone try to stop us," Jennifer answered.

Hammond gave half a nod. "I'd hoped to get us all on the first flight to Italy, but I've got no chance on that now. Unless you can pull a rabbit out of the hat somewhere."

Jennifer sighed. "Well, that's us stuck, then. Only thing left is a portal jump. And we've not enough protective clothing to go around."

Mary shook her head and stood in front of Kara. "Not to mention blind jump. Not happening." It was not up for debate. "Portal's way too risky."

Hammond looked anxiously to the squad, who looked confused at Mary's words. He then turned back to Kara, who shot him a stare of 'make this decision for yourself'. Appearing disgusted with himself, he started towards the terminal. After a few steps, he spun on his heels and called back at Kara, "They need you," then walked away.

"Well, that's just great." Mary seized Kara and Jennifer into a huddle. "You know, I could just *make* them put us on their plane, right?"

"And then what?" Jennifer asked. "You gonna keep that up for the whole thing?"

"I say let them go." Cristobal forced his way into the circle and offered his opinion. "We can get there first anyway."

"Well, the only reason I asked, other than the fact that tactical support would've been useful, was to get us a lift," Kara said. "As we said, we're not blind jumping again."

"You might not have to." Cristobal offered. "I can perhaps get us to the contessa's place at least. We port back from here to mine, then I can work on dropping us there."

Mary shook her head. "I told you, no. It nearly killed us last time."

"Perhaps because we tried to land on a person," Kara countered. "People move. Buildings don't."

The huddle dispersed into a standing circle. Mary and Cristobal looked at each other for a moment, clearly having the same thought. Then Mary addressed them. "Reckon you're right. Just a shame we don't know what we're getting into."

"It's risky," Cristobal added, "but it's that or let the police handle it alone."

"And we already know they can't," Kara agreed.

"Right," Jennifer said through gritted teeth. "But going through your portal's something I really shouldn't do." Kara started to get out of her jacket, but Jennifer slapped her to stop. "And then what are you going to do? Much as I'd have one less thing to worry about, you're not exactly going to sit on the side lines, are you?"

"Better I sit this one out than you do."

"But then who'll translate for us? I can't speak a word of Italian."

"It's not exactly a conversational visit, Jen." Mary stopped for a moment and then grabbed Jennifer by the chin and forced eye contact between the two. "Wait a minute—this isn't about the coat, is it? It's unlike you to be finding excuses. What's the problem?"

"You know what the problem is!" Jennifer raised her voice enough to attract the attention of passers-by.

"I don't." Mary loosened her grip and pulled her hand back. "Why don't you tell us, Jen?"

Jennifer twitched, then glowered at Mary. "Your world. It can't be good for me. When Violet came for me—"

Mary shook her friend firmly by the shoulders. "If that had been anyone else, they'd have been dead in a quarter of the time. You only survived that because you're you."

Jennifer shuddered as she remembered again those needle-like fingers jabbing into her, freezing her with a cold akin to none she had felt in her life. The other experience she cared never to repeat. But to go through any shortcut through lands of the dead . . .

I can't go through that again. I just can't.

People will die if you don't, and you know it.

A cold sweat ran down her neck, but she gently released herself from Mary's grip. "You're right. But I'd still rather we all went than left anyone behind."

"Go team!" yelled Kara, offering high-fives to the others. They all, Jennifer included, gave her a strange look, but indulged her. "Now, we've some catching up to do, but unless we've got another jacket, we're stuffed on that one. Damned annoying I don't have my passport. I'm at an airport, after all."

Mary's eyes lit up. "You've got enough for a flight though, right?"

"Yep, I can put it on a card."

"Right then. Back in ten minutes."

"Where are you going?" Jennifer asked.

"Loo," Mary replied. "Where'd you keep your passport, K?"

"I don't see how that's rel—" Kara started but then gasped. "Aha! Bedroom, strongbox in the wardrobe. Key's in the kitchen, top cutlery drawer. See you in ten." She gave Mary a hug. "And thanks!"

Mary winked, then headed straight for the ladies toilets. Jennifer grinned. They were going to love that one on the cameras.

~*~

In Cristobal's cellar, Mary and Jennifer witnessed the area he protected. The cold aura of foreboding proved much more subtle than that of Grenshall Manor. But then, the gate stood at half the size, too. The shadowy door bore a more elaborate design of curved arch and stylistic, almost embroidered edges.

Mary and Jennifer stood in admiration several steps away. Jennifer couldn't help herself when she gave a wry smile. "Kara would have been all over this, wouldn't she?"

"Totally. But I'll bet she's all over the complimentary first-class snacks right now. Good thing there isn't time for an in-flight film or we'd be down a team member."

"Nah. She'd kick herself if she missed the post-flight entertainment on offer."

As testament to the difference between the *Fantome Porte Noir* and the Grenshall Manor Gate Chamber, Jennifer stood just feet away from the hub of dark power without the slightest concern. However, no sooner had she realised as much than the thought occurred to her: it could equally have been a simple change in mentality on her part. Much had changed in recent days.

Cristobal raised a hand, a gesture of power, as he muttered words in his native tongue. The beautiful patterns shifted, and solid darkness retreated into the void within. With clear sight, it looked as if a door opened inward. "Step free," he said, and stood aside, prepared to go last. Jennifer advanced, ready to go first, but a thought hit her, and she turned to Cristobal.

"Maybe not getting there the easy way was a good thing," she suggested. "We don't have to worry about Customs and Excise through that monstrosity."

"Oh, yes. That means you can have this back." Cristobal grinned and pulled aside his robe at the waist. As Jennifer watched, a chill breeze whirled around him and a shadow appeared on his belt. In just a second, it took shape into a scabbard, a sword's hilt clearly visible. He handed her the weapon she had been training with. "And that's why I said I would look after it for you. There are some places modern technology simply cannot search."

Mary gasped, but then nodded and grinned as she worked it out. "You hid it in the Unresting? Neat trick. I hadn't even thought about that with *Tally's Peace*. That could've been awkward."

Jennifer played with the scabbard. "Now I feel properly dressed for this party."

"Then my work here is done." He gave a satisfied grin. "Good to know I can still teach you new pups some old tricks." Mary made a barking sound and gave a mocking grin. He rolled his eyes. "Jennifer, one more thing: you can only go to one place, no matter what, as long as you keep moving straight. Do not try to turn back; just keep moving."

"Keep moving. Forward, not back. Got it."

CHAPTER TWENTY-FIVE

Jennifer stepped through the open portal and felt an immediate cloying discomfort upon her. She walked from the light of the living to a place in which she could see nothing. She started to hyperventilate, though she could feel air to breathe, slimy as it felt on her lungs. And every part of her, covered by deathcloth or otherwise, felt as if a hundred icy fingers tickled her with oil.

For every second she spent there, the place seemed to slap her around the face with its sticky decay. She could see nothing in the absolute darkness, but could feel probing, poking, something akin to being licked in the face by a tongue twice the size of her head.

She barely noticed the sudden return of light as she dropped to her knees and emptied the contents of her stomach onto the stone upon which she emerged. Wiping her sleeve across her face, she shuddered at the smeared, black dust that clung to it.

She looked up to the click of a weapon being cocked. Before her stood an armed guard, dressed as one of Manta's own. He levelled his weapon at her, but visibly shook, his wide, startled eyes darting between herself and the open portal behind her.

Jennifer gathered her wits in a split second, and launched at the guard with all her strength. She barrelled him onto his back. A single blow eliminated the danger of him raising the alarm.

She regained her own breath. She looked out over the edge of a balcony that clung to a huge stone fortress. An ice blue lake, lush greenery and beautiful hills formed its picturesque backdrop.

But the guard couldn't have been the only one. Jennifer looked around, up, down, and behind. Luckily, the veranda stood high in the small fortress, which restricted the chances of much above her being able to see her. Behind her stood the open portal. No guard lurked beyond that. Fortunate.

The black door rippled. Through it first came Mary, then Cristobal. Jennifer placed a finger firm to her mouth and waved to demand them down. She waved again. *Now.* They obeyed the command and crouched as she moved silently towards them. She pointed at the unconscious guard. Mary drew a hand across her throat, the question in her eyes. Jennifer quickly shook her head.

Cristobal pointed and then held up varying numbers of fingers. Jennifer shrugged. She pointed back at the motionless body, then gestured behind her. Cristobal nodded and dragged the body inside. Jennifer then tapped her chest and held up two fingers, then the hand to order that they wait. Mary nodded.

Jennifer remained low and scuttled back outside, looking up. She spotted a stone lip above the open doors and adjusted her footing, then sprang up and seized the edge. She pulled herself over, crouched down, and looked around. A guard stood at either end of the roof, both looking out beyond the fortress walls. It would be difficult to reach one without being spotted by the other eventually. Left or right?

It didn't really matter. She scampered spider-like to her right and swiped her arm at that guard's ankles. She half caught him on his way down and, with her free hand, chopped at his throat and punched him unconscious. She turned to the other, who proved alert enough to turn at even that slight noise.

She reached him in three huge bounds as he raised his gun. Before he could raise the alarm, she dropkicked him in the chest off the edge of the roof and straight down. Glancing over only long enough to be sure of a safe landing, she leapt after him and controlled her fall as she hit the balcony just one storey down. She drove a forceful kick to his temple, enough to stop him wailing for a while anyway.

Movement behind. Another guard. He raised his weapon, but she charged at him and punched aside his aim, then buried her knee in his stomach and her fist into the back of his neck. *Area secure.* Or at least enough of it that they could proceed.

She ran onto the veranda wall and neatly leapt across to the next, jumped left into a handstand; rolled forward, stood up in front of Mary and Cristobal. They joined her in standing.

"Did you have fun?" Mary whispered.

"Useful warm-up," she answered. "Next job is to find ourselves a Kara."

"I can do that." Mary sniffed at the air. "Just keep me from getting shot at, yeah?"

Jennifer nodded, then removed the borrowed jacket, handing it to Mary. She replaced it with a Kevlar vest she stole from the nearest downed guard. She turned her attention to the man in the dark cloak. "Cristobal, go with her. Watch her back. Let's meet up again right here." He doffed his hat. The pair took three steps before disappearing from her sight entirely.

Jennifer chuckled. *She's like a bloodhound,* she thought, before mocking a sniff herself. But her smile dropped the second she did so.

She could smell something. A hyper-natural freshness. Blood, both ancient and new. Herbs and plant life of unfamiliar potency. The last time that happened . . .

She lowered herself to one knee and placed her hands against the floor, her focus heightened, just as had her sense of smell. With quick and quiet meditation, she attuned each of her other senses to the Primal strength. It was as well she did.

In the heart of the fortified residence, she discovered a glowing beacon of power from her world. Not a source, nor a gate, for she knew how to identify such with ease now. A distraction, perhaps, but not one to be readily ignored. Though connected to her own power, closer examination revealed a sense of suffering, strain, which made her feel feverish. The blood had not been spilt voluntarily. Someone had taken it by force.

She listened at the door of the open-plan room. Only the sharpest ears would have caught the sound of the minimal movement not far from the door. She held still, attempted to assess the direction, whether there were other such movements. As she focused, she could hear feet treading lightly against the stone flooring. She did not fear an exit through that door, but it seemed tactically unsound. Perhaps it would be easier to drop a floor as she had already.

The door burst open. She kicked the gun barrel away from her and hauled its yelping wielder in. She drummed in sequence at his head, throat and gut with her fists, then dashed to the wall, and leapt above the door. With immense strength, she suspended herself static until two more guards ran inside. As they ran past, she dropped on the second and easily dispatched the pair of them, then sprinted outside.

Two more. The element of surprise gone. Still at high speed, she leapt straight across the railings of the central spiral staircase and into a somersault. She caught herself on the next level down, held the railings with a firm grip even though upside down. Gunfire zipped around her, but the speed at which she moved, the hop, skip, and jump patterns she followed, left the shooters way behind.

She had barrelled through one of the gunners before she had even realised, already flying through the air and several steps past where she'd left him. She caught the bottom of the railing and made her body rigid, then hauled herself up by her arms. She arched her back and curled her legs tight until she could flip up and over.

The other got on to his radio—that one she couldn't prevent, but he wasn't going to finish his conversation. She planted her feet on the ground behind him, but he spun around. She ducked and grabbed his right wrist, taking all his momentum as hers to control, then rolled her body in and twisted him into a throw. His back bounced off the bannister and he flew over it. She lunged out to grab him, but misjudged the distance and snatched into the air as he fell, back first, several floors down. She smacked the ground, furious with herself as he crashed into the floor, worse than just unconscious.

Jennifer wiped a bead of sweat from her brow as she scanned for further hostiles. "He tried to kill you, remember?" she muttered to herself, as she found no others within sight. She returned her focus to the Primal energy within the place.

She followed her senses, sprung from point to point on the staircase, and landed in front of a brass door, a good couple of feet taller than her. She listened but heard nothing. Given that the door had been guarded more heavily than any other in the place, that she had found, her suspicions ran high. She stretched just her right hand, felt the familiar tickle as it extended into a full-weapon appendage. The action hurt to perform. Definitely unusual. She pushed at the door.

Jennifer heard a bang and witnessed a brief flash of overwhelming blue light. Her muscles seizing, she flew backwards and crashed into the staircase behind her. Everything turned upside down. Without thinking, she lashed her right foot outwards and caught the top of her foot on a railing. She looked around and found herself teetering through a hole in the balustrade. Smoke came off her singed skin, but she had healed as fast as she noticed. Her balance restored, she controlled her fall.

An electrified door. The contents of the room intrigued her. She dusted herself down after the unexpected lightning strike. "Primal gift," she muttered with a grin. She slid her feet and kicked hard to reach the other side of the gap on undamaged ground. She vaulted over it and returned to the door.

She could feel the lightning still coursing through her and shook herself out. It wasn't her first time on that count. With slow, focused breathing, she controlled the flow of the energy around her, and concentrated on thunder, rather than lightning. She stood just in front of the door and raised a fist, adjusted herself into a *kata*.

The energy surged through her with every movement, and she channelled its flow, grounding herself solidly from the feet and allowing the rest to flow upwards and into the prepared fist. With a furious shout, she stepped forward, and in the same move, hurled her fist at the door.

At the last moment, she opened it into a palm, but that palm may as well have been a speeding car. The door crumpled like a can and shot away from her. In the distance, she heard walls crumble, glass shatter and shouts as the door flew to the back of what looked like a large room, now missing most of two walls.

Jennifer counted two guards under the rubble. A third crouched and fired on her, but shaky hands wrecked his aim. She drew her sword and ran in, bounced off the rubble which she used as springboards. She landed to his side and, with a sweeping strike, disarmed her target. With the same momentum, she rolled into a roundhouse kick and laid out her opponent, unconscious.

When certain her immediate surroundings were safe, she returned her weapon to its scabbard and retracted her talon. Then, her eyes were drawn to the power they first sensed. Under the rubble, behind the door, she could see a glowing silver object of considerable size. Many pieces of paperwork with scrawling and sketches lay in the wreckage as she moved past, blown out of a wrecked strongbox. She shrugged and started to shift debris to get to what shone beneath.

After a moment, she shifted enough to see her objective. A suit of metal plate gleamed even through the mass of dust. She couldn't place it since it looked like none she had seen before. There was something . . . *futuristic* about its appearance, certainly no antique. Puzzled between this and the power it exuded, she dug further.

The second her hand contacted it, the metal, rigid enough to withstand the metal door and the rock fall, rippled.

"What?"

She touched it again. The same thing happened. The further she pressed, the more the metal liquefied. When she pulled her finger out, the chilled mercurial substance followed briefly, malleable at her will. She extended her senses. The flowing plate glowed in her sight, but more importantly, felt familiar somehow, *comfortable*.

With her vision stretched, so did she stretch her will. The liquid metal trickled up her arm, soon encased it, and continued to encompass most of her body. Though a part of her remained cautious, she felt no worry. Within seconds, the metal covered her, solidified, and was broad of shoulders.

She stood, barely restricted, and moved around almost as easily as if wearing loose-fitting clothing. It had even worked around her sword, the scabbard still an entity unto itself. She shook out her limbs, her motion unimpeded.

As she looked at the wall, she found herself facing a portrait of the Contessa D'Amato, but she wore no such armour, just a dark dress and a pretty, red necklace. One she'd seen before, but not on the contessa . . .

. . . on Cerise.

Before she had time to mull it over, movement at the door attracted her attention. She drew her sword and got three steps across before realising she recognised all three figures: Mary, Cristobal—and Kara. They each gaped at her in her metal regalia.

"You look awesome in every sense of the word," Kara stated.

Jennifer flicked her hair, flattered, but then scowled. "I thought we agreed to meet upstairs?"

"Wanted to know what the noise was, didn't we?" Mary answered.

"You could've endangered yourselves."

"Exactly!" Kara smiled. "Why should you have all the fun?"

"Because I can take it?" Jennifer retorted. Kara smirked and raised an eyebrow.

Jennifer walked over to the sprawled guard and relieved him of his body armour and spare ammunition. She took the weapon she had kicked out of his hand and handed both to Kara. "You know the rules: you go out on business, you dress for it."

Kara slid on the safeguards and checked the weapon over. Her eyes lit up halfway through her check. She hurried it along, then rushed past

Jennifer. "Here's a rule for you, Jen: if the bad guys leave a bunch of paperwork behind a fortified door, in a place you only get into by accident because you've smashed everything else around it, it's probably important." With that, she scooped up every piece of paper within sight.

"Looked like gibberish to me," Jennifer retorted.

"Just like most of the stuff I handle. Nothing's gibberish these days until I can prove it isn't about to ruin a city. Change of policy since last year."

"Can't argue that logic," Mary chirped.

Cristobal looked outside. He shimmered into an incorporeal form as he stood near the edge. "More guards to secure, I see?" He grinned, and then vanished entirely. Kara flicked through some of the mound of paperwork she had collected.

"Can we do that later?" Jennifer snapped. "Don't we have a museum to be getting to?"

"Quite," said Mary.

The others looked at Mary and shrugged. But Jennifer also nodded. "Let's get into position and take it from there."

"Fine," Kara said. "I just thought I'd check if there was anything that might be of use, such as this list of names here and—oh, hang on. Holger Winter's crossed off. The curator guy. And is that . . . *Vikash Sankram*?" She glared at one of the pieces of paper with some concern.

"Like, your university contact at Cambridge?" Jennifer asked. "Must be a different one. Come on, let's go."

Mary made to seize the papers from Kara, but stopped short just as she got a hand to it.

"You think that's weird. I'm sure I know that handwriting from somewhere . . ." She shook her head. "Nah, that's ridiculous."

"There are a lot of names crossed out here," Kara observed. "The contessa is one of them, which makes little sense, unless . . ."

"Come on, you lot!" Jennifer demanded. "Let's talk outside a place that doesn't belong to people trying to kill us."

"You wearing that outside?" Mary asked, tapping Jennifer's armour. It made the expected clanking sound and felt as solid as metal plate should have done, which slowed Jennifer's momentum.

"*Alice Winter?*" Kara blurted.

That stopped Jennifer dead. "*What?*"

"Alice Winter." Kara tapped at the paper. "The name's been crossed out. There are a number of names on the list crossed out. Vik isn't one of them. Nor is Doctor Nadeem Rahil . . ."

She trailed off into silence and ignored several attempts to get her attention from Mary. Eventually she snapped back into action. "Nah, couldn't be."

"Couldn't be what, K?" Jennifer asked, authority in her voice.

"Forget about it, it's daft."

She closed in and burned a glare straight at Kara. "No thought is daft at the moment. You said so yourself not a minute ago. And I haven't seen you look like that in a long time. So, what's up?"

Kara shook her head. "That's the same name as my old Arabic teacher. Wouldn't have paid it any mind if it wasn't for the other names I know on this list."

Jennifer shuddered. "And one *I* know. Not a coincidence, I'll bet. Mary, what were you saying about the handwriting?"

Mary quivered for a moment, but her face remained blank. "Just felt familiar, was all. Not a clue why, though."

"And the two names we know that are crossed out are confirmed dead." Jennifer stated. "So once again, we're in way over our heads here."

Kara nodded. "You got that right. They all have headings. Manta Court. Sibelle Court. Lyris Court. How many of these 'courts' are there?

Kara chewed her bottom lip. "There aren't many names not crossed off this list. Literally, just the ones I mentioned. I wonder; the robberies all took place in high-profile locations, all under the name of someone definitely dead. What are we missing here?"

"The two you know," Jennifer enquired. "One's in Cambridge and the other London, is that right?"

"No," Kara replied firmly. "Dr. Sankram has been abroad for about five years now, but never stays anywhere long. Remember just before I met you?" She turned to Mary. "I was in the States with him for a while. Dr. Rahil last taught at the University of Madrid about two years ago. He's been in Cairo since, but told me to keep it to mys—oh, the cheeky bugger!" She stamped her foot on the ground. "He *knew* someone was after him all this time!"

"Just like Alice," Jennifer added. Her fingers shot to combat length without her realising as she thought about it. The armour adapted automatically.

Mary's mouth dropped open as she darted back and looked down at Jennifer's hands. "I make it possible that all three of them did, then."

"You know, people really should stop trying to keep any of us out of trouble." Jennifer snarled. "We're going to find it anyway."

"Speak for yourself," scoffed Mary. Then she sighed. "Actually, you're totally right. There's not a trap in the world we can't blunder into."

"Trap . . . That's it!" Kara punched the air. "This whole thing's looked like a series of traps for everyone else on the list. Only they've gone to ground, haven't they? Whether or not the Consanguinity have got the Crown of Kings, they're also looking to finish the job with that list. We just happen to be the only ones fool enough to show up."

Jennifer pulled at her hair in clumps and paced around the wreckage. "And the police are about to walk into a bigger ambush. Manta just threw down a gauntlet for any remaining members of the Order of Winter. They'll either finish whatever Order members turn up, or just kill everyone there anyway, and move on."

"Leaves us little choice but to spring the trap," Kara concluded. "But at least we know they'll be there."

"Then we'd better not miss our invitation." Jennifer strode to the gap in which the door once stood and started to walk down the stairs. "We'll take one of their cars, if that's all right with our driver?" Kara smiled.

"You remember they're tracked, right?" Mary asked.

"I'm counting on it."

CHAPTER TWENTY-SIX

Darkness fell by the time they reached the National Archaeological Museum, Florence. Jennifer gave everyone specific positions, tasks that they were to perform if they were to have half a chance of success. They had to deal with being outnumbered and unsupported, their one possible ally in the police likely to treat them as hostile.

"You'll have the same problem as the other police, Kara," Jennifer instructed. "Body armour alone won't do you any good against any of the court. Two of them I've experienced personally and I still can't tell you which way it'll go. One of them I know next to nothing about. That may be worse. But I can only deal with the things I know about. So, you two," she pointed to Cristobal and Mary, "watch out for the Grey Lady. She doesn't need a second to kill."

Even me. And I don't know if this armour will stand up to that Wraithblade. But I can't tell them that. Not for what I've got planned.

"I want you two out of sight, full ghost. She can probably see you, but nobody else can touch you, so you're still at an advantage. Pick a good hiding place and it gives you another." The two nodded. "Kara, you remain within contact with one of them until we're engaged. And keep the deathcloth jacket on at all costs, in case Mary or Cris need to initiate a rapid extraction. Do you suppose the local police took you up on the evacuation call?"

"They have to take the kind of threat I phoned in seriously," Kara replied. "It's a little hard on them, but worth the risk over what they would've faced."

"Great. I want to know how they've been taking the power out all this time, if I get the chance."

"You and me both," said Kara.

"Actually, that's a good point. Cristobal, you stay on the rooftops with me. Mary, you keep Kara secure."

"And when Debussy's lot show?" Mary asked.

Jennifer pressed into the passenger dashboard hard enough to crush it. "They've no idea what they're walking into." She ground her teeth. "We'll just have to look after them."

"Yep." Kara bowed her head and the four took a moment to consider.

They agreed to go ahead with the plan, and each moved into position—Cristobal in the Unresting world but on a nearby rooftop, Mary and Kara in a recently evacuated house on a different side, and Jennifer above the house before which they had parked the stolen Audi. She figured she had a decent view of the important parts of the area from there.

Jennifer wished she had a little more time to appreciate the scenery, but a sightseeing trip would have to wait until another time. The part of town they had entered became deserted, word of a chemical spill clearing the area. She spotted Debussy's strike team, with an Italian task force, fanning out towards the front of the museum as a deterrent.

In the darkness, the hairs on the back of her neck tingled, a surge of power alerting her augmented Primal senses. The jolt reverberated around her head, followed by a stabbing scream. She clutched her head, and thought it might have been about to explode. She looked around for a possible source. Nobody else had reacted at all. A problem, then, exclusive to her Primal connection. She needed to keep herself together, now of all times.

Behind her, a *whoosh* and a crackle. She spun around. The tell-tale waft of deathly decay encircled her. She couldn't see her assailant, though. A flash of lightning engulfed the area and with it, the lights, the power, went out.

Within the flash, an armed silhouette appeared. When the flashes receded, she identified Cerise, brandishing an ornate metal sceptre.

Jennifer sensed a wave of humidity. Too late. A bolt of lightning flew from the weapon. It slammed into her chest and launched her backwards far through the air. She landed and slid to the edge of the roof. She scrambled for something to snag with her bladed fingers and hooked the edge of the wall with her left hand, but went over the ledge.

She slammed her right hand into the concrete and anchored herself against the fall. Her entire body quivered from the shock. She heard boots grind step by step closer to her, but they stopped, out of reach. Cerise loomed at range and examined her with a curious but detached look. She twirled the engraved baton and levelled the point at Jennifer's head.

"*Magnifique*," she said, attempting a forced smile. "The Armour of War. I've had that in my collection for some time now—" She put her free hand to her mouth, feigning embarrassment. "Goodness me, I *am* getting ahead of myself. *Lord Manta* has had it in *his* collection for a few years now. We haven't been able to figure out how to actually wear the thing. And yet, it seems to like you. Fascinating."

Jennifer pushed up, a moment too slow as Cerise deftly stepped forward and swung the staff straight into her face. The blow hit with real precision, testing Jennifer's grip to the full. A second swing left her teetering with one hand and a bloodied mouth. Cerise dared take a step closer. She squinted as she watched Jennifer flail. "It's uncanny. Maybe you *are* the Face of War after all."

The woman in the blood red dress evaluated Jennifer for a moment. "No matter," she scoffed. "Whatever the outcome, it serves just fine."

She moved to Jennifer's left, closer to the edge, then peered downward.

Jennifer glared at her. "What do you mean?" She swung her loose arm and returned her grip to the edge of the building. No sooner had she buried her fingers in, Cerise danced over and stamped her heel down with immense strength onto her left hand and drove it into the roof. Jennifer howled as bone cracked, the heel also pinning her in place. She knew she was a sitting duck, but attempts to free herself took time. Time that she didn't have.

Cerise gave a false grin. "Your rematch, of course." A crowing laugh, nothing artificial about that. Then she moved back and twisted the tip of the staff to aim at her again. "Of course, that all depends upon you surviving the fall."

Cerise closed her eyes and Jennifer saw heat steaming from the weapon. The air grew humid and her lungs dry as a sound like a gun-shot pealed out from the tip of the staff with a blinding flash. A bolt of lightning arced out and smashed into Jennifer's chest. She couldn't identify what hit first—the burning, the impact akin to being hit by a fast-moving motorbike, or the shrapnel of breaking stone.

Jennifer fell.

She looked around and saw the blur of a building a distance away. She gathered her will in a snapshot and expelled the plate from her in a liquid blast. Her mind could not get past falling. Worse, impact.

Her thoughts flashed to flight—to wings—like the Essence had given Mary . . .

Jennifer spread her arms and straightened her fall. She could hear a rip, felt her clothes tearing at the arms and her arms themselves feeling lighter. She flapped them once. Her descent slowed rapidly. A second allowed her enough control to evade a parked car. She stretched her legs with a small bend, braced for landing.

Her feet hit the ground. Too fast. She ran. Not enough. She rolled. Couldn't control it. Five, six, seven, eight, nine revolutions, then smashed through the glass of an evacuated house and head first into a wall. She slumped as she flickered out.

The blurry room spun. She couldn't have been down long. But importantly, she survived the landing. The wrecked lounge she occupied refused to still as she attempted to get up.

She'd just sprouted wings. So little time to absorb such a thought as she tried and failed to stand upright. The Primal Essence had been trying to get through to her that she could do more than grow weapon appendages. It felt similar, too.

Standing took two tries, but eventually a mantelpiece provided good support. She'd cut herself heavily on the glass, but no sooner had she noticed, her powers expelled it, piece by piece. After a few steps, entirely whole, she dusted herself down and exited the house through the front door.

She reached for her sword. *Gone.* She used her senses as a search-light for her abandoned plate. To the right. Maybe fifty metres away. The moment she tracked the location, however, those same senses became overwhelmed by many other energies.

The stifling, clammy stench of the Unresting loitered in the air in several places, unsurprising given the known combatants. Primal power exploded around her chromatic vision like a firework display, in addition to occasional fire of a weapon muzzle. Lightning flashed above her, no doubt that dread weapon Cerise brandished.

The strikes lit up a snapshot of the vicinity. Silhouettes moved into positions and dodged a number of attacks. Bullets whistled and howled in intermittent double bursts. She heard shouts in several languages. One curtailed abruptly and ended in a gurgle. That demanded her attention. She tried to ascertain the direction but could neither see nor hear over the deadly rave going on around her.

Her sight steadied, she stretched her claws and moved in a crouch to the spot she determined her armour to be. All the while, she endeavoured to remain alert.

Not alert enough. A figure burst from a house, a gun pointed at her. His yells were dizzying in the midst of the fray. She identified him as one of the *carabineri* from his carefully targeted fire, and slowly raised her hands above her head. She realised her mistake when she caught sight of her own shadow in the lightning. Her talons exposed. He took aim.

Two shots rang out.

The officer hit the floor, a hole in his temple and the side of his throat. Jennifer ran. Unable to see the shooter, she hoped her pace would be enough to evade the fire. Only just. Ahead, the morphing metal gleamed even within the shadow, and she called for it while she moved. It poured into two puddles. She dived at it, and it engulfed her during her forward roll.

Another Consanguinity guard ducked around a corner and replaced his ammo clip. Jennifer pounced, unnoticed, and slammed him to the ground as he turned to catch her flash through the air all too late. She knocked something off his head. Night vision goggles. She shattered his gun with one swipe of her metal-enhanced talons and brought the back of her fist down into his face. She rolled off him and got back on to the street.

The lightning flashed again. Movement above her caught her eye. Fast moving, cloaked shadow. It went dark again. Seconds later, a body hit the ground below where she had been looking. She ran closer to check, then gnashed her teeth. Another dead police officer. Not a mark on him that she could see.

She looked up again, this time with Primal sight, but only caught a trail where the Grey Lady had been. Another ghostly presence stopped and dropped something toward her. It glistened as it spun awkwardly through the air, but she sidestepped and seized the hilt of her falling sword.

Cristobal waved a salute and then vanished, his target clear. She returned the gesture, even though she knew she acknowledged thin air, then looked for other disturbances.

She did not have to search for long. Primal energy dazzled her as the ground rumbled and rippled ahead of her. She recognised the attack and leapt to avoid being flattened. It felt stronger this time. Buildings shook from the force and a police officer bounced head-first off the ground to her left. He'd probably survive as long as he stayed down. She turned to face the origin of the tremors.

"Manta."

She withdrew the talons and shifted into an offensive stance with her sword.

His eyes lit up as she stood in front of him. "You!" He flicked the safety catch of the submachine gun he carried and threw it aside. He then threw off his cloak and revealed the muscled Armour of Earth. The suit throbbed and pulsed in a bright brown to her Primal sight.

"Me." The self-proclaimed noble had her undivided attention. "And you've got this all wrong."

"I'm getting what's mine."

"You're being used."

"Stop stalling. I'm going to kill you, like they should have done the first time." She could hear the sneer more than see it from that distance.

"You haven't managed so far. And you're not listening to me."

"Why should I? You're *still* dragging your knuckles." He paused for a moment, studied her. "Albeit in a new suit."

"The Armour of War," Jennifer stated, bullish. "Take a good look. I really look like the portrait of the *Face of War* now. You should be worried."

"You have proven enough times you are no prophecy."

With that, he stepped forward and brought his foot down hard. The pavement burst and exploded in a line towards her, but she lowered herself for momentum and hurled herself forward, into a somersault. She landed right in front of him, brandishing her sword. Manta scuttled back a step and parried. She moved side-on to him. The tips of their swords crossed.

"On guard, then," she said, and launched a salvo of swift, snake-like strikes toward his head, his arm, his leg. Quick as they were, he parried each of them, then lightly tapped his foot. Jennifer staggered as the ground rippled, and he smelled blood.

He thrust as she tried to regain her feet, but she brought her sword to guard. Her footing remained disrupted though, and he exploited this by launching a series of probing attacks. She whirled and flashed her blade, remembering every step the experienced Cristobal had taught her.

His attacks stayed focused, but very aggressive, forcing her back. She used his momentum to her advantage and danced her way back to more control. Still he came, but she lured him out into the long street. With her free hand, she jabbed at him with a talon. Not a dent on his armour, but she had broken up his attack.

She gave a mighty lunge downward and forced him to block the strike. She whipped a blow under his exposed arm. He staggered, but got his guard up before she could press further. They both reset their balance, then Manta went for another small stomp.

Jennifer threw herself sharply to the ground and swept his trailing leg. He fell backward but rolled with it as she spun and flipped to get after him. She swiped on her way up, a miss. She still got to her feet faster than him, though. She used her inertia to make a fluid leap into a low flying kick at his head, which staggered him.

He took a few more paces back and growled.

"Are you ready to listen to me now?"

"I will not yield to you. Quit now, while you're ahead."

"I'm just getting started." She crouched and scraped her metal claw against the ground, a homage to his earlier insult.

Around Manta, the ground morphed, the air steaming hot. She didn't need her chromatic sight to feel the force of will he pointed through the suit, his summoning of Primal energies for an imminent attack. Taking no chances, she pulled her sword back and leaned herself down to one knee. The second she was down, she hurled her blade at him with great velocity. He turned it aside but underestimated the strength she'd put behind it. The deflection knocked him into a half-kneel.

Manta bellowed, louder than he should have been capable of, and pounded the ground with both fists. She steadied herself against the mini-quake which slowed her again. She followed the tremor, and leapt as if riding the crest of a wave. She sprung at his back, but he dodged and scooped up both swords as he returned to his feet.

No worries. A small effort of will and she had ten blades to his two. She ran at him.

CHAPTER TWENTY-SEVEN

The death sight countered the effects of darkness in the living world. Mary had taught herself as much over her months of practice. She could see the battle in light and shadow, life in motion, life taking life, death snuffing out light. With as much going on, she couldn't identify the level of success or failure, but her priorities remained in finding the greatest threat, that which only she and Cristobal could see.

In her death sight, that dark shadow buzzed near lights, and every contact put out another. Unchecked, the Grey Lady could end the battle in seconds. Mary had to do something about that.

But Kara appeared to have other ideas. They remained in cover, as originally planned.

"That wasn't an EMP at all," Kara reported. "An artefact. Above us."

"Yeah," Mary whispered over unnatural wind. "You'll have to get up there without being seen." She hadn't taken her eyes off the Grey Lady. Another police officer died with every moment she hesitated. "You want a shot at whatever that is? If so, we go right now, and we make it quick."

Kara looked around, nervous, but nodded. Mary remembered that Kara couldn't see her in the ghost form. Reluctantly, she grabbed Kara's hand and willed the shadow winds to wrap around them both. Within seconds, they reappeared on the roof.

They both spotted the armed redhead as she blasted a bolt of lightning downwards and across the street. A group of four clustered officers lit up, their bodies convulsing for a couple of seconds before they fell, smoking against rain which had just started. They never stood a chance.

A red-cloaked figure stood behind her, also wielding a staff. The shining golden weapon illuminated the wielder, but his face remained obscured beyond a stubble-strewn chin. He flicked it forward and a ball of flame smashed into another officer with force enough to snap his back as he fell.

Kara reacted quicker than Mary and raised her weapon. She fired a couple of rounds in Cerise's direction, but they bounced in a shard of sparks from a crackling bubble surrounding her they hadn't previously been able to see. The bullets zipped harmlessly off the ground, away from anything. If nothing else, it gained her target's attention, though.

The redhead twirled around, a sadistic smirk on her face. She levelled the staff at Kara, who threw herself aside as the lightning charged up. With a flick of her wrist, Mary blasted Cerise with raw Unresting energy, spinning her to the ground. Mary moved to press, but the figure in the red cloak unleashed a fiery hell in a wide arc between the pair of them. Even through Unresting sight, the fire's intensity blinded her.

"KARA!" she screamed, but to no answer. The heat of the living flames died out just as soon as they had appeared. But the silver-staffed woman remained in front of her, looking deeply unimpressed. "Hiding where you belong will not save you, death-walker," she seethed.

And then it dawned on her. The face, the voice, they were different, but the spirit remained the same. Foul, wilful, cancerous. If anything, it had deteriorated since they last met.

She hadn't met the woman at all, personally. But the familiarity became undeniable.

"I'm not hiding from you." She made her voice echo like an ancient presence. "You, however, are quite distinctly perpetrating a ruse."

The redhead remained unfazed by Mary's theatrics. "You sound like someone I once knew. Her meddling cost her dearly as well." She waved the staff and the Unresting air whipped into a violent storm. Mary tried to seize it with her will but the force caught her and hurled her off the roof. She clenched her fists and scrunched her eyes and shrieked a command to her domain, a demand to return to where she stood. As the shadowed ground approached, she returned to her original standing position and opened her eyes, just in time to see her enemy leap off the roof.

She ran to the edge of the roof and witnessed the woman fly down towards the museum, her path clear. Mary plotted a course to the ground ahead to intercept, then let the dead winds wrap around her and do her bidding.

Mary threw an arm out at the fleeing woman and made it solid as she caught her straight in the throat. Cerise landed on to her back. Mary lunged for the staff, but the woman took Mary off her feet with a chop to her ankle. Cerise stood and swung the staff hard into Mary's gut, knocking the wind out of it. She drove it again into a rib. Mary screamed. A third swing caught her jaw and left her dazed.

"Fine." Cerise threw the staff out of reach and produced the knife very similar in appearance to the one Mary already possessed. "I have precious little time, but more blood may prove useful. As will a chance to walk around in *your* skin, especially."

Mary refused to risk it. She flicked her wrist and directed a blast of

Unresting energy at Cerise's arm. The quick, weak blast smacked the knife out of her hand and sent it skittering away.

The words repeated in Mary's head. *In your skin.* The bodies missing skin in the Primal Realm. The place she called the Flayed Glade when seeking out Jennifer in the Primal Realm flashed firm in her mind.

As Cerise moved to retrieve the weapon, Mary stood and raced after her. She attempted a diving tackle. Cerise swatted her off, but she landed near the knife. She seized it. Cerise straddled her and held her wrist as the two battled for control of the blade.

That presence. All too strong to forget. Stronger than ever, in fact.

Cerise started to get the upper hand, and grasped the hilt. Mary held firm.

"I shall find another way . . ." Tally's last memory, as Guardian and dead relative. And Mary had already seen that the rules of aging didn't apply to everyone.

"The name Iris Grenshall mean anything to you?" Mary grunted.

Cerise raised an eyebrow as they struggled. "Why would it?"

"Because your daughter, Violet, rampaged around the streets of London last year. Nasty mess I cleaned up."

Cerise gained full control of the knife. Mary turned her mind to the murderous side of the Unresting void and allowed it to run through her. Her attacker drew back as if electrocuted. Veins swelled and rose to the surface of increasingly pale skin. Her knife hand came down, but Mary caught it and intensified her death grip. Cerise attempted to escape. Mary latched on, and they grappled to their feet. But with that contact, she instantly relived the entirety of Tally's final moments. And the true owner of the body before her.

The real Cerise Favager was a genuine healer. Red-haired, but she often dressed in blue. Lady Aurelia Raine chose to wear red, not her.

No, she preferred to not be referred to as 'Lady', not since the early 1900s, not since she fled Grenshall Manor after an interfering young whelp scuppered her plans. The necklace had power, that much was true, but she threw it away in the manor grounds. Such unpredictability in an artefact would thwart her again. She could not risk that.

She ran to India, and for a relatively small favour, gained a useful new companion. Shavana Singh. The troubled girl had killed, several times. The only reason she survived, in fact. Shavana told her she wanted to forget all about that, and the rest of her life. Raine gave her the chance. The cloak. No wonder the reminiscence of the Guide.

Decades later, the Manta family had served her, the Consanguinity well. Their misfortune, her gain. The child. If she could plant a seed early, he would serve a valuable purpose. Years passed. Perhaps someone of solid social station to finally convince him. Ah! A contessa! The time was right to change her living arrangements, anyway . . .

Vortext, that worm Cerise met at the hospital, it turned out had a talent even he hadn't been aware of. Easier to control it directly than bother to cultivate it. The sap would have had a conscience to deal with—just unnecessary time-wasting. She'd crush that weak will of his and keep him on a mental leash for the time being. And as for Manta . . .

The disguised Lady Raine shoved Mary away with the strength of several people. She trembled for a moment, but within seconds, her pale skin flushed back to colour and the usually lethal vein protrusions faded away.

"You sick bitch," Mary spat.

Raine retrieved the dropped sceptre and took aim. "Fine. A swift, expedient death it is," she said, and charged the weapon. "Lucky for you I can waste no more time with your likes."

Two gunshots close by rang out. Raine jerked back. Two more shots dropped her. Mary turned to identify her rescuer. Kara remained in a crouch, her aim firmly on the twitching body. Mary gathered the force of the Unresting into an intense shadowy burst she launched directly at her downed enemy.

The attack harmlessly dissipated against a spherical space around Raine. The woman rose, rolling her eyes. She snapped her arm forward and offered her own brand of lightning in return. Mary opened a wide rift of darkness between them to swallow it. As quickly as she closed it, Lady Raine had vanished.

~✶~

Cerise's lightning strike missed Kara, as did the column of flame that followed, but her evasion efforts sent her tumbling down a flight of stairs. She shook her head, reeling from the fall. A small orange glow at the top of the stairs burst into life and a stream of flame flew at her. She threw herself at the nearby door and crashed through, and yelped as the sting of the impact rattled down her leading shoulder. Her right foot felt suddenly warm. She looked down. Her shoe had caught fire. She beat her foot repeatedly against the floor until the small flame extinguished.

Her firearm lay out of reach at the bottom of the stairs. She sat up, about to crawl over. The figure in red took aim with the golden staff and she scrambled back, out of the line of fire. Her hand brushed against a corpse and she jerked away. Her enemy roared and threw his staff arm forward. She flattened herself and rolled to evade the assault. Her ribs jabbed into an abandoned rifle. She quickly checked the safety catch and levelled it at the doorway, then loosed a controlled burst. After the fourth round, the gun clicked.

It bought her time. She yelled and charged straight at him with the gun. He easily turned aside her attack with the staff and swung it into her stomach. She staggered backward and collapsed. The cloaked man gave a satisfied smile and somehow ignited the tip of the device. Unarmed, she cowered backward and prayed it would at least be quick.

Two shots rang out. The cloaked man staggered backward, and lunged his arm forward. Kara heard a man scream behind her. She lurched upward and grasped the staff with both hands. She pulled back and down until he fell on her. Kara held tight as his grip weakened, and eventually faded.

With a mighty effort, Kara forced him to one side and he slumped, motionless.

Kara's hands stung with the heat of the weapon, gripped in a position other that intended. She got off lightly, though. She gave a solemn salute of gratitude to the fallen officer whose sacrifice allowed her own survival, and clung to the instrument of his death, in the hope she could do some good with it.

~*~

Manta's two-weapon offensive came quick and brutal. Jennifer's parries, unorthodox weaponry, and rapid footwork proved more than up to the task at hand. She tested his own with jabs and swipes from a number of angles and got inside his reach advantage several times. She struck six precise attacks to chest and arms, but his armour held firm. Each time she gained the edge and tried to press her attack, he pounded the ground with his foot and slowed her.

His blades whirled through the air with unerring accuracy. Back and forth they stepped on a dance of precarious stalemate, neither giving ground by error. Manta's swordsmanship was exceptional, but his combat had hit a rhythm, which Jennifer noticed. She disrupted it with a feint and a backflip to offer him forward. A second flip kicked his off-hand weapon—her borrowed blade—clear of his grip.

Her talons blurred with speed and intensity and forced Manta firmly on the defensive. She shifted her feet with every flurry and overwhelmed him, forced him to alter his sword grip to a critical disadvantage. With her next attack, she slid talons between the blade and the hilt and rotated her body.

The momentum forced him to rotate if he wished remain armed. A swift, hard kick to the head took him off-balance. A second just above the elbow on a supporting arm felled him entirely.

Manta had one more trick up his sleeve. He bashed the ground with his gauntlets and it rippled around him. He rolled twice and spun to face her, then smashed a fist into the ground. The road exploded into a shower of rocks, each of which hurtled at Jennifer. She brought her arms up to guard and Manta made a staggering leap, which threw her backwards.

Jennifer rolled with it and turned it into a throw. She was already in the air when he landed on his back and she came down and plunged the blade into his plate. He half-dodged and the attack pierced the side of his stomach. Manta roared in pain, then clenched a fist and swung it straight into her plated stomach.

Her entire body quivered like jelly as the enhanced blow reduced her movement to wobbles. He followed with another couple of punches. The plate protected her, but the impact could still liquefy organs.

Every blow she blocked hit like a train, and numbed her arms. She accelerated her steps, skipped left and right, and Manta, determined to finish the job, kept going. She retracted her razor fingers and weaved further, encouraged heavier attacks.

Manta swung a haymaker at her head and she seized the opportunity to grab his arm, then sprang over it and threw him down to the ground. She held her grasp of him and lifted him, arching her back. As she pushed halfway up, the muscles in her limbs burned and she seized in place.

She screamed, and Manta fell away. He moved stiffly, grunted, but she couldn't at all. He slowly brought himself back to his feet. She watched helplessly as he gathered his sword, and plunged downward into her stomach. It made a loud clang as it skidded off her armour. He growled and hoofed a boot at her instead.

She twitched, but remained rigid as she fell sideways. The cramp became a secondary pain to the pounding howl in her head, as if someone had tried to rip her apart from the inside. She writhed and thrashed on her back like a fish out of water.

He brought a foot down on her stomach and the impact winded her. However, it had not flattened her as she had expected. Manta himself looked confused and then repeated his action. Thrice. "Even with the plate, I should have crushed you by now. But it looks like you have problems of your own." He raised his blade over his head with both hands.

"M-Manta. L-listen."

He shook his head. "No more talking." As he brought the blade down, she managed to force enough control into her right leg to slam it into his shin, skewing his strike. She scuttled out of his reach and retrieved her own weapon, just in time to parry two more heavy blows. He tapped a foot on the ground which forced her to fight just to stay upright.

"Strange. Seems my power malfunctioned. No longer."

He closed in for the kill, despite his laboured movement.

Compared to his malfunction, Jennifer had a total shutdown. The matters had to be connected somehow. She stood even as he stomped again and she wobbled backward. "Manta, listen to me. All the while you're fighting me, your crown is slipping away."

He glanced backward, but advanced, leading with another hard stamp on the ground. She felt a ripple but nothing like the magnitude of his previous efforts. His powers weakened.

As had hers.

Primal power. Disrupted.

She blinked into chromatic sight. Colours appeared pale, sickly.

"Seriously. Do you even know where the thing is?"

"It's in there." He pointed back to the museum behind him.

"Are you sure?"

Manta gnashed his teeth. "This was the last protected place. It can't be anywhere else."

"Except, perhaps, if one of your trusted court has it."

"They'll hand it to me."

"Really?" Jennifer advanced a step and raised her sword guard. "You don't seem so sure. You're winning here. Why isn't it on your head already?"

He twitched, looking back and forth and wavering on his feet. He then growled and punched a nearby building, which started to shake where it stood. He turned and ran.

Jennifer pursued, and the building collapsed in front of her. She adjusted her footing and bounced up to the top of the crumbling pile and then down, but Manta was nowhere to be found.

CHAPTER TWENTY-EIGHT

Jennifer offset the lack of light to the smells and sounds which lingered on the battlefield. Whiffs of putrid, burning meat made her gag as she wandered. Charred corpses and piles of ash lay on the ground where living bodies once stood. She almost tripped over a completely unidentifiable corpse, an officer doing his duty who never had a chance against an unseen enemy. She knew how he had gone, no doubt with a clear shot at one of Manta's lesser underlings only to be unceremoniously taken out by one of his best.

Screams of those still capable were few and far between, and mostly of an armed guard unit Manta had thrown away in self-preservation. One fight continued in the distance. She wearily dashed closer. By the time she got there, the firefight had descended into fists and feet, involving the only surviving police officer she'd seen. Debussy pummelled his enemy into submission with incredible speed and strength.

The powerhouse fumbled for his weapon and changed the clip. He levelled his weapon at her before he achieved a positive identification. His aim was far from steady. "Easy there, beastie," Jennifer said, her hands raised. "It's over."

It took some time before he slowly lowered the gun. "Wha-what just happened?"

She grabbed the strap on the back of his body armour and hauled him upright. "That's what I intend to find out. Stand ready."

His weapon hand still trembled. For her own peace of mind, she yanked the weapon and strap clear of his grip in one clean stroke. "Sorry, mate. You're not fit for rifle duty right now."

He didn't argue. He mumbled with a thousand-yard stare. ". . . My team. I gave—I gave the order . . . to regroup . . . it just hit them. One minute we were talking, the next, burning ash on the ground. Lightning. From nowhere. I've seen nothing like this. Nothing."

Jennifer squeezed him gently. It had to be the staff Cerise wielded. Though apparently metal, the armour she wore conferred some limited protection perhaps, though equally, Cerise may not have hit her with everything she had. From what he described, she had saved something particularly devastating for the four with Debussy, their presence enough of a threat to gain her attention.

"Mary! Kara!" she called out, at the same time as she expanded her senses. Some steps ahead of the pair, Kara emerged from a building, limping up a flight of stairs. Mary leaned against a wall, half upright and holding her ribs. Jennifer released Debussy and sprinted towards the others.

On her call, they turned to face her. Both of them looked preoccupied, mostly by her wounds.

"Manta's gone," Jennifer blurted. "I haven't seen any of the others since we faced off. I had him. Something happened. Something's happening. With the Essence. The keystone. I need to go back."

"So, open a portal and we'll follow you."

"Doesn't work like that. I don't need the keystone, but I do need an actual gate to get across." She stopped for a moment, concentrated. Streams of pale light and colour danced ahead of them. "There's one in the museum. I'm going in."

"Jen, before we go, there's something you should know." Mary hobbled closer and placed an arm on Jennifer's shoulder for support. "Cerise. She's not Cerise. She killed the real Cerise. That's—that's Lady—*not* Lady—Aurelia Raine."

The news stopped Jennifer in her tracks. When she had first been unconscious, it had been a far older enemy that had tried to invade her own mind. That all made sense. It also stood to reason that there had been one thing she'd experienced that would have proven traumatic even for that woman.

The memories of Violet's assault were very much on the surface of her mind at the time of her capture. If that had been one of the first things Raine had seen, even a stout old brain like hers would have been given cause for challenge. That it had affected Jennifer so badly would have been a shock to anyone's system. The combination provided a mental defence even Lady Raine would have found inviolate. At least once. Once was enough. "That explains a lot."

"It also means we may be up against the most dangerous person on earth right now," Kara added.

"Then I'm about to stake a claim for that title. Let's finish this."

Kara nodded. Mary pointed at Debussy. "What about him?"

Debussy looked up and waved them away. "Whatever you have to do to get the bastards who did this."

Jennifer, Mary, Kara, and Cristobal strode to the museum.

Nothing but a hole and rubble remained where an entrance door once stood. With even emergency lights out, Jennifer's cat-like eyes made everything look as if it had been bathed in moonlight. Kara had stolen a set of the night vision goggles which the Manta guards carried, to add to the strange golden fire staff once possessed by Raine's red-cloaked accomplice. That one hadn't been present in Manta's court. She would have remembered.

"If she's broken anything in the Etruscan section," Kara growled, "I want first dibs on her myself."

"You're unbelievable," Mary retorted.

"Seriously. Truly ancient wonders of the world in here and she tramples her way through like a common ram-raider. Doesn't give a damn about anyone or anything, does she? Should be bloody shot."

"That didn't work the last time," Mary pointed out. "But that'll be the least of her worries if I get hold of her."

"Can we just stop racing each other to enemy contact, please?" Jennifer growled. "We don't know what we're actually up ag—"

Mary threw hands up to block both Jennifer and Kara from taking another step. Like her, Cristobal had already stopped dead. "Something nearby. Bad."

Jennifer looked around. She couldn't see anything, but no sooner had she looked, she felt a chill wash over her. An Unresting threat, not her expertise at all, but she had learned to recognise that brand of danger. Kara had retreated, wide-eyed, as far as the door by the time Jennifer noticed her absence at her side. Kara probably hadn't even realised she'd done so herself.

"Kara!" she barked. "Come back!"

"Get down!" Cristobal ordered, and threw himself, and her, to the ground. Mary crouched. Though she couldn't see it, Jennifer felt something awful brush past the back of her neck. Every fibre of her wanted to flee, but she dug in, kept trying to find it. "What is it?" she asked. Already, Mary and Cristobal had formed a protective line on either side of her.

"What *are they*," Mary corrected, crouched as she scanned above them. "There's two of 'em."

"I can't see them."

"You don't want to."

"I need to. We're pinned and buying our enemies time."

"That's the idea," Cristobal whispered. "But these things are serious trouble."

"Then Kara can't stay there alone." Jennifer shifted into a crouch, and sprinted toward Kara. She heard an ear-shredding wail and something sliced straight into—straight *through*—the back of her armour. An excruciating cold numbed and felled her, a more paralysing blow than the attack had any right to inflict. She screamed, then sat up and reached for her back. She touched nothing but smooth, repaired metal, and her agony retreated to little more than a light sting.

"I've seen these before," Mary said, her voice calm, soothing. "Just stay down." The ghost walkers moved from their position, still crouched, and kept back-to-back, as if they'd been working together for years. Jennifer propelled herself backwards, to the frozen Kara, and pulled her down. It sounded like just in time, too. A *shink* sound flew over her head and several strands of Kara's hair fell from her head. She reached up to where the hair had been, and her petrified terror morphed into rage.

"Mary," she said, the accent back to her Manchester roots, "sort that bloody thing out. Now!"

"*Trying!*" Mary sounded like an aggrieved teenager as she pulled *Tally's Peace* from its concealment and stalked the invisible creature evidently somewhere above her. A thunderous roar exploded behind her and she heard something crash into glass cabinets everywhere. Jennifer indulged herself a look and saw Cristobal's staff smoking with darkness. At the other end of the hall, a huge, spectral creature stood and expanded its wings.

"That looks like you, Mary!" Kara yelled. Jennifer couldn't help but notice that important detail about it, its giant bat-like resemblance to Mary's manifestation in the Primal Realm almost uncanny. She restrained herself from comment, though.

Mary's eyes darted around, focused. She held up her free hand. "Hold that thought." Her body spun towards Cristobal and the knife shone luminescent in her hand as she charged and swung into the air, a dazzling arc in the darkness. In the light, Jennifer caught a glimpse of the other, an identical creature with a red glow around it.

A contrast of raw emotion filled the air in a tangible way that should not have been. The red a chunk of raw fury and the arc of brilliant blue light a solid embodiment of pure calm. The cool air dissipated and left the anger to linger in the air. Or rather, to fly around, sentient and on the rampage.

It wasn't in Jennifer's nature to sit out a fight, but the opponent was beyond her. Interference could be a fatal liability.

Cristobal attacked the downed beast as if whacking a training dummy, though he may as well have been for the damage he appeared cause it. It brought itself to its feet and with the speed of the wind, slammed a shoulder into him and sent him crashing backwards. Mary sidestepped to avoid him, her concentration imperious. She leaned right into a crouch and brought her weapon around to the trailing end with an arc of brilliant light. She stood and brought the artefact upward with her hands together in a prayer-like manner. "Cover your eyes," she ordered. Jennifer didn't argue.

Through closed eyes, Jennifer still saw the place illuminate as though Mary had captured the sun. Total and utter serenity flooded her mind and for a moment, nothing moved. Nothing needed to. A cool sensation flooded her mind, washed over her body and anchored her soul. Time froze, perfectly still, perfectly harmonious. She opened her eyes, and caught the room bathed in virtual daylight even as the fiery light faded. The shadow creatures ceased to exist.

"That . . . was . . . *awesome*," Jennifer gushed, like a star-struck fan meeting their idol in person.

Mary shrugged. "I thank you. Now, about that thought I told you to hold. I think I've worked it out. My form in the Primal world. That's one of Tally's memories. They were like the nightmare spectres. The things Raine used to keep near Violet's bed. It's an old trick of Lady Raine's, but she's got a hell of a lot better at it. I mean, they actually *hurt* now."

"Tell me about it." Jennifer's back itched at the mere thought, even though the wound had likely already healed.

"So, the Primal Essence assumed all ghost walkers look like that?" Kara asked.

"Can't be true." Jennifer shook her head. "Otherwise the Grey Lady would've shown up like that."

"How'd you know she didn't?" Mary challenged.

"The Primal Essence showed her differently. I—" She stopped talking as she spotted four skinless humanoids taking position behind glass pillars, each armed with assault rifles. "GET DOWN!" she yelled, just as they fired both in her direction and at Mary.

Behind her, Kara shrieked and flew backward. Jennifer turned and dashed toward her, no thought for her own safety. Several rounds hammered against her back and ricochets whistled past. She checked on Kara, who grimaced, but her protective vest took the volley in full.

Jennifer gave a relieved wheeze when she saw her friend was unharmed. In all the confusion, she'd forgotten about the body armour. Then she spun around and remembered that Mary wore no such protection. A hail of rounds flew into her—more accurately, flew straight *through* where she stood. She didn't so much as jerk from the impact. A closer look revealed she had shifted into a ghostly form in time to render the attack useless. "Still awesome, Mary," she muttered.

Jennifer drew her sword and charged straight through Mary's ghostly form, bullets bouncing off her metal encasing all the while. Jennifer caught her friend shiver as she ran through but swung her sword from her lower left to upper right.

The first of the fleshy enemies fell apart in two pieces. She ran a second through, then twisted a full circle and decapitated the creature. Though headless, it lunged at her. She rode its momentum and tripped it to the ground. She thrust the blade through where the bottom of its spine should have been, but it jabbed a foot into her shin and felled her, face-first.

The other two took aim at her head, but above her, two bolts of darkness threw the pair off their aim. Jennifer forced an effort of will and grew her metal claws, then hewed each limb clean from the body. She launched forward into a rolling attack. Her right talons stabbed a hole into the gut of the creature. She removed her hand, and whirled as she stood up and hacked the skinless monster to gobbets.

She then brought her arms up to guard her face and advanced as the monster emptied its clip on her. She stabbed her claw through its throat and pulled the thing down as she raised her knee. Its head snapped backwards as she drew the claw back and with her full might, threw a shredding uppercut. The remains of its body fell to either side of her and she went back to retrieve her sword. "Controlled aggression," she said to Mary. "Thank you."

Mary gave a weak thumbs-up before falling backwards against the pillar, solid to the touch.

"Oh, no. Tell me *you* didn't get shot."

The Guardian offered a feeble grin. "Okay. I didn't get shot." She slumped, eyes closed. Jennifer slapped her lightly, checking for wounds. "Come on, stay with me, Mary. Mary? Mary!"

"*Urrrgh.*"

Jennifer grabbed her chin. "I can't see anything on you."

"Told you . . . not shot. Resting. Those spectres . . . took a lot out of me, that's all."

Jennifer breathed a sigh of relief and drew her friend close in a hug, careful not to crush her. "You did a great job. But we're not finished. Can you go on?"

"Be fine in a minute. Go check on the others."

Jennifer did as asked. Kara had already returned to her feet and started to loot the skinless killers for weapons and ammo. Jennifer heard a "Yuck!" or "Eww!" every few seconds. She chuckled. As she approached the downed Cristobal, he shook his head and dusted himself off with a groan. She helped him back to his feet. "You did well there."

"Then why do I feel like I've just been hit by a car?"

Jennifer shrugged. She blinked back to her Primal senses and tracked the gate. "This way."

Reunited, they made it into the Etruscan Gardens and down a path, until they found a set of pillars collapsed in on themselves. With her vision, she observed multi-coloured sparks crackle and fizzle from the wreckage.

"No wonder it felt weaker than the last gate," Jennifer said, shaking her head. "They trashed it."

Kara clenched her fists. "I'm going to wring that bitch's neck."

CHAPTER TWENTY-NINE

So, now what?" Cristobal asked as they stared at the destroyed Primal Gate. Mary sat by them in an attempt to recuperate, but Kara stooped, cooing over it.

"Not helping, K," Jennifer grouched.

However, Kara's examination actually had helped. It told Jennifer that it wasn't just her Primal gift helping her to see. "Can you see all that, too?"

Kara turned and looked at her as if she had asked something incredibly stupid. "It's pretty hard to miss."

Jennifer dampened her Primal senses and noticed that the rainbow of sparks remained clearly visible. "Oh."

"That's it? '*Oh*'?"

"Yeah. *Oh*. As in, that's very bad. Whatever's going on at the other side of that gate has hit me, as well. And now they've scuttled it so I can't see for myself. As far as I know, the nearest other gate's somewhere back in France and we're no closer to figuring out what the hell they're up to. Our one chance to stop them and we've blown it."

Kara straightened herself up, utterly calm. "No, we haven't."

"How can you say that?"

"Because you led us here without any trouble. And I can see what you can, right there. So the gate can't be completely dead, can it? Or you wouldn't have picked up anything, let alone me. So, shall we try putting it back together again?"

"*We?*" Mary screeched. "Have you *seen* those bits of rock? They look like they weigh a ton. And I'm in no fit state to help."

"They probably do." Jennifer sounded happier about that fact than she had any right to, but crouched by the stones and weighed them for herself. She reached for the smallest of them, still needing two hands, and attempted to lift it from the ground. It did not move an inch.

"Er, Jen . . ." Kara muttered behind her. "Those sparks—aren't they bothering you?"

She hadn't even noticed until it was pointed out to her, but a kaleidoscope of colours lashed against her. Once she did, she held up a hand. The energy followed it.

"Jen?"

"Shhh!" She concentrated, felt the tingle of power ripple against her fingers like running water. She filtered her mind and let the energy swim over her hand. She felt a connection to the source of her power, though it seemed diluted, muddied somehow. Despite that, the rock she held grew lighter in her hand as she held it, and she lifted it with little more trouble than a medicine ball. By the time she returned to her feet, it felt more like a beach ball.

The energy palette grew pale, weak. As it did, Jennifer felt her own strength waver, but she redoubled her efforts and held the stone with one hand. The faded light field blasted at her like a sandstorm, not empowering her, instead grinding away at her every muscle. Sweat ran from her as she sustained her grip, twitching at first, and then teetering on her feet. With her free hand, she lifted one of the larger pieces upright, level, and back to its place.

The light intensified, grew more vivid, and as it did, her gift granted her a burst of endurance that cried out one overriding demand: *finish the job*. Within moments, she had returned the archway, a different style to the last and in keeping with its archaic surroundings, to its former glory.

When she placed the last piece, the cavalcade of energies trickled into the cracks and a low hum gathered into a raucous buzz. The inside of the gate shimmered as if she had blown a gigantic bubble through it, and then the light show faded and died. She stepped through the arch to a shower of sparks, but apart from that, nothing happened.

"Hmmm." She stretched her will, tried to invoke the strength required to pass through, and though the sparks gathered quickly, that remained the height of her success. The others watched on as she stepped back out. "So, that didn't work. Guess the gate's still out of service."

"It looked like it was at least trying," Kara noted. "Maybe it just needs more juice."

"Kara, I haven't got any more juice."

Mary raised a hand. "And the last time we walked through that same gate, we needed the keystone."

Jennifer examined the top of the arch. "That's why they took it." She then placed her hands in the gap above her and stretched, to the fullest extent of her height, reaching into the gap. "Can't do it."

"Can't do what?" Mary asked.

"Power the gate. It feels like there's nothing there."

Mary pulled a face. "Static gates are weird."

"What do you mean?"

"It feels a bit harsh to me that you have to be in specific places to get into your realm. Especially given you're a big deal over there."

"Nothing comes easy from the Primal Realm. But now that it's been weakened so much, it seems just about impossible."

"Isn't the Primal kind of parallel? Like the Unresting?"

"Well, yeah."

"You can't just pull a part of it open and walk through?"

"Can you?"

"You've seen me do it. But it costs me in energy. And you know where I get that from when I run too low on it. But it seems to me you're going to have to really push yourself. Give the Essence a jump-start, if you will. Quite literally, put your heart and soul into it."

"You don't think I have?" Jennifer snapped.

Mary folded her arms. "Not hard enough, no. From everything you've told me, from what I've seen, you've a lot more to give. That's our only chance."

"I've given it everything I have."

"Really? Because we're still standing here, wondering how we're getting across. You fail here, and we may as well jack it in and go home now. Come on, Jen. I've never seen anything stop you yet, when you get your back into it."

She stopped and turned back to Mary, weary and slumped. "I've never had to manage without the help I've been getting from there before, though."

"Hah!" Kara laughed hard.

"What's so funny?" Jennifer asked.

Kara stopped laughing. "You. Listen to yourself, Jen. How can you possibly be missing help you never really knew you had until you took an accidental trip to France? I mean, you've never let anything like that stop you before. You just dive in with both feet. Most people look to get their fitness up, they consider jogging. Jen skips about three stages and decides to leap tall buildings in a single bound.

"When I call you a force of nature, I mean it to every last breath. I don't expect a locked door, mystic or otherwise, to stop you. And deep down, neither do you. Kick the door down, Jen. Bad folk are waiting."

Jennifer met Kara's gaze. Her friend gripped her hand firmly and nodded. She looked over at Mary, who gave a thumbs-up. Jennifer felt herself choking, just a little, and rubbed her eye, hoping the others wouldn't notice. They did. She stretched and cracked her knuckles.

"Okay. Time we went back. I'm getting in. We're getting in. Because that's *my* turf, and if anyone wants it, they're going to have to come through me."

She spent several seconds drawing air into her lungs. Then, with one controlled effort from the bottom of them, she let loose a scream. A battle cry intended to be heard across worlds. And she held her bellowing note for almost a minute. By the time she stopped, the others had dropped to their knees, hands clamped over their ears. But the gate sizzled with the full range of her chromatic spectrum, lively, snapping and snarling.

"Something feels very wrong."

A surge of power rippled from the gateway and through Jennifer. Her knees buckled and she collapsed to the floor. The arch shuddered and each of the hastily repaired parts of the stone structure fell to pieces. She only just moved her leg before one lump almost crushed it as it hit the ground.

Jennifer screamed in frustration. "It's hopeless! I can't—I just can't do it." She leaned on to her back and rubbed tears from her eyes.

"You can." Mary took Jennifer by the hand and eased her back upright. "You can, and you will. I have faith."

Kara crouched and gently leaned a hand against her back on the opposite side to Mary. "As do I. Easy, Miss. We've got you."

"Damn right," Mary affirmed. "Now, see that knackered archway over there? It needs your help. A bit of Primal elbow grease. You nearly had it last time, I was watching. Just a few seconds more and we'd be through the other side, slapping folk who deserve it. You remember those Olympic weightlifters you saw, dropped the bar a couple of times? Three seconds. Three white lights. This is the same thing. Get that gold medal, sister."

Jennifer consolidated her balance and eased herself free of Kara and Mary's support. "I could have done, you know. Really. A rugby superstar in the making." She forced a defiant grin. "And it would've all been jolly hockey sticks, too. The world missed out. Just wasn't meant to be, was it? I had other things to do."

She diligently replaced every one of the collapsed parts of the structure and returned to her original position. She then channelled her will, her strength, thoughts of glories past, thoughts of what might have been had she had a more ordinary life, and reminders of just how good she felt every time she did some good in the world. And she'd done plenty.

She pushed back, determined to control the energies around her. After a few seconds, the other side became clear. Forest trees stood tall, grey and barbed of branch. Hostile. Demanding that they do not enter. Not the voice of her Primal Essence at all. The voice of the Essence came as but a whisper against the mind-ripping shriek above it.

"This isn't right. This isn't right at all." She turned to the others. "All aboard who's going aboard." Mary, Kara, and Cristobal gathered themselves and formed a queue. Cristobal strapped his staff to his back and drew his sword. Mary stood up, partially refreshed. Kara readied her rifle in one hand, golden staff in the other, and stood at the back of the three.

"Go!" Jennifer wanted to go first, but couldn't risk the gate dropping if she relaxed her efforts. Cristobal took point, followed closely by Mary and then Kara, and once all had passed through, Jennifer lowered her hands and ran straight in.

~ ✽ ~

Heavy rain battered them as soon as they emerged. Dark thunder-clouds rolled above, punctuated by regular flashes of lightning. Kara threw away her gun as it burst into flames and evaporated straightaway.

"Again?" she cried but watched as the smoke flew straight into her staff. She stared agape at it for a moment, then grinned.

Over the rain, Jennifer heard an echoing sob, and it troubled her greatly. Then she realised exactly where they had come in. All around, skinless, soulless dead hung from rotting vines in the trees surrounding the team, far more than had been described by Mary and Kara from their first visit.

The Flayed Glade, they called it, and she could see why. The place stood as a travesty to everything else she knew of the realm, an affront to the defenders of the living and the dead, a grey, sodden embodiment of misery and sorrow.

At the farthest end of the glade, sinuous, blood-red vines rose up and detained a naked woman covered in spiral tattoos, with her back to them. The source of the sobs, and the reason, lay right in front of them. They were no louder than whispers, but throbbed against her skull as if a hundred voices yelled. She clutched her temples upon hearing each one.

"Essence? What's going on?"

The Essence body looked up. As it did, one of the trees shambled into a different shape, appearing to crouch even at its massive size.

From one of the branches, a familiar redheaded, red-dressed woman leapt and landed gracefully between the Essence and Jennifer and her team. She smirked wide and strode towards them. They all drew weapons, other than Mary, who barged her way to the front of them. "It's okay," she said, bullish. "I'm a massive nightmare thing here. I'll stomp her into the ground."

Only now did it dawn on Jennifer that Mary's manifestation hadn't happened that way. If anything, Mary looked like an unblemished version of herself here, a pale goddess in a complimentary white dress and boots with a mane of glorious raven black hair and almost glowing blue eyes. The Essence no longer feared her, and instead, allowed her to manifest in an idealistic form. Another long-gone memory that probably didn't belong to Lady Grenshall. Either of them.

"Mary, about that . . ." She ran to her, grabbing her by the hand. She lifted it, and Mary had the same realisation. "Aww, crap."

"Why do my guns keep doing that?" Kara asked, mostly to herself. "And why is the staff still—oh, hello . . ." The tip of the staff burned like a torch, and the rest remained exactly the same as it had before.

"Not now!" Jennifer chided, as the red figure stopped several paces in front of them. Jennifer enhanced her senses. The figure didn't *feel* familiar. In fact, it didn't feel like anything at all. And unlike the Cerise or Lady Raine she'd seen before, the person who stood in front of her had no discernible weapons or jewellery. It was like a shell of the woman she'd encountered previously. She took a step back. That was *exactly* what they faced.

Around them, the dying vines disintegrated entirely. Each of the hanging bodies dropped to the ground.

And then, they stood up. They advanced and surrounded the four.

"Okay," Jennifer said, trying to keep her composure. "Really not good."

"You don't say," Mary whispered as she mimicked Jennifer's retreat.

The sobbing grew louder. Jennifer fought for composure as the noise tore through her head once more, but the sight of the Essence, the friends she had dragged into peril, consolidated her will. The four united and formed a circle of their own, far smaller but concentric nonetheless. "Does it speak?" asked Kara, a question directly to the Cerise shell.

It pointed at each of them and counted aloud. "One, two, three, four." It bowed, then beckoned the skinless to close in on them.

The wailing grew overwhelming.

"I want to go over there," Jennifer stated.

"We'll come with you," Mary said. She equipped herself with *Tally's Peace* and held it in front of her. The blade appeared as a bright, but not burning light in Mary's hand. But then Mary leaned back as if repelled. "Of course. It's not a weapon, now, is it?" She replaced it in its holder, looking far less concerned than she might have done.

"Your powers stopped working?" Jennifer asked, at the same time as she waved her own blade.

Mary bobbed her head a couple of times as she pondered an answer. "Only some of them. And I knew about those." She blinked, her eyes instantaneously taking on the inky black properties, but then she thrust a hand forward. Jennifer watched as the ground blackened underneath Mary and flooded her in shadow. From the tip of her leading hand, black fire vaporised the nearest puppets with ease. "And it doesn't wear me out here, either. Right, go!"

Jennifer broke and charged toward the trapped Essence. The Cerise-shell stepped into the way. Jennifer tackled it down to the ground. Then, something completely unexpected happened. The skin simply burst from the body and launched straight at her, at a velocity she could not avoid. On contact, the skin slapped all around her and wrapped first around her face. Everything went dark. No space was left to open her mouth or breathe.

She hit the ground and writhed to escape the suffocating attack. As she tore at the skin, it rapidly reformed and kept her trapped. She ripped, it wrapped, but she stretched for breath as she battled the extraordinary assault. Through flashes of sight, she saw the rest of the skinless charge at the others, and only Cristobal's rapid sword hand stopped them from caving under the weight of numbers.

The flesh struck again. She scrambled to her feet and scraped and scratched and spun around to rid herself of the ruinous thing. She felt herself grabbed, held as it squeezed harder than ever. Her strength, her resistance, faded as she ran out of ideas. Armour proved no good whatsoever against such a uniquely wretched peril.

Armour.

I'm still wearing it! Maybe . . .

Jennifer ceased her struggle, instead diverting her focus to the liquid suit underneath the wicked husk. With one thought, she demanded the protective Armour of War to expel. In one movement, it obeyed her command, exploding into a star shape. With it, the skin stretched and ripped to match, and the armour shook the suffocating death clear from her.

The force also proved sufficient to break the hold of the newest skinless creature, the body previously harbouring Cerise. She wasted no time with a firm back kick and went for the sword she dropped in the struggle. In a swift stroke, she despatched the wretched thing and turned to her friends, just in time to see the swarming creatures go up in a wall of flame on one side, and disintegrate into a shadowy flame on the other. It looked spectacular, but incredibly freakish at the same time.

On the brighter side, Kara held a pole which burned stronger at one of the tips. At the freshly created gap, Mary's hands burned with shadow. Cristobal cleaned up some of the flaming skinless with rapid, controlled strikes.

The smell nauseated Jennifer. The others reacted similarly. Jennifer held a hand to her mouth and staggered to the kneeling, sobbing Essence. Once she stood over her, she could see a further flesh vine which bound the construct's hands together. That in itself shouldn't have bent the will of an entire realm, but there it was.

She hacked the Essence down and pulled it back up to its feet. The entity still sobbed. At such proximity and able to see it, Jennifer shuddered, almost crushed from what she witnessed.

"Essence," Jennifer pleaded, "it's okay. I'm your Champion, remember? I'm here now. *We're* here."

It stopped the wailing and examined her, its eyes rolling back as they had previously. Then they flashed a sinister red and the facsimile bore fangs. It hissed at her and she fell backward. Its leafy hair mutated into green and black snakes, and they snapped and snarled around her head like a modern Medusa. Razor fingers shot out, twice the length of Jennifer's ever were, and the construct felled everyone with a deafening, agonised wail.

Jennifer scrambled to her feet and held the sword to the construct's throat. *"ENOUGH!"* she bellowed. "We're here to help. Get it together."

The being gave a bestial, panicked scream and backed away. But soon, it reverted to a form more familiar to Jennifer, and gave the most penitent of looks. "So sorry!" it spoke, a whisper on the dead vines. "She-she trapped me here, and—"

Jennifer dropped her sword and walked to the construct. She stroked her hair and offered an arm to comfort it. She wasn't sure if that would work, but there was no harm in trying. "It's okay. We're going to take care of it."

"She was going to 'take care of you'." The distraught construct rose. "Left me here to feel you all die. That's what she said to me."

"Why didn't you stop her?" Jennifer asked, concerned as to what they were up against.

"The crown." Jennifer suspected she'd hear those words, but she knew nothing about how. "The mortal-made artefact. She has claimed the place as her domain, now. I—I can't control—I can't *be* . . ." The being spluttered. "Sh-she's been through here before, always offers sacrifice I can't refuse. For it, I am bound to extend her life. She has her own gate key, but I cannot defend against her. Even less now. Many tricks. Many artefacts. They affect many realms. The crown grants her dominion over them."

Mary and Cristobal looked at each other, the same question burning in their eyes. "Even ours?" the Guardian said.

"I know little," it replied, "but almost certainly."

Jennifer shuddered. "She never intended Manta to have it. If he ever knew what we just found out, she was happy for him to fall by the wayside."

Whatever the outcome, it serves just fine.

"Manta's just a patsy," she mumbled. "And so was I. Lady Raine's not worried about a whole lot these days between the immortality, the lethal bodyguard, and the ability to walk around unnoticed."

"And the people who *did* notice," Kara added, "have one by one been taken out of the picture for good. She's had access to a bunch of these artefacts from the beginning."

And then it dawned upon Jennifer. "Florence wasn't the whole trap. That was just to soften us up and take out enemies on both sides. If we didn't get through, she'd have been happy leaving us there. Now that we are . . ." She turned to the Essence. "Raine and the Grey Lady. Are they both still in here?"

"She's just reached another gate."

"Then close it. Don't let her through."

The construct shook its head. "I can't stop her. Not now."

"Do everything you can. And get us straight to them. We have to end this here, now."

The Essence gave a vengeful smile. "I am no longer bound here. I *can* do something."

"Seriously," Jennifer ordered. "*Everything*. That means ditch the body and stop talking to us." She turned away and headed for the gap in the glade. But as she did, the skinless bodies not disintegrated by Mary stood, still burning. The rotting vines animated into movement and slithered towards them. Behind them, more emerged, perhaps dozens.

"And I will ensure your power does not falter as best I can. I cannot hold our quarry for long," the construct said, whilst already starting to sink into the earth. "They already know you are here. This is *her* doing. Hunt them down."

"Go," Cristobal said, and moved into a battle stance. "This is my business."

"Mine, too." Mary's arms burned with dark flame. "This can't continue."

"Your business is much older." He skewered the closest skinless with a series of deft strikes. "All of you, go!"

"Fine." With little more than a shrug, Mary threw up a wall of ghostly onyx flame. It immolated the remainder of the first rank and slowed the rest. She turned, her eyes burning, and started to walk to the edge of the clearing. "Thanks. For everything."

Jennifer shook with annoyance, evidently reluctant to leave him, but little time remained. "Don't die."

"But my staff . . ." Kara started, then considered her words, ". . . only means we have flaming skinless freaks to contend with—fine, I'm coming, too. Cris—what Jen said."

Jennifer made a rapid value judgement. Kara would hardly be safe, whichever course she took. She'd more than earned the right to her choice. The Primal Champion roared in frustration. "All right," she conceded, but gathered her will as she spoke. The Armour of War, now free of its terrible skin, heeded her call and the puddle crawled until underneath Kara. Then it rapidly formed around her. Kara squealed. "What the—?"

Even Jennifer was unprepared for the conclusion. The Armour of War did not form as a suit of plate, but instead became one with Kara's skin, turning her silver but with no further impediment. Jennifer believed it would do the job she required. "If you're coming with me, you need every chance you can get. Now, come on."

The battle began. Thus, so did the race.

CHAPTER THIRTY

Jennifer took in the landscape as she purposefully led the others in the direction of the violators. It wasn't hard. The trail the enemy left had been far from subtle: trees felled and rotting, rich and fertile landscapes dulled, withered and decayed.

Only now did Jennifer realise the extent to which the Primal Essence had been weakened, restricted, and beaten down. The image of the Flayed Glade, Raine's own image, had imposed itself upon every step they took.

The devastation got to her, but she—they—still had a job to do. Her personal shock would have to wait. Better still, she would find the source of her outrage and channel it well.

The Essence seemed determined to offer one final act of defiance, even as it languished, sapped and battered, in a grave state. Kara manifested against the bleak, despair-ridden backdrop as a gleaming metallic version of herself. A brilliant aura surrounded Mary, her lambent form angelic light against the plague of darkness around her.

Jennifer took heart in knowing that was just what her friends both did these days. Win or lose, their brilliance radiated from within. She didn't need chromatic enhancements to see that.

Like a mystical bloodhound, she led them through a drenching deluge to the eye of the storm, the top of a valley where below, a brooding tempest raged at the other side of a chasm at the edge of her vision. A lengthy, gnarled wooden suspension bridge separated them from a figure in the distance, whose silhouette periodically burned into their sight with each blinding flash of lightning. A second figure silhouetted halfway across, standing sentinel against any who would dare cross.

The Grey Lady.

The three looked over, then peered at each other as they identified the situation in more detail. The assassin's purpose was clear. The furthermost figure—Aurelia Raine. Jennifer's Primal senses overwhelmed her as the Promethean schemer brutally suppressed the Essence of the realm.

The raven-haired woman held a silver sceptre and wore a matching circlet. The sceptre exploded with blinding light as she stabbed it into the sky. The chasm warped. A gate arch blinked into existence for a few seconds, then crumbled and fell into the void below. They watched the same thing happen several times. The landscape warped and shifted with nauseating frequency, and Jennifer sensed the colossal clash of conflicting forces at war with one another.

Raw energy wafted from the circlet in waves of malevolence, every pulse of it making her legs tremble. The Essence wouldn't be able to hold out for much longer. The gate Aurelia Raine battered and bullied would give way to her demands in moments.

"How are we going to play this?" Kara asked.

Jennifer knew her more than well enough to be aware she had a plan, but she trusted the Champion enough to defer. She didn't like to let that level of trust down. "They're in *my* place now," she answered, total assurance in her voice. "So, they play by my rules, or else."

"Are we taking these two bitches down or what?" Mary sneered.

Jennifer could feel the power of the Essence caving under the assaults. "Raine's guard dog won't let us anywhere near that side." She flexed her sword and stepped on to the bridge, then called upon the source of her strength. "But we've got unfinished business, her and I. You two should lock that gate."

"How do we get across?" Mary asked.

Jennifer knelt, pressed her hands into the earth, and focused hard. The Primal Gift called faint in her mind, but she latched on to it, sent a mental distress call for it to keep going just a little longer, and called upon it for one last favour. Within seconds, her skin grew itchy and her hair morphed into a toughened, brambled and wiry knot. For her discomfort, though, Jennifer felt significantly tougher. Then, she stood and turned to her friends, smiling with freshly-grown fangs.

Jennifer placed a reassuring arm on Mary's shoulder. "Fly, of course. Just like you always have here." With that, she turned back and strode toward her nearest enemy.

Against the shadow, Raine's guard stood fast, the onyx blade almost invisible between crackles of lightning. Jennifer closed purposefully on her enemy, not once taking her eyes off her mark. Though the hood obscured the woman's face again, she could feel her opponent's undivided attention, just as she gave hers. Jennifer grinned and raised her weapon arm. She pointed the tip of her blade directly at the cloaked figure. "No more name calling."

The Primal Champion felt the strength of the earth below flow through her as naturally as blood, as clear as the air around her. She raised her foot inches off the ground and slammed it down, then leapt back on to the ledge. The air in front of her rippled, and the bridge did likewise. As each plank flew upward it splintered into a thousand pieces. Her enemy's charge ground to a halt as she shielded herself against a shower of wood, but she seized a length of rope on the way down.

In the blast, Aurelia Raine's relentless assault on the Primal gate ceased as the brunt of the attack smashed into her. The ledge she stood upon crumbled beneath her feet. She caught herself on an intact section of planking as she fell and held firm, both to the failed bridge and to the sceptre.

"NOW!" Jennifer ordered and waved Kara and Mary forward. Mary looked at her, puzzled. Jennifer held her eye in silent assurance. After a couple of seconds, Mary grinned.

A mighty energy surged from the crown across the chasm, and the landscape reshaped at Raine's whim. Rock jutted out from under the woman's feet and shaped into the form of a set of stairs, which she climbed with great nonchalance.

"Oh, come on! That's not fair!" Jennifer grumbled. "But two can play at that game."

Jennifer mentally apprised the Primal Essence of the situation and within seconds, the ground shook. Treetops occupied the chasm where previously nothing but a drop to oblivion awaited. As Jennifer watched Mary whizz past with Kara in her arms, she saluted and took that as her cue. She sheathed her blade and threw herself at the nearest treetop. Over to one and then the next she bounced and flipped with rhythm, grace and balance, until almost to the other side.

Raine had already disappeared through the gate, but Mary released Kara and the two sprinted the few steps required to escape and pursue. The Grey Lady appeared from nowhere and kicked Kara flat. Before she could follow up, Mary threw a blast of dark fire at the assassin. Her enemy dodged with the ease of an expert killer. She turned and closed on Kara's protector.

Jennifer finally closed in and launched her own sword with everything she had at the Grey Lady's head. The cloaked warrior turned and deftly parried the weapon out of the air. It proved distraction enough. Jennifer launched herself into the air and came down, talons out, at the ghost walker. Another parry altered the course of her landing and her enemy, quick as the wind, launched into a combination of strikes.

Jennifer weaved and rolled out of the way, her distraction complete and her friend saved. As she rolled, the Grey Lady lashed out with a kick which left her flat on her back at the edge of the drop. Jennifer lay at the mercy of the destroyer, who brought the Wraithblade up for the kill.

"Jen! Catch!"

Kara threw Jennifer's dropped blade towards her with reassuring accuracy. Jennifer caught it with her left hand and brought it up just in time to block a certain killing blow. She twisted her body and jerked her enemy off-balance just long enough to return herself to one knee. She threw her hand in the direction of the gate, urging her friends on as she held off the deadly enemy.

The Grey Lady threw back her hood. In the Primal Realm, her face appeared skeletal, almost mummified, decayed, flies and maggots lurking in the orifices, skin tough and decomposed almost to bone. She reeked of death, which wafted towards Jennifer in a revolting miasma, but there stood a problem from which a Primal Champion could not falter. Desiccated skin cracked and fell as her enemy offered a decrepit grin. "Try it." Her voice sounded as knives scraping on metal. "Taking your pathetic life will amuse me."

"And it looks like laughing might do for you, too. What's the matter? Not enough fresh blood lately?"

The Grey Lady rolled her eyes. Ash flew away as she did so. "*She* uses blood. No good for me." She looked down in admiration at her dreadful Wraithblade. But something caused her to frown not long after.

"Problem?"

The answer Jennifer received came by way of a growl. Then the Grey Lady charged. She lunged and hacked with terrifying speed, but Jennifer parried with efficiency of movement, equal to each attack. She rode the assault and then countered with precise and powerful but probing strikes. Her opponent did not give her an inch.

The two reset their footing and adjusted their range, then went at it again. The Grey Lady stepped and thrust, stepped and slashed, her offensive lightning fast and unpredictable, but Jennifer controlled her retreat well, dictated their dance with targeted jabs. Neither opponent slipped; neither gave ground willingly. For an opponent denied the benefit of her greatest weapons, the assassin still proved formidable.

The others were through the gate. She couldn't say safely, for Raine proved the deadliest enemy they had ever faced. But dealing with the Grey Lady in the Primal Realm was Jennifer's best chance.

Then it occurred to her: perhaps she could trap her opponent in the Primal world and aid the other two unopposed.

She disengaged and retreated backward, looking for a point to spring from the gate. Of no surprise to Jennifer, her opponent denied her the space. She leapt into a somersault strike with the onyx blade and came down with speed and force. Jennifer jumped sideways and rolled to evade the cleave. A nearby branch sliced clean off where she landed. The Grey Lady propelled herself up and back—straight at the gate.

Jennifer roared with frustration. She brought herself back to her feet, spring-boarding herself straight through the portal in close pursuit.

Immediately, she leaned back in a limbo pattern on the other side and slid to avoid the ambush she anticipated. The Wraithblade swung back at her at full strength and she parried in a fighting retreat from the almost invisible barrage of slashes.

She heard a clang on the ground and only then spotted that her own sword had been sliced in twain at the blade. Jennifer threw herself straight into a series of backflips. She rolled sideways just as her opponent vanished into the darkness.

The edge was no longer hers. Time, just, to gather her surroundings. It was possible that would prove a vital tactical assessment: natural darkness—a real disadvantage against her current adversary, and the wreckage of a room she had entered previously.

They were back in the Contessa D'Amato's self-styled palace, the same room she started in. Debris remained, the veranda still an open run, but that meant no new weapons, just the hope that the Grey Lady still gave her full and undivided attention to her. If not, and Mary and Kara were nearby, things were about to get even messier.

~ ✲ ~

As soon as she passed through the gate in pursuit of Lady Raine, Kara felt a great difference in weight on the armour she borrowed. It remained as if tailored to fit her perfectly, but not the second skin it had been previously. Her movement slowed as gravity bit hard. She recognised the shambled residence of the Contessa D'Amato. Their enemy was nowhere in sight, but even lacking in preternatural talent, Kara still felt an old, malevolent presence.

However, Mary availed herself of her abilities, and scanned the area like a consummate night hunter. Her head darted around in a predatory manner, and she gave a now customary sniff. She stopped in her tracks, a grave look on her face. "Not sure what, but there's some bad juju around here."

"Given known company, how is that news?" Kara rooted around at the door and listened for movement. A moment later, she heard a heavy clattering. "Down there." Both of them ran down the first flight of stairs, but Mary shifted into a shadowy, ghostly version of herself. "Seriously," she said in an echoed whisper, "it's something different. And not in a good way."

"All the more reason we need to poke our noses in."

They reached the door, an eerie, neon-like glow of coloured light shone strong enough to illuminate the floor on which they stood. Inside, their enemy stood in the centre of an elaborately patterned set of three concentric circles, orange, green, and orange again. Outside the circle at four equally spaced points lay symbols of elements clearly recognisable as earth, air, water and fire. Directly outside those, another four unknown symbols.

"Just like Antoine's tattoo," Mary said.

"Yes. Yes, it is."

Streamers of illumination stretched from the outer patterns into the centre. It directly pulsed to the circlet on the head of Lady Raine, who stood static and awash with fiery, eldritch light. Kara attempted to step closer but found her efforts repulsed. Mary fared no better. Kara prepared her fire staff and aimed it toward the centre.

As she did, the occupant of the circle spun round and faced them with a smile. Mary vanished from Kara's sight completely, but it was clear that Raine was tracking movement to her right.

"I wonder what it is you two believe you are about to achieve?" she asked. Her movements carried about them the elegance and fluidity of over a century's practice. Her manner remained calm and precise, not a hint of concern as she swept a silky mop of hair out of her face and exposed cold blue eyes.

Kara folded her arms. "Lady Aurelia Raine. You have a lengthy history of troublemaking, so unless you're about to tell me you're actually *saving* the world this time, we're going to have to ask you to stop."

Raine did indeed stop, but more out of amusement than fear. She looked almost impressed. "And what if I do not?"

Kara hesitated for the briefest moment. She had tried so hard not to offer the slightest sniff of blood. "Well—well, then we'll have to stop you."

"*You* plan to stop *me?* A primordial being with the power of a god lies dying at the hands of the power I possess here. Power you clearly know nothing of."

Kara aimed the staff with a wavering arm. "I know how to use this."

Raine snorted. "Do you, though?"

Kara glared at her enemy. "The thing is, we *know* you, Aurelia. We can quite literally see right through you."

"If only you did." With that, she raised her sceptre and swung it as she might a sword. Kara heard the quietest of whistles above her head—or, at least, where she had been standing. She sat on her backside. Mary's faint incorporeal form briefly flickered in and out of her sight.

"I thought as much." Lady Raine smirked. "Honestly, have you come here to thwart me or replace me?"

Kara dusted herself off and looked around quizzically. Mary had saved her, but Lady Raine declined an opportunity to press her advantage. "What's that meant to mean?"

"Saved by your pet medium. And no doubt you scorn me for having likewise."

"She's no p—" Kara started, and then realised the trap and bit her tongue. She waved a gesture for Mary to take over, though without knowing where she actually stood.

"*Pet*?" Mary spat, an echo around the chamber with a dangerous tone. "Not everyone keeps slaves, Lady Raine." Kara felt the light of the circles fade, only for half a second, then return as before.

"And yet here you are. You hold dominion over the dead, and yet you wait upon her command. How does that make you otherwise?"

"We're all in it together, her and I. Friends. But you wouldn't know anything about that, would you? You, who would raise your own child for nothing more than a human sacrifice."

The resentment in Mary's disembodied voice scraped against Kara's insides. Raine appeared to take no notice, but scanned around as if tracing the movements of a fly.

"Those who hide with ghosts rapidly become tiresome to me."

The circles dimmed again for an instant. At the same time, the blood red jewel flashed bright. Just as quickly, Mary stood outside the circle, clear and solid, looking somewhat perturbed. Her hands flushed with Unresting fire, an act which only served to amuse their enemy further. "We should all converse together, yes?"

"No more talking." Mary unleashed the dark fire in a direct blast, but she leapt back and Kara braced as the contradictory freezing heat lapped harmlessly outside the circles before petering out entirely.

Raine shook her head in disdain. "I ask again: what is it you propose to achieve here?"

"You first." Kara raised her own staff and pointed it, wary of the fact that Raine stood within the protective ring. Despite the fact that she had operated the staff with the simple will to burn back in the Primal

Realm, here it worked differently. And she hadn't figured out how yet, so she just had to try and keep her enemy talking.

The ritualist simpered and played with the sceptre in her hands. "I suspect, too, that even if I proceeded to demonstrate, you would not have the right of it anyway."

"Tally had the right of you a long time ago." Mary stalked around the circle like a cat by a tree, watching and waiting for an opportunity to pounce upon its prey. "What's changed so much since you rampaged through London with the *Grenshall Teardrop*?"

Raine's self-assurance flickered as she glared at Mary and examined her thoroughly, with total curiosity. "Tally Grenshall. What do *you* know of that meddler?"

"Oh," Mary pulled out *Tally's Peace*. "You know . . . *family* business." She closed her eyes and focused in a manner Kara had become familiar with of late. The appearance of the knife distracted Raine further.

"Ah, you recognise that, eh?" Kara taunted, just as Raine threatened Lady Grenshall with the crackling staff. "As my friend says, this conversation's over."

"Pity. I was just—"

Raine's words were cut short as the talismanic knife grew white and then expelled illumination as bright as daylight. Kara covered her eyes at the last second, so as not to alert Raine, but then fell on to her back as the ground shook underfoot. Whatever Mary had done definitely had their adversary's full attention.

The blazing beam faded and, though Lady Raine rubbed her eyes and writhed in pain, the illumination in the surrounding coils and tiles flickered and died in one stroke. Strange sparks fizzled in a circuit and the room grew almost insufferably humid. Lady Raine staggered and waved the sceptre around with reckless abandon. Kara ducked as the air whipped around her any time the artefact waved in her direction. Even an inaccurate slash could have caused severe injury, she decided, and she could see her enemy recovering.

Kara lifted her own weapon and pointed, but it emitted no fire. She had no hint as to how to operate the staff to the full. She willed it, *wished* it, to belch fire, but it either ignored her or refused her.

She saw Lady Raine take a slow and wobbly aim at Mary, who, drained from her massive gambit, seemed sluggish to react. Cursing, she ran into the inactive area and raised the staff to a more martial stance. Though off-pace, Raine managed to change her aim and point the sceptre straight at Kara instead. The plated Kara tried to alter her footing, but a surge of buzzing energy whammed into her. The strength of the attack lifted her off her feet and she bounced off the wall behind her.

Stunned, the room spun around her. The lightning failed to fade, and after just seconds, the liquid plate expelled itself, still crackling bright blue. As she sat forward, she spotted Lady Raine holding the sceptre towards her, lightning accumulating and lashing around the blue orb at the top.

As she looked on, Mary raised her free hand and bowled a bolt of black lightning at Raine. It quickly dropped the crown wearer, but the dark energy redirected and swam around her head, into the circlet. Mary stumbled to one knee. Raine grinned as she put the sceptre onto a holder on her belt. Instead, she pulled out her knife, the twin of Tally's Peace—save for the ruby and the absent *Grenshall Teardrop*.

Kara tried to get up but fell straight away. Mary then lifted her knife high, an attempt at defence. It wavered in her arm, but she remained determined. Lady Raine slashed at lightning speed straight at her throat.

Mary's blade lit dimly. Raine's strike missed by some way, little more than a feint, but Mary's movement remained slower than her opponent's. Another attack. The blade smouldered with weak light again. Once more, Raine flew wildly off-target. It really ought to have struck true. "Interesting," she observed, a hint of frustration in her voice.

She gave Mary a sharp kick in the stomach, then slashed several times. Even off-balance, *Tally's Peace* shone and Raine could not dispatch her victim. One blow glanced against Mary's arm. Raine's weapon glistened and dripped a single drop of blood on the floor. The rest disappeared into the tip of the blade.

Kara shook herself and then stood. Raine tripped Mary to the ground and then crouched over her. A knee pinned her blade hand, her free arm gripped her throat.

"I tire of this, death walker," she hissed, and drew the knife up, ready to plunge.

"NO!" Kara yelled. She levelled the fire staff, burning with the desire to put her enemy down, damn the consequences. A column of fire belched from the tip.

Flame obscured Kara's view and rapidly engulfed the entire room. Through it, she spotted Raine walking through the crucible, shaking her head and patting down her arms. "Touché. It appears we have reached an impasse. Your mighty armour will probably protect you, as mine will me. Not certain about your pet, though. I wonder if she will bleed out before she roasts?" With a few yelps, she barged through the fire and out of the door.

Kara looked for a gap as the flames rose in a tall, circular wall around her. On another side of it, she knew Mary lay on the ground. She called her name loudly but to no response. She ran for the hole in the prison of flame but stopped in her tracks as a creak above warned of the burning beam which dropped straight in front of her. The fire circle closed.

Kara, the Armour of War, and Mary had all been separated, and Kara, unsafe and growing increasingly hot, contemplated a wasted death in the centre of the burning ring. She glowered at the golden staff with the utmost disgust.

CHAPTER THIRTY-ONE

Primal senses at their height, Jennifer picked up the faintest trail of the hiding Grey Lady. Though she wanted to help the others more than anything, her adversary did not have escape in mind. Rather, Jennifer stalked her chosen prey. The two had swapped roles in their deadly cat-and-mouse feud. The sniff she caught told her the assassin had looked to go up rather than down, and with the Wraithblade against her, death followed all too easily. She'd either have to change the game, or the game would be up.

Up.

Her eyes, no doubt feral yellow, itched with neurosensory overload, most of it below her. But her nose told her that the scent of a thousand deaths lingered above. She got out to the veranda, leapt onto the balcony and in the same motion, hopped back to the ledge above the ceiling and climbed to the rooftop.

Death moved closer. Jennifer unleashed her claws and drew ready, crouched, eyes out for trouble. It stalked behind her, but she feigned ignorance, carried on crab-walking forward, to the centre of the roof. She waited for the inevitable lunge . . .

. . . and still the Grey Lady moved faster than her. Though she turned, the blade plunged into her, colder than ice but hot as the sun.

Her opponent lost her grip as she missed vital organs, but the excruciating attack tortured Jennifer to almost crippling proportions. She roared as she fought off incapacitation, and remembered that she had only taken the obvious effect of the weapon thus far.

At that, she felt the second, a violent agony that she had experienced once before, when the body of a dead woman and the soul of a crazed girl almost killed her. The sickening soul drain pulled from the lodged blade at the centre of the wound and all across her mind and body, but she fought it, refused to allow it to take hold.

She turned to the Grey Lady, back to her original appearance of youth without emotion. The foe betrayed a startled look. Jennifer had moved just in time. And though few lived to battle their soul being devoured, Jennifer's previous experience helped her to fight. Her strengthened connection with the Primal Realm empowered her further.

As the Grey Lady reached to retrieve her weapon from Jennifer, the ground shook underneath them. Despite their best efforts to remain balanced, it took both combatants off their feet. Both rolled and maintained control. Though the blade tore at Jennifer's very life force, without a wielder to guide it, her soul held intact.

The Grey Lady came for her again, though. The weight of death slowed Jennifer, but against an unarmed opponent, her claws drew blood. The Wraithblade ran a cold finger down her soul and continued to distract her, although she stood against a foe she could ill-afford ignore. Wasting no time, she lashed out and forced the Grey Lady backwards. The billowing robes hampered Jennifer's strokes, but she backed the woman close to the edge, almost victorious.

Jennifer collapsed, as the wound at the side of her stomach, the chill touch of the blade, screamed and tore at her mind and body until she could take no more. She retracted her claws instantaneously, then put her hands around the hilt of the sword. It felt slimy, repulsive, the taint of the Unresting making her sick to its touch. Debilitating. Worse. She held the hilt tight and with strength of body and mind, pulled the sword out of her.

Immediately, she found herself relieved of that exclusive brand of agony, felt her wound start to knit itself back together, albeit more slowly than others. But that consideration became secondary to the feel of the Wraithblade in her hands.

The chilling stain of death crawled to the back of her mind; instead, the joy of the kill surfaced. It would be so easy to plunge the blade into the Grey Lady and take her strength as her own. After all, her enemy had done the same for decades.

Just thrust and hold, feel the rush of life flow through you.

In the corner of her eye, smoke. Fire.

Her friends. Down there.

Kara. Mary.

The impulse she felt. One that the Lady Grenshall had fought many times. The abominable device she held in her hand wanted that, not her. It fed its owner, but it fed itself, too. The weapon wanted to kill.

She could kill. That wasn't a problem.

"No!"

She pulled back her arm to throw the Wraithblade far behind her, but the Grey Lady caught her with a snapping hand and charged her off her feet, on to her back. Jennifer used the momentum to keep rolling and try to land on top of her enemy, but the killer's experience saved the pin. They stopped with feet pushing against the floor, locked in a grapple, each determined to gain advantage over the other.

The woman's cloak flapped in the air around her and confused Jennifer's attempts to find purchase, whilst her enemy gained grip in an arm lock. She pressed down, Jennifer's strength more than matched by masterful technique, and the pressure made her eyes water. She shuffled her legs wide and then around the back of her enemy's neck before applying pressure of her own. The two struggled, rolled, scratched and shoved, anything to gain a definitive advantage over the other, but the two remained deadlocked.

Both intensified the pressure on their holds, to see if the other would give, but nothing. The smell of smoke wafted from below. Jennifer thought of her friends. She reshaped her right hand to razors and threw it upward, into a gap in the cloak. Her opponent released her hold immediately, but Jennifer did not. She could feel the Grey Lady weakening.

The assassin responded with a number of snake-like punches to Jennifer's head and throat, but she held her relentless grip. Instead, she jabbed again with the claw. Her enemy shrieked. A drop of blood trickled from her mouth. Jennifer stabbed again, but her attack got blocked and in a fast but final effort, the Grey Lady twisted her arm at the wrist with everything she had.

As she heard a snap, Jennifer let out a monstrous howl and thrashed her body sideways, freeing the both of them. She slapped the ground with her good arm and screamed as she focused her mind on healing, but watched her enemy stagger, bleeding, towards the downed Wraithblade.

Jennifer forced herself up and pursued. The Grey Lady dropped into a forward roll and seized the weapon. Jennifer kicked hard, straight into her enemy's wounded stomach.

The Grey Lady almost smiled as she flew straight over the ledge and down. Jennifer teetered forward, but put out a hand to prevent herself from joining her enemy in her fall.

She caught herself upside down on her toes and pressed against the wall with her functioning arm. She closed her eyes and held herself absolutely still. With all her strength and a great deal of concentration, she remained rigid and spent several seconds knitting her worst injury back together.

When she opened her eyes, she found herself alone. An attempt to stretch her senses ended in dizziness and nausea, a terrible combination. She looked instead for a more natural solution and to her left, found a protrusion in the wall. Below, a window exploded. Smoke and flame splashed against her face, a reminder of her most immediate problem.

She wriggled her feet, crawled and pushed repeatedly until she reached the point. She gripped the wall anomaly and gave herself a moment to allow the blood to rush away from her head, then looked over at the burning window.

She drew upon her strength and memories of her exploits through the Primal Realm to give herself power and form. She felt her hair tighten to wire and her skin harden as she considered the heat from inside, which she could now feel against the wall.

No more preparation time remained. She adjusted herself and leapt sideways, to the burning window ledge, and pulled herself up and inside. From out of one mess, she ran straight into the fire.

~ ✱ ~

Jennifer wondered if it was wrong that the second her feet hit the inside of the building, she smiled, relishing the challenge. But she immediately dropped into a crouch. The smoke obscured her vision and hampered her efforts to get through. She scanned the fire with her chromatic sight and her eyes burned with every blink. She spotted the gaps she sought, worked out the distance to the walls, and the best exit route. She bolted for it.

Jennifer kept every movement limited to one step, one touch, as she leapt, rolled, vaulted, and slid through the room until she reached the door. A broken beam aflame snapped and fell, barring her way. Not for long. She retreated several steps, then burst forward, straight through the centre.

Into the central corridor, at full speed, Jennifer gripped the staircase and flipped into a somersault. Her feet touched the lower railing before she safely hit the floor.

She sensed Mary and Kara in the room ahead—she could find them anywhere—but black choking smoke and a wall of flame blocked her way. She backed to the staircase, then propelled herself up and over the obstructing wall.

She landed directly next to a bleeding and unconscious Mary. It looked such an innocuous cut, but for some reason, it bled like a severed artery. Jennifer's Primal eyes allowed her to determine Mary's true condition. Even with Mary's already unique reading, her life signs appeared weak. She had seconds—no time to take her outside the fire to heal.

Jennifer placed a hand on the wound, another on to the ground, and then concentrated. She could feel the heat—and in that came Mary's salvation. She placed her grounded hand into the nearest patch of fire. She felt the flame but did not fear it; it lashed at her hand but did not burn. She channelled its energy into the hand on her bleeding friend. Mary's pale skin hissed and smoked as Jennifer's touch began the healing. Even with the Primal conduit, the wound fought her, insisted upon staying open.

"Essence, if you do nothing else for me ever again, help me save her." She clenched Mary's hand tighter.

The blaze flickered and went out in patches around the room. As it did, the blood ceased to flow and the gap in Mary's arm closed. Jennifer slumped and fire leapt from her hand. The exhausted flame reignited everywhere and her hand grew red and blistered.

Mary's life signs remained unchanged, and she lay motionless. Jennifer prodded and shook her in an effort to revive her, but her friend would not stir. At another side of the blazing ring, she heard screams and thumps.

"MARY!" Kara yelled. "Stay with me." Kara choked and spluttered and Jennifer looked up in time to see a segment of the roof shudder and lurch downward.

Jennifer scooped Mary up and hoisted her onto her shoulder, looking for a gap. Nothing clear. Jennifer's lungs filled with smoke and she too started to choke in the cloying atmosphere. Her eyes streamed and the heat began to tug at her skin. She had to get through but could not risk wounding Mary further.

An explosion knocked her backward, and she twisted to save her burden from burning. At that moment, something brilliant glistened against the raging orange light and alerted her senses.

The Armour of War.

She crawled, Mary on her back, to the protective plate, then deposited Mary onto it. Jennifer commanded. The armour obeyed. The metal warped and slithered across its target and in seconds, the strange suit encased Mary, once more adapted into a perfect fit for its wearer.

Jennifer stood and hauled Mary back as the bashing behind the wall of flame slowed. The roof creaked. She gritted her teeth and dashed straight into the column of fire, screaming all the way. She placed the protected Mary down as she patted and dowsed herself, then searched for Kara. Her friend collapsed to one knee and coughed uncontrollably as the smoke overcame her.

The fire raged. The column whirled around in a superheated cyclone. Any question that the blaze had been natural evaporated with its behaviour. It was *trying* to kill them.

The roof shuddered and crumbled. Jennifer seized Kara and forced the three of them into a crouched brace as the floor above fell in around them.

Her strength fading, Jennifer began to lose hope. She had nothing left to give. But as she slumped to the ground, she felt the fire whip around her, not in attack, but to give her power. No, *fuel*. The age-old conflict within the element's nature touched her personally. She embraced it.

Primal energy surged through her, as it had when she first met the Essence. Her fatigue dissipated, and one word—no, thought—throbbed at her mind repeatedly.

SURVIVE.

She sensed that the Essence had won its own battle. Her gift operated freely, her connection with the Essence as solid as it had ever been. She called upon it once more, a request for the might of the Earth that she had used on the other side of the gate.

As the roof attacked, she raised her arms and caught the largest part of the ceiling. With all her might, she held it overhead and deflected the rest of deadly debris. Once that passed, she felt that link, the connection from which she knew came all her early power, and channelled it into one internal focal point. She lifted both of her incapacitated friends off the ground, and jumped.

Jennifer leapt as high as her extra encumbrance allowed. As she landed, she expelled every ounce of her summoned will.

The floor shattered underneath her, just as intended. Straight down they fell, away from the worst of the blaze and into a quieter room.

Though the fire licked after them, she'd bought them a precious few seconds.

Mary inhaled air in one heavy breath and woke with shrouded eyes. Her veins stood prominent and dark against almost blue skin and she eyed Jennifer with grave hunger. Jennifer had seen that look before, in the eyes of the creature that put her out of action for months. The difference lay in the recognition—not from her, but from Mary, who shoved her away and onto her back the moment she became cognizant of it.

"Get away!" Mary wheezed, and weakly crawled backwards, distancing herself from the others. She trembled as she fought the vicious hunger, Jennifer could tell from where she stood. The sight served as a terrible reminder of one of her own worst days.

But it served, too, as a reminder of her best. Two friends who in different ways had saved her life now asked her to return the favour. Jennifer grimaced as she quickly considered the one chance of getting everyone out.

She walked to Mary and stood over her. At her will, the protective shell around Mary melted into a puddle beside her and reformed into its static state. She took Mary by the hand and held tight. "Whatever you need," she said, wincing as she did, "but try and leave me standing."

"No, I—" Mary spluttered, but Jennifer simply gripped tighter.

Jennifer twitched. "Do it now, in a way we can control. Better that than you turning on Kara."

The weakened Guardian of the Gate looked up, almost tearful, about to ask if she was certain. Jennifer vigorously nodded. She allowed Mary to adjust her hands, so she held Jennifer instead of the reverse, then drew in air at speed.

The grip grew ice cold, colder, *unnatural,* unbearable, and Jennifer shrieked as the terrible touch of death ran up and down her spine and shook her beyond physical punishment. Her knees buckled as life force drained from her. But she remained the Primal Champion, and had significantly more to spare than most. She watched as her own veins darkened, and felt a nauseating tug against her soul.

Mary threw Jennifer clear with tremendous force. Jennifer trembled for a moment but felt her strength returning, however slowly. Just another injury to heal. She lifted her arm and called the Armour of War back to herself. It took its perfect fitting, contemporary form, and the mystic fire erupted around her. She looked at Mary. "Are you strong enough to jump now?"

"I am, but I still can't—"

She cut her off. There wasn't time. "Take Kara. Grab her and go." Mary gave a single nod and did exactly that. Though the flame burned hotter than ever, Jennifer breathed a sigh of relief. Those two would be just fine. Now, she just had to catch up.

As she took two rapid steps to the veranda, a mighty rumble shook the ground. The remainder of the ceiling collapsed, along with the floor on which she stood. With nothing to grab, she fell with it—several floors down.

CHAPTER THIRTY-TWO

Wedged between collapsed rock, Jennifer awoke, spluttering and aching everywhere she could feel. She could *feel*. A good start. A regular pounding of the ground, hard enough to make it tremble, was not so good. Worse still, the cause approached her with slow, heavy steps as the Armour of Earth made its presence felt. Through her blurred vision, she saw Gianfranco Manta striding toward her, sword drawn.

He yelled; she could only assume, from his vitriolic utterances, that he swore in Swiss-Italian at her as he advanced. She did catch his words in English as he shattered the rubble in his path with a single stomp. "You! You ruined everything. Now, you're going to die!"

Jennifer's plate hissed with steam as a driving rain cooled her and her armour. She saw double as she parried the blows Manta rained down on her. She raised her arm more out of instinct than design as he hammered at her over and over again. The Armour of War held firm, but her arm grew heavier with every strike. However, trapped, slumped forward, she had nowhere to go, little to do but thwart his attack.

And at least try to reason with him.

"Manta!" she cried, still turning aside his strikes. The strength the plate conferred on him told with every hit as each time her arm did not rise quite as high as it did the time before. "I told you! It's not *me* breaking your plan. Cerise, the contessa—they never existed. Not to you, anyway."

The contessa. Once she uttered the words, his tired weapon arm lowered. It wasn't like she could free herself without lowering her guard, anyway. The non-existent noble still struck a nerve with him, though. Manta steadied himself, aimed a blow more for accuracy than enraged force.

"If it was me who screwed things up for you, tell me where the crown is," Jennifer pressed. "Think, man. You're not an idiot. Who do you think took it?"

"LIAR!" He thrust the sword at her exposed neck. She snatched the blade at its tip and gripped tight, her hand holding him still. The two wrestled, neither gaining the upper hand. He swung his other hand at her face.

At the same time, she shoved hard and twisted with her blade arm. His blow glanced at her cheek with enough force to dull her senses. She retained her grip on the weapon as he lost his on the hilt. She tossed it to grip the hilt, but fumbled the effort and dropped it on the ground. As Manta regrouped, Jennifer grew her razor fingers on the free hand and slashed into the air to halt his advance.

A standoff. If he reached for the sword, or tried anything else, she had him. Time to talk.

"The fact is, neither of us are wearing it. It's not under this pile of rock I'm buried under, either. Like I said, you've been had. Big style."

He pondered for a moment. Or at least, that was what Jennifer thought initially. As her vision straightened, a spectral protrusion from his chest became clear. His mouth widened and he gasped for breath. Unsuccessfully.

"You know, that has always been his problem." The bulky, armoured Manta fell to one knee and revealed Aurelia Raine, carefully guiding the Wraithblade with him. "Obstinate to the point of untrainable. Well, I have no further requirement to indulge his idiotic wheezes."

She pulled the weapon from his back. He looked pale, his eyes blank, as he slumped forward and crashed into the ground. "However, I *do* have further use for his plate. Especially seeing as your armour refuses to cooperate."

She paused, a pleasant thought evidently occurring to her. "That said, I have yet to attempt to use the *Unification* upon it. Honestly, what kind of title was the 'Crown of Kings' anyway? A simple tale to romanticise his prize. That he governed his life around it kept things manageable, and kept him from asking its true purpose. Not enough about him to remain useful, really. You, on the other hand, would make an outstanding lieutenant. If only I thought there to be any chance of your fealty."

Jennifer fumbled with her trapped arm in an effort to free herself, to no avail. "Well, well. Something we agree on."

Raine chuckled and nodded as she took a step back and started to mutter incomprehensible words. Jennifer felt nauseated with every syllable. The Armour of Earth fell into its component pieces and appeared to sink into the ground without trace. Raine examined the Wraithblade briefly before raising it in an attacking stance.

"A pity. I suppose I should deal with you before I return to business. Funny. I forgot just how heady a devoured soul from this thing feels as it rushes through you. Quite addictive, if not managed correctly."

Jennifer prepared to guard, but knew it to be one last futile act of defiance. Even the Armour of War wouldn't save her from that blade's fatal touch.

She felt a tingle down her spine and a hellish howl screamed around her ears. Searing flame of pure darkness smashed into Raine, from whom a flash of orange blinded Jennifer for several seconds. When her sight returned, Mary stood to her right, ethereal and enshrouded in a burning, void-like aura. Her voice echoed around the air.

"If you want to harm her, first you have to come through me." Although she tried to hide it, her legs buckled and her arms trembled as she tried to raise them towards Raine.

Raine unsteadily brought herself up to a crouch. The necklace she wore glowed like lava before fading out. She looked down at it, then sighed and fumbled a switch of weapons to the lightning sceptre. "Have it your way."

Jennifer felt an intense heat blast past her from behind. A brighter flame. Another familiar voice entered the fray: Kara. "And you'll have to come through me, too." Kara stepped past her, pointing fiery death directly at their enemy. "So you know, I'm getting the hang of this thing. Next time, I won't miss."

Raine smirked, though her breath was heavy. They'd *hurt* her. If only Jennifer had been free to move. If only Mary had one more attack in her. "I am sure of it."

As Raine raised her sceptre, the sound of police sirens warned of their imminent arrival. She feigned a shrug. "No matter. I hope you like what I've done with the place."

Kara threw a ball of fire at Raine. At the same time, Raine pointed her sceptre downward and a flash of lightning chained from her proximity towards them. Jennifer closed her eyes. When she opened them again, a flame burned where Raine once stood. But their enemy was nowhere to be seen.

~*~

The police arrived before Kara and Mary could help Jennifer out of the rubble. Soon, a column of firefighters descended upon the blaze and set to work putting it out. The three friends anxiously watched the emergency services work as they remembered the one remaining party member still missing—Cristobal. Last seen in the Primal Realm, he had aided their own escape. They had no time to aid his.

The polyglot Kara brought the police up to date on the situation—to some extent. Kara became animated, distraught, and it did not take fluency in language for Jennifer to understand she had a delicate juggling act between providing a satisfactory story as to why the old building had been razed to the ground, and giving the unwitting authorities something plausible to work with.

Jennifer chuckled at the realisation that Dr. Mellencourt was becoming something of a dab hand at such matters, just as she helped DCI Hammond come up with a suitable tale to allow London to continue sleeping peacefully at night.

But Florence might have been a more difficult gig. The location hardly lent to terrorism, at best leaving a choice between mindless arson and an aggravated robbery attempt. Frankly, Jennifer wondered if it might have been easier to have just told them the truth.

Mary twitched, poised for a worst-case scenario, but Jennifer placed a hand on her shoulder and laughed again. "She's putting it on," Jennifer said in a low tone in Mary's ear. "She's tougher than the pair of us put together.

Mary turned her head and snorted. "You've got that right. Brave to the point of stupid sometimes."

Jennifer shook her head. "Nah. *Never* stupid. Bats in her belfry, for sure. But never stupid."

The two murmured in agreement. "Let's hope nothing changes there. If she loses form now . . ."

"You don't have to tell me."

They watched Kara intently for several moments as she blustered and pointed at the wreckage. Kara wandered back towards the other two and gave a discreet 'Okay' gesture. "I told them our house party got way out of hand," she told them. "Sometimes you're just best off going with the truth."

"What about Manta?" Jennifer asked.

"He's been wanted for some time. I couldn't think of a better reason for a party to get out of hand, myself."

"They'll want to question us more in a bit then?" Jennifer asked.

"Once they've finished looking for the three I reported missing, yes."

"Three?" Mary asked.

"Yeah. The Contessa D'Amato, her chief servant, and Cristobal."

"You saw her walk right through the fire like it wasn't there," Mary griped. "So, I don't think we'll find her."

Jennifer ground her teeth. "And I didn't get a chance to see where the Grey Lady fell," she seethed.

Mary's eyes darkened with the sight of death. "I couldn't miss her, even if recently dead. Not here."

A cry came from the firefighters, a furore of motion from all of them around a side of the building. The three friends heard a clang and they all looked to see what happened. Jennifer enhanced her sight, and identified the noise as a sword hitting the ground. An old sword. From Toledo.

"Cristobal!"

They sprinted closer, and Jennifer cast the obstructing police officers aside. From under some melted rubble, an incorporeal cloaked figure crawled, much to the confusion of the first on the scene. They backed away as the other three ran in.

Mary burst ahead of the others and became almost invisible against the smoke and the night. She reached her hand through the debris and pulled him clear. He returned to full solidity and looked up with a smile. His clothing was tattered and blood-soaked, wounds prevalent almost everywhere. He coughed blood, then collapsed.

Jennifer caught up, placed hands on him, and identified numerous injuries about him. She tried to summon the energies of the Primal Realm, but all around her, the firefighters blustered and shouted. Kara attempted to intervene, but soon the police crowded, too, ushering her out of the way. Mary interfered with those haranguing Jennifer though and got to her first. "It's okay," she said, almost relieved. "His charges won't let him die."

Mary stood rigid and snapped her fingers. The act called the winds of the dead to her side with an ease unfamiliar to Jennifer. She let them rush around her before she raised her hands and took slow, controlled steps towards the emergency staff. Jennifer took a step behind Mary herself, the lifeless parallel world taunting her with an unsubtle reminder of that which came for everyone. She stood behind the focus of the attack, and for that felt grateful.

Sure enough, the operatives all backed away, cowed and herded, without hesitation, question, or need for communication in a common language. "He looks after them," Mary explained under her breath. "Just in a different way to me, is all. Perhaps I can teach him mine."

With Cristobal's health less of a concern, Jennifer turned her attention towards other matters. Kara still coughed, but her health did not look problematic to Jennifer's most enhanced vision. She put an arm around her friend's shoulder and walked her backwards.

"What do you suppose Raine meant by that?" Jennifer asked. "Whether we'd like what she did with the place?"

Kara scratched her head for a moment. "No idea. Everything looks nor—" The burning, collapsed palace hardly represented normality. "The Primal Realm. Could she have been talking about that?"

Jennifer vigorously shook her head. "The Primal Essence is back to its old self. I can feel it. Thanks to Cristobal and you two, she held out."

"Give yourself plenty of credit, too."

"No time to boast."

"Less time for humility. Raine certainly didn't have any . . . Oh, no."

"What?"

"That crown she's got." Kara squinted, rubbing her chin. "Crowns. Royalty, leadership, command—of course! Focal point, centre of circle, command. Elements. The wearer of a crown controls a realm—of course. But if that's the case, the symbols could correspond to other realms. But there were four symbols. Four realms. Assuming we're at the centre, that is."

Mary turned to the other two. "So, wait—are you saying that what happened with that Flayed Glade could happen to my place as well?"

Kara frowned. "If my guess is correct, it would seem so."

Mary's face dropped. "Have you any *idea* of the things she could let out of there? Because I've been looking around for almost a year, and I still don't fully know. I doubt she broke a sweat summoning those nightmare spectres."

Jennifer nodded in agreement. "I need to check on my place as soon as I can. The gate in there is off-limits to her now, though. I'm changing the locks." She squinted and expanded her perception. The gate remained in energy if not in structure, but the area had too much attention to search properly.

"Now what?" Jennifer asked, her words coated with anger. "Where do we go from here? The trail's gone cold."

Kara tapped her feet in thought, irritable. After a moment's hesitation, she waved a hand, danced a finger through the air. "Yes, we do. The list. There are two names left on it. People I know. We find them before the Consanguinity do."

"Er, team . . ."

Mary drew their attention to the fire, no longer a mansion in structure but instead a growing, swirling, burning tornado. The authorities retreated from it with haste. Her Primal connection screamed at Jennifer, as if the flame lapped against her directly. But she snapped out of her distress when she saw Mary clutching her head and screaming too. She grabbed Mary and looked into her onyx eyes, then shook her gently. "What is it? What did you see?"

"It's what I *can't* see. It felt like several Gate Chambers just flew open at once."

As if by confirmation, Cristobal sat bolt upright with a loud cry and heavy breaths. He looked over at Mary. "Did you—? I—?"

"I know," Mary replied.

"Several places. Outside my place."

"I *know*."

Jennifer looked over at them, but distraction came in the form of the mildest speck of light in the distance. It drew her attention to one of the police cars. A flicker of flame reflected against a telescopic sight. One of the officers aimed in their directions.

"DOWN!" she screamed, and everyone dropped quickly, like accustomed professionals, but two *thwips* in rapid succession preceded yelps from Mary and Cristobal. The officers adjusted their weapons, ready to shoot again.

"Kara, check on them," Jennifer commanded, and then ran at the attackers. The other police each took aim as their colleagues had and shouted at her, but she couldn't understand a word. She willed the Armour of War to provide her a visor, and with speed built up, leapt up and forward to avoid the barrage which came at her.

Kara bawled in Italian at the police, who could barely be heard over the gunfire, but she screamed desperately, repeatedly. Jennifer landed at the other side of the car. The officers taking cover there stepped into a fighting retreat from the armoured Jennifer, switching weapons and hitting her with repeated and consistent volleys.

The plate held as bullets whistled and sparked off her. Still Kara screamed, her words evidently confusing the objects of her tirade, but Jennifer's two remained on the offensive. She closed in on them with ease.

She grabbed their weapons by the centre, flicked her wrists around, then shoved them both backwards. She threw the guns behind her and pressed on. One had time to draw a sidearm and emptied the clip at her. Jennifer snarled and kicked the weapon out of his hand. He held his injured fingers and cried out as she seized and dragged him, then with her spare hand, grew a weapon of her own. She kicked the second gunman in the chest and held her claw to his throat. She let the face plate dissipate and gave him an international look. *Your move.*

"Hold them up!" Kara yelled.

"What?"

"Hold them up! The commander wants to ID them."

Jennifer retracted the claw, seized the downed officer by the throat, and lifted him. She released the other squirming officer and slapped him with the back of a metallic fist. He fell backwards, out cold, and she gathered him into a head lock. She then did as Kara requested, moved to the cluster of armed officers and held them forth for clear sight. After a moment on his radio, the commander nodded to Kara, who had closed in.

"He hasn't seen them before in his life," Kara croaked. "He checked in and they're not who they said they were. The two IDs they have are for police killed weeks ago on an armed robbery."

Jennifer threw them to the ground. "How's Mary?"

"Missed anything vital. Quick recovery, likely. Quicker if she fancies it."

"Does she?"

"Hell, no. She's scared of what she'll do to anyone who volunteers."

Jennifer's eyes lit up. "You should tell them that. Then we'll ask them some questions before they get locked up."

Kara had a moment of realisation, then turned to natter at them, pointing at the downed Mary and miming the exact threat about to befall the uncooperative. Jennifer loved Kara's ease of explanation when she felt like it.

The police impersonator spat in Kara's face as he answered her in clear insults, then finally uttered three words which even Jennifer heard clearly. Pure hatred blazed in his eyes. "*Sei senza speranza.*" Kara held a hand up to stop Jennifer before she'd even thought about how she planned to punish him for that one. She respected her friend's wish.

Kara wiped her face on her sleeve, never taking her eyes off him. She then drew her fist back and smacked him hard. "I'll *tell* you when I think we have no hope, dickhead." She shook out her fist and stood up. Jennifer gave her a wide berth as she walked away from him.

"We have a few serious issues to take care of, and a legacy to uphold. So, what do you say we get the band back together?"

Mary gritted her teeth. "What are you talking about?"

"The *Order of Winter*. They—*we,* have a job to do. Let's get to it."

THE END

ACKNOWLEDGMENTS:

Debbie, my chief cheerleader

Mum, because, you know, mum.

Penny, McKenna, Heidi, Tori, Dale. See this here book? What you did for it? Thank you!

Rachel, for taking me a step closer to an Oscar nomination.

The Tea Society. Growing stronger.

Cristian. Thanks for the help early on.

Chloe, for making yourself my minion.

And YOU! If you're reading this, you're obviously awesome and for that, I'm truly grateful. Stay tuned.

ABOUT R. A. SMITH:

R. A. Smith lives in Manchester, UK with his girlfriend. Among his extended family, he counts two considerable war gaming armies and several bears, including Sir Arthur and Frost. A keen gamer, he is equally happy rolling a set of dice or suiting up in plate and swinging a sword at his friends. He can also be found on game consoles, and is generally unable to dance, shoot or kick a ball.

Smith loves his cars and has a long list of things he wants to drive while he still can. He gained an M.A in Creative Writing from Manchester Metropolitan University and worked as an editor in his old student magazine.

ABOUT XCHYLER PUBLISHING:

At The X, we pride ourselves in discovery and promotion of talented authors. Our anthology project produces three books a year in our specific areas of focus: fantasy, Steampunk, and paranormal. Held winter, spring/summer, and autumn, our short-story competitions result in published anthologies from which the authors receive royalties.

Additional themes include: *Mr. and Mrs. Myth* (Paranormal, fall 2014), *Out of This World* (Fantasy, winter 2015), and *Losers Weepers* (spring/summer 2015).

Visit **www.xchylerpublishing.com/AnthologySubmissions** for more information.

Other anthologies from Xchyler Publishing:

Shades and Shadows: a Paranormal Anthology, by Eric White, Ginger Mann, Scott William Taylor, Marian Rosarum, R. M. Ridley, Scott E. Tarbet, E. Branden Hart, Neve Talbot, and J. Aurel Guay; edited by Terri Wagner and Jessica Shen, October 2013

A Dash of Madness: a Thriller Anthology by M. Irish Gardner, Elizabeth Gilliland, Sarah Hunter Hyatt, Breck LeSueur, F. M. Longo, Ben Ireland, David MacIver, and Tim Andrew; edited by McKenna Gardner, July 2013

Mechanized Masterpieces: A Steampunk Anthology by Aaron and Belinda Sikes, Alyson Grauer, Anika Arrington, A. F. Stewart, David W. Wilkin, M. K. Wiseman, Neve Talbot, and Scott William Taylor; edited by Penny Freeman, April 2013

Forged in Flame: A Dragon Anthology, by Samuel Mayo, Brian Collier, Eric White, Jana Boskey, Caitlin McColl, and D. Robert Pease, edited by Penny Freeman, October 2012

Look for these releases from The X in 2014:

Primal Storm, Book II of the urban fantasy series The Grenshall Manor Chronicles by R. A. Smith, January 2014; sequel to Oblivion Storm.

Kingdom City: Resurrection, a Book I of a dystopian fantasy by Ben Ireland, February 2015

Vanguard Legacy: Reflected by Joanne Kershaw, sequel to the paranormal romance *Foretold*. March, 2014

Conjectrix, Book II of the Vivatera fantasy series by Candace J. Thomas, May, 2014

Tomorrow Wendell, an urban fantasy by R. M. Ridley, June 2014

Accidental Apprentice, a fantasy by Anika Arrington, July, 2014

To learn more, visit **www.xchylerpublishing.com**

Sneak Peak

MOMENTS IN MILLENNIA:
A FANTASY ANTHOLOGY

By Samuel A. Mayo, Ben Ireland, Michael Cross,

Candace J. Thomas, Fischer Willis,

Neal Wooten, and S. P. Mount

~*~

THE CARTOGRAPHER
BY SAMUEL A. MAYO

The rumble of the aether drive engaging punctuated the still air aboard the Cartographers' Guild ship and woke me up. I should have been used the sound by then, but it always bothered me. It meant that I would have to go to work. Don't take that for laziness; I could plough through a day with the best of them. It was the type of work it heralded that I didn't like.

Other people came to the Guild, not the other way around. Merchants, diplomats, generals, kings. It didn't matter who they were. Even basic supplies and materials arrived via regular trade shipments. So, if the Masters felt convinced that an incident required travel through the aether stream, something big was going down. "Big" did not begin to cover it. "Galactic" might come close.

I tossed back the blanket, swung my legs around and sat up in my bunk. My head began to swim while my stomach did a backflip. I had to swallow hard to keep from heaving. Twenty-three years aboard the ship had done nothing to help my spatial orientation. I eventually belched and felt better.

A freckled face surrounded by a mass of tangled red hair appeared from the bunk below and looked up at me with amusement.

"Again?" it said. "Dirt lubber forever, eh?"

"Shut up, Burke," I said and kicked down at him. He narrowly dodged it.

He laughed and yanked on my leg, nearly pulling me from the bunk. I shook loose and jumped to the hard iron floor. My stomach turned again, but I kept my face straight. Burke didn't need more ammo.

"Quit jerking around," I said.

I stretched every bit of my medium build, went to my locker, and popped the latch. I quickly threw on my khaki pants and white long-sleeve shirt and pulled out the dirt-brown jerkin issued to all third-tiers. The jerkin had short sleeves and a stiff high collar that came halfway up the neck.

"What are you doing?" asked Burke.

"Getting ready."

"Why? They haven't called us yet."

"But they're going to."

Burke grunted, put his hands behind his head and lay back down. "It's not like we'll do anything."

"All tiers must be prepared to assist in any event—"

"Bah! Don't quote that crap to me." He sat up. "That's your problem, Conner. You care too much about the letter of the law. That's why you're still a third-tier."

I grimaced. "I care because the Masters care."

"Whatever."

As I fastened the fourth and last clip on the jerkin, the round speaker near the door to our room crackled.

A female voice from it said, "All tiers report to the drafting room immediately. Repeat. All tiers report to the drafting room immediately. Failure to comply will result in Class Three punishment."

That spurred Burke into action. He shoved me aside getting to his locker and began grabbing his things in a flurry. Taking care to avoid the wiry living ball of chaos that Burke had become, I deftly grabbed my leather boots and—the most important thing—my tool case, before shutting my locker.

Burke, trying desperately to pull on his pants, was doing a one-legged hop across our tiny room as I headed for the door.

To my back, he said, "Aw, come on! Don't leave me here."

I ignored him and grinned to myself as I turned the handle and exited the room. I'm sure I heard him curse me from the other side of the heavy door.

Other third-tiers began to fill the narrow hall of the barracks. A few were fully clothed like me, but most had one piece of clothing or another barely hanging on as they moved awkwardly down the hall. It would have been comical had I not known what awaited anyone who didn't make it to the drafting room in time.

Despite my room being farther back in the barracks, I led the pack of third-tiers into the concourse. Practicality ruled the design of the Guild ship. The concourse served as a hub for traffic between all areas of the ship. Brown jerkins flowed in from the three hallways while a third stream of blue jerkins flowed out from the second-tier barracks.

"Conner!" Matthias had seen me and used his thick frame to move across the flow and walk beside me.

"Where's Burke?" he said.

"Still pulling on his pants when I left," I replied.

Matthias shook his head. As a second-tier lead, he was responsible for four third-tier cartographers. Burke and I made up half of his group. Kaja and Savry made up the other half. Since they had been scheduled to work the second shift, they were likely already in the drafting room.

"Do you know what's happening?" I said.

Matthias shrugged. "Not at all."

Though I had at least three years on him, he had a scowl on his face that made him look older. I could tell the alert bothered him. This, in turn, bothered me. Second-tiers usually had some inkling about why the Guild ship moved.

The concourse became noisy with conversations that I guessed mirrored our own. The mass funneled into the large opening that led to the drafting room. The din quieted as we neared the entrance.

Entering that room had a strange effect on people. It was as if it imposed a will of its own over its occupants. It wanted to let you know that, no matter what you did, no matter what tier you were or how well you performed your duties, it would be there long after you were gone, still serving its purpose. You could never outperform the room itself.

The ground floor of the drafting room, also known as the third tier, spread wide. It was the largest open space on the ship, even bigger than the cargo hold. A grid of evenly spaced wooden drafting desks made a ten by twenty grid. A pair of long tables flanked either side of the desks. Two small chairs sat within each u-shaped work area.

The walls of the third tier were made entirely of large drawers, each with a brass handle and cardholder. Metal ladders led up to several levels of catwalks crisscrossing the room, allowing access to the drawers higher up. Lanterns with electric bulbs formed their own grid between the drawers, emitting a golden glow over the whole room. Metal posts with these same bulbs shot upward from the floor in between the desks in a similar fashion.

On the far side of the room, the edge of the second tier stopped right at the top of the drawers along that wall. It contained smaller desks, but much nicer chairs and more room to maneuver. All of the second-tier desks butted up against the railing so that the group leads could look down on us third-tiers to make sure we kept working.

Above the second tier sat the first tier, but none of us knew what it looked like. The only door we could see led to a small landing that jutted out over the open air. From the floor, we would occasionally see a first-tier wander out and look down, their golden yellow vests standing out against the dark gray walls and ceiling. When the Masters addressed us, a rare occurrence, they did so from that landing.

On that day, all of the tiers collected on the bottom floor. As I scanned the room, I smiled a little. We were all on the same level. Brown dominated the scene, with plops of blue here and there, and less than a dozen dots of yellow. I even saw two of the orange-shirted engineers. The rest were in the engine room, keeping the radioactive core that powered the ship's normal systems from killing the rest of us. The white-robed aether-drive alchemists were understandably absent. It was just as well. Those people gave me the creeps.

Matthias and I crammed into the space in front of desk C7, alongside Kaja and Savry. The two women occupied the chairs of the work area. They had covered their maps with butcher paper to make sure no one accidentally ruined what they had just spent the better part of twelve hours drafting.

"What's happening?" asked Kaja.

The way she posed the question sounded as though she blamed Matthias and me for the alert. She was on a tight deadline to rework a map of a sector of the Bohemia star cluster circa 1873. Kaja always seemed a little on edge anyway. Like many of the cartographers, Guild collectors had picked her up as an orphan at the young age of ten. Apparently, Kaja had been a runaway from slavers. The Guild had saved her that day, and she served them with fierce loyalty.

While still fairly pretty, her thin frame and sharp facial features only added to her aura of intensity. So did the scar underneath her left eye.

"No clue," said Matthias.

"Where's our redheaded step-child?" said Savry, smiling.

Where Kaja was hard and dedicated, Savry seemed the exact opposite. Which was not to say she was incompetent. Her work was decent, but only when she wanted it to be. She came from nobility, a dynasty with close ties to the Cartographers. Her parents had placed her in the Guild's care as part of some arrangement, but she never knew the details.

What she lacked in dedication she made up with a warm personality. Plus, with curves in all the right places and bright blonde hair, she was easy on the eye. Everyone liked Savry. Well, everyone except for Burke. She didn't seem to care much for him either. Why this was, one could only speculate.

I stuck a thumb toward the hallway that led to the concourse. "Back that way somewhere. He was having trouble with his pants."

Savry giggled. Matthias vainly suppressed a chuckle. I even detected a hint of a half-turn corner of the mouth from Kaja. As if on cue, an elbow jabbed into my low back. Burke's face appeared just over my left shoulder.

"Thanks, dirt lubber," he said with a hiss. "I just barely beat the enforcers."

"But you did beat them, ass," I replied.

He tightened his jaw and looked as though he would hit me again. Matthias stepped up. He stood almost a head taller than Burke and liked to use it when the need arose.

"Knock it off," Matthias said in a harsh whisper, "or I'll give you a Class Three myself."

Burke loosened his jaw for a split second, tightened it again, and looked down.

"Fine," he sulked.

A loud voice boomed over the whole room. "Cartographers."

Everyone looked up to the platform in astonishment. We all knew that voice—deep and gravely, full of command, demanding respect. We heard it on the edu-vids, the audio lessons, and in the "encouragement" messages that played on repeat in the galley.

Grand Master Cartographer Erasmus Penderbrand.

Though he had to be in his nineties, the man did not look a day over sixty. His large, muscular frame was the envy of men a third of his age. The black robe he wore contrasted with the stark white of his long hair and beard. He stood tall and proud, with his hand clasped behind him as his cold, grey eyes scanned the room. They paused just long enough on mine to make me feel both proud and afraid. Proud to have a strong leader such as he, but afraid of what lay within his mind.

One thing struck me as odd, however. On either side of the Grand Master stood members of the exploration unit, clearly designated by their crimson hooded jerkins and array of tools and weapons strapped to their bodies. They reminded me of the time I tried out for the explorers. Thanks to my weak stomach, I failed the physical fitness portion of that exam, but I did learn a few of their tricks along the way, so not a total loss.

When he finished his visual circuit of the drafting room, Erasmus said, "A grave situation is upon us all. The Argonaut Empire is on the verge of war with the Old Earth Dominion."

A collective gasp issued from the crowd, including me. The Argonaut Empire was a military state with powerful warriors and vast interstellar fleets. They had, in a relatively short matter of time, gobbled up a sizeable stake in the universe. Their involvement was no surprise; they fought everyone.

However, the Old Earth Dominion was another story entirely. The Dominion encompassed the Milky Way and most of the neighboring Andromeda galaxy. Where the Argonauts were brash and impulsive, the Dominion was steady, slow, but eternal. A war between them would be a physical manifestation of an unstoppable force meeting an immovable object. Both metaphorically and actually, the level of destruction would be astronomical.

"The focus of their grievance," said Erasmus, "is a claim on Mother Earth itself."

This time the crowd didn't gasp. We erupted. All of the tiers on the floor turned to one another with exclamations of confusion. More than a few curses shot across the room. Kaja and I exchanged disbelieving looks.

"Silence!" commanded Erasmus.

The room instantly obeyed.

He continued, "I understand the incredulity of the Argonaut Empire's claim. However, I have reason to believe there is some validity to it. Given the seriousness of the situation, I have decided that we shall intervene in this matter. Both sides have agreed to our involvement. An excavation team is to be assembled. The task: determine proper ownership and ancestry. This will require the support of every one of you. Cartographers will process the information brought to us by the excavation team the moment it arrives. All other work ranks inferior to this priority."

Erasmus cleared his throat. "The excavation team will not only consist of the exploration unit, but also an Antiquarian agent and one of the desk teams."

Furtive murmurs came from the floor. Matthias and I exchanged concerned looks.

"Their drafting skills will be essential in this mission." Erasmus looked down at us. I suddenly felt like vomiting. "Desk C7, are you up to the task?"

In unison, all heads on the ground floor turned to us. The silence was deafening. I had to swallow hard to control my stomach.

Matthias, slightly dazed, stammered out, "Y-yes, s-sir."

Erasmus nodded. "Report to briefing room seven immediately. Everyone else, dismissed!"

~*~

The Guild had a variety of spacecraft that performed different functions. Most were small vessels designed for ship-to-ship transport. A few were more specialized. The *Tartessos* was a landing craft designed for planetary travel. The exploration unit had their own ship, the *Iram*, outfitted with an aether drive and armaments for long-term assignments. They must have felt that our mission was short enough that we would not need it for this trip.

"We're really going back in time?" said Burke for about the fifth time since we boarded the *Tartessos*.

Matthias angled his head back toward Burke, with more than a little exasperation. "Yes! Now, shut your trap. Are you done with buckling in?"

Burke tugged at the left strap of his five-point harness and made a face at Matthias.

"Lord, help me," our group lead muttered as he faced forward again. "Kaja, Savry? You ladies all right up there?"

Savry breathed in sharp. "Define 'all right.'" She had been the most nerve-wracked of our team since the announcement. Her face had gone pale in the drafting room and still had not regained its color.

"We're fine, Matt," said Kaja. She shot Savry a look a mother would have given a stubborn child.

"So you say," Savry shot back. "I hate space travel."

Matthias looked across the narrow space between our seats. "How're you holding up, Conner?"

I gave him a thumbs-up. "I've thrown up three times since yesterday, so I'm good."

The second-tier chuckled louder than I expected and shook his head. "Glad to hear it." He cleared his throat and then leaned in close so that only I could hear him. "I know this opportunity means a lot to you. Know that I am going to push for all of you, especially you, Conner, to get second-tier. It's the least you deserve."

I said nothing in reply. Instead, I nodded and sat back in my seat.

Truthfully, I had mixed feelings about the whole thing. On one hand, Matthias was right. After being passed up by several third-tiers that I had helped train, I finally had an opportunity to prove I could handle second-tier duties. On the other, my nerves were a mess, more than just the spatial orientation.

The whole mission seemed strange. Desk teams almost never went on excavation runs, and the idea of tearing a hole in the fabric of reality just to act as a glorified zoning board did not sit right in my stomach. In fact, a sense of unease planted itself in a small section at the back of my mind.

Someone brushed past us. I looked up and saw Tumek, the lead tier of the exploration squad, moving toward the cockpit. He stopped just before the pilots' seats and turned to face us.

Any other time I'd seen them, exploration squad members had their hoods drawn and a black breather mask covering the lower half of their faces. Tumek had pulled back his hood and removed his mask, revealing a hard face that had seen more in its time than it should have. He had a thin, muscular frame and no hair on his head except for his black eyebrows. His gaunt face and hooked nose made him look like a raven.

Black leather straps crisscrossed his chest, each one supporting a tool of his trade. Two of them held long, double-edged blades, sheathed. Another pair held a series of pouches containing all manner of secret powders and potions. The last two held a different item on each. One had a cylindrical metal casing that protected their maps, while the other, a bulging rectangular pouch, held the explorers' most important tool: the Rhodian Astronomic Compass. The device used complex inner gear works combined with aethereal alchemy to allow temporal-spatial orientation. Encased in a rectangular wooden box with brass trimming, they also looked pretty snazzy.

In a rough voice—and higher-pitched than expected—Tumek said, "None of you have had training in the field, and yet I am still responsible for you." His eyes fixed on me longer than the other as he said this. I shrank back and avoided his gaze. "Do exactly what I tell you, when I tell you. Any deviation will result in severe punishment. Is that understood?"

At our briefing, we learned from Sokar—an Antiquarian representative—that the dispute arose from a discovery by an Argonaut survey team in the Colchis Nebula. The Golden Fleece Treaty had purportedly been signed millennia previously, between the Hadrian Hegemony, the founding nation of what would eventually become the Old Earth Dominion, and Argo, then a fledgling planet, after it had waged a short-lived and intense war for independence.

The Argonauts claimed it promised them eternal rights to not only their own region of space, but also a time-limited stake to a portion of land on Mother Earth. With billions of people and abundant natural resources within those particular regions, the Dominion understandably disagreed and called the treaty a forgery.

To resolve the issue, the Antiquarian League agreed to sponsor a Guild excavation into Earth's past to survey the regions owned by the Hegemony at the time of the treaty's signing. The results would then factor into the apportionment given to the Argonaut Empire, if indeed the treaty were authentic.

Tumek turned away from us and took the co-pilot's chair on the right. Savry looked back at Matthias, even paler than before. He held up a palm and nodded to reassure her.

From the seat behind me, Sokar said in his smooth baritone, "Don't worry, pretty girl. Old Tumek talks mean, but he is nothing if not dependable. He'll take good care of us." He then picked up the thick book he had been reading, and resumed studying its text.

Savry smiled weakly as her face flushed. "Thank you, sir."

Of anybody, Sokar seemed the most out of place on that mission. His clean, pressed clothes contrasted with the drab appearance of the ship, the explorers, and us third-tiers. The coat and slacks he wore were so white they almost glowed. The gold trim along the hem and high collar of his coat accentuated the sheen. The brass buttons seemed to shine at all times, no matter the lighting. The Antiquarian League had tasked him to oversee the mission and attempt to ascertain the validity of the treaty. His vocation, clothes, brown skin and sharp, blue eyes worked together to give him an air of mystery and intrigue.

The Antiquarians were an odd bunch. They performed a similar function to the Cartographers, but dealt with artifact preservation. As such, they always had a strange gleam in their eye that suggested hunger. Many thought of them as thieves with special privileges. They shared an especially intense rivalry with the monks of the Great Library. The Library was a group tasked with guarding ancient texts and technology, something that at times put them in direct conflict with the Antiquarians.

Suddenly, an old, wiry man in a brown tattered robe stormed into the seating area. "Mister Tumek!" he shouted. "I insist that I come aboard. This *woman* won't let me."

Tumek's right-hand explorer, Vorra, grabbed his shoulder, and yanked him around.

"That's because you don't belong!" she insisted, almost spitting into his face.

The man, his eyes looking as though they would pop from their sockets, shoved a large piece of parchment in Vorra's face. "*This* says that I do."

Tumek emerged from the cockpit and stepped quickly to the pair. He tore the parchment from the man's hand and studied it. His eyes widened and then narrowed as he read it again.

Through clenched teeth, he said, "Let him on board, Vorra." He pointed a finger at the man. "If you do anything to jeopardize this mission, don't think your status will save you."

"Tuh!" replied the man. "If anything, I am here to make sure you do your job properly."

Tumek grimaced. To Vorra, he said, "Make the necessary adjustments for one more passenger." He then returned to the cockpit.

The old man looked up at Vorra. "Well? You heard him. Unhand me."

Vorra shoved the old man into his seat and released her grip. She stomped to the aft of the ship to finish preparations for departure.

The man straightened his robe and seemed to notice us for the first time.

"What are all of you staring at?" he demanded.

Sokar, who hadn't looked up from his book, said, "It's to be expected, Brother Fergus. They've never seen a monk of the Great Library in the flesh."

Brother Fergus scowled and scrunched up his nose. "When I heard you were involved, I insisted to the Head Librarian and to Erasmus himself that I come along. This matter is too important for the Library to be left out." He jabbed a finger toward Sokar. "And I'll make sure you don't pilfer any artifacts."

The Antiquarian turned a page of his book and smiled. "Wouldn't dream of it, Fergus."

Fifteen minutes later, preparations were complete. All of the passengers had oxygen masks over their faces and headphones strapped on. Vorra joined Tumek in the cockpit, taking the pilot's seat.

I leaned to one side so I could watch. Only the cockpit showed a view outside the ship. At that moment, all I could see was the double-doors of the hangar. Since windows served little purpose on the Guild ship, I rarely got the opportunity to see open space. I relished those moments.

Vorra spoke a few words into her microphone. Moments later, the double-doors shuddered and slowly began to separate. The black canvas of space appeared. Stars, quasars, and nebulas served as pigments for an invisible artist's brush as the picture grew ever wider.

"Everything okay, Conner?" said Matthias.

I realized that I had been holding my breath. My face felt flush. I shook my head to ward off the feeling.

"Yeah," I said. "Just enjoying the view."

Tumek's voice came over the headsets. "Sit back and stay still. If you aren't used to space travel, it can make you sick if you're not careful."

"Or in Conner's case, no matter what," said Burke.

"Shut up," Matthias and I said simultaneously.

Vorra placed her hand on what I guessed was the throttle and increased the output of the *Tartessos'* nuclear drive. The ship steadily pushed its way through the hangar and out into open space. As it did, the air in the ship felt, for lack of a better word, tighter. Once the Guild ship's artificial gravity no longer affected the *Tartessos*, things within the shuttle shifted, including my stomach.

I let out a long, slow breath. I refused to do anything that would make the rest of the team think less of me. I did not want that punk Burke to be right.

The ship drifted up and began to turn to starboard. An arc of blue appeared at the top of the cockpit window. It quickly turned into the lower portion of a sphere.

Earth.

I couldn't help but smile. The planet had been my home for the first five years of my life. Well, not that particular Earth, but another version. I wondered how different it would be. I wondered if another me would exist at the same moment I did. Those in the know told me it was unlikely, but that did nothing to hinder my imagination.

We spent a good while drifting closer to the blue planet. In that time, Tumek and Vorra busied themselves in the cockpit turning knobs and flipping switches. At one point, Tumek popped open a box-like compartment situated in the exact center of the console. He then placed his RAC inside and closed the compartment.

"Compass secure," he said over the comm. "Engaging time displacement."

A violet light appeared around the edges of the box. Simultaneously, a translucent filter of the same color coated the windshield. From the briefing, I knew that this meant within moments we would travel into the aether stream. Time travel required a series of steps through the aether, each one drawing the traveler ever closer to the exact time and place they wished to visit.

The *Tartessos* shuddered for several seconds. The shaking stopped and the violet filter disappeared. Then, gravity took hold as we began our approach for entry into Earth's atmosphere. Steadily, I began to feel pushed farther back into my seat. The pressure continued to rise. Outside the cockpit window, a dull red glow appeared just around the nose of the *Tartessos*. Gradually, it became orange and then turned to an intense yellow-white. It was as if we were inside a giant fireball heading straight for the ground.

Suddenly, my head began to swim. The ship swirled all around me, stretched, and then compressed. I felt the contents of my stomach revolt and make for my throat.

Darkness flooded my vision as I threw up into my mask. Just before I lost consciousness, my only though was, '*crap.*'

~ * ~

"Conner? Conner, wake up."

Right after someone said this, I felt a hard slap against my cheek. It stirred me from my dark world.

My eyes couldn't focus properly, but I could tell by the regulation-cut black hair and facial structure that Kaja was looking straight at me.

"Oh, hi, Kaja," I said feebly. "I ha-had a crazy dreeeeeeeeam. W-we were going to M-moffer Earf."

My vision cleared enough that I saw Kaja roll her eyes. She turned her head to the left and said, "He's awake, Matt. But, he isn't worth much at the moment."

I scowled. "Thasss n-not very nice Kaja. I'm perf-f-f-fectly f-fine."

I tried to stand. Before I had gotten halfway up, my legs failed me, and I collapsed.

"Wha' happen'?" I asked. "And why is muh mouf gross?"

"You got sick and fainted, dirt lubber," said Burke.

"And you're s-still an ass. But at least I'll get better."

From somewhere nearby, Matthias and Savry laughed. Kaja smirked, but quickly suppressed it.

"Here," she said and extended a hand

I grabbed it and let her help me stand. The weakness in my legs didn't last long, a few minutes at most, and soon I was moving around just fine.

Matthias handed me my frame pack. "Glad you're all right. However, we need to get moving. Tumek and the others moved on ahead to set up camp. We stayed behind to make sure you were okay."

"Thanks, Matt," I said, strapping the waist buckle. I chewed my lower lip. "Sorry I lost it."

He clapped a hand on my shoulder and smiled. "Don't worry about it. Come on."

I followed him to the cabin door. To be honest, I felt like a weakling. I had promised myself I would be tougher than that. Nervous as I was about the mission, it was a chance to prove myself. First test, failed. I tried to shrug it off as we stepped through the opening.

The scene that spread out before me as I stepped down the ladder was one that would stay with me forever. Rolling green hills, punctuated here and there with gray rocks stretched on and on until they gave way to high, snow-capped mountain ranges. The mid-afternoon sun shone brightly across a clear blue sky. I took a deep intake of the cold air and let it out slowly. Memories came flooding in. None of them good.

Savry looked back up at me and said, "How does it feel? Like home?"

"Not quite," I said, forcing a smile. "But close."

She returned the smile.

The girl seemed in a more confident mood now. Happy, almost. I did not want to ruin it.

"Come on," said Burke. "I want to catch up before it gets dark."

"Agreed," said Matthias. "Let's move out."

He took the lead and struck out for a tall hill not far from the ship. As we walked, I looked back at the *Tartessos* and stopped. Before they led the advance party, Tumek and Vorra had covered the ship with a cloth that blended in with the surroundings. I had not seen them before when I exited the ship. Those explorers really knew their stuff.

"Where and when did we land?" I asked as I caught back up.

"A remote part of Colchis, tenth century B.C.," said Kaja. "Sokar and Tumek think it should keep us concealed from civilization long enough to complete our excavation."

I tried to correlate that to the maps I knew of Mother Earth, but could not quite make the connection. "I worked mostly in the eighteenth and twentieth centuries A.D."

"This region eventually becomes part of the Georgian Kingdom in 975 A.D.," said Matthias. "Right now, it's populated by wandering tribes."

"How in the world did you know that?"

Matthias grinned. "Brother Fergus mentioned it in the middle of another rant against Sokar."

"I can't get a read on that guy. Why do you think that monk's even here?"

"The Library and the League hate each other. Probably feels like they're getting one-upped."

"I don't know. I think there's more to it."

"I agree with Conner," said Savry. "The guy seems a little off."

"Of course he's off," said Burke. "He's a Library monk. Those guys never go anywhere."

I cocked an eyebrow. "And we do?"

"You know what I mean."

I chuckled. "No, Burke, I don't."

He turned suddenly and slid off his pack. He stepped right up to me and said, "You know what? I've had about enough."

"What's your problem?"

"You are! You think you're so smart, but how is that you're older than the rest of us and still a third-tier, huh? Tell me that."

"That's enough, Burke," said Matthias as he grabbed the redhead's shoulder.

Burke shook it off. "No, it's not, Matt. I want to hear it, Connie boy. Why are you such a pansy?"

I started to slide my own pack off, when out of nowhere another pack slammed into Burke's chest and sent him tumbling down an incline. His eyes looked wild as he looked back up at Kaja.

The thin girl stood with her pack still hefted up. "Stuff it, Burke!" she yelled at him. "We're here to do a job. Now take off your panties and man up!"

The rest of us just stared at her.

"Nice shot, girlie," said Savry.

I grumbled something about not needing help. Kaja shot me a withering look, and I shut my mouth.

After several tries, Burke got to his feet and silently retrieved his own pack. The rest of our hike was fairly quiet and uneventful.

I took in the countryside as we walked. In the distance, I noticed a thin stream of smoke rising up the clouds. I resisted the urge to strike off toward them. The chance to observe an ancient civilization in action was almost too irresistible. I satisfied my curiosity by stopping and pulling the spyglass from my pack.

Even with their camp magnified, I couldn't make out much. From the little I could see, they seemed much more organized than the wandering tribe Matthias had mentioned.

"What are you staring at?" asked Savry.

"Just taking in the local culture."

I collapsed the spyglass and returned it to my pack.

"Or staring at girls," Savry said with a coy smile.

I bumped her shoulder. "Shut up."

Dusk approached as the camp came into view. It was nestled between two rocky cliffs halfway down a narrow valley. According to the quick overview on camping they had given us, it served as a prime location. Concealment from the elements and, more importantly, from ancient peoples took priority.

Between breaths, Savry said, "Could they have picked somewhere farther away?"

Matthias laughed.

"They did it for a reason," said Kaja.

"Yeah, I know," said Savry. "Just wished we could have landed closer."

That reason had to do with the quirks of fine-tuning travel through time and space. That wonderful substance, aether, allowed us to break the laws of physics and travel across all dimensions within the multiverse. The material still wasn't fully understood—where it came from; how it even came to be; mysteries even the best alchemists had yet to discover. It appeared where and when it wanted, seemingly at random. People found pockets of the stuff in places as varied as their cupboards, the hearts of glaciers, and the open vacuum of space.

However, aether could be unwieldy. In untrained hands, it could do crazy things. Sometimes people wound up with different pieces of their bodies across time and space. Some were still alive even. It was no small wonder the alchemists were the only people allowed to manipulate the stuff in any substantial way.

Our explorers used a tiny amount of aether inside their compasses. When combined with our maps, they could activate an aethereal portal to go to wherever they wanted. Distance played a factor. The closer you were to your destination, the less likely the portal would back-fire.

We temporarily lost sight of the camp as we stepped down an incline. At the top of the next small rise, I looked down at the campsite and stopped. Matthias and Kaja sensed it, too, and stared with me.

"What is it?" said Savry.

"Something's off," I said.

"Where is the team?" said Kaja.

"Good question," said Matthias as he pulled off his pack.

From one of the side pockets, he produced a spyglass. He placed it to his eye and studied the camp.

"The tents look fine," he said. "The portal circle has already been mark—" He took in a quick breath of air. "Someone's running across the camp."

"Who is it?" said Savry.

Matthias' mouth open and closed. "It's Fergus. He's bleeding."

Kaja and Burke cursed.

"Why is he running?" I asked.

"I don't know. I don't see anyone else around."

As I saw the small figure of Brother Fergus make his way across the camp, thoughts fought back and forth in my mind. *Should I help him?* said one. *No, stay up here, where it's safe,* said another. The second voice seemed louder and made better sense. Then Fergus tumbled to the ground.

I started down the incline.

"What are you doing?" said Matthias.

Without looking back, I said, "He needs help."

I soon heard footsteps right behind that quickly caught up. A quick glance told me it was Kaja.

"Guys, stay back here," shouted Matthias. "We don't know what happened yet."

"Matt's right," said Savry. "Come back!"

Kaja and I ignored them.

From above, I'm sure we looked like a pair of drunks, running first this way, then that. The rocky and uneven terrain made the going tough. We had to jump and dodge every other step. More than once, I had to climb up an outcropping and then turn to help Kaja up.

At the second of these, I jumped when Burke appeared at the bottom of the outcropping next to Kaja. We eyed each other for a long moment, but didn't say anything. I helped Kaja up and then held a hand down to Burke. He took it and stayed with us the rest of the way to the camp.

When we reached the edge of the clearing where the tents had been pitched, we slowed. While we were eager to help Brother Fergus, Matthias had a point. We didn't know what had happened. A measure of caution guided the next few steps. We stopped behind a small mound and surveyed the area.

This close to the camp, we now saw signs of struggle. Flattened grass and upturned dirt littered the clearing. Seeing no one other than Fergus, I left the safety of the mound and rushed to the monk's side. The old man lay face down on the ground.

"Brother Fergus," I said. I placed a hand on his shoulder. "Brother Fergus, are you all right?"

Suddenly, the monk's arm swung back and struck my right temple, knocking me sideways.

"I'll kill ya!" he said, almost screeching. "I'll kill ya all!"

He cocked an arm back. To my horror, he held a huge rock, ready to dash out my brains.

"Fergus it's us," I said quickly.

He didn't seem to care. His arm swung down.

I tried to roll to dodge, but I didn't have to. Another rock saved me. It crashed square into Fergus' face. Blood gushed from his nose and he crumpled to the ground again.

I looked up and to my surprise, Burke stood there breathing hard. He had ditched his pack, picked up the rock, and thrown it straight at Fergus.

He had saved me.

I let out a breath. "Nice throw."

"Don't mention it," he said. "Ever."

As I got to my feet, Kaja went to Fergus.

"Careful," I said.

"I don't think he's going to get the drop on us this time," she replied.

Fergus groaned and rolled onto his back. The Library monk began muttering. Words came out randomly, disjointed.

"I knew it would go wrong," was the first complete sentence that came out his mouth.

"What went wrong?" said Kaja.

This seemed to stir Brother Fergus. "The . . . the summoning. Didn't look right. Even before they started."

"The summoning?"

Kaja looked up at me, eyes wide.

"No way," I said.

Burke joined us. "'No way' what?"

I shook my head in disbelief. "They summoned the portal without us."

Burke's jaw dropped. "But we still had calculations to make! Maps to redraw! Their maps weren't right yet!"

Then Fergus said something that galvanized our collective attention.

"Cartographer . . . traitor."

"What did he say?" said Burke.

Kaja leaned closer to the monk's face. She shook him. "Fergus. What do you mean? Fergus!"

Then Brother Fergus' eyelids slowly closed.

We stared at him, no one saying a word.

Burke broke the silence with a curse.

"Yeah," I said.

A shout from behind made us all look. Matthias and Savry had followed us after all. They stopped when they caught sight of Fergus' bleeding face.

"You killed him?" said Matthias. He directed the accusation at Burke.

"He would have killed me," I said.

"And anyway, he's not dead," said Kaja.

"Besides," I continued, "we have bigger problems."

Matthias cocked an eyebrow. "Oh?"

Before I could say anything, Kaja said, "Someone summoned a portal without corrected maps."

"Ho-ly—"

"I know!"

I looked at Kaja, and she gave me a look that I had seen countless times before: shut up. Burke recognized it, too. He and I exchanged a brief glance but said nothing.

Savry shouted at us from near the tents. "Hey, guys! I found another one."

Burke, Matthias and I moved to her. Vorra. The explorer lay face up on the ground with her hood pulled partway back, a hole in her head.

"Geez," said Burke after a few moments.

Matthias let out a breath. "Well, there's nothing for it. We'll move her body over there." He pointed to Fergus. "And let's get him under one of the tents. Night's coming and it'll get cold. We'll get some sleep and decide what to do in the morning."

I nodded. "Agreed."

~*~

As we sat around the betavoltaic heater at the center of the camp, no one said a word. The sun had long ago gone down. We each had pulled on under-layers and wool parkas to keep warm. The heater had supplied us the means to cook a meal and boil a pot for tea. I still had some at the bottom of my cup, though I was sure it had become ice cold.

I looked up at the sky. On that clear night, I could see the ebb and flow of the Milky Way galaxy. I imagined myself as an early tribesman in the area, wondering just what the heck lay up there. My mind drifted back to the camp I had seen earlier. I tried to understand what it was about them that seemed odd. It didn't make sense. I mean, how in the world would I know what a tribesman in Colchis in tenth century B.C. looked like?

I glanced back at the tent behind me. Brother Fergus lay as we had left him, motionless. We made sure to cover him up. Kaja had even taken the time to clean him with a blanket, which surprised me a little. I'd expected something like that from Savry.

Matthias sniffed hard and stood. "We need to get some sleep. I'll take first watch."

"No, I will," I said, shooting a quick glance to Kaja. "My nerves are shot and I won't be able to sleep for a while."

Our second-tier looked at me and frowned. "Have it your way. Burke?"

The redhead was staring at the heater. He didn't look up as he said, "I think I'm going to keep Conner company."

"What, you guys buddy-buddy, now?"

If Matthias was trying to make a joke, it fell flat. No one laughed. "All right, then. Guess I'm the only one that cares to sleep. Don't stay up too late, lovebirds."

"I think I'm going to bed, too," said Savry.

"Finally," said Matthias. "Someone else has some sense. Have a good night."

Savry turned to Kaja. "You coming?"

"In a minute. I want to check on Fergus before I do."

Matthias headed for the freshly designated the "Man Tent", while Savry headed for Woman Tent.

As soon as they had both zipped their respective flaps, I scooted closer to Kaja.

"What was that about earlier?" I said in a whisper. "Why'd you shut us up?"

Burke leaned closer but didn't move otherwise.

Kaja glanced back at the tents. "Fergus said that a Cartographer was a traitor."

"And?"

"And I trust you two more than them."

I had to keep from laughing out loud. "You can't be serious. Matthias? Savry? No way."

"Savry hasn't ever really had a heart for the Guild, you know that."

"And Matthias?"

"You know better than anyone Matthias would cheat if it got him what he wanted."

Her eyes stared straight into mine as she said this. I bit my lower lip and looked down at the heater. She was picking at an old wound, but with good reason. I had been passed up for second-tier promotion in favor of Matthias. I was hurt, but shrugged it off at the time, thinking my own lack of confidence was the deciding factor.

However, some strange things emerged shortly thereafter. Several of his map designs looked suspiciously like my own—designs that had helped him secure second-tier. On the surface, I waved it off as coincidence. Besides, I had no way of arguing. Who would have believed me anyway? Nevertheless, I still had that nagging doubt at the back of my mind.

"There was no way to prove that."

Kaja scoffed. "Why do you do that?"

"Do what?"

"Shrug off what he did to you."

"What would you have me do, Kaja?"

"I don't know. Anything besides roll over and take it."

"I thought we were talking about traitors here, not my lack of advancement."

She shook her head and fell silent.

"What do you think happened up here?" said Burke, thankfully changing the subject.

I shrugged. "No idea. But, a traitor makes sense. How else could they have known where we'd be?"

"They who?"

"Whoever attacked the camp."

"What if it was the explorers?

"That doesn't make sense. Why go through the trouble of setting up camp and then killing everyone after the fact?"

"I don't know. To lead us on?"

I shook my head. "If they wanted everyone dead—which includes us, by the way—they could've done it right after we landed. Or they would have waited until we got here. No, I think someone else did this."

"That Sokar guy? He didn't look that tough."

"At this point, it's all just speculation."

"Yeah."

We fell into another long silence. Burke stared at the heater for another fifteen minutes or so, and then went to the Man Tent.

A little later, Kaja said, "I didn't mean to bust your chops. Sorry."

"Don't worry about it. You're probably right anyway."

"I just . . . Conner, you deserve to be second-tier. I complained to Palatin when they picked Matthias over you."

I cocked an eyebrow. "You argued with a first-tier? For me?"

As though it struck her for the first time that this is what she had done, she turned away. "Yeah, I guess I did."

She was going to say something else when she turned back, but she met my lips instead. It surprised her, I could tell, but she didn't turn away. Instead, she pulled in closer. We stayed that way for, I'm sure, a long while, but not long enough.

It never is.

When we parted, we stared at each other for several minutes in silence. If I could have captured the feeling of that moment and bottled it up, I would have.

"Why don't you get some sleep?" I finally said. "If—when we get back to the Guild, we can—"

"Shh!" she said.

I felt a little crestfallen. The moment ruined. "Well, sorry, I didn't mean—"

"Shut up!" she said in a harsh whisper.

Then I understood. She had heard something. I heard it, too. Footsteps. Voices.

I got to my feet, taking care to stay crouched. I nodded in the direction of the sounds. They came from somewhere along the cliff wall, in some far back corner of the area.

Kaja pointed to the mound we had hidden behind when we first arrived at the camp. I nodded. We crept to the spot as fast we could without making any noise. The glow of the betavoltaic heater was not enough to let us see the entire camp but, near the fringe of its glow, I caught sight of a leg. A white pant leg.

I leaned toward Kaja and whispered, "Sokar."

She clenched her jaw and nodded.

Then something happened I didn't expect. Another figure stepped close to the heater. It was hard to see thanks to the way the shadows lay across the clearing, but this I could tell about them: they wore a long fur robe and matching hat. The glow of the heater caught the side of a wide blade peeking out from under their coat. I had seen that outfit before, but where?

The newcomer said something to Sokar, but I couldn't make out what. Then he did something that made my stomach drop. He pointed to the tents.

The two men moved to Man Tent first.

I started to move, but Kaja's hand held me in place.

"Wait," she said.

Why was she telling me to wait? The guys were in trouble. A terrible thought crossed my mind right then. Was Kaja the traitor? Was it her plan to distract me until her partners showed up?

At the same time, I wasn't sure what I would do if I did try to intervene. I had no weapons on me and the fur-wearing man would have sliced me in two.

They unzipped the tent. After some shouting, Burke and Matthias emerged and went to the heater. Fur-man stayed with them as Sokar went to Woman Tent. Moments later Savry screamed. Again, I wanted to bolt up and again Kaja put a hand on my shoulder. This time I stayed put on my own, but my mind began accusing Kaja again.

What was I to do?

Sokar shoved Savry into the same area as the boys.

He then shouted at them loud enough that we could hear. "Where are the others?"

Our fellow Cartographers, bless them, all shook their heads.

He started to rage a little, but the other man quickly shut him down.

"Calm yourself!" he shouted.

My heart sank. The voice belonged to Tumek.

"I understood Vorra," continued the explorer, "but killing them buys us nothing. It's due to arrive at any minute. Then it won't matter if they know."

Sokar seemed to consider for a moment.

He said something that sounded like, "You're right."

Suddenly, a loud clap filled the valley and made us jump. I accidentally kicked a rock over. It made a horrible, horrible clacking noise. I prayed the clap had masked it.

When I looked back across the camp, Tumek had doubled over. He said something that was likely a curse and then fell to the ground, dead.

Sokar stepped into the light and pointed something at Savry's head.

"Now, tell me," he said, "where are they?"

"I'm here!" I shouted. "Please, don't shoot."

I couldn't take it anymore. I couldn't let him kill Savry. If nothing else, I bought us a few seconds. Bought Savry a few seconds. If Kaja were the traitor, she would have to decide what to do now.

"Conner?" said the Antiquarian.

"Yeah, it's me. Just me."

"You're alone?"

"Yes."

"Move over here."

I obeyed.

I took as long as I dared to cross the distance between us. Hoping, praying, that something would save us.

And then, the sky exploded.

A swirling mass of purple and white light materialized in the air several hundred feet above us. It lit up the entire camp. Strands of purple swept across the landscape, warping and twisting everything in its path. I knew then what I saw: an aethereal portal. But why was it so far up in the sky? And why was it so big?

Sokar looked directly at the portal and began laughing. I could barely hear him over the cacophony of the portal.

"Do you see it, children?" he shouted. "Is it not beautiful?"

"What have you done?" I shouted back.

He turned to me. I could see the white teeth behind his terrible smile. "Wait and see, boy. Wait and see." He looked back up at the portal. "Only a few seconds now."

Something emerged from the portal, but I couldn't tell what, at first. It simply looked like a dark shimmer against the portal's light. The thing grew larger as something started to come through.

My jaw dropped.

What came through the portal looked to be made entirely out of tentacles, like those of a giant squid. However, it was not like any squid I had seen in textbooks and edu-vids. The creature was gargantuan; it covered nearly a third of the night sky. It had no identifiable eyes, nor a mouth. An angry, deafening roar emanated from it, making me cover my ears. One of its tentacles slammed into the ground, sending rock and earth skyward. However, rather than fall back down, the debris stayed suspended as if frozen in midair.

"Behold, the future," said Sokar.

"What is it?" I said.

"A creature of pure aether."

I blinked at him. "What?"

"Where did you think the aether pools came from?"

"No one knows where they come from."

Sokar grinned again. "You are wrong."

He then aimed his weapon up at the creature and fired. The bullet struck somewhere one of its tentacles. The creature moaned. From the point of impact, a liquid began to dribble out. I squinted, trying to understand what he meant. Then I did.

Aether. The creature's blood was pure aether. Then I understood Sokar.

"You're trying to harvest it," I said.

The Antiquarian's grin widened. "Such a smart young man you are. Yes, I want to harvest the creature. It took a long time, a lot of money and some clever rummaging through the Library, but I finally tracked this one down. After that, it simply became a matter of finding a way to take advantage of the Cartographers' technology."

"The Antiquarians won't get away with this." I tried to sound defiant, but I was sure Sokar wouldn't buy it. "The Cartographers will learn what you did here."

"The League has no idea what I'm doing and the Cartographers won't be a problem." His grin dropped, and he took a couple of steps forward. "Not after I've taken care of you."

He aimed the pistol at Savry again.

I rushed forward. "No!"

But it was too late. The gun fired. Blood shot out from the exit wound of her head. Savry dropped to the ground, dead.

I stopped and collapsed to my knees. How had this happened? Kaja! Where was she? I looked back to the mound but saw no sign of her.

"One down," said Sokar.

Suddenly, Matthias roared and jumped to his feet. He charged Sokar, his head down like a battering ram. He took the Antiquarian off-guard. Matthias clipped the man's shoulder, spinning him around. Sokar wheeled around and dropped the pistol at Burke's feet.

"Grab it," I shouted.

Burke quickly scooped up the gun, but instead of shooting Sokar, he fired a round at the still-moving Matthias. Our second-tier took one more step and then plopped to the ground.

"Well, that was exciting," said Sokar.

"Burke," I said. "What . . . what the hell?"

Burke actually looked apologetic as he said, "This is not quite how I wanted it to go. I had hoped your sickness would have lasted longer. And that stupid monk just had to jump on board. I could have spared Savry. I actually liked that chick. We had a thing once. Did you know that? It was good, too, but not good enough for her apparently. And Matthias . . . well, I think I did you a favor."

"None of that matters! You've just killed him!"

Burke grinned. "You're right. It doesn't matter. Not when I have that." He pointed up at the creature.

"You're the traitor."

"Bingo! Sokar needed a draftsman inside the Cartographer Guild to understand how they worked and to help run interference if necessary. I wasn't alone of course. We needed Tumek," he kicked the explorer's body, "to help give credibility to the find. And, by the way, there never was a Golden Fleece treaty. To be honest, I'm surprised anyone fell for that trick. With my artistic skills and Sokar' experience with ancient artifacts, it was an easy fake. Even the Argonaut envoy fell for it. Erasmus still posed a potential problem. He might not have picked our group. But with you on the team, I imagine he would have done it anyway."

Memories flashed back to me again.

I am five years old. Dominion troopers gun down my mother and father right in front of me. I am crying, and their bodies will not respond to my pleas. Mommy? Daddy? Why won't you get up? Please, get up! A shadow looms over me. Cold, gray eyes peer down into mine. The man is huge, with long hair and a thick beard. I could tell even then that he was a hard man. But something inside cracked the shell that day. Whatever he saw in me made him break down. He didn't cry. He didn't say anything. He just picked me up and held me in his massive arms.

And then, he made me a Cartographer.

"The man always had a soft spot for you," said Burke. "Giving you opportunity after opportunity. You know what?" He looked thoughtful. "I'm going to give you one more opportunity, Conner."

"Burke, what are you doing?" said Sokar.

"Relax. Let me do this. Look at it, Conner. Do you still not see what it represents? What if we could harness the aether whenever we wanted? Think of the power one could wield in this universe. In all the universes. Never mind prestige and wealth. What happened to you, you could make it so it never happened to anyone ever again." He pointed at Savry's corpse. "You could save them. You could save everyone. Even your parents."

His words flew around inside my head. They alternated between making sense and sounding completely insane. I stood there looking at Burke, looking at the bodies of my fellow Cartographers, looking up at the poor creature whose powerful blood would be harvested.

Then something else caught the corner of my eye.

I locked eyes with Burke and smiled.

"You know what? For all this talk and showboating, you're still just an ass."

The redhead snarled and aimed the pistol at my head.

That was when she struck.

She timed it perfectly. It sliced right through Burke's wrist. A nice, clean cut.

Burke screamed as he grabbed his arm and dropped to his knees.

Their attention focused entirely on me, neither Burke nor Sokar noticed Kaja moving in close. While I stood off with them, she had crept over to Vorra's body and took her weapons.

Kaja turned to face Sokar, but the Antiquarian, though rattled, was ready for her. He produced a dagger of his own, a curved blade with an ivory handle. The way he handled it and the way he stood suggested an experienced combatant. Kaja would be no match for him. I ran forward and went for the pistol.

An enraged Burke lunged at me. Adrenaline must have been pumping like crazy through his body. He punched me hard in the gut with his good hand and then dove for the pistol. I coughed, trying to suck in air, but I had to keep trying. Burke's fingers touched the handle of the gun, but got no further. I tackled his legs, making him crash face-first into the heater.

He screamed as it cooked his skin. He pushed and rolled away. It gave me enough time to pick up the pistol and step to him. His eyes wild, he looked up at me as I aimed the end of the barrel at his head.

"Connie boy, please."

"I hate being called that."

I pulled trigger.

I felt nothing as the pistol jumped in my hands. The bullet effortlessly pierced through the right side of Burke's forehead, killing him instantly. He deserved worse. With my instincts and adrenaline still in command, I looked up at Sokar and Kaja. He had knocked away her knife, but she refused to back down. She held a huge rock in her hands, deflecting a pair of hard blows from his knife.

I lifted the gun and said, "Stop!"

Something about my voice must have made an impression. Sokar' eyes went wide when he saw me with the gun and Burke's dead body on the ground. He dropped his knife.

"On your knees," I said.

"He-he said you were soft," said Sokar. "Said you were a good guy." He smiled. "You're a good guy, right Conner? You won't shoot me, will you?"

I looked to Kaja. "Nope, I won't."

Kaja nodded and then slammed the rock into the Antiquarian's temple. His body hit the ground with a thud.

"That's for Savry," she said and spat on him.

I then looked up at the aethereal creature. From down there, it looked beautiful, majestic even. Out of the corner of my eye, I saw Kaja sidle up next to me. I was vaguely aware that she grabbed my hand.

"What do we do about that?" she said. "I doubt the locals will have missed it."

I stared at it for a long while. I then said, "We send it back."

Kaja looked up at me wide-eyed. "How? We don't have the right equipment."

I pointed to Sokar' corpse. "I bet he has the maps." I pointed back to Vorra's body. "And she still has her compass."

"Conner, if we get it wrong . . ."

"I know. But is it worse than letting it stay here? Sooner or later, it will do more than inspire a cave painting."

"Do you remember enough to use it?"

I smirked. "We'll find out, won't we?"

It didn't take long to find Sokar' maps. But we quickly hit a snag. They were old and in an ancient language that neither of us recognized. On top of that, none of them seemed to connect with the other. It was a strange mélange of star charts, political maps, and even a timeline.

"Great," said Kaja, exasperated. "We can't even read them!"

But I felt strangely calm about it. "Give me a second." I scanned the symbols scattered across the map. Their arrangement seemed strange, as if they weren't really a language.

Then it struck me. "We're not supposed to read it."

"Say again?"

"We're supposed to unlock it. We can't read the symbols because they aren't another language. They're part of a code. Look, this point here. It's the constellation Draco. With that I think I can work out the rest."

A noise came from above. The portal began to undulate. More swaths of purple swept down, distorting the landscape.

"The portal's becoming unstable," said Kaja.

"I'm working on it."

I moved quickly from point to point across the maps. I had to get the exact coordinates and exact time to the millisecond that Sokar and Tumek had dialed in to return the creature to its own realm.

Kaja yanked me back as a tendril of purple light whipped by inches from my face.

I let out a breath. "That was close."

"Just finish it already!"

Two more points to go. I had it!

I placed the compass on the star chart and adjusted for correction across all dimensions. I then turned the dials of the RAC to the right coordinates.

A golden light enveloped the compass and my hand. The light then shot out in all directions. I watched as it began to climb up to the sky, swallowing the purple light of the portal as it went. It crawled across the aethereal creature's body.

It began moving back through the portal. A new song came from the creature. A happier one.

It took a full minute for the body to finish crossing the portal's threshold. The moment it did, all light went out, leaving Kaja and I standing in the cold, dark night.

We stayed standing there for a while, staring at the spot where the portal used to be.

"Well, that was something."

Kaja and I turned to the sound of the new voice. "Fergus?"

"More or less," said the monk, rubbing his face.

He sniffed hard and stepped into the dim glow of the heater. A scratch surrounded by an ugly, dark smudge ran from one side of his nose, over the bridge and down the other side. Otherwise, he looked unhurt.

The old monk then looked around at the bodies on the ground.

"Nasty business. I tried to warn Erasmus about Sokar, but the old fool didn't seem concerned. Said he already had his best man on it. Always so frustratingly cryptic, that man. Do you know what he meant?"

I shrugged.

"I do," said Kaja with a grin.

"Care to share?" I said.

"Nope," she replied.

Fergus made a sound somewhere between a grunt and a sigh. "I'll make sure the report reflects the truth of what happened here." He looked down at Savry and Matthias. "It's the least they deserve."

"Thank you, Fergus."

"Don't thank me for doing what is my duty to begin with." He cleared his throat. "But, you're welcome, all the same. And young man, I don't say this often, but if you ever think about becoming a Library monk . . ."

Kaja answered for me. "He's already spoken for."

"Oh?"

"Afraid so," I said. "To the end of my days, I am a Cartographer."

~ * ~

Read all seven short stories in Moments in Millennia, available January 2014.

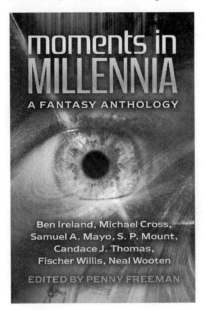

26374102R00275

Made in the USA
Charleston, SC
04 February 2014